Red Flags

A collection of stories

By

JAMES NELSON ROEBUCK

Copyright © 2020 James Nelson Roebuck

All rights reserved.

ISBN: 978-1-9162766-1-1

FIRST EDITION

All characters and events in this publication, other than those clearly in the public domain, are fictitious and any resemblance to real persons, living or dead, is purely coincidental.

All rights reserved.

www.green-cat.co

This book is sold subject to the conditions that shall not, by way of trade or otherwise, be lent, resold, hired out, or otherwise circulated without the publisher's prior consent in any form of binding other than that in which it is published and without a similar condition including this condition being imposed on the subsequent purchaser

CONTENTS

1	The Lines	1
2	Hairballs	27
3	Rise Up And Be Strong	63
4	The Hotel That Fell Into The Sea	113
5	Caravanning	139
6	Basher Baiting	169
7	Old Boy	213
8	The B.I.L.F	237
9	The Doghouse	269
10	Strange As Folk	307
11	Red Flags	359

RED FLAGS

FOR WILLIAM

semper paratus

THE LINES

Good-natured pleading was getting me nowhere. He must have heard it all a thousand times before. As I wheedled on, he appeared lost in contemplation of something amusing taking place at a point just above and beyond my head. Perhaps I should have surrendered there and then; accepted that further resistance was useless. I am, after all, by nature a mild, pragmatic man with an aversion to lost causes. But that dismissive smile playing on his face acted as a gauntlet thrown down, goading me on.

'Your name, then!' I heard myself huffing. 'I'm going to report you for unreasonable conduct! This ticket is totally out of order, and you know it! At least I have a right to know your name.'

Unusually tall, he took a gangly stride nearer and stood looming over my own five feet four inches. For a moment, I was back in my placard-waving student days, gazing up at one of those giant policemen who, in memory, always seemed to preside over whatever demonstration was going on at the time. The uniform he was wearing had a strong whiff of the past about it, too. Black, immaculately pressed, with shiny silver buttons, it belonged to an age when even traffic wardens took pride in the apparel of public service. From under the peak of his cap a long, questing nose, red and moist with the rawness of the winter morning was sniffing me out. The only blemish on this Uber-Warden persona were the flushed cheeks. Their schoolboy rosiness looked silly on a man I took to be in his early sixties, as though he'd been rouged up for some younger part in a Christmas pantomime. In fact, they reminded me of a boy I'd once known at school but couldn't quite place.

RED FLAGS

'I am not obliged to give you my name, Sir,' he said in the tragically imitable vowels of my home town.

Despite this near comical nasal whine, I sensed myself up against a powerful mind. England teems with people whom life has sadly misplaced: bricklaying Oxford dons; bus driving physicists. In any other circumstances I'd have felt sorry for the bastard. We were near contemporaries after all. What fine tweaking on fortune's rails had shunted me off to university and a career in television; he to a lifetime patrolling the car parks of this Midland's backwater?

But I just couldn't let it go. The sight of the ticket on the windscreen set me off again. I began to repeat myself, no more convincingly but louder.

'We're allowed five minutes added time! I shouted to you! You saw me coming! You had the option to not do this!'

The smile broadened to that of an adult humouring a small child angling for one treat too many. Again, it set off a tiny bat squeak of memory, as if I'd experienced some version of it before.

'For Christ's sake,' I blundered on, 'it's Monday morning! Look around you. How can I be inconveniencing anybody? The goddamn frickin' car park's two thirds frickin' empty!'

The Americanisms, legacy of a lengthy spell in New York, prickled in my ears. I'd already started checking myself for pretentiousness, always considered the worst of sins when returning to my 'roots' as a younger man. A mere three days and the place had already got its claws into me. I felt it pricking my bubble just as it used to forty years ago when, full of myself, I'd come down from Cambridge to sign on for my summer job at Carstons (Pride of the Midlands- Brewers of Fine Pale, Mild and

RED FLAGS

Bitter Ales).

'I would kindly request that you modify the strength of your language, Sir,' he said, disappointedly.

'I'm sorry but surely...look...I just popped into the library to find something to read. I'm in the town on temporary business, although I was born and bred here,' I said, hoping to appeal to his civic pride. 'I didn't have a card. It expired ages ago and it took longer than I thought to issue me with a new one. Simple!'

It might have sounded dodgy, but was all perfectly true. My father had died at a grand old age. I, an only child, had returned to arrange his funeral and begin sorting out his estate. For many years, I hadn't been back for anything longer than the briefest of stays. He'd always enjoyed excellent health and revelled in his independence, preferring to stay with us in London. Then, with no warning, he dropped dead, leaving me choc-full of guilt and thwarted filial love. In the turmoil, I'd not brought enough books with me. So, I gave myself a break from sifting through the sad detritus of bereavement, drove to the library and found instead a sort of drop-in centre come coffee shop for the old and not very well off. Poorly dressed people sat pecking at banks of computers. Books seemed incidental to the place. The strictly enforced silence I remembered from schooldays had given way to carefree chatter. There had been problems concerning my identity. What I assumed would be a simple thing became a great kerfuffle. When, finally, I'd been issued with a card, my request to be pointed in the direction of the French Literature section drew a blank. It was no more. No call for it. I left in a temper, having spent more than ten minutes trying to 'self check-out' on the 'system' a translated copy *A La Recherche du Temps Perdus*, the original of which I needed for a feature I'd been working on before the hospital called. And now this!

'Your leisure activities are no concern of mine, Sir.'

The smile now melded into an expression of good-natured puzzlement. Despite the bitter cold of the morning, his appetite for the fray was unquenchable. An icy, ill-tempered wind was lifting the tails of my overcoat; plucking at the flaps and epaulettes of his nostalgic warden's get-up. It brought with it the pong of brewing that on certain days lingered famously over the town like a huge and not wholly unpleasant fart. One of us was going to have to crack sooner or later. I decided to play my ace in the pack. I didn't want to. I am not - and never have been - given to self-advertisement but I'd nothing to lose and there was no one else around to hear me.

'I suppose, it's because of who I am?' I said (I've acquired modest celebrity recently, presenting a late-night TV Arts Show). 'Is that it, eh? Want to take me down a peg or two, eh? Go down nicely with your mates in the canteen that.'

In my particular case, on balance, public recognition had caused me nothing but the kind of grief I was now getting. It came too late. I didn't have any strategies (as they say these days) to deal with it; didn't, in fact, want it. It wasn't my idea to use my surname - Trowell - in the title of the show. As I said to the head of programming, the only appeal it was likely to have would be as a gift to nasty reviewers with their post-modern jibes, and so it proved: ('Far from popularising serious art, Trowell, in painful weekly scoops, is merely digging its grave with this trite attempt at relevance' etc. etc.). But she insisted the thing needed a nice homely touch. The casual grazer of the late-night channels must not be put off by anything *too* arty. *Time For Trowell* it became, as though I were synonymous with the whole of Art.

'Your name is of no concern to me either, Sir,' he whined with increasing pleasure, 'the registration number of your car is all I require.'

'Aha, the car! That's it!' I crowed, gesturing towards the lemon yellow 1964 E-Type Jag, my one extravagance in life. Next to my wife and children it's the thing I love most.

'It's the car that's got your goat, eh? I bet if it was a Ford Focus, a Honda bloody Civic, you wouldn't be slapping this on me, would you?' I said, plucking the ticket from under the jag's chrome windscreen wiper and waving it under his nose. I was letting go now. I knew I'd lost. In the war of attrition between the forces of petty order and the ordinary man there is only ever one winner. The trick is to remain neutral.

'It is indeed a very beautiful car, Sir,' he said, 'but unfortunately it has committed an offence and by law you must pay.'

Then he astonished me by saying something in Latin, the gist of it being that justice could not be allowed to show favour. From his gaze it was clear that, for whatever reason, this was supposed to bind us together as men of erudition. I was completely thrown. My resistance finally collapsed.

'OK,' I said in a weak attempt at sarcasm, reading *his* registration number. 'OK, Warden number seven two zero four two five, I'm going to appeal this. You'll be hearing from me.'

'Very good, Sir,' he said, beginning to disengage. Then, like a mime artist breaking out of character, he suddenly became what I took to be his real self. It was shocking; frightening, almost. 'Do you know, Sir, I think on this occasion I *will* make an exception. The name is Paul Gervis.

Oh, and I hope you don't mind me saying that,' – and here he amazed me further by pointing at the book in my hands and switching to flawless and beautifully accented French – 'one day I hope you may be blessed with the author's memory, for at present it is a faculty you would appear to have mislaid.'

With that, he turned on his heels and bent his tall, gangly body into the wind, arms behind his back as though skating in slow motion. And then I knew him. A picture flagged itself up in my mind; a picture of me as a boy in school uniform, skating after him.

'Gervis,' I cried, horrified, 'Gervis...I'm sorry...I didn't recognise...' But the wind whipped my words away and he was gone.

*

The house was as cold as the mortuary where, sobbing like a child, I'd identified my father a few days before. He'd refused all entreaties to have central heating installed. 'Going soft, he said, "was the first step on the way to being dead." It had worked for him. He'd cheated the Grim Reaper for ninety-two years. In the sitting room, I put a match to his antique gas fire. As always it flared in my face with an angry pop, sending me reeling backwards. I swore, cursing the 70s flock wallpaper mother had chosen just before her stroke, the faded curtains and galumphing armchairs. Without him in it, the place's eccentricities were no longer amusing. Closing the door to let the heat build, I made my way to the even icier upper reaches of the spacious Victorian villa that for over half a century had been home to the town's Physical Education guru and oldest surviving war hero: my father; my titanic father. A fresh rash of guilt spread over me. How could I have let his memory be so readily eclipsed by the morning's encounter? Shouldn't I have been mourning him harder; with the same single-mindedness *he'd* applied to everything he'd done in life? Traces of this doggedness, lasting until his death, were all around me in the streaky, self-painted walls, patterned on the stairwell with the handprints of his defiant groping (he refused a chair lift to last). Risking amputation, I wrestled with his homemade folding ladder and head butted my way through the trapdoor to the loft. It was hard to believe that any object could have survived years of such blistering cold, but there it lay: my trunk. Inside, all was in the meticulous order of my schooldays. I went straight to the bottom:

General Work Book

Form 2A 1966

D. Trowell

The lines were there in their hundreds:

I must not indulge in verbal intercourse during assembly

I must not indulge in verbal intercourse during assembly

Impersonation is the lowest form of mongrel wit

Impersonation is the lowest form of mongrel wit

The last page of each marathon of wrist stiffening tedium was stamped:

P. Gervis

Head Prefect

Abbot Beyne Boy's Grammar School

I knelt in the gloom and smell of bat droppings as if at prayer, trying to connect the distinctly weird traffic warden with the dashing wit, scholar and athlete I'd carried about in my head for over four decades.

Gervis had been his cohort's most brilliant prodigy, garnering cups, records, awards with an insouciant ease that had even the Masters in awe of him. I remembered my father, still Head of P.E. for the first two years of my time at 'The Beyne', had treated him with the easy confidence of an equal. This was no small compliment. The Digger, as he was inevitably dubbed, was by that time possibly the most revered figure in the town. Generations of boys had already felt his bracing enthusiasm; rugby, cricket, tennis clubs; his galvanizing presence as player, coach, President. Few were the sporting committees that had not experienced his firm hand on their rudders.

As the son of such a sporting man, much of my childhood had been spent accompanying him on playing fields, scampering between the legs of Colossi. So, when Gervis entered our form room that bright September morning in 1966, I wasn't prostrate with quite the same awe and fear as were my classmates. I'd met him before, informally, whilst still at junior school and so knew we were in for an easier time.

Each form had a Prefect assigned to it. They were given ridiculous powers. A propensity for exercising them could result in untold hours of pointless drudgery with the occasional beating thrown in *pour encourager les autres*. On the vagaries of character depended the tolerable survival of a whole school year. Fortunately for us, Gervis had a reputation for good humour and fairness that bordered on laxity. His mind, it was assumed, was on higher things. Extremely tall and lithe, in his immaculate blazer with its blue and gold braiding running up the lapels, he stood before us to deliver his inaugural address, our Form Master 'Waggy' Wagstaff cowering in his shadow. The cheers were genuine. Then, as was the tradition, he led us in a rendition of the school song. It could be heard breaking out all down the corridor, until the whole mad Gothic pile of a building was loud with

>'Deus Nobiscum, God with us
>
>Be this our ensign yet
>
>Our forbear's deeds victorious
>
>Oh let us not forget...'

Easy to snigger now. Back then it was still possible to take seriously things like devotion to duty; heroism, pride in one's school, patriotism. Older, striving boys like Gervis who embodied them were free to be worshiped. And worship I did. A kind of pre-sexual love quivered in me at the sight of him. On afternoons when the whole school was set free to watch the 1st XV take on some bitter local rival, I would be pressed to the touchline in adulation, cheering my lungs out as he drove the team forward, the opposition clinging to him like jackals on some noble stag. Once, I even picked up his discarded, sucked-out segment of half-time orange and put it away in my blazer pocket to keep in a jar. Even more cringe-making was the peon I submitted pseudonymously to The Cygnet, the school's magazine. To my astonishment, it actually made it into the Christmas term edition of 1966; the first thing I ever got published. Here it was, my twelve-year old's doggerel:

> *When Gervis takes the muddy field*
>
> *The valiant foe is forced to yield...*

Of course, I couldn't share my joy. I'd have been crucified. I wasn't a creep, quite the reverse. I had a gift for mimicry which was always landing me in trouble. So it was that, in the course of impersonating my idol's pensive, skater in slow motion walk he whipped round and, with unruffled good humour, dictated the lines that were now before me. I was mortified. How to explain it had been out of devotion? No matter. Later, he took me quietly to one side and bending down, his rosy face close to mine, explained in Latin that justice could not afford to be partial, *'justitiam minime iniquum esse oportet.'*

Death sows an unhealthy introspection in those left behind. It had been bad enough my father going with the suddenness he'd always hoped for but probably never believed would happen. Now this other death of a happy illusion really shook me. I felt cheated. How, once, could that half-mad man met earlier, have been Gervis? A terrible violence had somehow been done to a life.

The incurable documentarist in me insisted on an explanation, but where to start looking? I'd completely lost touch with my own school friends. I knew the school had a website because my father had phoned in a state of agitation to inform me that he'd been told he was on it; and should he take legal action. But, of course, there was no wifi in a house where the television had been regarded as suspiciously new-fangled.

I continued to brood, until two days later while I was nodding over my Remembrance of Time Past, the phone rang at eight in the evening. Swathed in blankets smelling of mothballs, I scuttled to the farthest arctic reaches of the hall where it had been located for maximum inconvenience. Expecting my wife's voice, I was peeved to hear another.

'May I speak with Mr Duncan Trowell, please?'

'Speaking.'

'Mr Trowell, may I offer my deepest condolences. Your father was a great man.'

'Thank you.'

'Please forgive this intrusion at such a sad time for you,' the voice whined nasally on (was nobody immune?). 'My name is David Green.'

'I'm afraid...'

'You will probably remember me,' he laughed nervously, 'as Piggy Green. I was a Prefect in the Upper Sixth when you were in the 2nd form, I believe.'

'Actually, my memory's a bit hazy these days, Mr Green, but please go on.'

'No matter, Mr Trowell. Getting to the point, I manage the Old Boys' website. A labour of love. Now, please cut me off if you think this is in anyway an intrusion but I was wondering if you might have any photographs of your father that we might be able to scan and use? Of course, I fully understand if at this distressing time...' There was something Uriah Heep-ish in his tone that set my teeth on edge. I was on the point of making my excuses, when I remembered Gervis would have been an exact contemporary of his.

'How extraordinary,' I said, brightening, 'I was just thinking the very same thing.'

'Your father was such a character at the school, and in the town at large,' he went on, relaxing a little. 'A truly gigantic figure. It would be a tragedy if his life weren't secured for posterity.'

'Well, I think that might be stretching it a bit far...er...'

'Call me Piggy, Mr Trowell. Everybody else in the town does, ha, ha.'

'But yes, er, Piggy, I agree. I suppose it would be a shame if my father were to miss out on internet immortality.'

'Splendid,' he said, eager to close the deal. 'When might I be able to call on you?'

RED FLAGS

I looked around me and shivered. With each passing day the house seemed to be taking on the quality of an exhibit in one of those depressing Heritage Museums found in parts of England that have had their reason for being taken away: The Way We Used To Live.

'Actually, the house is in a bit of a mess at the moment. Not the most welcoming of places. Perhaps we could meet in a pub somewhere?'

'Even better. What finer venue to have a good chat and honour your father's memory? He liked a pint, I remember.'

'He certainly did.'

'Do you know The Dog? It's my local.'

'Vaguely, yes.'

'It's at the bottom end of Station Street.'

'Of course. I remember now.'

'Wonderful. Shall we say tomorrow, seven-thirty?'

'Fine. I'll bring along whatever photos I think might fit the bill.'

'Marvellous. Just ask for Piggy. I certainly won't have any difficulty recognising *you*,' he said, the Heep-ish note returning. 'May I say how much I've been enjoying *Time For Trowell*. I've never been the arty type but it's really opened my eyes to so many interesting and entertaining things.'

'Thanks. It's what it's there to do,' I said, genuinely grateful that someone in the town had finally acknowledged I had an existence other than that of my father's son.

'Until tomorrow then, Mr Trowell.'

'Sure.'

Replacing the receiver, I found I *did* remember him. Short, fat, with a stubby upturned nose, he'd been a sort of Anti-Gervis. One of the many who should never, under any circumstances, be given the slightest shred of authority. He'd made 2C's life hell.

The photographs wouldn't be a problem. There was a whole mosaic of them spilt out over the dining table. (How epic the lives of that generation now seem.) I made my selection.

*

The Dog had re-invented itself as a Real Ale pub. Or perhaps it had just stayed the same, banking on a revival of enthusiasm for what pubs once stood for: good beer, no intrusive music, pleasant service. The landlord, a man with Dickensian mutton-chop whiskers that didn't seem out of place, pointed me in the direction of an alcove next to a proper coal fire. The years had not been kind. Spread across the entire width of an unforgiving wooden bench sat a man of truly monstrous proportions, drinking from a pewter mug.

'Piggy?'

'Mr Trowell!'

'Duncan, please.'

With great effort, he struggled to his feet to shake my hand. Here, it was clear, was a man who waged an exhausting battle against gravity every minute of the day.

We settled behind our beer, the properties of which proved, as ever, a useful conversational ice-breaker. I realised it had been the phone that had imposed on my mind a picture of oleaginous servility. Phones do that. Heep had vanished, replaced by a nice, jovial fat man. Having surrendered to his condition, given up the ghost of ever returning to the land of the normally proportioned, his eyes seemed to be popping with pleasure at his managing to be anywhere at all. Gone too, was the Piggy

RED FLAGS

of the Upper Sixth. Nastiness more than likely born of self-loathing had given way to a comfortable self-assurance. He had made a small fortune in steel and settled down to retirement in the ranks of the Barmy Army, following the England cricket team all over the globe. He laughed about having to book two adjacent airline seats when on campaign. He wasn't joking; he could afford it.

I'd anticipated an evening of tedium as the price of investigation and found myself instead being hauled out of morbidity by his conversation. The pints kept coming. We began swapping anecdotes about my father that gave me pleasure rather than pain. It turned out the website was not a geeky life's obsession but one of several projects taken on to keep a lively intelligence occupied. The Beyne of our boyhood assumed its appropriate place in time. We even found ourselves swapping affectionately, lines of the rousing song we had bellowed unambiguously all those years ago:

'"Our school has stood the test of time/ The centuries have crowned her" haw, haw haw! Wait...waaaaiiiit...yes... "Through earnest zeal to heights sublime/ Her sons have risen round her". Your turn...'

'Easy... "Fair play and hard health giving toil/ And strong united will/ Make us good seed in this fair soil to sing God With Us still..."arf, arf arf!'

And here we both joined in, warbling off-key the final crescendo, 'Deus Nobiscum...Deus nobiiiiiscuuum!'

I'd almost forgotten the reason why I'd consented to come when, in the silence following our choral exertions I said, 'Whatever happened to Gervis, I wonder? You remember, Gervis, the school's all-time star pupil. He was in your year, wasn't he?'

Piggy took a long pull at his tankard, as if arming himself.

'Ah, Gerv! Now that *is* a story.'

'Didn't he win an exhibition to Oxford? Modern Languages, I seem to remember. He was my hero. I ended up reading exactly what he did. He was a 'shining light'; the incarnation of all that the song bangs on about. Went on to join the great and the good somewhere, I should imagine.'

'Quite the reverse,' he said.

'Tell, tell.'

'There was some kind of breakdown in his first year.'

'What, Gervis? Breakdown? I don't believe it. He seemed such a colossus.'

'He was always a bit highly-strung, you know. Like his brain was overloaded with too many things. He never was quite one of us. All the same, it came as a surprise. I remember that first vacation. We were all back working the Christmas post for a few extra bob, down the Fox and Goose every night. You know.'

'I remember it well.'

'We were all full of ourselves. University was like being born again for most of us. My first term at Salford! The freedom! The girls!'

'I remember them, too,' I said. 'The old Girls High might just as well have been bloody Narnia for all the chance we had.'

Piggy took another pull at his tankard and went on, 'But Gerv seemed to have shrunk. We tried to get him to talk about Oxford, but he didn't want to know. He kept going on about the school, you know, reminiscing. Who wanted to reminisce about the bloody place when we'd just left it? That comes later, when you're an old fart.'

'Odd.'

'Very. Me and my mates couldn't wait to leave. Some of us set fire to our blazers on the last day after we'd been down The Kings Head. It was a ritual, a rite. Gerv was horrified. He loved the school, see. Really loved it. I'm no psychiatrist but I reckon he'd been such a star 'til then that it came as shock when he got to Oxford to find himself in a whole galaxy of them, if you know what I mean.'

'I do. I had a bit of a wobble myself at Cambridge. Not that I'd put myself in the same class as Gervis. He was a complete all-rounder. A supernova all to himself.'

'His mother didn't help, I shouldn't think. God, what a dragon! How she drove him on. Imagine carrying all that weight of expectation around with you. He was from very 'humble origins', was our Gerv. It was the D.H Lawrence scenario. She placed all her hopes in him but never praised his efforts. Just drove him on. Again, I'm no Sigmund Freud but I reckon the school, with all the adulation he got there, was a sort of substitute for the love he never got at home. When it wasn't there anymore, he was lost.'

'At least my old man didn't saddle me with all that. Left me to my own devices, he did. Another?'

'Why not. It isn't often I get to talk about these things. Really taking me back, it is.'

I took myself off to the bar. A sadness settled in me as I stood waiting my turn. For most of us it takes half a lifetime of steady disappointment to do away with promise. By that time, if we're lucky, we've got things, money, family, to take its place. Gervis on the other hand had fallen straight away like a young officer fresh in the line on the Somme, and never come back.

'I remember, now!' Piggy said as I set his tankard down. 'The Easter vac' we didn't see him at all. He'd stopped coming to the pub. Then that summer he had a job, like the rest of us. His was a conductor, a 'clippy' on the buses. We'd see him on a Saturday night as we rode into town for a piss-up. His uniform was immaculate, nothing like the other clippies. He'd ask us where we were going, in French. When we tried to talk to him, he'd answer back in French. We thought that maybe him being at Oxford and all that, we weren't good enough for him anymore and that was his way of keeping his distance. So, we sort of gave up on him. We should have twigged something had gone wrong. Pete Turner said he bumped into him walking by the river one day, and he was wearing his school blazer, talking to himself. I suppose we thought that was how a genius was supposed to behave, if we thought anything at all.'

'Odder and odder,' I said, letting him go on.

'Then, when I came back for a quick visit that autumn, there he was, still working the Number 2. He'd dropped out.'

'Jeez, what a horrible waste.'

'It gets worse. The buses had to get rid of him. To start with it must have been a laugh having what should have been an Oxford double first doling out the tickets. All his 'Messieurs' and 'Mademoiselles' probably went down well to start with. But in a town like this you're going to come up against some local lads who take against you. Despite all the rugby and other heroics, Gerv was a gentle soul. Wouldn't hurt a fly. But that side of him changed too. He started getting into fights. He'd go berserk apparently. Dave Brookes saw him once. He said it was like watching a cornered animal. And Gerv was a big strong lad. You can imagine the mess.'

'When did you last see him?' I said.

'Oh, it was nearly twenty-five years ago now. About the mid-eighties. He was working as a traffic warden.'

'My God, what a waste,' I said, thinking to myself how long life was if you got it wrong; how terribly long. 'What a sentence for a brain like that. What torture.'

'Oh, I don't think he was unhappy. Just not all there. You don't have to talk to people much. Just dole out the parking tickets. Which is what he did to me as it happens. I couldn't have been more than five minutes over time, so I chased the bloke down and found Gerv. He was perfectly pleasant, although it was hard to tell if he really recognised me or not. He still had those rosy cheeks and exactly the same hank of hair was sticking out from under his cap. I tried to use the 'old school tie' but he wasn't having any of it. Just said something in Latin, which I didn't understand of course, then walked off.'

'You know,' I said, using my last reserves of researcher's guile. 'It's the most remarkable coincidence but I'm pretty sure I saw someone like Gervis doing his stuff in the car park by the library.'

'Not possible,' Piggy said, draining his tankard. 'He got given the boot years ago. There was some incident involving violence again. It made it into the Evening Mail. I even think he was sectioned somewhere.'

I said 'goodbye' as he was stuffing himself improbably into a taxicab, a performance the Pakistani driver was well acquainted with judging by his patient smile.

'Goodbye, Duncan,' he said waving regally. 'I shall be there! We shall all be there!'

RED FLAGS

*

'There' was St. Stephens Parish Church, a late Victorian religious barn, all spikes and gables. It stood on a knoll overlooking the village like a mad aunt who'd forgotten where she was and why she was there. In his last decade my father had taken to 'popping up' occasionally to join the sprinkling of people who still knew what 'evensong' was, although he was not in the least bit religious in any spiritual way that I could make out. I think he did it more out of a sense of public duty. "Help keep the old place ticking over," he'd said. "Either that or a Carpet Warehouse." He found the Vicar sympathetic, "Indian chap. Very pleasant fellow." "Hedging your bets, Dad," I'd said, and we'd laughed. He had a healthy sense of his own mortality, my father. Dunkirk, Monte Casino, D-Day; he knew more than anybody we aren't put on this earth forever.

'We' turned out to be what looked like half the town. As our cortege passed through the graffiti scrawled on granite gates (*Albion Posse...Riverside Boyz*), people were still streaming up the path in the pouring rain. Cars choked the surrounding streets.

'Good grief!' my wife said, sitting beside me in the black Mercedes following the hearse. 'I had no idea.'

'Neither had I.'

I felt that liquid sensation in my bowels which in my case always heralds the prospect of public speaking. My talking image on the screen never ceases to amaze me. That smooth, urbane dwarf is not me. I'm a bag of nerves.

My daughters were impressed too, in their teenage way.

'Wow, is this all for Gramps!?'

'Nah, it's for the Queen, stoopid.'

'Big gig, Dad!'

'You could put it that way, but I wish you wouldn't.'

They began fussing with their hats and checking their make up in little mirrors.

It was clear to me straightaway that I'd misjudged the mood. For some wishy-washy reason I'd envisaged a sort of celebration of a good man's long life. I hadn't banked on the weight of *their* grief. He'd touched hundreds of lives, taught thousands of boys. For a lot of them he'd been the last living reminder of their 'Halcyon Days'. Most were now old themselves. But here they were, boys again, bowed in silence, summoned to appear before The Digger for one last time. It was standing room only for some. They lined the walls and crowded the font at the back. The organ mewled in dignified sympathy. On rubber legs I paced slowly behind the simple coffin, wishing I'd left the oration to the Vicar. In full rig, The Reverend Favill was waiting for us up in the pulpit, a fakir with stage fright. It was probably his biggest 'gig' too. There was a smell of rained-on overcoats and mothballed suits. Necks were craning. In an age of pointless celebrity, I'd become the town's most famous son. Squeezing out what I hoped was a smile of gratitude for their having come in such numbers, I beamed it meekly around. Some smiled back, shyly. Piggy, stuffed into his aisle seat, gave me an encouraging little wave. We took our own seats at the front to the left of the coffin, which I still couldn't quite believe contained my father. How small it was!

'Dearly beloved, we are gathered here today in the sight of God to remember and celebrate the life of Richard Trowell...'

A hymn: The Old Rugged Cross.

The reading: John 4:3 'Do not let your hearts be troubled...'

It was galloping by and I began to feel more and more like a spectator. Then, 'I'd like now to invite Richard's son, Duncan...'

Clumping my way to the lectern I began to feel rather sick. The three large whiskies I'd had before we set off had gone stale in my head. I cleared my throat and a giant rasping noise filled the place. My few, scribbled notes appeared to have transformed themselves into some kind of impenetrable code. How could I, of all people, have been so casual in my preparations on this, of all occasions? Me, 'Trawler Trowell', as I was known for my appetite for detailed research. From the off the register was all wrong, far too breezy. It was the tone we'd always bantered in, father and son, emotions, feelings, kept at a safe distance. The joke I made about how many in the congregation would have 'passed through The Diggers hands' with its not so veiled reference to the corporal punishment of their schooldays, fell horribly flat. The times had moved on. Even they were conscious of its more sinister contemporary connotations. As my voice boomed and blundered on through the over amplified PA, I could feel the disappointment swelling. I was not living up to my billing. Then, as the thing was coming to a close, an awful noise went up from somewhere at the back of the sea of faces. At first it was a continuous animal yelping of pain. Heads swivelled on arthritic necks. At length it settled to a low, ululating wail of grief. It wasn't difficult to pinpoint who it was coming from. A tall and willowy man was rocking back and forth in his pew: Gervis. Next to him sat a dumpy, matronly-looking woman half his age. She was trying to calm him down by stroking the hump of his back.

'Job done,' I said to my wife miserably, in a pause between shaking hands as we, the family, stood in the portico receiving condolences. The mourners were streaming back down the knoll to their cars and taxis. I looked for Gervis but he'd been hustled away. Piggy dragged himself towards me like a giant ambulant wineskin, full to bursting.

'Well done, Duncan,' he said. 'You did the old man proud.'

'Hardly. I was bloody awful.'

'Not *that* awful. Very sticky wicket. Not easy.'

'Pretty bloody awful all the same.'

'Did you see Gerv? Did you *hear* Gerv?'

'Good God, was that Gervis?' I lied. 'I thought I recognised him. I'd rather like to speak to him. I don't know why. I just feel I ought to.'

'I doubt if you'll have the honour. That's his outing over for the year, I bet. Listen, you're busy. We'll have a good natter when the dear old fellow's finally up there with the angels. See you at the club for the wake of wakes. Family time now.'

I liked him even more and found myself regretting I'd cut myself off from the town and all these nice people.

Our cortege set off again, crawling through the village and then accelerating as we hit open country. As we approached the crematorium, black smoke was going up into the grey sky from one of the chimneys. The sight of it brought the whole thing home. A life was going up in smoke and shortly my own father's, would follow it. I began to cry, silently, for the first time in the proceedings.

We filed in and there stood the Reverend Favill again, as though he'd conjured himself out of a hat. Music of a non-funereal nature was playing; Glen Miller's In The Mood. My father's last laugh. Right through into his early eighties he could still perform a stately jitterbug. It had been his party piece at the annual Rugby Club Ball, amazing the younger ladies who queued up to be hurled about the dance floor. I tried to smile but couldn't. The few people there, his 'inner circle' of friends, all much younger than him, had their faces twisted out of shape too, set somewhere between laughing and crying. No matter how rationally you packaged it, it was still a sad business which had to be got through. Taking my seat, I gave them all a stolid look of thanks. Thanks for coming. Thanks for seeing it through. Then things became suddenly brisk and business-like, like I imagine an execution to be. Another hymn: Bringing In the Sheaves. A quick prayer and before I knew it, it was '...we commend his soul to God in the hope of everlasting peace,' and the neat folds of curtain were closing round the coffin.

'Nooooooo!'

The cry drowned out the mewling of the organ. All heads couldn't help but turn to look behind. It was an obscenely intrusive noise, an explosion of raw grief out of all proportion to the loss. After all, my father had not been some youth taken in the prime of life.

He stood at the back by the door, the dumpy young woman beside him barely reaching up to his chest. In the much smaller confines of the chapel I could make him out clearly. He was wearing some kind of blazer which looked homemade. Gold and blue braiding had been clumsily stitched to the lapels. Tears were pouring over his rosy cheeks and down into his mouth, contorted in pain.

'Nooooo! He was the last! The last!'

'That's enough, Paul,' his partner soothed in a practiced sort of way.

'He was the last! Who shall walk beside me now? Who shall I be now?'

'Paul, that's enough I said!'

He shook her arm from his. For a moment I thought he might make a bolt for the curtains, although by now there would be nothing behind them. But he stayed where he was, rocking on his heels. I noticed his trousers were a good six inches too short for his legs. You could see the tops of his socks.

'Who shall I be now? Who shall I be now?' he wailed with the abandon of a spoilt child denied an ice cream. His partner made to steer him away and out of the door that we would shortly have to exit through ourselves. He shoved her to one side.

'Who shall I be now? Who shall walk beside me now? What is left of me now?'

I'm not the kind of man to call on in a crisis. I was paralysed, caught in a no man's land of conflicting feelings; outrage at the intrusion, the ruining of the moment, and deep sympathy with his pain. Then, still howling, he began to march down the aisle with great, mad strides of his gangly legs.

'Paul! Come back here this instant!' the woman cried as if to a dog chasing sheep in a field.

I'd never really been called upon to display physical courage before. The extraordinariness of the situation surprised the instinct in me. I stepped out of our pew and barred his way. If it came to blows, I'd have to take them. There was no one there sufficiently physically imposing to hide behind.

'Pull yourself together, Gervis,' I heard myself bark in the voice of my father. It stopped him in his tracks. He stood looking around him as if woken from a dream.

'This won't do, Gervis! This simply will not do, will it!?'

'No, Sir,' he said.

'Man of your stature should be setting an example, not crying like a baby.'

'Yes, Sir.'

'So, Gervis, take this down,' I said, smiling kindly now. It was a line from Pliny that I'd had to translate for my Cambridge entrance exam, resurfacing after forty years.

'Excessive grief does not become the stoic mind.'

The effect was immediate, as though some bolt of electricity had passed between us. His features rearranged themselves into those of a rosy cheeked schoolboy, eager to please.

'Two hundred if you please, Gervis: 'Excessive grief does not become the stoic mind.''

The dumpy young woman was now tugging at his elbow, apologising profusely. I noticed she was wearing some kind of nurse's uniform under her black coat.

'I'm so, so sorry, Mr Trowell,' she said. 'It's all been my fault. I should have known he wasn't up to it. But he insisted. You insisted, didn't you, Paul? And you promised to be on your best behaviour!'

Gervis drew himself up to his full height. Looking down his long, fine, Roman nose he said,

'I consider myself suitably chastised already, Deidre,' and skated her back up the aisle and out of the door.

*

He found my London address. Easy enough to do, I suppose. A

few days later a brown envelope landed on the doormat as I was drinking my morning tea. It contained an exercise book, the first ten pages covered in his beautiful copperplate handwriting:

Excessive grief does not become the stoic mind

Excessive grief does not become the stoic mind

I kept the house. I didn't want to cut myself off from the town completely, and it can only go up in value anyway. I use it as a holiday retreat and when I'm there, I visit. Some days, when his medication is right, we chat away for an hour or so in French. He panics a bit when it's time for me to leave. He has trouble projecting his mind imaginatively beyond the here and now, so he thinks I'm going away for good. This is very common in paranoid schizophrenics, I'm told. That's why I usually leave him with some pithy and reassuring aphorism which I order him to copy out. It seems to calm him down and gives an excuse to exercise his beautiful schoolboy's hand. I keep the exercise books in my trunk in the loft.

HAIRBALLS

1

'In the Museum of Natural History at Kuching,' Tim said in that posh neigh of a voice he put on when holding the floor, 'there's a glass case containing a perfect crocodilian hairball. It's about the size of a small cannonball, the colour of hashish, and it's all that remains of your landlady's first husband.'

The three of them laughed, rather savagely Peter thought, baring their unpleasant yellow middle-aged teeth. This made him feel every bit the innocent abroad. He'd not long arrived and was especially in awe of the old hands he came across. Back in ninety-one he was a young man, still in his twenties. Anyone over fifty seemed packed full of wisdom and experience he could never hope to attain. Founding fathers of the University's Department of Zoology the Three Wise Men, as he called them, had been midwives to the country's emergence from its primeval jungle, and all over the world before that. Brunei was Peter's first foreign posting. He was anxious not to appear gauche. So, when he mentioned Haja Rosni's name and they let out a collective guffaw, he felt himself blushing. Had he made some elementary slip in pronunciation or nomenclature of the kind which pedants (they could be incredibly pedantic on points of local knowledge) live for?

She was his landlady and, trying to display a little worldliness himself, he'd said that he found her attractive. In truth, it was more than that. Although she was a few years his senior, he was in love. Half-Malay, half-Chinese, she possessed the petite tropical lusciousness he'd started dreaming of as soon as the contract came through. "Goodnight Ladies! Goodnight you beefy English ladies. Goodnight!" he congratulated himself mentally, letting the kids riot as he drudged out those last months at The Meadows Comprehensive. Hello...?...Hello, Haja Rosni!

'She's helping me to settle in,' he'd said, cryptically, his sixth tin of Tiger bringing out the bloke in him.

'What's her name?'

'Haja Rosni.'

Once they'd calmed down, Tim claimed poll position of beginning at the beginning of what he called a 'bloody good yarn". At the time, Peter had no idea he was to play a part in its unfolding; 'In the Museum of Natural History at Kuching...'

'Don't forget the watch, Tim,' Eric said.

'If you'll only give me the chance, Eric!'

'Yeah, give him a chance, Eric!' said Dan. 'Fair play!'

Stuck with each other's company for so long, they had a tendency to bicker amongst themselves in public. It didn't help that all three were scientists, given to that semi-autism which stems from needing to be proved right, or wrong, all the time. There was a touch of the Music Hall about them, too; the suspicion that it was all an act, but that the act had taken them over, like the Marx Brothers, and they couldn't stop hamming it up. Since he never saw them apart, it was impossible to get beyond the vaudevillian facade. To Peter, they existed as a single entity, in hilarious exile from their individual selves, and perhaps because of this he began to look forward to meeting them at The Orchid. There wasn't much else in the way of company, anyway. You couldn't be too picky.

'As I was about to say, before I was so rudely interrupted by our little friend (Eric was as short as 'Tiny' Tim was tall), the case also contains a watch, laid beside the hairball. Its hands give the time at 4.36 p.m.; the exact moment of the attack since the watch was not water-resistant, almost certainly the time of the unfortunate spouse's death. A twenty-foot croc would have killed him instantly. My money would have been on a punctured heart. The incisors of a giant that size would have penetrated his sternum with the ease of a stiletto. Dead before he was spun.'

Tim scratched at the scab on his scalp, the aftermath of his most recent operation. He was being slowly devoured by melanoma, a condition he regarded with a curious scientific detachment as offending bits of him were cut away.

'Let me get this right,' Peter said. The conversation had taken one of those jagged turns that often threw him. 'Haja Rosni's first husband was eaten by a crocodile?'

'That's about the long and short of it, blue,' Dan said in his Australian bushman's voice from under his bushman's hat. Like Tim, he had brown, leathery skin, the result of decades of field work in blazing hot places. All that was missing were the dangling corks.

'Why on earth would she go to the trouble of preserving the hairball and watch like that? Seems a bit macabre, no? She comes across as pretty normal to me.'

They exchanged one of their knowing looks especially reserved for neophytes to local lore. Eric took up the thread in his flat, no nonsense Yorkshire tones, which jarred with the rather camp-looking yachting cap he always wore (he had a boat he'd sail inexpertly from time to time when the mood took him).

'Revenge, most probably. She's as hard as nails under that doe-eyed exterior. The first Mr Rosni was, by all accounts, a bastard. A rich bastard, but a bastard all the same. She was only fourteen when she was given away. Arranged marriage of course. Her father was a Hakka Chinese from Guangdong. Came over to work the rubber plantations along the Sarawak coast, escaping The Great Helmsman. Married a native Iban, barely out of the jungle, and a fine looking one if the offspring is anything to go by. Both dirt poor. Hairball, prior to his untimely demise, was some sort of merchant-entrepreneur, a Muslim, but a drinker. Her parents must have had their eye on the main chance. Didn't have any qualms about giving her over to a violent drunk. He knocked her about something rotten.'

'Hang, on,' Peter said, 'you're going too fast. How do you know all this stuff? Not from her, surely?'

'The woman,' said Tim, 'is notorious. In a place as small as this, you can't escape a...how should I put it?... *colourfu*l past.'

'So how *did* she end up getting widowed? I mean what *were* the circumstances? How did Haji whatever his name was manage to get himself eaten by a croc? Not an exceptional occurrence for a jungle dweller, admittedly, but for a merchant...'

'This is where we start to put the pieces together. If our vertically challenged friend would care to continue...'

'Thank you, Your Honour. The popular reconstruction goes something like this,' Eric said, pulling at the ring of his umpteenth Tiger and filling his glass. They were inside the 'bar', for a change. It was the top floor deluxe suite of the hotel converted for the purposes of clandestine drinking now the 'fundos' had got their way and turned the whole tiny country nominally dry. Normally they'd have been out on the terrace taking in the canopy of moonlit treetops but a booming discharge of celestial guns behind the clouds warned of an electrical storm on its way. The sky was a light show of white and blue flashes. At such moments the air would be crackling. You could feel it tickling your skin, feeling you up for the kill. Death by lightning was quite common. They were doing the sensible thing.

'She must have got wind on the jungle grapevine that a man-eater was on the loose around the system of ponds in the hills out of town. Worked its way up from the Pelaban River, most likely. Moves were afoot to build the holiday lodges that are there today. She took him up to have a gander. Told him she could get him on the inside of the deal, probably. Help him persuade her headman to take the bribe. As Tim, our Lizard King, will tell you, you can keep a croc local by leaving bits of rotting carcass around, just like you'd keep a cat if you needed it for mousing. She knew he couldn't swim. Whether she pushed him in, nobody will ever know. The police certainly couldn't pin anything on her. She turns up all floods of, excuse the pun, crocodile tears a day later and they pile in the Land Rovers to hunt the bugger down.'

At this point Dan jumped in to claim his share of the telling.

'And you know what they used to finish the bugger off?'

Peter spread his hands wide in a gesture of surrender to his habitual ignorance. The evening was showing every sign of turning outlandish. Evenings at The Orchid often did. He'd come out for a few tins before an early night and end up at two in the morning with the car in a storm drain, looking into the eyes of a giant monitor lizard.

'They blasted the bastard with every type of gun they could lay their hands on. Nothing doing. In the end they had to call the army in with grenades. Frickin grenades, I tell you.'

The entry of firearms and explosives into the story had a special appeal for Dangerous Dan. His great passion was for shooting anything that moved in the jungle. Barbeques at his villa were apt to be of an exotic nature ('Python, anyone!?'). The ring and little finger of his left hand were missing.

'Miracle there was anything left of the fricker, once they'd finished.'

'But there was,' Peter said, 'and I find it extraordinarily odd she should want to preserve the bit of it that was her husband in a glass case for all to see.'

'You are,' said Tim, 'familiar with the Iban and their rather singular ways, I take it?'

Peter spread his hands in surrender again.

'Head-hunters. A less sentimental bunch you cannot imagine. Compassion is something anthropologically alien to them. It doesn't exist. Can't be allowed to exist in their world. They simply leave their old and sick behind to die. The misfortune of others excites neither pleasure nor sympathy. It's all the same to them.'

'You mean they're hard little bastards,' Dan said.

'Precisely, my convict friend.'

There was something too of this quality Peter had noticed in the pupils he taught. The school, built on a plot hacked out of jungle hillside on the furthest fringes of Bandar town, was for children of parents who, although supposedly urbanised still lived mentally in and for the jungle. The pupils themselves would often be up all night hunting rare birds for their feathers. They'd sometimes offer him samples as a bribe for letting them sleep in class. He'd noticed that nothing - teasing, bullying, beating, could induce them to cry.

'Haja Rosni,' Tim went on, 'comes from such stock. Her grandfather would have been spearing the enemy and the grandmother hanging the heads out to dry. The whole Islam thing is only the thinnest of thin skin deep. She might have kept the hairball as a sort of trophy and then got bored with it; donated it to the museum as a final twist of the knife. Then again, she might have been completely indifferent and just let whoever discovered it hand it over for money. Who knows how her mind operates? The point is, she was hardly in mourning.'

Peter's lonely nights in Haja Rosni's rambling villa were already febrile with fantasies of her stepping out of the shapely western dresses she preferred and into the huge double bed he lay sweating in. Now, a fresh vision of her as native to the jungle had been added to the erotic mix.

'When did all this happen?' he said.

'Four thirty-six p.m. October 11th 1974,' Eric, reeled off.

'Good God. That was my tenth Birthday!'

Again, they bared their yellow fangs and laughed.

'What are the chances of that!?'

'Three hundred and sixty-five to one,' Tim said. 'Roughly the same odds as the fiscally challenged Yorkshire pygmy here getting his round in.'

Peter excused himself and headed for the bogs. They were situated in the bathroom of what was once the en-suite master bedroom, where the pool table was kept. As he stood relieving himself he experienced a sudden attack of mild euphoria. Life, a dull affair on the whole up until then, had begun to feel dramatic. Like Alice and her Wonderland, he'd been floated down from the world of properly ordered things into this odd little hothouse of a country, where nothing was as it should be. And now it appeared he was in love with a putative murderess from a head-hunting tribe, and she, a married woman some eight years his senior, quite possibly in love with him. How many people he knew back 'home' could say that of themselves?

Returning to his seat he found a fresh can of Tiger waiting on the table. Popping it, he picked up the thread, eager to know more.

'So, did she inherit?'

'A packet,' Eric said. 'Sold up in Kuching and made her way here just as it was taking off. Bought a string of little shops. Had no problem finding another rich bugger to tie the knot with, either. She was still in her teens and must have been an absolute stunner. He was a 'penguin', a Pengiran...royalty,' he added in explanation. 'The twentieth cousin removed from the top man, something like that, so it put him about half way up the Sultan's family tree by my estimate. Wasn't short of a shekel now the oil was really flowing.'

'Wasn't?'

A collective nod and grin. They were enjoying themselves enormously.

'You mean the current Mr Rosni is not the second Mr Rosni.'

Another nod and grin, as if to a village idiot.

'Boa Constrictor?' Peter hazarded. 'Rogue elephant?'

'Nothing so dramatic this time,' Eric chuckled. 'Over to our digitally deficient Spider Man there,' he said, pointing to Dan. 'But before we continue, shall we go outside? Looks like the storm's rolled over.'

They took up their usual seats on the terrace. The Orchid was set up on a spur in the river, in dense jungle. From up in the penthouse, it felt as if you were riding a carpet over billowing waves of green. The storm had emptied the clouds and a fresh, chill moon hung over the treetops. There wasn't a breath of wind and the moronic yell of the jungle was doubly loud. Although he wasn't quite aware of it yet, Peter was falling in love with the jungle, too.

'*Lycosa atrax robustus*, one of the most poisonous arachnids, pound for pound, going,' Dan said, settling into his chair. 'You won't have known Tom of Tom's Ridge fame?'

'Died on the Hash a few years back?' Peter said. This time he wasn't completely in the dark. Dan was referring, he knew, to a veteran 'hasher' who'd croaked it in action. The Hash was a form of cross country running through jungle, following a paper trail laid down by the 'hares' beforehand and ending in copious consumption of Tiger at the finishing post. He'd done it once, and once had been enough. Roughly half way round, at the top of a ridge, he'd been greeted by a man in full Jeeves the Butler get up, proffering a tray of gin and tonics in memory of Tom. That was the precise spot where he'd collapsed and died.

'They thought it was a heart attack at first, naturally. But the autopsy showed paralysis of the nervous system leading to sudden death. Cause: our little friend *Lycosa atrax robustus*, better known as the Borneo Blueback Fungus Spider. Incredibly rare but one of those things. And even frickin' rarer in a dry urban domestic environment. The little buggers don't normally stray from the hot, wet and steamy. Why would they? Nothing in it for them. The second Mr Rosni was found dead in bed. According to her, she woke up in the morning to find herself next to a corpse. Nice touch. Could have been her. Oh boo hoo hoo etc. etc.'

'And the Rosni financial empire gets another great shot in the arm?'

'Got it in one, our Man from Mansfield,' neighed Tim. 'There'd been no children. Perhaps Hairball had seen to that with his brutality.'

'And now we're on to hubby number three,' Eric said. 'But she's got to be extra careful this time because the man who currently shares her bed is Haji Bendaya. Not only a Penguin of some standing but ex-Chief of Police to boot. That's how brazen the woman is. Seduced him during the investigation itself.'

'Rich as Croesus?'

'Naturally.'

'So,' Tim said, wrapping up, 'the moral of the story is, especially in your case: do...not...have...carnal...knowledge of *La Rosni*. Not if you want to wander this earth for your full three score years and ten.'

*

He ignored the warning. His infatuation grew with her increasingly frequent visits. Each time she showed up it was in a fresh outfit lovelier than the last. That she wanted him he was certain. The fact that she was married, an older woman, only served to inflame his own need to have her. He began to listen out for the protesting screech of her car as she crashed inexpertly through its gears on the way up the winding road that lead to his ridge top villa. She drove a rare and expensive, low slung two-seater. With a squeal of brakes, it would come to rest in the driveway next to his distinctly shabby looking Korean tin box. Then she would spend a good half a minute revving the engine, summoning him to greet her. This he would eventually do, barefoot and sweating on the porch, having put on a t-shirt for old-fashioned decency's sake.

On the day that things went up a gear, the excuse was an inspection of the new water storage unit. Its predecessor had ended its life spewing streams of orange rust. The heat and humidity ate into everything. Things were always breaking down. There was no shortage of perfectly innocent pretexts for her calls.

The unit was in the garden, a patch of scrubby vegetation fighting a losing battle against the encroaching jungle. There was a monkey perched on it, insolently regarding their approach. She shooed it away.

'Blaay monkeys. Blaay everywhere.'

Her English and the voice it came out in, was as unclassifiable as its owner: a mix of 'pukka' Empire-speak instilled by old style elocution lessons, and a highly personalised version of Desperate Dan's 'Strine twang. Had she taken an Australian lover in the past? Was it possible that Dan himself, in younger days, had had, in Tim's phrase, 'carnal knowledge' of her? It wasn't beyond speculation, Peter knew. He wasn't *that* innocent. For some reason she had terrible difficulty with the consonant *d* when occurring between two vowels so that words like bloody - a favourite expletive which peppered her conversation - were elided into a single elongated syllable.

'Blaay hot t'aay,' she said, inspection over. 'Can I come inside? A drink would be nice. Got any gin?'

She herself made absolutely no concessions to the new fundamentalist order. Her tastes were aggressively western. Having grown up dirt poor, she wasn't going to let a bunch of beard-wearing killjoys stop her enjoyment of the good life that had fallen into her lap. She was wearing a blue knee length dress belted so as to accentuate her tiny waist, and matching sling-back shoes. Peter was sweating (he was always sweating). Her light brown skin was dry and the long black pelt of her hair hung perfectly straight. The heat seemed powerless to dishevel her as it did his female British colleagues (not he suspected, particularly presentable in more temperate climes). He was reminded of that line by Kipling: 'I've a neater sweeter maiden in a greener cleaner land'.

'You're in luck. Jackie arrived last night,' he said. 'Thanks for putting me on to him.' Jackie was his Chinese 'milkman', one of the taxi drivers now doubling as bootleggers since the ban.

'My pleasure,' she said. 'Anything I can do to help, just ask me.'

'Anything?' he said, raising an eyebrow, taking his cue.

She laughed in that surprisingly harsh, rasping way he'd noticed before. He suspected that life with Haji Bendaya, luxurious though it might be, was not exactly unbridled fun.

They made their way to the kitchen where she stood, leaning back on the table, watching him fix the drinks.

'Cheers!' she said, taking the tumbler full of gin and tonic.

'Cheers!'

For once, nothing was wrong with, or needed adding to, the house. They were suddenly at a loss for conversation. Peter smiled. She smiled back with her perfect white teeth.

'That's a nice dress,' he said, goofily.

'Thank you, Peter.'

'What material is it?'

'I honestly don't know. Perhaps you could tell me. Come and feel it if you like.'

He crossed the few feet that separated them and held the

material of the capped sleeve between his fingers, rubbing it lightly. Before he could say 'chiffon', she took his hand and bit it, quite hard. He was thrown into confusion. Had he gone too far, or was it a playful gesture? Perhaps it was she who was confused, torn between the urge to kiss him and the need to hold back from the precipice. The kiss which eventually did come wasn't in the least bit practiced, as he'd have expected from a woman thrice married. But neither could he say he'd 'never been kissed like that before' because the experience was very similar to being nibbled and licked by the small dog he'd once bought for company during the lonely hell of his teaching practice year. It would go bonkers when he got home from school, jumping and wriggling in his arms, just as she was doing.

'Ow! Slow down.'

'Sorry,' she said, drawing back.

Then he bent his knees so she no longer had to stand on tip toe and squeezed her body to him, covering her mouth with his. He felt her heart beating incredibly fast, like a little bird's heart. When they disengaged, she went straight to the window, peering out anxiously, before drawing the blinds. There were always Indonesian gardeners, watchmen, workmen on the prowl; imported labour, very poor, looking for leverage. An uneasy feeling of being watched all the time was compounded by the knowledge that they despised you. Their smiles meant nothing. They smiled permanently. It got on Peter's nerves. It obviously worried Haja Rosni too.

'No need for that. Let's go upstairs,' he said, and within a minute they were tearing off each other's clothes like lovers in a bad French film.

Never before had he felt such fierce sexual need in a woman as when her perfectly proportioned, almost miniature body was writhing under his that first time. At the moment of climax her eyeballs rolled back in their sockets as though she were casting out demons. Spent, he rolled off her.

'Blaay hell!'

'Nice?'

'Incrayble.'

'For me too,' he said, stroking the leaf-shaped motif of lifted skin around the protruding belly button.

'Does it mean anything?' he said, once he'd got his breath back.

'Nothing. Silly jungle stuff. My mother. One day she took me back to the tribe for cutting. She was worried if I didn't get cut, I'd never get pregnant. All stupid.'

'And all the Islam stuff?'

'I do what I'm told, when I'm told. The rest of the time...'

Peter got up and fetched their drinks and cigarettes. They sat smoking, drinking and chatting with an ease that surprised them both. Then they made love again, before it was time to shower together with refreshingly non-orange water. Once dressed and groomed, as if nothing had happened, she jumped into the two-seater and roared off down the hill with a cheery wave.

There was no phone in the house, so her visits were nearly always impromptu. Sometimes Peter would be there, sometimes not. It kept things fresh between them. He never asked about her past. Whatever she told him came without prompting. She had no fond remembrance of her previous two husbands, to whom she referred as Bastard Number 1 and Bastard Number 2, and who'd, happily, died, one drowned in an accident the other of heart failure. Tim's warning seemed absurd. He simply couldn't bring himself to believe what they'd said had any truth to it. They'd been hamming her up for their own amusement. People *did* die young in Brunei and even younger back then. The first husband had been an alcoholic, prone no doubt to the usual calamities of the species, the second enormously fat. Nothing could have been more natural.

'And Number 3?' he said once, after their lovemaking.

She just laughed. Peter laughed, too. When, a few weeks later, he told her he was planning on spending the Eid break in Kuching, he thought he saw a shadow of suspicion darken her face but put it down to him going away and leaving her for a week. They'd become very close very quickly.

*

He took the boat. It was the most adventurous thing he'd done in his life. The packed little cruiser chugged past water villages perched on stilts along the river banks, a wall of thick emerald jungle gleaming on either side. Then, out into the South China Sea, huge thunderheads of pure white cloud boiling up in the blue sky. For a day and a night, it hugged the coast in a series of short hops, pulling in to tiny settlements along the way to disgorge and take on board a shifting cargo of babbling Malays and their mysterious bundles.

At last they entered the broad sweep of the Sarawak, straining against the current, and docked in Kuching. Peter was back in the world of the White Rajas he'd spent much time researching. The pinks, lime greens, ochres of their palaces and neat colonnaded public buildings sparkled amidst the palms. 'Coolies' scampered barefoot over the docks bent double under huge loads.

Peter bounced down the gangway and into the tangle of streets adjoining the stinking fish market where he had a couple of early morning Tigers before making for his hotel.

The Hilton was brand new. He stayed there the whole week, venturing forth each day into the heat and chaos on a giant wheeled sit up and beg bicycle he rented off a Tamil, retreating at dusk to the luxury of the cool hotel. He was having his cake and eating it.

On his last day, the museum, closed for Eid, opened. He got there early before the crowds. As a rule, museums, galleries, exhibitions of all kinds, left him bad tempered and exhausted. On this occasion he couldn't wait to get through the doors to find out if The Three Wise Men had been having him on. After about a quarter of an hour of pacing by glass cases full of petrified, angry looking wildlife, just when he'd started to congratulate himself on his lack of gullibility, he found it.

On a faded piece of card, in ink turned brown with time, the curator's neat handwriting read:

These are the remains of Haji Salim Hao Liu, killed by 'Buyung Senang' - the largest crocodile ever recorded in the state of Sarawak - at 4.36 p.m. October 11th 1974.

It was just as Tim had described: a perfect sphere, the size of a small cannonball and the colour of hashish. Beside it lay a rusted, old fashioned wind-up watch with the hands showing the time recorded on the card. There was nothing more; no information as to who Haji Salim Hao Liu had been or how he had ended up in the belly of Buyung Senang.

He stood gazing into the case, transfixed by the horror, the absurdity of it all. He pictured her, a wisp of a sixteen-year old standing obediently behind the cunning merchant, already counting the money he could make by turning the place in to a wealthy tourist's paradise. Then the violent shove in the back, the splash, the cries for help turning to shrieks of horror as the massive jaws clamped down and the tail began to thrash; the water turning crimson then, silence, and the girl that had grown into his lover skipping away to her tribe in the jungle.

It was all preposterous, he knew, but now his mind couldn't rest. All through the journey back it throbbed along with the engine of the boat, turning the thing over and over, again and again.

*

Mid-morning, the day after he got back, he heard the familiar wrenching noise and squeal of an engine in vehement protest at being made to climb such an incline still in third gear. Then, the other squeal of brakes and, 'Parp! Parp! Parp! Vroom! Vroom! Vroom!'

He stopped frying the egg he was cooking for a late breakfast and headed for the porch. This first sight of her for over a week, waving from the open-topped car, confirmed he was still very much in love. She seemed more beautiful than ever. Their lovemaking took on a new intensity. He felt confident that lying in bed, spent, their intimacy somehow legitimised the question:

'In the Natural History Museum at Kuching,' he said, doing his best to sound casual, 'I came across a hairball, the remains of someone called Haji Salim Hao Liu. He was eaten by a crocodile. Didn't you say that was the name of your first husband?'

She betrayed not the slightest flicker of surprise.

'I told you. He died in an acci-ent.'

'But not *that* kind of accident.'

'You never asked.'

'Couldn't you have buried him, or something?'

'There was nothing left to bury.'

'The hairball?'

'You can't bury a hairball. Ri-iculous.'

'Well couldn't you have just thrown it away?'

'I din't see it. One of the policemen must have sole it to the museum.'

'But you could have objected.'

'Why? He was a blaay bastard. He used to rape me.'

'So, if I get eaten by one of those boa constrictors everyone's talking about up in Bukit Shabanga, you'd have what's left of me put in a glass case.'

'No, you're different,' she said, laughing. 'And besize I'm going to eat you first.' He felt her lips working their way down his torso and left the matter there.

The affair settled down into something almost approaching comfortable. She appeared to have very few commitments in her married life and little to do other than amuse herself as far as the tiny backwater of a country would allow. Of course, they couldn't be seen out together. Their paths crossed outside of the villa only once. It was one of those big gatherings to do with education at which minor royalty was required to earn its keep by sitting on a stage pretending to listen to various speakers droning on. Peter was astonished to see her up there, an entirely different person but equally stunning even in national dress (a kind of badly fitting floral tablecloth with matching headscarf), sitting beside her husband. He was exactly as Peter had pictured him: a soft and pampered-looking man old enough to be her father. He felt no jealousy; only a sense of irritation that he was getting in the way of what could have been fun, a 'proper' love affair. To be able to speed along jungle lanes together in her car from one speak-easy to another -The Smiling Cat; The Happy House - was something they could only dream of. Afterwards, balancing a plate of chicken and rice, he caught her eye through the crowd. She refused to acknowledge his smile. Not long after this she arrived in an unusual temper.

'He knows!' she said.

'Jesus. How?'

'I think he's had me followed. It won't be the first time.'

'How did you find out?'

'He told me last night.'

'Has he told anyone else? I mean is he going to turn you over to the Fundos?'

'Not a chance. Too much of a scannal. Besize, he's got no photographs. No real proof.'

'Nobody else knows?'

'Only his personal guard. The one who probably followed me. He would never say a word. Too dangerous for him.'

'What's going to happen to me?'

'Nothing. If I stop seeing you he'll leave you alone.'

'But I can't stop seeing you. I love you.'

'An I love you, but its blaay impossible now.'

'But this is ridiculous.'

'I know. But he's a powerful man.'

'Can't we do anything?'

'You do nothing. Don't try and contact me or you certainly will never see me again. Maybe something might happen to him. Who knows?'

She displayed no self-pity or tearfulness, merely handing him the draining board that had been brought along as pretext for her visit then, without any kind of final goodbye, got back into the car and sped away.

*

Peter had to move house 'to be nearer to his school', he lied. Life went back to being sexless, but worse than before. In the past he'd found it easy, or *easier*, to go without once he'd got back into a single man's habits. In the wake of a passionate affair he discovered it was close to torture. He'd got used to pouring himself in to her. Now all the energy, love, need, that had been flowing out of him to her became dammed up again. He found it hard to concentrate. His performance at school was at best perfunctory, something he couldn't afford since he was still on probation. He found himself shouting at the pupils in genuine, as opposed to professionally modulated, rage. He slept badly, waking at every belch of the gecko lizards stuck like jelly babies to the sweating bedroom walls. Drinking commenced at two in the afternoon as soon as he got home from work and just carried on, pointlessly.

So, it was already half-loaded, a couple of months after they'd parted, that he drove the pink Korean tin box through the twilight of a Thursday evening on his way to the border with Sabah. Thursday nights, the start of the so called three-day weekend, were always Borders Night. Friday was a chance for the locals to catch up on their piety and for non-believers to catch up on their drinking. He'd then return to school on Saturday, a duty undertaken with as little seriousness as possible on all sides, before soaking through what was left of it and then, Sunday. The trip to the borders was to stock up on supplies for the binge, as well as to start things off with a bang. Sabah, belonging to the Malaysian Federation, wasn't dry. A generous quota of 'duty free' was permitted to the *hawaja*. The spirit of enterprise entirely lacking in its oil-rich neighbour had ensured that along its borders a number of shanty towns had sprung up; shacks strung between the trees selling booze, barbeque and sex in the most unhygienic conditions imaginable. It was the Wild West, about as far removed from the ordered greyness of England as could be imagined. Peter loved it.

The box beetled its way along the plain into a blood orange sunset. He had the windows down and an iced Tiger in his hand trailing outside. Tangy veils of bonfire smoke hung over the rice fields with pretty girls in broad conical straw hats tending water buffalo up to their haunches in mud. The place had besotted him to an extent that the thought of returning to his old life under leaden English skies made him feel sick. There was no reason why he should have to return but sometimes, unbidden, the coffin lid of memory would swing open and the corpse of that dead existence come staggering towards him, arms outstretched. He began to volunteer for tedious extra duties at school with a view to making himself indispensable. In the interests of sexual pragmatism, he'd even begun to make overtures to one of his fellow ex-pat teachers.

It was more straightforward to cross the border on foot, leaving the car on the Brunei side. Out of sheer bloody mindedness the parking lot was located a quarter of a mile up the road. The aim was to make the process of booze procurement as unpleasant and difficult as possible without actually banning it all together. There were forms to fill in in triplicate. Punch ups would sometimes break out in the queue of shouting drunks jostling to get back across before the gates came down at ten thirty. But it was all worth it for a few hours of madness at Lingy's.

Everyone had their favourite shabeen on the other side and theirs was Ling's Place or 'Lingy's'. It was a wooden tree house teetering on bamboo stilts above the jabber of food hawkers below grilling their meats of suspect provenance. The rickety stairs were almost vertical. Peter heaved his way up into the treetops where the Three Wise Men were sitting in their favourite corner.

'Evening chaps.'

'If it isn't the Magus from Mansfield!' Tim neighed.

'Park yer Pommy pedagogue's posterior over here and get outside one of these,' Dan shouted, lobbing a tin of Victoria Bitter at him like a grenade. It looked as if they'd been there since mid-afternoon.

'I'm here on a mission to find some witty and enlivening company,' Peter said, 'so perhaps you could point me in the right direction.'

They no longer frightened him. Now he'd been fully adopted, he was allowed to give as good as he got.

'You're going frickin' nowhere, you Pommy prick.'

Peter was looking down the barrel of one of Dan's twenty tinny blasting moods.

'Sidaaan! We've got some news for you.'

He sat down.

They were grinning and exchanging those infuriating looks which preceded their bits of juicier news.

'Well?'

Whatever it was, it was clearly too big a gem to impart straightforwardly.

'You have my ears, gentlemen.'

More grinning.

'But not my indefinite patience.'

Tim was the first to crack. 'Have you ceased to peruse the obituary columns of The Bulletin?'

'Never was an avid reader,' Peter said.

'Then I suggest that you become so.'

'And how, in the greater scheme of things, might that add to the sum of my enlightenment?'

'By informing you, for one thing, that your ex-landlady's husband, Haji Bendaya, now romps with the sixty-seven vestal virgins.'

'You mean...?'

'Shuffled off this mortal coil,' Eric said.

'Departed this vale of tears,' said Tim.

'Six feet under,' Dan said.

'When?' Peter said.

Tim handed him a soggy copy of the paper, open at the relevant page. One whole sheet was given over to a panegyric mourning the passing of the fat man he'd seen nodding off on stage a few months back. He remembered how she'd given him a sharp dig in the ribs. His soft, puffy features were set against a background depicting what Peter took to be the average Bruneian believer's vision of heaven. A strangely alpine vision in which dead loved ones welcomed the newcomer with outstretched arms, against a backdrop of snow-covered peaks.

'Heart attack?' he said, fumbling in his head with the new reality.

'He doesn't exactly look like a carrot juice and gym man, let's face it.'

A positive riot of grinning ensued.

'Now come off it, chaps, you're not going to tell me she enlisted the help of the animal kingdom to speed him on his way. Not again. It's getting far-fetched.'

'What don't you do in these parts when parking your car overnight?' Eric said.

'Leave your windows open.'

'Because?'

'Snakes like the warmth.'

'They do indeed. Especially the Orange Borneo Tree Viper, deadliest of the deadly. Little bugger loves it, especially if it's provided by Haji Bendaya's Bentley.'

They laughed their savage laugh.

'So, he forgot to close his car window, an Orange Borneo whatever got in, he disturbed it, it bit him, he died from the poison. Why should Haja Rosni have had a hand in it? Nature's perfectly capable of obeying its own instincts without her having to put her oar in.'

Tim was on his feet. 'Ladies and Gentlemen of the jury,' he blared, 'I put it to you that the deceased lived in precincts of palatial modern splendour wholly unsympathetic to the needs of serpents. I put it to you further that the car in which the deceased met his unfortunate end was garaged nightly by his personal guard, a man of unimpeachable loyalty and conscientiousness. I put it to you, in short, that the chances of a serpent curling up to sleep in the front passenger seat of a deluxe Bentley in such a meticulously swept and supervised environment without the aid of human intervention are next to zero. No, Ladies and

Gentlemen of the jury, the serpent was there because the accused put it there, leaving the windows open to feign authentic access and egress. She put it there in order to cause the death of her husband, thereby inheriting his estate, and regaining the freedom to pursue a career of lustful intrigue unparalleled in the most depraved annals of antiquity, let alone Bandar Seri Begawan.'

'No!' Peter found himself on his feet and shouting. 'That's not true and you know it!'

'Steady on, blue,' Dan said, 'or we'll have to bind you over for contempt of court.'

'Is there going to be an investigation?'

'Very unlikely,' Eric said. 'The lady is, of course, hysterical with grief for the time being.'

'Well there you go then,' Peter said, unconvincingly. He'd given himself a way and knew it.

'She's too powerful now. And seriously rich enough to be able to choose who she wants to marry next. Mark my words, she'll be wearing her widow's weeds for however long it takes to create the right impression but once they come off, oh boy, will she be hunting. You'd better watch out, boy.'

They laughed again then abruptly stopped. Peter felt a presence behind him and swivelled in his chair. A woman was standing there, a picture of bedraggled wretchedness. In his excitement he hadn't even registered the booming of the daily evening thunder; the rain drilling on the tin roof. Water was pouring off it in a translucent curtain. The woman's hair was matted and mascara was running down her cheeks.

'Forgot me bloody umbrella, didn't I,' she said in her full-blooded

Birmingham accent.

'Natalie!' he said, 'Pull up a pew. Let me introduce you to the chaps.'

The evening wasn't a total disaster but a subsequent one, ending in bed, was. Then the same thing happened again, or rather, didn't. The affair fizzled out as meekly as it had begun. He didn't care. His heart was elsewhere and one Friday morning, not long after the scene at Lingy's, it leapt to the sound he'd been half craving, half dreading to hear. Faintly, from about a half a mile away down the ridge, there came the tortured scream of a car engine being thrashed, getting louder, getting closer.

2

> To: DesmondoD@tmail.com
> Subject: HAIRBALLS-A SORT OF STORY FOR YAH
> October 11 2022

'In the Museum of Natural History at Kuching,' he says, like he's giving some sort of lecture, 'there's a glass case containing a perfect crocodilian hairball. It's the size of a small cannon ball, the colour of hashish, and it's all that's left of my wife's first husband.'

King Hilarious, Desmondo! You have to check this oldster. We're in a time warp. Nothing's changed in The Orchid since The Age of Wham, and this Peter dude holds the key to the Teleporter. He was here before the internet. He was here before the *mobile phone*! He has got to be heard to be believed. Especially on ten tins of Tiger.

He laughs to himself. The teeth are a car crash - total wipe out. (Have these ancients never heard of dentistry?)

'Would you care to hear the story of my *wife*?' he says, chuckling this time at what I suppose they call a 'pun'. We've only met once before and we're already besties. We're on to the tall tales. I get the feeling he's a bit cracked, sitting up here on his own night after night, year after year. I'm a very captive audience. There is nowhere else to get a beer. The No Fun Party has wiped the floor with all opposition, and never has a party been truer to its manifesto. Mr Whitey has elected to hop it rather than face the full blast of the wrath of the righteous. The only ones left are top techies like us, Desmondo, nutters left on the bus like Old Pete, a few grizzly oil men passing through and a sprinkling of local Chinese who still dare to bend the elbow.

'Sure. Beam me up, Pete,' I say, 'and mine's another Tiger.'

He lumbers off to the 'bar'. I check the Specs are working. The streaming is hardly of the best but, yep, it's all out there and on the Pad too. I'm already getting incoming. Naughty I know, but someone's got to put this stuff out. Not everyone gets to come across specimens like Old Pete. Sharing is caring. I'm just doing my bit for connectivity, as you well know my dear Dezzy. Seeding the cloud.

It's so freakin' humid I worry about the hardware sometimes. It wasn't made to withstand this kind of battering. Neither was I, but it won't be forever. A year tops, The Foundation said. Well enough time to set up their own primitive version of the Learning Zone and teach the natives how to use it. Then it's Teachasaurus Rex R.I.P. and offski for me. Out of this festering hole. The things we do for coin of the realm.

'Yes indeed,' he says, hoisting his elephant's arse back into its chair. 'Be sure to pay your respects to Haji Salim Hao as soon as you arrive. Did me the great favour of getting himself eaten by Buyung Senang, the largest crocodile ever recorded in the state of Sarawak.'

He gives me one of his 'what do you think about that?' stares, which the Specs are picking up perfectly. He doesn't have a clue. I don't think he even carries a *phone*. I give him one back which says 'absolutely fascinating. Please continue.' Which he does. He doesn't need much prompting. He doesn't need *any* prompting.

'Now, the more inquiring mind might ask itself 'How does a merchant, a town dweller, get eaten by a beast like that'?'

(Check the fossil-speak. King Hilarious! Richard Coeur de Lion!)

'It might, Pete,' I say. 'In fact, mine was thinking the same thing itself.'

'The sort of fate likely to befall some jungle bunny, but not the man of considerable means who was my dear lady's first alleged victim.'

'Victim?' I say.

'Aha! I see I have your ears,' he says, chuckling, and starts rapping some very odd stuff indeed. Turns out his missus was suspected of doing Haji whatshisname in. Turns out she was a 'jungle bunny' (not my words Constable!) herself and practically fed the dude to the croc. Turns out nobody could pin anything on her and she ended up with all his boodle. Now, I'm thinking, if this is all true, you're married to a killer my old son. I know we're time travelling and People of the Earth are still dancing round the pocket calculator as if it's fallen from the stars. I know that in such a world, strange and improbable things happen but *come on*: men do not go waltzing down the aisle with alleged murderesses. No smoke without fire and all that. Bit of a boner stoner, for one thing, unless you're a serious Kinkster. This is what I put to him.

'Credulity,' he says in his lecturing voice, 'is the handmaiden of a timid intelligence. I prefer mine not to run with the herd. I draw my own conclusions, make my own judgments; something of an anachronism I know in this Brave New Information Age. Apropos of which: will…you…put…that… bloody thing away!'

(Henry VIII!)

'You mean you think they were talking bollocks,' I say, pocketing the Pad. (For some reason it really gets his goat when I'm dealing with incoming. He 'craves' as he puts it, my 'undivided attention.')

'If you choose to put it that way, yes. And, no, I am not a *Kinkster*. Just a man who happened to fall in love with the first Head Huntress he clapped his eyes on.'

He chuckles and gives me another of those 'what do you think about that, aren't I the great adventurer?' looks.

'No, the origins of my skepticism were to be found in the rather dubious source of my information. There were some very colourful characters around back then. Yarns were spun. People talked to each other for pleasure, believe it or not.'

And he's off again. This time it's some rap about three very weird dudes even older than him who once held sway in the Mead Hall of Middle Orchid and did spout wondrous tales from the Telling Stool. That kind of guff. All stiffs now apparently. One drowned when his yacht went down in the South China Sea leaving old Pete and the other two clinging to the wreckage for a day and night. One shot himself through the head, by accident, apparently. The other died of gruesome natural causes, nursed in his final days by Old Pete himself. He fishes out a photograph (a *photograph*!) of the four of them in some sort of tree house drinking beer. It's all faded and yellow but you can make them out clearly enough. Old Pete is Young Pete, of the same vintage as yours truly, although he's sporting an extreme barnet that makes him look like that bloke we did for 'A' Levels. George something (I'll google it later). The other three Weirdsters are King H. Charles I: a dwarf in a sailor's cap, a psycho looking Crocodile Dundee, and a beanpole of an English aristocrat with what looks like the map of the world on his skull. They are smiling and holding up tins of Tiger to the camera. I am, for a moment, strangely moved, they being brown bread and all.

'Dig the rug, Pete,' I say, tres New Romantic. 'Wouldn't have made much of a hairball though, if Mrs P had decided to have *you* fed to the crocs.'

This doesn't get the laughs I was expecting. Goes down like a led zeppelin in fact. He looks more than a tad put out.

'Of course,' I say, trying to make amends, 'plenty of raw-material for a decent sized one these days though.'

This goes down even worse, and he starts stroking his rug, nervously. He goes in for the geriatric Jesus look some of these real old timers think befitting, which is a shame because, with a bit of scissor work, a general cutting down on the amber fluids and cow pies, he'd be quite a distinguished gent. He's tall and square of jaw and the rags are quality for these parts. Not the usual tropical fruit fight and baggy shorts. Back in the day he must have been a hit with the ladies.

I think I've thrown him off his stride. Or maybe he's just forgotten what he was saying and why he was saying it. Happens with fossils who are partial to the sauce, I've started to notice. So, we leave his wife with blood dripping from her hands and I shift to a topic which never fails to grab Pete: Pete.

'What do you actually do, Pete,' I say, genuinely intrigued. 'I mean for coin...?'

He starts moving his hand about like he's trying to wave away a bad smell.

'Married it my boy. Married it,' he says.

Turns out the Head Huntress wears the trousers. Owns half the real estate round these parts and is not unknown to certain institutions of a Swiss nature either. So, he had an eye for the main chance. Not quite the nutter on the bus I took him for. Respect.

'OK,' I say, warming to the man, 'so boodle is bountiful. No need for the Petester to bend to the plough and the more power to his elbow for that. But what does he do to wile away the hours when not tanking the Tiger?'

'He accomplishes himself.'

'And how might he do that?'

Another bit of hand ballet. This time like he's penning lines in the air with one of those quill things.

'He writes?'

He nods.

'Anything in particular?'

He points inwardly to himself then spreads his hands wide, which I suppose is intended to mean him, life and the mysteries thereof although it must be a pretty limited oeuvre if he means life round these parts. It and he stopped evolving about the same time as that croc he's so fond of, Buyang whatever. It gives me the willies. I can't work out how he gets through time; how he navigates it. He doesn't surf, game, text, spec, tweet. I suppose he must read, by the sound of it; books, but there's only so much of that you can do before going off your rocker.

'Anything published.'

'It would appear,' he says, 'I am fated to join the ranks of Kafka, John Kennedy O'Toole.'

So he's just tossing himself off then.

'Ever thought of going E?'

'If you mean the internet,' he says, all shock and horror, 'then I can safely say I'd prefer to stick red hot needles....'

But he doesn't get to say where he'd prefer to stick them. Instead, his eyes start bulging and his head starts moving about in a sort of circular motion.

'You alright, Pete?' I say, thinking he might have popped a vessel.

'Hello, darling,' he says. 'It isn't Friday, is it?'

I look over my shoulder to find a woman standing behind me. This I take to be Mrs Pete.

'Are you going to offer me a seat an intra-use me to this young man or do I have to blaay stand here all night?' she says (she's got some sort of speech impediment).

'Of course...of course, darling. It's just that I wasn't expecting...I mean you never come up except on....er...' And he jumps up and starts rumbling chairs about.

She sits down like she's Cleopatra and the terrace her royal barge. I notice those few left aboard have all gone quiet. Here is one sassy lady. She's old, obviously, but kind of *new* at the same time. There's not a wrinkle on her. If she's been under the knife then whoever was wielding it must be a supreme artist. They usually emerge from the bandages looking like they've been embalmed, but there's no Egyptian mummy look here. And the dentistry; the grooming! Perfection. A yummy granny, if you're reading me Dezza, you GILF monster, you!

Introductions over, Pete rumbles off to the bar in search of G and T. The Specs are off. The lady demands respect.

A bit of fencing: the heat; how I am coping. Then, 'I hope he hasn't been boring you,' she says, fishing a cigarette out of an exquisite little clasp bag. I supply the flame and, leaning towards her get a delicious draught of something very expensive indeed.

'He doesn't get a lot of company these days. All his old friens are dea or have left and nobody wants to come here anymore.'

'He was telling me.'

'God, was he?'

'Afraid so.'

'I like to travel. To get out,' she says. 'The British passport helped. I suppose that was one thing to be grateful for.'

'I can see,' I say, gesturing to the gorgeous sheath of Chanel fellating her petite body (Down Dezza! Down!). 'Paris?'

She flashes the naughty, furtive smile of the serious fashionista who is feeding her habit far too seriously.

'He won't come with me. Says he can't fly. It terrifies him. He hasn't left here for blaay years. I don't think he could cope anywhere else. Like most of the natives. Since my third husband died I've been free to get out as often as I can. I suppose he's been telling you all about me and my husbands. He does it to everyone when he's been drinking. Anyone who'll listen. You can tell me. I won't take it out on him, the poor thing.'

'We got as far as Mark 1,' I say. 'Not a nice man. An unusual ending.'

She laughs in a surprisingly harsh and manly way.

'It was a happy acci-ent. I was much too young to be given away to such a brute. I *was* young once, if you can believe that.'

'Oh, I can,' I say, 'I can.'

I'm intrigued to know how Marks 2 and 3 snuffed it but Mark 4 comes wombling back with the necessary and we have to break off.

'So what brings you here, Steve?' she says.

'Steve's in the business of estranging us from ourselves, darling.'

'Shut up, Peter.'

'Educational Technology,' I say.

'ET go home!' Pete says in a funny voice, pointing from his chair at the stars.

'Now if you don't stop it, I'm going to tell them to close the bar and take you home early.'

He puts a finger in his mouth.

'Sowwy!'

'I don't suppose he tol you that I own The Orchid.'

'He did not.'

'I bought it so he'd still have somewhere to go. The previous owners were going to sell out to the Beards. God knows it doesn't make me any money. What do you think of it? Frightful?'

'Could do with a lick of paint.'

'You're right. I've been thinking the same for ages, but Peter won't have anything changed.'

'Then again, eighties retro's all the rage at the moment.'

'Really Steve? You know about these things?'

Pete is looking very uneasy, grinning and moving his head like he's following a tense, slow-motion rally at Wimbledon.

'Did interior design at uni.'

'How fascinating.'

'Yeah, but it doesn't pay like ET does.'

'Even so, you might be able to advise me.'

'An absolute pleasure.'

'When should we start?'

'No time like the present,' I say.

Pete is starting to look queasy, like the drink's gone bad in his head all of a sudden.

'As a disciple of Parmenides I feel I must protest!' he says.

'Oh, shut up, Peter. And stop talking in blaay riddles. You really would like to help, Steve? I'd pay of course.'

'Please, Roz,' I say, looking hurt. 'Please.'

'Excellent!' she says and claps her tiny little hands.

We scan each other, to Pete's evident horror. I spark her another cigarette.

'Where are you staying, Steve?'

Taking a leaf from the Petester's book, I gesture expansively to my soon to be gutted surroundings.

'Peter! You never told me Steve was staying in this blaay dump.'

'The matter of his residence was never raised.'

'Well it has been now, and I'm not having him staying here a day longer. You know perfectly well we have villas lying empty. Why can't you do your job for a change! Isobel is empty up on Bukhit Serikan. Beautiful view. It's where Peter lived when *he* first arrived.'

Pete has gone a funny colour, with a face like a football manager who's just seen a three nil lead thrown away. He's stroking his rug ten to the dozen.

'I'm sure Steve is perfectly capable of arranging his own accommodation, darling,' he says.

'Nonsense! You will bring the Bentley tomorrow morning and show him round.'

'Of course, darling,' he says, looking now like that last second of injury time losing goal has just gone in, the ref's blown, and Pete United are relegated for the first time in their history with the loss of several zillion quid in Prem money.

It's a Louis, Dezza! A Louis Quartoze!

More anon. Opportunity knocks. Keep yah posted.

Byeeeee !!!! And give my love to Real World!!!!!

RISE UP AND BE STRONG

1

Bill shouldn't give in so easily to that know-it-all from the brewery, barging into me and laying down the law. Public Relations Officers are what Carston's calls them these days. Just because they've given you a fancy name and a badge doesn't make you Wyatt Earp, dearie. I've done without a 'juke box' for near on a century and I can do without one now, thank you very much. It's not as if the music's anything to write home about, anyway. You couldn't dance to it even if you tried, and as for the words...!

Something called I Can't Get No Satisfaction is what we all have to listen to at this precise moment. The latest 'Number One in the Hit Parade', apparently. 'I can't git nooo sadisfacshurn...' Lover, try serving three hundred pints of bitter a day, draped in flock wallpaper, you'd soon change your tune.

It's all part of a 'modernisation drive' according to His Nibs.

'We've got to get the youth out of the coffee bars and into the pub, Bill. It's the youth that's the future of the licensing trade.'

Something of a truism, I'd like to point out, along with the fact that I've always attracted more than my fair share of young gentlemen. Indeed, it wouldn't be stretching things to say that I've gone out of my way to nab them as young as I can (behaviour that's got me the odd slap on the wrist from our gallant Boys in Blue over the years).

'If you think so, Mr Shepherd,' Bill says, rolling over like a puppy.

'Please, call me Dave, Bill.'

'If you think so, Dave.'

All this chumminess makes me queasy. We're all of us supposed to be equals now that Mr Wilson's in charge, with his pipe and his Macintosh. The Common Man is quite the latest thing.

How Bill managed to do what he did in the ring is one of life's great mysteries. He might be a bruiser, all cauliflower ears, shorn off eyebrows and mashed in nose on the outside but inside he's a marshmallow, a great big softie. People take advantage. I've tried telling him ever since he hung up his gloves and took me on not long after the Second War, but will he listen? Result: they've carted Mabel's piano away to make room for this monstrosity and everyone has to suffer everyone else's favourite racket. Bernard says it's happening everywhere. The latest craze is piano smashing competitions. They're not needed anymore. 'Barbarism' is what he calls it.

Anyway, Mr Bossy Boots PRO doesn't have to lecture *me* about seducing the youth'. There's never been a problem on my side. I've got a Snug. It's the Snug that pulls them in. It's tucked away round the back, so any passing 'Tit Head' - as the naughty things will insist on calling our local constabulary - can't just poke his head through the front door and feel their collars. That gives straight on to the Saloon, full of my Rowdies, where any sensible copper fears to tread. The Smoke Room with its side entrance is the domain of my Ancients rattling their dominos about, so he'd feel pretty silly looking for under agers there. Then, he'd have to traipse his great big muddy size elevens through the carpeted Lounge, something his own mother would never put up with. Hence, I always start my young gentlemen off in the Snug. All tucked away, snug as a bug in a rug. Grammar School lads, mainly. Generations of them. Hundreds of bright young things all blurring into one now I'm getting on, although I never forget my special ones. I know we in the trade are supposed to be impartial but I just can't resist a certain type: tall, well-off, well-built young blondes with nice little noses. Narrows the field somewhat but they will keep sauntering into my life every twenty years or so and I'm powerless to resist. There was that lovely poet, son of a Vicar, just before Victoria died. Beautiful head of hair on an oarsman's body. Left me for a Cambridge Don. I didn't dare expose my tender side again until my Captain arrived, fresh out of his teens, to storm my defences again. He was killed on the Somme. I only got to see him in uniform once. Then, as if I hadn't suffered enough, that American airman in the last war went and married a local trollop and took her back to Kansas. Sometimes I think it would be better if I just turned my back on love. Then another one comes along and sweeps me off my feet. It's his 18th today.

'Happy Birthday to you. Happy Birthday to you. Happy Birthday dear Tilly. Happy Birthday to yoooooouuuuu!' his mates are yodelling over the Strolling Bones, or whatever they call themselves, coming from the Saloon. And – be still my racing heart - he's blushing. Jonathon Tillbury – Tilly to his friends – last in the line of the Tillbury Chains dynasty stretching back to the Industrial Revolution, is a blushing eighteen today.

'My shout,' he says, composing himself, and with a new manly swagger of those snake hips, makes his way over to the hatch. 'Eight pints of bitter for the Birthday Boy, Maureen,' he commands legally for the first time, letting a bit of Black Country trespass on the posh vowels he got from all those elocution lessons Tillbury *pere* paid for.

'And while you're at it, give us a kiss.'

He puts his head fully through the hatch, and puckers a pair of plump, rosy lips in mock- anticipation. A yelping of approval comes from his mates behind. Maureen, more at home fending off like propositions from her own kind in the Saloon, tosses her head and drops her eyes, all bashful in the face of this young squire from The Big House, as the Tillbury pile is known.

I've been extremely lucky with Maureen. If any girl was born to pull a pint it was Maureen Burns. She's a looker, too, Bill says, which I suppose she is, although I'm not the best of judges. The fairer sex is all much of a muchness to me and we don't get many specimens in here anyway. I'm a man's pub.

She's wearing those white 'kinky' boots up to her knees, little pleated mini-skirt and a blouse that's positively trumpeting her bosomies. The Dusty Springfield peroxide loaf is an advertisement for the kind of hairspray that would laugh at a force ten gale. A barmaid's barmaid is our Maureen, born to the pumps. She's got a gob on her too, when she wants to use it; normally on my rowdies. Gives as good as she gets, but on this occasion, faced with the puckered cherry reds of the gorgeous Jonathon, she's momentarily lost for a vulgar riposte. I think there might be something going on. I detect a little *frisson*, even though she's a couple of years older and from up the Estate.

'Ask me when you've got rid of that bum fluff on your chin,' she manages finally, in the broadest of broad.

'Whoooaaah!' go his mates, 'you're in there, Tilly! Pop your cherry!'

'I popped it ages ago,' he says.

I'm not so sure. To hear them talk you'd think they were putting it about like Lord Byron, which might be true of a few, granted. We are, after all, supposed to be 'entering a new age of promiscuity'. I read it in

The Times over Bernard's shoulder in the Lounge. But with Jonathon, I have my doubts.

'Here, Bill,' Maureen bawls over the din (it's a Friday night and I'm packed to the rafters), 'there's a lad in the Snug says it's his eighteenth birthday. Can't be right can it, cos he's been coming in for near on two year?'

Bill's mangled bruiser's face appears in the hatch and, through its mashed in nose he snorts out the time honoured: 'You...little...bleeders! I'll 'ave you one day, I swear I will.'

'Arf! Arf! Arf!' they go, as always. 'Too late now, Bill. Horse has bolted.'

Bill withdraws, shaking his head and they return to their youthful banter.

The Snug's a cozy little room, as the name suggests. It's got two tattered leather banquettes dating back to my conception. They face each other like a mini House of Commons debating chamber, so they tell me, the better to promote vigorous high-minded debate in that vigorous high-minded age to which I was born. There is no mystery about my age or provenance. I was a planned pub. Temperance was stalking the land, new churches going up everywhere, so the breweries thought they'd fight back by giving the working man a decent space to drink in for a change: spacious, clean, with proper conveniences in place of a reeking bit of wall. Perhaps trying to catch something of the pioneering industrial spirit of the times, Carston's had me christened The Navigator. On June 7th 1877, the fashionable glaze of my claret brick walls shining in a hot mid-morning sun, I opened my doors to the public and was instantly condemned to live a lie; to pretend to be something I am not. You only have to look at my sign: a brawny rustic in rough breeches and smock, shouldering a pick and shovel, smoking a clay pipe. That's not me! That's not me at all! I'm a Prince of Orange, a Royal Oak, at the very least a Rose and Crown. What I am *not*, is a Navigator. It's so unfair. Look at that King's Head in the market square with her half-timbers and hanging baskets; little tart. Bernard says they're wasted on her, the kind of drinker she's getting in these days. "You get a much nicer class of drunk in the Navvy," he says. "Never judge a book by its cover." Which is a sort of compliment I suppose. At the end of the day, none of us really chooses what we become. Bernard, above all, knows that. He's got such beautiful nails and wears scented cravats.

There's nothing high-minded though in what they're going on about, House of Commons or no House of Commons. And the language! It's "bloody" this and "bleedin'" that. Shocking in boys so young. The clothes though, now of these I *do* approve. Where they get the money from is anybody's guess, but I'm glad they do. The lines are so much more...more flattering, shall we say; the fabrics and colours so much lighter, brighter. A breath of fresh air from those Teddy Boys dripping grease all over the place. Yes: thank the gods of taste and hygiene- it's goodbye Brylcream and hello nature again! Let those lovely locks flow as they did in Oscar and Bosie's day.

It's a hot September night and not a tie to be seen. Shirts are open at the chest. Trousers are worn snug and low on the hip, with the faintest hint of a flare creeping in at the ankle. Jonathon's are mauve! How incredibly daring. They were a birthday present from his older sister who lives down in London.

'Got them on the King's Road,' he says. 'The King's Road's got everything.'

'Have you been, Tilly?'

'Not yet. But I'm going. Half-term hol. Just you see. My sister says she'll put me up for the week. She's got a flat in Chelsea.'

He's a lovely boy, but just a tiny bit given to boasting, which is understandable perhaps, what with the start he's had in life. He's got such big, such 'don't fence me in' dreams. Touching, really. That and the little poems he writes. He showed one to Maureen not long back, when he'd had a pint too many. Said he'd dedicate it to her if she'd wear that tight sweater she had on the other night. It was about love. A bit fruity from what I could make out over her shoulder. She read it and called him a 'mucky little devil' but I could tell she was flattered. Popped it down her bra, when he'd sat down again. Something's going on, definitely. I can feel it in my pipes.

'It'll be a kind of rehearsal for when I get to Imperial College,' he says.

This is pushing it, even for Jonathon. He's not the brightest button in the box, by all accounts, academically speaking; just scraped his way in to the sixth form with the aid of expensive private tuition.

'What's that?' some cruel wag pipes up. 'Do I hear squadrons of pigs doing victory rolls over our beloved Navvy?'

'Arf! Arf! Arf!' they go.

Bitch! And on his birthday, too. He looks all flummoxed.

'Yeah, you've got to *earn* a place at Imperial,' says another, twisting the knife. 'With this,' he says, tapping his skull. 'You can't just *go* there.'

How nasty boys can be to one another. Almost as cruel as

children. 'Little savages' they are, Bernard says. He knows, because the Coach and Horses out on the Stafford Road has started letting them in before 8 p.m. Even built some kind of giant boot in the beer garden for them to play in, or on. They're not coming near me, and that's straight.

'Booger yow,' Jonathon says, beer and pique getting the better of those elocution lessons. Hardly Oscar, but spirited all the same. 'Whatever happens, I'm not sticking around this dump. I'll go tramping if I have to. Or abroad. You remember that lad three years above us that was always getting expelled? Remember, The Beak washed his mouth out with a soapy flannel at assembly, for swearing? I bumped into him last year and he'd just come back from grape picking in France. Said he'd made enough to go and live in Morocco for the winter and then in the spring he'd got a job lined up working on a campsite in Provence. No reason I can't do the same. I'm not letting my old man tie me down like his did to him. Tillbury's can stuff its chains up its you know what.'

'Isn't that what George Orwell did?' one of the brainier ones says.

'What? Stuff chains up his jacksy?' Jonathon says, rallying.

'Arf! Arf! Arf!'

'Tramping,' says the brain box, patiently. 'He was from a well-off family but he turned himself in to a tramp?'

'What for?'

'So's he could write about it.'

'Well, I might do the same.'

'You've got to learn to *spell* first, Tilly!'

'Arf! Arf! Arf!'

And on it goes: the timeless, feeble ragging of the very young, each generation exercising just that little bit less restraint than the one before. Why can't we be more kind to one another? Why is kindness so hard to practice? I ought to ask Bernard. It's the sort of thing that's up his street. He fancies himself as a bit of a philosopher, when he's not doing that eternal blinking crossword of his. Any road up, let them have their fun. They'll have plenty of time to learn restraint, what deference means, when they're stuck in that lower management job with Carston's, or Briggs', or Tillbury's, with a nagging wife and another kid on the way, and years and years of the same stretching ahead. A few might escape, a very few, and I hope from the bottom of my cellar that Jonathan's one of them. He's a lovely, lovely boy but it would be selfish of me to keep him for myself. Fly! Fly away! As must I. I'm having a makeover tomorrow. All part of the modernisation drive. Off with this dreary flock and into…? We shall see. I'm all of a flutter. Time gentlemen, please! Time, please! Time!

2

I've decided to do a little stocktaking every ten years or so. Keep myself up to date. In step with the times, which are 'a changing' as that American folk singer keeps reminding us. He must be well past his sell by date now, although he certainly had a gift for prophesy because back in his day, no one could have dreamed that what's coming out of the noisemaker *a ce moment* would have been possible, let alone permissible.

'God save the Queen/ And her fascist regime,' some lout is snarling.

Now I'm all for freedom of expression, like the rest of us. It is, after all, what I'm here to promote, along with spreading a bit of merriment around. No one's ever called me a prude. But I can't help thinking, hang on a minute, ducky, I know the Horse Guards like to dress up a bit and the Boys in Blue got a little carried away during that miner's strike not so long back, which did for our nice Mr Heath, but hold up; that hardly makes HMQ Benito Mussolini, does it? It's stretching things a bit. And as for her being 'married to a Mormon', well, the Church of England would never have allowed it. Or perhaps I'm going a bit deaf.

It's from something called Never Mind The Bullocks, which also contains a 'track' called Anarchy in The UK, so Bernard says. I don't know about the UK, Bernard dear, but if what's happening in the Saloon is anything to go by it's certainly making inroads here. There's a man with a safety pin in his *nose*! He's sitting with a woman who's got pink hair done up in spikes and black lipstick. I thought it was fancy dress at first, for the Jubilee, but apparently not. I blame it all on Nigel. He can't keep order like Bill used to. Bill was a big softie but you wouldn't argue with him, not unless you fancied retrieving your falsies from the lavatory bowl in the morning. Nigel, on the other hand, looks like he couldn't knock the skin off a rice pudding. In fact, I think his wife knocks *him* about. I had a peek in the bedroom. Every inch the slutty harridan, she is. You should see the state of the living room! I don't think the sideboard's seen a duster since Bill's Mabel died and he retired to Mablethorpe. Mind you, to watch her carrying on with some of the blokes in the lounge – single or married, it's all the same to her - you'd think that butter wouldn't melt in her mouth. Bernard sent her packing with a flea in her ear though, I'm happy to say. Maureen hasn't got any time for her either. I'm not quite the happy house I used to be, but who said life was all wine and roses.

That new young rep from Carston's thinks I'm the bees-knees, whatever's going on behind the scenes. My barrelage keeps going up year on year. Despite us being, Bernard says, what some 'Dago' calls the 'sick man of Europe,' the average working man's got more to spend on beer than ever before, even though he's on strike half the time. It doesn't add up. The housekeeping's all to pot. There's going to be a reckoning, mark my words.

Jonathon's back, so that's a relief. When he said he was going on a *plane*, I nearly had kittens. He's all sun tanned and wearing a gold medallion on his chest. My King Midas.

'You really ought to go to Torremolinos when you can,' the piece he's currently squiring says to Maureen. 'The sun shines every day.' (It certainly has on you, dearie. You look like you've been dipped in toffee and put under a blow torch.) 'No more caravanning in Skegness for us, 'ay Johny?'

Notice, the *us*. She's really got her claws in to him, this one. There have been others – he's still a very good-looking boy – but he's managed to brush them off. This one means business, though. She'll stop at nothing, I can tell. You only have to look at what she's wearing. A white linen pencil skirt and matching blouse, so thin and clingy you can see her knickers and bra. Common as muck, even though she is a member of the Tennis Club.

'What the lady wants,' Jonathon says, slurring just that little bit, 'the lady gets.' Then, leaning over and nearly pitching forward off his bar stool, he gives her a slap on the rump.

'If she's a good girl!'

'Johnyyyy!'

'Urgul. Urgul. Urgul,' he goes, in a way that doesn't suit him at all. He's getting coarser as each year goes by. Turning himself into something he's not. Or something else is.

Maureen, to whom Torremolinos might just as well be the moon, says, 'I fancy Corfu myself.'

I can tell she's jealous and of course, with a husband on the sick and three little ones to feed, she's got about as much chance of getting to Corfu as Bernard, in the booth next door, has of finishing his blinking crossword (couldn't he leave it alone, just for once, on this day of days?). She did what they all do from up the Estate, got up the duff with a local welder or whatever, married, and stayed exactly where she was. And I had such hopes for her. She might talk common, but she's got a bit about her. Always has had. I caught her reading Cosmopolitan the other day, and she wasn't just flipping the pictures. I used to hope that, once it became clear Jonathon wasn't cut out for that glittering academic career he'd pencilled in for himself, he might leap the great class divide and… But then it was too late. Barry or Gary or Cary was on the way.

Mind you, she's kept her figure. I'll say that for her. It's bigger, but in all the right places. I suspect my rising barrelage is not all down to my warm and accommodating nature. There aren't many Maureens manning the pumps these days. I'm lucky to have kept her.

The minx, Diana's her name, brushes aside her dreams of the Burns clan toasting themselves on some Aegean shore with more exotic reveries of her own.

'Of course, now Johny's been made a full Director we might be spreading our wings further.' Jonathon flaps his arms obligingly: a swan taking flight. 'I've been looking at brochures for Hawaii.'

'Book it Danno!' he says and collapses in fits of laughter. It ends in him coughing his lungs up, which is what happens of course if you get through forty Embassy a day. He needs somebody to tell him he can't coast forever on all that rugger and running he did at school. It grieves me to say so but Jonathon Tillbury, once king of track and field, is getting out of shape. His shirt's straining at its buttons. His face is going puffy. Gone is the chiselled jaw. It's what you get if you're in the Lounge Monday to Friday regular as clockwork six till eight. He's an after-work drinker, if what his old man gives him to do can properly be called work. Brings his Telegraph in, goes through it methodically then leaves it behind for the next bloke, which is thoughtful of him. Where he goes after that isn't my business. I'm not the jealous type anymore. It's enough that he's stayed faithful all these years. I didn't ask it of him. Quite the reverse. It would have been wrong to have tied him down, but since he insisted on doing it himself, who was I to complain?

'And another thing,' she goes on (and on and on. Oh, how she goes on! Can he not see what lies in wait? He used to have imagination. All those little poems he used to write. Can't he use what bits are left of it to picture the hell he's got coming if he doesn't stop thinking with his you know what? She's a stunner now, alright, in a common sort of way, but when she's gone to seed what's left but a pair of lips flapping their twaddle?), 'we won't be coming in here *quite* so much, will we Johny.'

This touches a nerve.

'I've been drinking in the Navvy nearly every day since I was a lad,' he says, bristling manfully, 'and I'm not stopping now.'

I'm moved. Whatever spell she put on him during their two-week romp in Torremolinos, it can't stand up to mine.

She realises she's overstepped the mark and backs down. For now. Cunning little minx.

'Anyway, I'm off to powder my nose,' she says, getting down

from her stool.

'Don't be too long, princess,' he calls after her, drooling as she picks her way on six-inch heels over my best shag pile.

'Like two melons doing the samba,' he says under his breath, just loud enough for Maureen to hear. He's always at it, trying to make her jealous. I don't think he's ever forgiven her for getting herself a life of her own, just when his started shrinking. Whatever happened to him after he failed all his 'A' levels and went to Paris, he was never the same when he came back, tail between his legs. It's easy to be big in a small town. He had big dreams, but the world was bigger. He backed down, sharpish. It gave him a fright. He's a small-town boy, although he won't admit it. He knows his place. Whether he was ever really going to make a move on her is debatable, though. All that sixties talk about 'free love and the classless society' was precisely that round these parts, just talk. In a small town like this, there's still a fair bit of forelock tugging goes on. Tillburys don't mate with girls from up the Estate. Not unless they want to get themselves disinherited. No, I don't think he's ever forgiven her, not because she got married to another bloke, but because he couldn't bear to see her change. He wanted everything to stay as it was when he was on the brink of conquering the world. Like a lot of dreamers who end up doing nothing but dream, change in others hurts. It's why he doesn't keep up with his old mates anymore. They've moved on. Moved away. He clings to me instead, and aren't I the lucky one. I have to pinch myself sometimes.

'Behave yourself, Tilly,' Maureen says, 'or I'll have to report you for sexism.'

'Whatism?' he says.

'Sexism. What you just said was a sexist remark. Degrading to women.'

'So a bloke can't pay a bird a compliment anymore.'

'Not if it objectifies the species in purely sexual terms.'

'Flippin heck, Reen, you swallowed a dictionary or something?'

'I've joined the Open University,' she says. 'Sociology. I've always fancied giving it a go.'

This really throws him. It throws *me*. Out of all the people in the room, Maureen on her fag break, a Sovereign Gold hanging off her lips, formidable cleavage reposing on the bar, is the last person you'd have down as a scholar. I always thought she had something about her but not quite that much. As Bernard says, 'never judge a book by its cover.'

'But you can't,' Jonathon squeaks in disbelief. 'You've got three kids to bring up. You left school at fifteen. You're a barmaid.'

'That's what it's there for, people like me. Anybody can join. Maybe *you* should give it a try. You might have better luck this time round. Perhaps you're a late developer.'

'You saying I'm thick or something?'

'What I'm saying, Tilly, is it might do you good. Give you an interest. Give you something to do instead of boozing and chasing after skirt.'

'I read the Telegraph every day. Cover to cover.'

'Hardly makes you Ludwig Wittgenstein.'

'Everything a man needs to know is contained within the pages of the Telegraph.'

'To think you used to write poetry. Remember?'

'I lost my muse,' he says, and goes all quiet for a moment.

RED FLAGS

The skirt he's currently chasing regains her stool with that self-satisfied wiggle of the woman who knows she's got her man. Like a hen that's just laid an egg.

'I was just saying to Reen how we've done the old girl proud,' he says, gesturing at my bunting. 'Nigel's really gone to town.'

Indeed, he has. I'm bedecked, outside and in, with little plastic Union Jacks. I feel quite festive. It takes the eye off that awful purple and lime green striped outfit I've been stuck with since sixty-five. Sometimes I feel like mutton dressed up as lamb. Honestly, I'm ashamed to be seen in it; cheap, tatty, not to mention dreadfully *passee*. At least my flock had a certain dignity.

'Turn the sound up, Nige!' Jonathon shouts through to the bar, 'she's about to speak.'

I've had a telly put in especially for the occasion. Colour, too. It's four in the afternoon and I'm still open. Packed to the rafters in fact. Special license. Takes me back to before Lloyd George decided to give us all an afternoon nap. Hard to imagine how I'd cope without my siesta these days. I'm wilting already, but 'once more to the pumps dear friends'! We all have to do our bit for queen and country. She certainly looks pleased enough.

'My husband and I...'

'Wonderful!' they all go, once it's over.

'Where would we be without her?'

'Twenty-five years! Who'd have thought it?'

'God bless her.'

And I don't want to sound churlish or take anything away from her Big Day, but you'd have thought somebody might have remembered another anniversary. I never expected flowers. Just a little thought here and there. But even Bernard's forgotten. Forgotten that a certain someone not a million miles away is a Hundred Years Old Today!

3

I've got a new sign board next to my front door. It says:

Hearty Traditional Fayre Served Daily

12-1.30 and 6-8

Children Welcome In Our Playroom

I suppose it had to happen sometime. No point in swimming against the tide. The new rep from Carston's did his best with Nigel but he wasn't having it. Stuck in his ways.

'I'm a pub, Peter, not a bloody restaurant! And I'm certainly not a bloody kindergarten.'

'Nigel. Nigel. Nigel. How many times do we have to tell you the old fashioned boozer's on its way out. Cost-price margins are shrinking and all our surveys indicate a big socioeconomic shift in client demographics. We have to be more customer-driven.'

'Come again?'

'There's not enough profit in beer and women aren't prepared to be left at home with the kids anymore and they need to eat.'

'Well can't they go somewhere else?'

'The Navigator's one of our bigger premises. The lounge will do nicely for the catering side of things and we can convert the stables into a playroom for the kids.'

'Over my dead body.'

'Hopefully that won't be necessary, Nigel.'

It wasn't. He went meekly in the end. To be replaced by the current 'mien host' who is a fat little ex-army cook who likes to tell jokes all the time and insists on everyone calling him Smiffy. Familiarity is running amok. And besides, you don't give yourself pet-names, they get given to you. Giving *yourself* one is the mark of an insufferable egotist. Like those disk jockeys on the radio he has blaring away in the kitchen all day and night. The Hairy Cornflake. The Kid.

Smiffy calls himself 'the wizard of the Micro-wave', which is a new gadget that means we don't have to cook anymore, although Jonathon insists on proper food. He has steak and chips with all the trimmings nearly every night, sitting on his usual stool at the end of the bar in the lounge. Lady Di, as he calls her, 'can't boil a bloody egg,' apparently. They've had to get a cook in so young Nathan gets some proper nourishment, poor little mite. He can't see much of his dad either, because his dad practically lives here these days. He used to go home on the stroke of eight but now he's in till closing time most nights, which is nice for me, I suppose, although he's getting worse than my rowdies in terms of his intake.

'Throw your arms around the world at Christmas tiiiyuurm!' he sings along to the noisemaker's current Number One, waving his fork about. I don't know about the world, Jonathon love, I feel like telling him, but they'd certainly have problems throwing their arms around you. You're enormous.

He's passing through what Maureen's taken to calling his 'Roman phase'. At least I hope it's just a phase because it's so unbecoming. Prosperity of this order doesn't hang well on him. Since Old Man Tillbury passed on and he took over the firm proper he's changed.

'Getting too big for his boots,' she says. 'Pride comes before a fall.' You don't need a degree in Sociology to see that, Maureen dear.

'Feed the wuurhuld, let them know it's Christmas time! Feed the wuurhuld...'

Smiffy, who's wearing a Rudolph the Red Nose Reindeer hat, which goes perfectly with his own glowing whisky conk, cuts him off.

'F*** the world, Jonners. I've got my work cut out f*****g feeding you!'

The language! In the Lounge! From the landlord! And notice how it's all Jonners this and Smiffy that now, like a couple of comedians. The other customers don't like it. A good pub, according to Bernard, is a perfectly functioning democracy. It has its social types and classes, which belong to its different rooms but each is treated with equal respect and attention. A good landlord never has favourites. The way he, Smiffy, is going about it, I'm being turned in to, as Bernard puts it 'a private club for the privileged few'. This is in keeping with the times, of course. I saw it all coming. The housekeeping was all to pot. The working man was getting above himself. I don't mean like in the 30s. He had good reason then. I was the first to welcome Red Ellen and those Jarrow marchers. But that Red Robbo was just pure mischief. We were becoming a laughing stock and now our Mrs Thatcher's taken him, the working man, down a peg or two. The trouble is though, soon there won't be any work left for him to do. She's gone over the top. Half the foundries have closed round here. It's beginning to bite. My rowdies are thinning now the redundancy money's been spent. Maureen's husband's been out of work for near on two years. She's back on five nights. That job she's got as a social worker hardly brings in a part-time wage. Jonathon, on the other hand, is sitting pretty, like most of them in the Lounge. Tillbury's rode out the storm. Those firms that are left have got the pickings. For the time being anyway. But I don't think Tillbury Junior's got the old man's touch. He'd been riding on his coat tails for too long. Not tough enough. Wants to be liked. That's verdict coming from the Saloon.

To me, he's still an innocent, despite the swagger, the golf, the pastel coloured lambs-wool sweaters, Jaguar and all the other trappings. Perhaps it's just the memory of when he first walked in with his mates and, because he was the tallest, in his gruffest voice, cheeks ablaze, ordered four pints of Carston's and ten Number Six. The flush of triumph on his sixteen-year old face when Maureen looked him up and down, winked and started pulling the pints, I'll never forget it. Anyway, time will tell, like it always does. The main thing is he's still mine, for better or worse, richer or poorer. He hasn't left me for one of those village pubs that seem to be all the rage now with the hoi-poloi, like that Shoulder of Mutton. Little trollop, with her horse brass and 'fine dining'. So, in the meantime, I'm happy to let him play the great Captain of Industry (as Bernard calls him) when he's had a skin-full, which is most nights.

Steak and chips polished off, he settles to a familiar theme, 'Trouble was, Smiffy, we'd been over-manned for years. The Unions were running the show.'

'No Unions in the army, Jonners,' Smiffy says over his shoulder, as he pours them both double scotches from the optics (he's a Top Shelf landlord if ever there was one). 'Never did us any harm when we were giving the Argies a kicking.'

'Precisely. 'Excuse me Pedro, but can you hold up shooting at us whilst we negotiate terms for double time'. I'll give you an example.

Summer holidays. Before Mrs T, about a third of our shop floor was off over July and August and we had to replace them with students. The Union insisted on us taking them on at normal rates. Insisted we couldn't maintain production targets without temps. So I used to just poke my head through the door of the Snug and whistle. They used to think Christmas had come early.'

'I bet they did.'

'Why? Because they knew they had to do bugger all. The foremen thought they were getting one over on me, but I had my eye on them. When they weren't smoking and playing cards, they were wheeling barrowfulls of old chains backwards and forwards from one end of the floor to the other. Who could blame them? I'd have done the same. But it meant I didn't have to be Pythagoras to work out that we could function perfectly well on two thirds of the force. Which is what we do now. Which means we're still in business.'

'Which the mines won't be if Scargill and his lot carry on like they're doing, Jonners. The enemy within, as the Divine Margaret says.'

'I've got no liking for the woman, Smiffy, don't think I have, but she's got a point. That bugger wanted war and now he's got it.'

'All she's trying to point out is that you can't have your cake and eat it,' he goes on, which is a bit rich coming from him these days. 'You can't go around behaving like the Revolution's already arrived, expect to get paid a brain surgeon's wage just for digging stuff out of the ground *and* expect people to want to buy it at four times the price they can get it elsewhere. It just doesn't stack up.'

'Quite the orator,' Maureen who's been listening over by the sink, says. 'There's a rush on in the Saloon, Smiffy. You expect Sally to cope on her own whilst you stand here gassing to Mr Tory Boy?'

And off he goes. You don't argue with Maureen these days. At forty, she's become formidable. That degree she did boosted her confidence. She always did have a wicked gob on her when she wanted but now it's educated as well. She can silence my Rowdies with a single quip. They don't dare take her on anymore. Put her in the ring with Mrs T and you'd see some fur fly.

'I hear old Lawrence is standing down at the next election,' she says. 'Why don't you put yourself forward, Tilly? You're certainly making all the right noises these days.'

'I'm with the common man, Reen, and you know it,' he says, sparking up his heaven knows what number Embassy of the day with a gold lighter. 'I pay my workers a fair wage for a fair day's work.'

'What's left of them.'

'That was the old man. And he was right. We couldn't compete. Orders were drying up. Better half a shop floor than no shop floor at all. You bleeding-heart social workers haven't got a clue. It's a dog eat dog world in business and it's no use being a poodle.'

'What species of canine are you then, Tilly?'

'A Pit Bull Terrier,' he says, and snaps his jaws at her so the flesh on them wobbles.

'Not going home tonight?' she says, lighting a Sovereign. They could be a comfortably married couple out for a drink, if there wasn't a bar between them. They *should* be a comfortably married couple. I've been saying it for years, but no one will listen. He rolls his eyes wearily.

'To Lady Di?' he says with a kind of shudder and gulps down his whisky. 'She'll be there preening herself like some mad bird of paradise with her hair in curlers waiting for me like a spider in the bath.'

'A mixed metaphor if I may point out, Tilly.'

He's stopped trying to make her jealous. She's more of a confidante now. Even looks like she belongs at the end of a pier telling people's fortunes (Bernard's words, not mine). Heavy mascara is back, along with big hair and proper skirts. Very becoming. She knows how to make the most of herself, does Maureen.

'I don't care. That's what it feels like. She's there in the morning in her dressing gown and face cream and she's still there at night in her dressing gown and face cream. And before I leave she'll start asking me for things and as soon as I get through the door she'll start asking me for things. It's always things. We never chat about stuff, like I do with you. It's always things.'

'Well it is Christmas. Season of giving. Things.'

'Talking of which, how are you fixed, Reen? I mean for the kids. I mean, a few oranges and choco-bars in a stocking won't cut the mustard these days like it did when we were nippers. I mean, it's an expensive time of year. I mean...you know...you've only got to...you know...'

She pats his hand, whilst nobody's looking.

'The best Christmas present you could give me and the kids, Tilly, is to stop Smiffy filling you full of whisky. Stick to the beer. The hard stuff doesn't suit you. Some blokes aren't cut out for it and you're one of them.'

He goes a bit misty-eyed at this. Whisky unbuttons him. He's not a natural top shelf man, and I've been getting worried myself; noticed a tremor in the hands when he first comes in. Makes it difficult for him to locate those lovely lips and get the first sips down. How many hundreds have I seen?

'I think you might be right,' he says, 'but it's hard out there, Reen. Especially since the old fellah went. Sometimes I feel it's just me against the world. Honestly, I don't know what I'd do without you and the Navvy.'

She gives his hand another pat and sails off in the direction of the Saloon where there's a fight broken out. Why, if it's The Season of Goodwill, do they always end up knocking each other about more than usual? 'Do they know it's Christmas time at all?' How very apt.

4

They told me to take a holiday. I've never had a holiday in all my hundred and eighteen years, but they said I was looking a bit off-colour, needed a bit of pepping up. When you get back, you'll feel as good as new, they said. As good as new! I can hardly recognise myself! It's like I've had one of those strokes that Bernard had. I'm myself but not myself at the same time. The old Noisemaker's gone, for starters, replaced by something called a video box. Not only do we all have to listen to everybody else's favourite racket, we have to watch the flaming artist performing it on a flaming great screen as well. There's a tall thin young man up there at the moment - quite nice actually, I have to admit, with a proper shirt and tie - singing about Common People, and I think: how true, dearie. How very, very true. Because we're all common people now. All mixed up together, like Noah's flipping Ark. There was a reason why I had a Saloon, a Smoke Room, a Lounge, a Snug: because people are different and like to stick to their kind. Now I'm just one great big barn they're all lost. They don't know where to sit or stand or how to behave or what to wear. What's left of my Rowdies are effing and blinding all over the place and my Ancients rattling their dominos back at them and

RED FLAGS

Bernard can't read his paper in peace and it's all a flaming mess and to top it off they're making me stay open all day. At my age you need a nap in the afternoon; a little siesta. I can't cope.

When Jonathon walked in after a month away, I threw my doors wide at him; I'd missed him that much. They say absence makes the heart grow fonder. Mine was going like the clappers but instead of the loving reunion I'd been picturing he went berserk. Said he was leaving me. Started calling me every name under the sun: common; cheap; crass; a brainless, characterless corporate knock off. Jonathon, I tried to say, don't blame me, blame Carston's. They lied. Sold me behind my back. I'd been with them since I was named. I thought we were one big family. And they sold me like a common…a common football player, to the highest bidder. Trusty Taverns. Blame them, blame Carston's, but don't blame me. He wouldn't listen, of course, so it was a good job Maureen was there to calm him down. I couldn't remember the last time I'd been so moved, watching him scratching his head, pacing the new carpet trying to work out where he used to sit. Bernard said, rather unkindly, that it was like watching an elephant trying to retrace its ancestral migration route. (I suppose he is rather large these days, but hey, ho, more to cuddle up to.) He finally settled on a stool at the end of the bar, which he's made his own I'm relieved to say.

It's a special night tonight because Nathan's stopping by on his way to wherever he's going to celebrate his 18th. (That trip to Torremolinos bore accidental fruit, if my basic arithmetic still serves me right. Shotgun wedding if there ever was one. She knew what she was doing.) His dad doesn't get to see much of him since the divorce. Lady Di took him to the cleaners once she saw which way the wind was blowing.

Tillbury Chains had been on its last legs for years, although to be fair, they said, he kept it afloat for longer than was in his own interests. It was the last of the old foundries to go. He did his best. He couldn't find a buyer, not even for the plant. All he got was scrap and land value, which she snapped up along with half the Big House. He had to remortgage and turn it in to a B and B. How the mighty have fallen! Jonathon Tillbury running a common lodging house.

    Of course, Maureen said she'd seen it coming a mile off. In your crystal ball, Maureen dear? Like you saw that windbag Kinnock leading us all to the Promised Land a few years back? Our nice Mr Major put you right there. Sometimes I think you're getting a bit too big for *your* boots. You've never been the same since you've been on the radio. And did I get a word of thanks? It was me that gave you the leg up. You wouldn't be on the airwaves every Wednesday night, dispensing homely wisdom to the tried and troubled if it wasn't for me. Maureen's Tea Break would never have seen the light of day if you hadn't been brought up a barmaid. That degree in Sociology was just window dressing. I know we're supposed to call you a 'bar person' now but a proper old-fashioned barmaid was what the local studios were after and it was me that taught you all you know. So, don't go making out that it's you that's doing *me* the favour. We're stuck with each other. We belong together. Besides, you'd miss the company. I know you would.

    'Any sign of Lord Lucan today, Reen?' Jonathon says.

    'Nope,' she says, laughing. 'Although there was a corroborated sighting yesterday. At least the draymen thought it was him but the cellar was dark, so they might have been mistaken.'

    It was Jonathon who came up with the name Lord Lucan for my

current *mein host*. On account of him being well-nigh impossible to locate. Trusty Taverns don't go in for tenant landlords like Carston's did; too costly to get rid of. They employ Managers instead and pay them a wage like any old jobsworth and like any old jobsworth they do as little as they possibly can if nobody's watching them, which is most of the time because Trusty Taverns don't go in for reps or PROs, either. They prefer accountants who don't actually work for Trusty Taverns anyway. They answer instead to Albright Holdings, an American company which owns Carston's, which belongs to Trusty Taverns. My head's in a tizzy with it all. I don't know whether I'm coming or going, but everything's 'dunky hory' Bernard says because they've given me something called a Mission Statement. When I found out, I thought the Sally Army was making a comeback, but no: it refers to the words on a Ye Olde scroll affair painted above my bar. They say that once you pass through my portals, Trusty Taverns guarantee you will be assured of...

A friendly welcome with a smile

Quality food and drink at reasonable prices

State of the art entertainment

Unbeatable comfort

...so that's alright then.

I can just about hear over the din of that young man who's telling us common people that common people laugh and drink and fornicate because they've nothing else to do. Speak for yourself, lover. It wasn't always so. Back in the fifties we had ballroom dancing and pigeon racing and stamp collecting and work's outings. We had Piscatorial Clubs and

Dramatic Societies and Working Men's Institutes. There was a lot more going on.

'Honestly, I know Smiffy was a bit over the top with the hospitality but at least he was on parade,' Jonathon's saying.

'With his hand in the till.'

'Alright, with his hand in the till from time to time, but at least he was manning the pumps.'

'Drinking the place dry.'

'He was alright, was Smiffy.'

'He was a criminal and an alcoholic.'

'Steady on, Reen, the quality of mercy is not strained and all that...'

Since The Fall, as Bernard called it, he's become nicer. A bit less full of himself. At least while he's sober, which tonight doesn't look like it's going to be for too long. He's tanking up to face Nathan. Tanking away the guilt. That mysterious little Thai woman he's got running The Eyrie (as The Big House is now commercially known) is going to have her work cut out tonight. She comes and fetches him in a taxi when he's had more than the usual. It's a sort of sixth sense she's got.

'What time's Nathan coming in?'

'About now,' he says, then roars to the whole assembly, 'Talk of the devil...! Here he is! Here's The Man!'

From the off you can tell I'm the last place on earth he wants to be seen in. The 'youth no longer find me attractive. I'm all 'you can't do this and you can't do that'' these days: ID cards and signs up everywhere telling them they're not welcome. All for their own good, apparently. Keep them off the demon drink. Honestly, as if a few pints of bitter once or twice a week ever did a young lad any harm.

He's all done up for his big night out, scrubbed and shiny. A lovely lad but not a patch on his dad at the same age. Like a lot of them, he's going to fat already. I've never seen so many fat people about. Where did they come from all of a sudden? It's as if they've been sent from somewhere else to take over the world. Maureen says they're called 'Wobblies'. They 'graze all day, like cows in a field'. It's got something to do with 'chronic lack of self-esteem'. If you say so, Maureen dear.

'Happy 18th son,' Jonathan says, lurching as he gets down from his stool and giving him a big boozy hug. 'What you having?'

'A Coke, please.'

His dad makes a face like he's having his leg pulled and knows it.

'Do my ears deceive me, Reen, or did my son just order a Coke on his 18th birthday?'

'Nothing wrong with your hearing, Tilly. Ice in that, Nathan love?'

'Yes, please, Aunty Maureen.'

She's not his real aunty, of course. It's what he grew up calling her on account of him spending his formative years in my Playroom waiting for his dad to finish putting the world to rights. She used to take his pop and crisps out.

'Now hang on. I'm not having it. It's not natural. You're of age now. A pint of Carston's, Reen.'

'I don't drink, Dad.'

'What do you mean, you don't drink?'

'He means he doesn't drink. Some people don't.'

He looks genuinely upset. I think he'd been picturing dad and son going head to head on the pints and chasers, all past crimes of neglect washed away by my miraculous waters. You can't have your cake and eat it, Jonathan love. You can't have been an atrocious father and expect oodles of love just because he's come of age.

He knocks back his own pint and chaser anyway, orders another, and begins to get all nostalgic for his own vanished youth.

'I don't think we had 'Coke' back in 65 when I had my eighteenth, did we Reen?'

'We had ginger beer.'

'You remember mine? Me and the lads jammed into the Snug.' He gestures over to The Carvery which is where it used to be. I still feel it sometimes, like a phantom limb. 'Absolutely kaylied. They had to carry me home.'

Nathan, clearly not one for the Bacchanal himself, tries to be suitably impressed but it's all a bit awkward. Conversation is hardly flowing. There's something not right with the tone. I pick up on these things. To jolly things along his dad decides to spring his big surprise and pulls a badly wrapped flat oblong object out of his inside jacket pocket.

'Happy Birthday, Nat...'

'...Go on...open it...'

'...It's a mobile phone.'

'I know. Mum got me one last year.'

'Well you've got two now. One to call your mum and one to call all the totty you'll be chasing down La Bamba. You can't fail to pull with one of these. It's all switched on and stuff and I've got your number written down here so I'm going to go to the phone box across the road and we'll give it a test run.'

He crashes out through my doors.

RED FLAGS

'You mustn't be too hard on your dad, Nathan,' Maureen says. 'He lost practically everything, you know. He's no saint, but he does love you. Talks about you all the time.'

'But he's so...so pig headed. Keeps going on and on about me getting a girlfriend and how when he was my age he was this super stud. He won't listen to anything I say. He just doesn't understand. Won't understand about...you know...'

'Well maybe it's about time to put him straight. You're a big boy now.'

We're all waiting round this thing called a mobile phone. I've heard of them, but I've never set eyes on one before. I don't think Maureen and Bernard and the rest of them have either. It's about the same in size and shape as those 'walky-talkies' you'll see the coppers using now. (If you can find one, that is. They've vanished from the streets. It's called 'community policing'.) Anyway, suddenly it starts making a horrid buzzing noise and moving about on the bar like a dying fly. We all give a little jump. Nathan prods it and we hear Jonathon's disembodied voice which sounds tiny, as if he's on Mars, not just over the road.

'Testing. Testing,' it goes, then, 'Is that perchance Nathan Tillbury esquire?'

'It is,' says Nathan, squirming.

'The very same Nathan Tillbury who's about to go on the pull with the new mobile phone his old man very thoughtfully provided him with?'

'God.'

'A mobile phone shortly to be filled with the names and numbers of the finest, sexiest fillies ever to frequent La Bamba Club?'

Nathan rolls his eyes in horrified despair.

'Dad,' he says, 'haven't you worked it out by now?'

'Worked what out?' says the voice, losing its Martian bonhomie.

'Why are you in denial, Dad?'

'Denial?' What are you on about, Nat?'

'I'm gay, Dad,' Nathan says and, leaving the mobile phone on the bar exits through my back doors.

'Ha! Ha!' goes the voice, in a hollow, melodramatic sort of way. 'Auntie Maureen's little joke, no doubt.' Then, 'Nathan. You, there…? Nathan!...'

Maureen gives it a prod and puts it out of its misery. Everybody looks a bit sheepish, except for her. I'm not quite sure I heard right. Did he mean he's one of those young men Bernard says they have in such abundance down in London? Men who like men? It hardly seems conceivable. They can't exist round these parts, surely. Where would they meet each other? Not in here, and that's for sure.

A minute or so later there's a great crashing of my doors and Jonathon enters like the baddy in a bad Western, looking for trouble. Word's got round already and a few of my Rowdies (in their tracksuits and training shoes as though in permanent expectation of some much anticipated athletics event for fatties that never seems to arrive) start nudging each other and sniggering. He sweeps the room with a terrible stare, which is actually quite scary. The eyes were a bit bloodshot already so they look really murderous now. His face is an angry red, the veins on his nose standing out more than usual. His big meaty fists are bunched at his bursting sides. He makes a B-line for the bar, wagging his finger.

'It's you that's put him up to this, Reen, I know it. Filled his head with all your touchy feely stuff about being true to yourself and your instincts and all that bollocks you talk on the radio. Well I can tell you now, no son of mine's going to be a bender just because some jumped up little tart from a housing estate's told him he's one.'

'Come off the stage, Tilly,' she says, calmly. 'They don't give Oscars out just for being a wanker.'

This gets a laugh from the cheap seats.

'A perverter of young minds, that's what you and your kind are!'

'I can't hear you, Tilly, your mouth's full of shit.'

'Hur. Hur. Hur.'

He really is getting a hiding.

'A tart with a bleeding heart! I should have never let him near you!'

'When you've put your brain into gear, we'll talk about it.'

It blows over. These things do, in my considerable experience. And besides, he needs another drink. He sits there brooding over a couple more pints and chasers with that sulky, martyred expression on his face I know so well. By the time the Karaoke Man arrives with his infernal machine it's turned to one of his Cheshire Cat, fixed grins of mystification he hides behind when the world has him completely flummoxed.

The Karaoke Man is, I suppose, part of my 'state of the art entertainment'. I've got a raised area now, a sort of little poop deck, where he sets his stuff up and then starts daring people to get up there and sing along to songs with the words removed. Several lists - Your Musical Menu - are distributed beforehand for people to choose what takes their fancy and then they send up chits of paper with their choices written on them and wait their turn. It gets me quite nostalgic for Mabel, thumping away at her old Joanna. "Any requests?" she used to say.

"Come on, don't be shy!" And up they'd come: If You Were the Only Girl in The World; White Cliffs of Dover; Whispering Grass. Something's gone wrong in the intervening years, though. Back then people could sing.

I notice Jonathon, a notable abstainer on a normal night, is poring over the menu, chuckling to himself. One of my fat female Rowdies finishes (...i'll tell yah wadda want wadda really really want...) and he weaves his way over to the deck and grabs the microphone.

'You're supposed to wait your turn, mate,' says Mr KM.

'Satisfaction!' booms the Tillbury baritone, like the voice of God. Mr KM, taking a good look at the size of him, doesn't demur. The music begins and Jonathon starts yelling atonally to the words popping up on the screen:

'I cayunt git nooo...sadishfachsurn...I cayunt git nooo...girly acshurn...'

At the same time, he moves around the tiny stage like a deranged baboon. It's a sight both awesome and pathetic to behold. I want to throw a blanket over him and drag him away to where he can't do any more harm to himself. But I can't. Then it happens:

In answer to the repeated complaint regarding his general inability to obtain satisfaction by conventional means, one of my Rowdies yells above the din.

'You ought to start batting for the other side then, like your lad!'

He stops. The music gallops on aimlessly like a runaway horse that's unseated its rider. With astonishing speed and athleticism for one so large, out of shape and drunk, he vaults the guard rail of my poop deck, grabs the Rowdy by his tracksuit top and attempts to headbutt him. The Rowdy wrestles himself free and one of those scuffles ensues that used to be so common in my old Saloon and outside my front door at chucking out time. With an uncanny sense of timing, Lord Lucan decides to grace us with his presence for the first time in days and, showing more managerial steel than I'd given him credit for, shouts, 'Oi! You two! Out! Now! You're barred!'

The full significance of the pronouncement takes a while to sink in. How many hundred times have I heard the dread words pronounced without turning a hair of my shag pile. Rough justice for rough people. One must harden one's heart for the sake of good order. But this is Jonathon! This is Jonathon Tillbury, I try to say. Jonathon Tillbury of the Tillbury dynasty. Jonathon Tillbury who I've loved since he was a boy. Jonathon Tillbury who's stuck by me through thick and thin; through my moods, my strops, my violent changes in décor. You can't tear us apart like this: throw him in to the arms of some tart like that Duke of Argyle! I might never see him again. Please! Please my Lord, I beseech you!

But he is all deaf ears and cruel resolve.

'Yes! You heard me! Out! Now! You're barred.'

5

There's a bad smell. It's been hanging about me for a couple of years now, a nostalgic whiff of the days when bathing was a weekly event at best. I thought advances in personal hygiene had got rid of that lingering odour of unwashed bodies and unlaundered clothes, but clearly, we're regressing. Bernard, bless him, is fighting back with his scented cravats and richly pomaded hair. He keeps himself as fragrant and dapper as ever despite being on his last legs, dragging himself in on that frame of his. He's fighting a losing battle, though. It won't go away. I keep trying to point it out to Philip, my new *mein host* - the fifth I've had since 'the fall of The House of Lucan', as Jonathon called it upon his triumphant return - but he won't listen. He's too busy dreaming up new schemes to try and get people to drink in me. The latest is a Bring and Buy Auction every Wednesday night. As if a few knick-knacks are going to roll back the years and have me packed to the rafters again. It's more serious than that. A kind of pestilence is stalking the land. We're dying off, according to Bernard's Times, at the rate of three hundred a month. The Rising Sun went last week, a drawn out and painful end, opening and closing with every new manager that tried to breathe a bit of life into her. Just when it looked like she might be a going concern again, Trusty Taverns came along with their accountants and put the rents up until no one was prepared to help her anymore. Left her to rot, they did. A couple of months before that it was The Loaf and Cheese. The Loaf and Cheese! Who'd have thought it? She was always bragging how popular she was. They were both getting on, admittedly, but even so...

Then it comes to me in one of those blinding flashes of pure genius I get every fifty years or so. It's the Smoking Ban that's doing it. Before the Smoking Ban, I was wreathed in the fragrance of the beautiful weed. The gorgeous exhalation of millions of gaspers and fags and tabs and snouts and pipes and – my personal favourite– Panatelas, had kippered my walls for a century and a quarter. Without it I'd have stunk to high heaven in the old days. I'm ponging *now* and we're in the 21st! *And* there's hardly anybody in. *And* half of those that are in are out, anyway, smoking. Smoking in that extraordinary Pagoda one of my few remaining Rowdies - a carpenter - built so they could all do outside what they used to do perfectly happily inside. It's got a heater and everything. They've even installed a telly so they don't miss a moment of Big Brother.

When the one half of them comes back in from smoking the other half goes out. It's in out in out all flaming day, like the flaming Okey Cokey; not that anyone would remember *that* these days. My Ancients have vanished completely. They and their dominos seem to belong to another world. Where have they gone? It's got to be the Smoking Ban that's doing it. Someone should tell that shifty looking Blair fellah before it's too late.

Apparently, the whole idea is to protect 'bar persons' like Maureen, which is just plain ridiculous because she spends more time in the Pagoda than she spends in me. But I'm still lucky to have her even if she does only do a couple of nights these days. For the company mainly, she says. Since Kevin finally succumbed to his asbestosis and the kids moved away. Money's not a problem now she gets a little pension by way of compensation. It's the company that matters. The Navvy's like family, she says. "A supremely dysfunctional family but a family all the same." I'm moved.

One person who doesn't frequent the Pagoda anymore is Jonathon. After his second heart attack the Doc read the riot act. It was either giving up the fags and booze or shaking hands with The Grim Reaper. A 'no brainer' he says now, although at the time it was a narrow squeak. It was painful to see him trembling every time he came in.

The main thing is, he's still here. I thought I'd lost him: kept getting reports from Maureen and Bernard and Nathan and even a few of my Rowdies who'd visited intensive care that there wasn't much hope. He was hanging on by a thread and I felt so powerless; couldn't even send flowers. But he came through and he's here. We're still together. Still an 'item' as they call it these days. In sickness and in health and I can't help thinking how serious illness, if withstood, survived, can return people to what they were. How they rediscover the nicer bits of themselves. He's recovered his figure. He's quieter, a bit more thoughtful, like when he was a boy. I suppose because he nearly died, he's having a second life and I wonder if I'll be so lucky if I get struck down. I've been off-colour lately. Feeling drained; empty. Devoid of merriment. Perhaps it's the onset of middle age but I've started to dislike the way I look, too: my sofas and chairs are herniated, my tables chipped and scratched, with isolated knots of people (if I'm lucky) sitting round them pecking at their various pocket devices as if even talking's too much of an effort these days. If they're young they tend to wear hoods for some reason, like a lot of flaming monks on a vow of silence. The Karaoke Man doesn't come anymore. If anyone can muster the energy to program the video box what comes up more often than not is a gang of angry looking young men wearing a lot of gold ornaments and bragging about how rich and successful they've become and the unpleasant things they've had to do to other people to achieve this. Meanwhile, their concubines shake their enormous bottoms at them, presumably in celebration. Very occasionally we're treated to a lesson on firearms. Tonight, we've got something called Rap das Armas, a song in praise of Magnums, Barretas, Madsens and even a type of hand grenade. Dickson of Dock Green wouldn't stand a chance. No wonder you don't see any coppers on the beat anymore.

'Would you mind turning it down a smidgin, Phil darling,' Nathan says, 'or I'm going to get one of my headaches.'

'Or off,' says Jonathon, then, holding up his glass of red wine, 'My name's Jonathon Tillbury and I'm an alcoholic. Cheers!'

And he takes his first sip of the night. He's allowed two glasses, no more. So he brought his own glass in which is twice the size of the ones Trusty Taverns provide.

'Dad! Do you have to say that every night I'm in? You're becoming a parody of yourself, you know that.'

'Talk about the Pot calling the Kettle black,' he says.

There's been a mending of fences. A *rapprochement*, in the words of Bernard. They barely spoke to one another for years after Nathan 'came out', as they say. Then the Grim Reaper came knocking and I suppose it was seeing him lying there all helpless, with tubes sticking out of him. We're all innocent when we're sick, or sleeping. Even a twenty stone bigot like Jonathon Tillbury. A cynic might say that it had something to do with Nathan calling himself 'bi' now, which means he's a man who likes men who likes women at the same time, apparently. He's even got a steady girlfriend, although why Jonathon should find this preferable to his being straight 'gay' is beyond me. It seems like cheating. A more likely explanation is that Nathan decided he liked drinking after all since he liked manly men and manly men, as he pointed out, tended to drink beer so he thought he might as well join them and ended up getting a taste for it. In fact, he took it one step further and went to a 'uni' and got a degree in Brewing. (You can get a degree in anything these days, it seems. There's even something called Meeja Studies, although I personally think the occult has no place in formal education.) He works for Carston's now, who still supply my waters although, being owned by Trusty Taverns (who were sold by Albright Holdings to the sinister sounding Black Consortium) I'm obliged to put on at least one Guest Ale. We're not allowed to call it 'beer' anymore. It has to be 'ale', which strikes me as odd since you'll never find anyone saying 'do you like ale?' or 'I fancy going out for a few ales tonight.' Anyway, it's one of my Guests he raises to those plump

Tillbury lips tonight.

'Very hoppy,' he says, teasingly. 'Full gravity but light on the palate.' And takes another long, satisfying pull.

'Pack it in, Nat.' his dad says. He misses his beer terribly. He's still in mourning for it. He was, is, a thirsty man.

'Full of bite yet smooth as velvet.'

'Stop teasing your old man, Nathan,' Maureen says. 'You're supposed to be giving him support, not the DTs.'

'Do you know,' Jonathon says, 'Since I had to knock it on the head, I actually dream of beer. I'm not kidding. You were in one the other night, Reen. You're pulling me a pint, all lovely and foamy, and you hand it over, and I go to take a pull and I can't. There's something holding me back.'

'Like Prometheus chained to his rock,' she says, and Bernard, a few yards down the bar looks up from his crossword and gives a knowing chuckle.

'Whatever,' Jonathon says. 'How were those courgettes I gave you the other night?'

On the doctor's advice he's taken up growing vegetables. For the exercise, since he had to stop running the The Eyrie. The Big House is flats now. He lives in one and rents the other four out. The final remains of two centuries of capital.

'Lovely. I had them with a nice béchamel sauce and some gammon. Are you coming round for your tea tomorrow?'

'Wild horses,' he says. 'Especially if it's steak and kidney.'

I'm rather enjoying this homely banter. It's not exactly University Challenge but at my time of life there's nothing wrong with wallowing in the ordinary, the humdrum, the domestic. I'm getting a nice warm feeling in my pipes for the first time in ages - good 'vibes' as they say - when Bernard starts making a funny noise and pointing at the local evening paper which he reads when he's given up on the crossword.

'What's that, Bern?' Jonathon says. (He's ever so patient with him.) Then, 'Bern, you alright?'

It looks and sounds for all the world like he's having another of his strokes. He keeps mouthing sounds which aren't quite words and pointing at the paper. Phil gets there first and snatching up the filthy rag begins reading what Bernard's trembling finger was trying to point out.

'Bastards!' he cries. 'Bloody lying bastards!'

They all gather round.

'What is it, Phil? What's going on?'

He begins to read.

'...Trusty Taverns have announced further offloading of licensed premises...in response to customer demand, the company is to further rationalise its food and beverage operations...vital to liquidate existing assets in order to improve service in expanding areas...units due for liquidation....The Grapes...The Railway Inn...The Navigator...'

Jonathon's turned as white as a sheet.

'They can't,' he says.

'They can,' Maureen says.

'They have,' Phil says.

'They've what?' I want to say. I don't understand. It's clearly got something to do with me, but it's written in gobbledegook. 'What do they mean by 'due for liquidation'? I can't be up for another makeover, surely? I only had one fourteen years ago!'

'Liquidation!' Phil shouts, obligingly, very red in the face. 'Bloody liquidation! Why can't the lying bastards speak the queen's bloody English for a change? Why can't they just say the chop, the axe? Why can't they just say 'in order to make lots of money for ourselves we're going to leave entire communities without entertainment by turning all our pubs in to flats and houses'? Why can't they just say we're killing off the Pub!? And I've tried so hard! I've tried so hard!'

I feel my pipes go icy cold. My pumps, walls, furniture swim in and out of focus and I begin to see things that can't really be there: Men with blackened teeth in frock coats and stove pipe hats drinking from pewter tankards and through my windows, cab horses trotting through yellow fog in the street outside. An electric tram sweeps round the corner, the top deck crammed with men in bowlers and flat caps and women in hats with parasols and they all wave and inside my Rowdies are in khaki uniforms, singing, then nobody's singing and half of them aren't there anymore and I feel this terrible sense of loss for someone who left me one day in his khaki uniform and never came back. I see hungry-looking men marching past my windows and then they're in khaki again and a tall, delicious blonde in a different sort of uniform leaps out of a car, comes in and bowls me over with his American voice and lovely manners, and then there's a huge celebration with everyone drunk with joy and then that aching feeling of loss again until he appears for the first time in his cricket flannels and sunburned summer cheeks. I see him framed in the lunchtime light of my doorway as he swaggers towards the bar and orders me to serve him and his even younger-looking mates and I do although I know I shouldn't and Jonathon, he says, Jonathon Tillbury, pleased to meet you and this feeling of utter powerlessness comes over me even as he coarsens, fattens, sickens and ages until he's saying over and over again 'they can't! they can't! they can't!' and I want to reach out and comfort him and say we've had a good life together and tell him what he's meant to me, but I can't and this terrible tiredness is dragging me down and the last thing I remember is an amplified auctioneer's voice going, 'a pound for this wonderful pair of curling tongs, hardly used.....in their original box...come on gents...give the wife a nice surprise...do I hear one pound ten?...last bid...no...alright...going...going...going...gone!'

And I remember thinking, is this it? Is this how it ends? Not with a bang but with a crimper?

6

If there is an afterlife, a heaven, then I think I must be in it. I read somewhere in one of Bernard's books that there's a thing called reincarnation. It means that you don't die, you just come back as something else and the state of that something else depends on how good you've been in your previous life. If, for example, I'd been really bad I could have come back as that atrocious little slut The Pig and Whistle, dolling out remaindered beer on the cheap to blokes from up the Estate with dubious roofing businesses; getting raided by the police every other week for illegal substances. But I haven't. I must have been good because instead, I've come back as what I was a hundred and forty-two years ago, when I first flung my doors open to the world. I've got my Saloon back, my Smoke Room, Lounge and Snug. Some of my beer comes straight out of my barrels. I've got a coal fire in every room. I've even got sawdust on my floor in the Saloon. As if all that wasn't enough, I am heaped with laurels too. There are plaques over my bar awarded by an organisation called CAMRA, which Jonathon says is short for Campaign for Ridiculous

Ale-bores, although I think he's being unkind. They proclaim me as Regional Pub of the Year on three occasions and my waters have garnered prizes up and down the land. From Land's End to John O'Groats, my name sounds in the ears of these strange people with their beards and kagools. Even Nathan's got one now. A beard that is, not a kagool. He spends most of his time wearing a leather apron to go with his steel capped boots. Contrary to what his dad says, this is not 'fetish wear', but a practical necessity when heaving barrels of beer about. These days he's not 'gay' and he's not 'bi'. He is – and he claims to have invented the term – simply 'guy'. He doesn't have the time for a 'relationship'. He is, he says, 'married to The Navvy', which is a sort of back-handed compliment I suppose (although you could have asked first, Nathan dear). Giving off a strong smell of hops and yeast he pokes his head in to the Snug where his dad's getting some help with the Metaphysical poets from Maureen. She's supervising the 'A' level studies he's doing at the Tech. Making up for lost time. 'Having another go', as he puts it. 'Keep the grey matter ticking over' now that he's in his seventies.

'Could you do me a favour, Dad, and nip to the brewhouse. Check on the temperature of the mash tuns. I'm supposed to be interviewing a new apprentice, if he can be bothered to turn up.'

This new arrangement still has my head swimming from time to time. I have to keep explaining it to myself to make sure I'm not just dreaming.

When Trusty Taverns decided to have me put to death, I entered a state known as 'pubatory', whilst the powers that be decided my fate for all eternity. It was a terrible, terrible dark time of emptiness and loneliness, my windows boarded up and scrawled on with graffiti. I was on the point of becoming part of a 'brownfield development site' when Bernard came riding to the rescue on his mobility buggy. He'd been retired from the Town Hall for years but still had a bit of clout and started asking embarrassing questions. Demanding to look at certain deeds and documents and so forth. Digging up the dirt until it came to light that somebody, for an undisclosed fee no doubt, had conveniently overlooked the fact that I was something called a Grade 2 Listed Building, which means that no one can get rid of my bricks and mortar, ever. My function can be changed but not my edifice, a 'state of affairs that would have thrown Aristotle,' Bernard said. There were shenanigans, threats, even attempts at bribery but he remained steadfast; my saviour. He even made a trip down to London on a train to deliver a petition on my behalf. Jonathon and Maureen went with him. They took along a reporter from the local Evening Mail which had taken up my cause, too. The photo of them together outside the Houses of Parliament has pride of place over my bar.

In the end, the effort proved fatal. He had a stroke on the train back. He died saving me! I miss him terribly. He gave me my education. But it was his time.

The plan was hatched at his wake. He was speaking to them from a higher plane, they said:

By selling the Big House and moving in with Maureen up the Estate, Jonathon would raise the cash to buy me off Trusty Taverns. Having lost the battle to have me erased, ploughed into the ground for filthy lucre, they were sure they'd jump at the offer. Then Nathan, whose talents were languishing at Carston's, was to convert and extend my stables into a 'micro-brewery', there to concoct the waters that were to make me famous throughout the land.

Suddenly I was flooded with light and given life by expert craftsmen who still possessed the ancient skills necessary to restore me to my former glory. My re-opening was wondrous to behold. June 7th 2014 will go down in history as the day the little people fought back and won. The day a mortal blow was struck against the faceless giant of global corporatism. That's what Jonathon says, although I think he's milking it a bit. We've moved on. I'm a business now. A Limited Company. It's 2019 and there's money to be made.

'Just give us ten more minutes, son,' Jonathon says, 'whilst I nail this Donne feller.'

'Ten minutes max, Dad. Half a degree out and Navvy Christmas Old Thumper's down the drain. Literally.'

'Alright! Alright!'

'Now where were we, Reen? 'Where can we find two better hemispheres? Without sharp North, without declining West?' That's a metaphysical conceit, right?'

'Correct.'

'But what does it meeeaaan?'

'You should know.'

She fishes out a bit of yellow paper, all tatty and worn with lovely old-fashioned handwriting on it, done with an ink pen.

'Your eyes are windows to *my* soul,' she reads,

'Your breasts twin peaks of my desire

Your hips the seas on which I roll

Your thighs contain celestial fire...'

'Who wrote that?' he says.

'You, when you were sweet seventeen. You dedicated it to me. I've carried it around with me ever since.'

'Good grief,' he says, going all grave and thoughtful. 'Why did it take us so long, Reen? It was obvious we were made for each other. Why couldn't we just come out with it? Why couldn't we admit it? All those years wasted.'

'They weren't wasted. We always had the Navvy to keep us on course. It was just a question of life sorting itself out. You had yours and I had mine. It wouldn't have been right throwing everything out the window. We had to wait. That was *our* destiny.'

(Pass me that tea towel someone, I'm filling up).

'Perhaps you're right,' he says.

'I know I'm right,' she says, 'because here we are, without sharp North, without declining West. A perfect sphere. Get it now? It's one of the easier ones.'

He leans over, and very slowly, very gently puts his lips to hers.

Just as I'm going to blub, a flaming great racket starts up from the Smoke Room. As well as being a mobile-free zone (I've got pictures hanging everywhere of Lord Kitchener pointing and saying 'Your Mobile Doesn't Need You'), I've been decreed an artificial music-free zone too. No Noisemaker; no video box. Instead, I have 'folk nights' during which folk who don't resemble other normal folk get together and, on a collection of primitive instruments, scape and bang away at songs nobody's ever heard of. There is one, however, that's quite rousing in an antiquated sort of way. It's been adopted as my Anthem. To be sung, they say, to a pub that knows what it is and what it's for. They're at it now, in Irish accents for some reason; a little bit rude for them, or it could just be my hearing which is getting worse by the day:

'Navigator, Navigator rise up and be strong

The dawn it is here and there's work to be done

Fetch your prick and your shovel and your old dynamite

For to shift a few bums of this earth we delight'

Though flattered, naturally, a tiny smirk of irony comes over me. These people wouldn't recognise a shovel if one jumped up and hit them on the head. My Rowdies on the other hand wouldn't have any problem, but they've all gone; gone somewhere else, although nobody seems to know exactly where. Nobody fights in me anymore. Tracksuits with trainers are no longer worn. Language is invariably restrained. Drinking, though immoderate, seldom leads to drunkenness. I'm profoundly grateful for this, my new life, of course, but I can't help thinking at times, just at times, that it's all a bit, well, a bit...tame.

These heretical musings are cut short by the entry of a gorgeous young man whose hair, facial accoutrements and rough clothing suggest he's just walked off the set of Game of Thrones. I feel a sudden pressure and then melting sensation in my pipes. He's six foot five, built like Thor, with the kind of regular little nose those Nordic types have. His hair flows over his broad shoulders in ringlets of gold. Nathan scurries up to him, all of a flutter.

'Jason?' he says escorting him to one of my more private booths where, with great difficulty, he attempts to focus on his touchingly short Curriculum Vitae instead of the gorgeous looks.

'It says here you went to Charterhouse?'

'Yah,' says the lad.

'It's not Jason Douglas-Warren of Douglas-Warren Concrete

fame, by any chance?'

'Yah, I know. Weird, right. I should be at Cambridge or Oxford or Durham and all that. But that's the point. I don't want all that. I want this. I want to *do* something. I don't want all that academic stuff and I don't want to go into the family firm. I want to learn a trade. I love pubs. Real pubs and real beer. Please don't stereotype me out of this.'

'No, no, no, no. I'd be the last person to do that, believe me. It's long hours, though. You are aware of that? Very irregular.'

(Shut up! Shut up! You might put him off!).

'I'll work whatever hours it takes, Mr Tillbury.'

'Nathan, please. It's very physical. Not at all like you might imagine.'

'I swear I can handle it…Nathan. I rowed for my House.'

'I'm sure you did,' he says, with a hungry, appraising gaze.

There's a pause during which the lad flashes the most meltingly winsome of smiles. It seems to last an hour. Then Nathan says,

'Jason Douglas-Warren Esquire. Let's get down to business. I'm going to introduce you to The Navigator.'

And I feel myself go all week at my pumps. There's a warm, wobbly feeling in my cellar. Falling in love again…never vanted to…vat am I to do?...I can't heeeelp it…!!!!!

THE HOTEL THAT FELL INTO THE SEA

In the summer of nineteen fifty-eight, at the age of nine, Timothy Seaton fell in love for the first and only time in his life. On the second Saturday in August, the family bundled itself into a tiny Austin A30 and set off for the resort on the North Sea coast where they spent their annual holiday. They left at dawn, briskly, the departure taking place in silence so as not to, as Mrs Seaton implored her noisy husband, wake the neighbours. They had not long moved to their own house in the quiet lane and Mrs Seaton was terrified of making a bad impression.

'So you expect me to push the ruddy car up the hill, Alma?' Mr Seaton said under his breath.

'Schhhhhhhh! They'll hear you Ron. And mind your language.'

The car was packed the evening before with military precision and neatness. It had a small boot into which went the pushchair, cricket bat, football, all the kiddies' clobber and a canvas bag of tools in case of breakdown. Two leather suitcases and Ron Seaton's old army valise were stowed on the luggage rack, covered with a green tarpaulin. Oil, tyres and radiator were all topped up. Wheel nuts were checked and the fuel tank filled to the brim. Nothing was left to chance. Because the Seaton's were off! Off on...

'Holidaaaaay!' Mr Seaton roared, as soon as they were up the lane.

'Oh Ron,' said Mrs Seaton, still in her twenties, laughing and happy, 'pipe down! You'll wake Janet.'

Janet was Timothy's three-year old sister, stashed beside him on the back seat, asleep in a cardboard box. Timothy was wide awake; as awake as a boy could be because holidays made everything special and different.

'Holidaaaay!' his father roared again. Then, 'Pour me a coffee, Alma.'

His mother reached down in the brown leather bag at her feet and pulled out a thermos flask the size of an artillery shell. The car was filled with the aroma of Camp Coffee mixed with a good splash of whisky: the smell of the start of holiday.

'Can I have some this year, Dad?' Timothy piped up hopefully.

'Sorry old son. Cannot oblige. It's got whisky in it, see. Dad's little holiday treat.'

'But I'm nine now!'

'Oh go on then...'

'Ron!'

'A little sip won't do the lad any harm.'

'Only a tiny sip, mind,' his mother said, beaming and handing him the Bakelite cup. 'We've got to make it last. There's over a hundred and sixty miles to go!'

Distance was precious to her since she'd married a man with a car. Where she'd come from people took trains or coaches, if they went on holiday at all that was. But they, the Seatons, were pitted against a hundred and sixty miles, alone. It was the car which made the journey magical. Timothy felt it too. At that hour, as they left the grimy Midlands' town behind and broke in to open country, theirs was the only vehicle on the road and, on straight stretches, Mr Seaton swerved the Austin from side to side in an ecstasy of freedom, making his wife squeal with pleasure. He was a high- spirited man.

There were frequent stops along the way. The first was in Sherwood Forest where, the year before, in the course of pulling off the main road to obey the call of nature, Mr Seaton had discovered a sort of dell with four tree stumps, almost in a ring, one for each of them to sit on.

'Is it still there, Ron?' Mrs Seaton called after her husband.

'Still here, darling. Just like it's been waiting for us all year.'

'Come on chickens,' she said, breaking in to a run, and swinging the picnic basket, 'We're having breakfast in our dell. Seaton's Dell!'

Mr Seaton loosened his tie. Soon it would be put aside for two whole weeks. Holidays gave you license to do that.

'Crack open those sandwiches, Mum,' he said, 'before I have to set upon *you*.' And he clasped Mrs Seaton from behind in a bear hug, pretending to take a bite out of her neck. She had been the prettiest of all the girls in the typing pool before he married her and took her out of it.

'Ron! The children!'

Timothy giggled bashfully. He was just on the cusp of understanding. Janet chased butterflies, falling over on the thick carpet of grass. The morning was fresh and sunny. They ate the cold bacon sandwiches, which always seemed to taste even better on holiday.

'Go and play with your sister,' Mr Seaton said to Timothy once they'd finished eating, 'whilst your Mum and I have a bit of a lie down in the sun.'

Timothy wanted to ask why it was that adults liked to lie down in the sun whenever they could but didn't because that might be classified as 'answering back' and anger his father whom he loved and feared in equal measure.

The penultimate stop to stretch their legs and give the engine a chance to cool was at the foot of an escarpment called Staxton Hill, which had a one in four gradient. Once up it they were on the moor that carried them on the final leg to the sea. There was no guarantee they *would* get up it though. Last year a cylinder had blown and Mrs Seaton had to steer whilst her husband, son, and two sympathetic motorists who'd stopped to lend a hand, pushed the car up the last stretch. Timothy had swelled with pride as his father shook his hand as he'd done with the strangers, congratulating him on a job well done. And off they went again, limping along on the two remaining cylinders.

Mr Seaton checked the oil for the umpteenth time. After making sure the road ahead was clear of traffic, he lit a Senior Service and, smoking furiously, hurled the car at the hill. Half way up, the engine began to squeal. It felt, at the steepest point, almost as though they were about to roll backwards. Then, as if an invisible giant hand had given them one last helping shove, they broke over the rise and were gathering speed again.

'We did it!' Timothy shouted. 'Goodbye, Staxton Hill!'

'And hello, the sea!' his father shouted back. 'Bet I see it first this year.'

Another hour of beetling over the moor and there it would be. They played the game every year and every time Timothy won. This year he was quietly instructed by his mother to let his sister win. It was all 'part of growing up,' she said. As they got nearer, an odd seriousness settled over them, almost as if they didn't want the journey to end.

'The sea!' Janet said, finally, jumping in her box and pointing.

'That's not the sea,' Timothy said, 'that's a field of cows.'

'Timmy, what did I tell you?'

'Yes, but it's not fair.'

'Don't answer your mother back!'

Then, all of a sudden, it really was there, filling the V of a steep-sided valley with its sparkling hugeness. Timothy's heart lifted in his chest and for a moment he was speechless with wonder.

There was one final stop for a 'cat-lick' to make themselves 'presentable'. Timothy squirmed as his mother flannelled his face, combed and parted his unruly mop of blonde hair. Then she made up her own face in the rear-view mirror whilst Mr Seaton smoked another Senior Service and thought of amusing things to say to Gigi, their landlady.

It had been some years since the Seaton's had had to bow to the regime of a boarding house. Mr Seaton had done well with the town's evening paper he'd joined shortly after the War, to the point at which the family could afford the one week rent on a holiday flat. This occupied the top floor of a grand three storey late Victorian house on the more exclusive south side of the resort. The owner was the spirited widow of a clothing manufacturer who had died of a weak heart. She was very much not the respectable landlady. There was no 'Mr' this and 'Mrs' that with her. It was all Gigi, Ron and Alma. Still a handsome woman, she liked to flirt mildly with Mr Seaton, who was a handsome man. Mrs Seaton didn't mind. It made her feel even prouder of her husband and anyway, when you were on holiday you shouldn't worry too much about fuddy-duddy stuff like back home.

After his usual rigorous inspection, Timothy was, as always, ecstatic that nothing in the flat had changed. The fluffy pink eiderdown on his bed, mustard-coloured tea cups, galumphing furniture, smell of varnish and mothballs: all as he remembered it. The only difference this year was he'd have two weeks, not one, in which to savour it. In the winter his father had become the editor of the paper. The job came with quite a bit more money. They could also afford to rent a beach 'chalet'.

'Just think, Timmy,' his mother babbled excitedly as they unpacked. 'No more humping stuff down and back from the beach. No more worrying about the rain. We'll be able to go down every day now. If it's raining, we'll be snug and dry in our cozy little chalet.'

On holiday, to give Mum 'a well-earned break', Mr Seaton took charge of breakfast. The first morning, Mrs Seaton reluctantly left him burning toast and walked Timothy down the esplanade to where the shop selling beach stuff was. Every year he got a new bucket and spade. It was a clear, fresh, breezy day. The white fronts of the grand hotels sparkled in the sun. Down below in the great sweep of bay, the sea gave off its muted roar. Timothy was bursting with impatience to get on to the sands which were perfect for the intricate sculpting of castles. This year, because he'd 'shot up' as the shopkeeper remarked, he got a bigger spade, which was pointed and shaped a bit like a heart but still bright red. Spades were always bright red. A blue spade would have been stupid. His bucket was made of plastic, not tin. He wanted one of the new brightly-coloured beach balls also made out of plastic but his mother said he'd have to wait. On the way back he received his first treat: a small carton of fresh double cream from the dairy shop which was the richest, most delicious thing he'd ever tasted.

After breakfast, Timothy was loaded up like a packhorse with towels, sweaters and bathing suits. Now he was nine he had to 'chip in.'

Mr Seaton, wearing light grey flannel slacks and an open necked shirt, carried on his broad, muscular shoulders a canvas bag full of all the elaborate paraphernalia two weeks of being by the sea required. Mrs Seaton, barelegged, long chestnut hair swinging free, wheeled Janet along with the big strides her tennis pumps allowed. They always took the winding path down through the Italian Gardens and tunnels of laurel bushes. As they got nearer, Timothy began to taste the salt in the air and heard the sea booming against the sea wall, which meant that the tide was in; perfect for morning swimming!

They collected their key from the man in the blue and white striped hut who was there every year. To Timothy, this was the yearly miracle: not only did the place never change but the people stayed the same too, doing the same jobs in the same shops, cafes, huts and cabins, as if the whole thing were a clockwork toy come alive just for his return.

'Isobel, number twenty-three, blue door, top tier, the one on the end, nice and quiet. Have a lovely time!'

The chalets were in rows of six on either side of a grand set of steps leading up from the beach and ending at the Clock Tower Café which sold delicious cream teas and milkshakes. Halfway up, Mrs Seaton paused to look down on the bit of the sea wall where, only a year ago, their deckchairs rented daily, they'd jostled for space with the crowd. Briefly, she experienced the swelling sensation that her life was on the cusp of breaking through in to something less ordinary than she'd ever dared to imagine.

The family in the chalet next door, named Betty, had arrived just before them and was in the process of staking out its bit of concrete paving with the deckchairs provided.

'Lovely morning,' the mother said cheerfully.

'Looks like we're going to be neighbours,' her husband, a big jolly but intelligent looking man said, and Mrs Seaton was relieved.

'A pleasure, I'm sure,' she said in her best voice. (In her teens her parents had scraped and saved to send her to elocution and dancing lessons.)

A girl of Timothy's age was blowing furiously in to the valve of an inflatable airbed. With her spare hand she gave him an unselfconscious wave which made him blush, not out of shyness, but eager expectation. Although he tried to pretend otherwise, especially at school, he was a sensitive, secretive boy who, although he couldn't say so, preferred the company of girls. And here was one he might have all to himself.

Mr Seaton opened the padlock and flung open the blue doors. There was a strong smell of wood; of salt, sand, and deckchair canvas. For a moment, even Janet stopped prattling as the whole family, crammed inside, observed a reverent silence, as though they'd entered an empty church.

'Look Ron,' Mrs Seaton blurted finally, 'it's even got a Belling stove!'

'It did say so in the inventory, darling.'

'I know, but a Belling stove...plugged in to the mains...and a bread bin...and cups and plates. It's a proper home from home.'

They set about unloading their stuff, got into their beach costumes and once settled outside Mr Seaton, in his easygoing way, began introductions properly. The neighbouring family was called Parker: Harry, Dorothy, Jenifer their eldest daughter and Thomas their three-year old son. There was jovial surprise at the coincidence that the two sets of children were, give or take a few months, of identical age. The Parkers, from the North East, were 'very well spoken', Mrs Seaton commented later to her husband with approval. Harry Parker was something special to do with mining and, by the sound of it, quite high up in the National Coal Board. They were also staying for two weeks, as they always did, at the Radcliffe Hotel. You could see it from where they were: a red brick, turreted, Victorian Gothic mansion stuck out at the end of the promontory which marked the southern tip of South Bay. It stood alone in its own substantial grounds. Crouching on the cliff top behind a wall of trees bent double and combed back by gales, it had a purposeful air, as though it was there to defend something.

'Won't be there in about sixty years, by my calculations,' Mr Parker, a geologist by training, said impressively. 'The cliffs round here are mostly shale. Eroding fast. A great chunk of them just beyond the hotel came away in the winter.'

All this time, Timothy and Jenifer, as befitted young children, were not speaking until they were spoken to. Instead, they pretended to be interested in what the grown-ups were saying, whilst eyeing each other shyly. Jenifer, tall, thin and gangly in her bathing suit, had a freckled face built around a strong nose and widely spaced, remarkable green eyes, one of which had a very slight, satirical squint. Her black hair was cut in a tomboyish bob. Timothy was a blue-eyed, squat young boy with a thick blonde mop of hair perched above his short back and sides, as though it had been stuck on the top of his head as an afterthought.

At last, after agreeing with Mrs Seaton, Mrs Parker said in a mock-chiding voice, 'Well, what on earth are you young ones hanging about here for! There's a whole beach down there with rock pools and crabs and starfish and heaven knows what, so off you go!'

Freed, the two children grabbed their buckets and spades and went racing down the steps, like a pair of spaniels let off the leash.

'I know a special place to build a castle,' Jenifer said, taking the lead at once as they scampered across the beach away from the crowds that were beginning to colonise it now that the tide had turned, licking the sand smooth and even.

'Why's it special?' Timothy said, panting behind her.

'It's hidden behind the rocks and the sand's stickier.'

'How did you know it was stickier?'

He was a pedantic, bookish boy, much given to reciting facts and always wanting to know why things were as they were. His mother said he was going to be a policeman one day; a chief inspector, although he wanted to be a dress maker, like her. To watch her working at home: pins in her mouth, face set in a fierce frown of concentration as she piloted the clattering sewing machine, was one of his secret pleasures. He loved and feared his father as he was supposed to do but it was his mother whom he truly loved.

'Because I *suspected* it was.'

Timothy knew what the word 'suspected' meant but had never heard it used before by someone his own age. It shut him up.

They reached the rocks: an alpine mountain range in miniature, stretching back to the sea wall and sloping down to where they were swallowed in the sand. Waves were still breaking on their lowest point. Jenifer, her bucket around her arm, began to climb.

'Shouldn't we wait for the tide to go out a bit further? We could go round them then,' Timothy said, timidly.

'Don't be a scaredy cat,' Jenifer piped down at him. 'I know a secret path. We've just got to get over this first bit.'

So he began to climb too, and she was right. They followed a narrow zigzagging fissure stinking of seaweed and after a second ascent found themselves looking down on a smooth, empty stretch of yellow sand. Timothy, of course, had seen it before from the cliff tops, but he'd never been allowed to explore it on his own. In previous years he'd been told to stick to the main beach; stay in sight. Now he had a companion his horizons, so it appeared, were permitted to expand. He felt himself growing intrepid in her presence.

From up at the chalets, the two mothers stood looking down on the moving sticks of their children piling up sand. Of about the same age and both nearly ten years younger than their husbands, they had managed to keep their figures and were showing them off in newly-bought bathing suits.

'They certainly seem to have hit it off, Alma,' Mrs Parker said. 'I may call you Alma?'

'Please do, Dorothy.'

'Dot, please.'

'My Timmy's a funny little boy, Dot. He's not shy with girls at all. He seems to prefer their company to that of boys. One would have thought he'd grow up sporty like his father but he shows no interest in football or cricket. I sometimes think Ron feels a little cheated. My view is one shouldn't interfere. Nature will take its course, I'm sure.'

'How, odd,' Mrs Parker said, 'because Jenifer's the opposite: a proper little tomboy. If there's a tree to climb she's the first up it. Always making up adventures for herself and others. Likes to beat the boys at their own game.'

Having helped dig a moat and made a great heap within it, Timothy was out of breath. Jenifer worked at a furious pace and he found it hard to keep up.

'Can we stop a moment and plan how to sculpture it?' he said.

Jenifer left off shoveling and flinging sand like a machine and stood with her hands on her hips, legs apart.

'Can we stop a moment and plan how to sculpture it,' she parroted back in a whining voice. 'No, we *cannot* stop. It's not half the height it's got to be. So get digging!'

Far from feeling belittled by the command, Timothy experienced an odd, slavish surge of gratification in surrendering to it. He began to dig with renewed fury.

Finally, it was proposed that Camelot was to be the model for the finished structure. 'King Arthur and His Knights of the Round Table lived in it,' Timothy said, parading more facts. 'About twelve hundred years ago during the dark ages before William the Conqueror conquered England.' Jenifer accepted without contradiction and, for the second time in their short acquaintance he became flushed with a new pleasure: that of imparting successfully to a girl he liked, in tribute to her superior ignorance, facts he thought exclusive to himself.

The mound of sand was smoothed, squared and trimmed into three levels, narrowing towards the top. On each ledge they placed a series of turrets in the shape of Jenifer's bucket, the corners defended with larger ones sculpted from Timothy's. It looked good enough to eat, a man walking a dog said, stopping to light his pipe and offering them boiled sweets from a paper bag.

'Go away or I shall scream,' Jenifer said.

Up at the chalets the two fathers stood sentinel, smoking and chatting easily. They were both sporting, practical, ex-infantry men who had seen a lot of fighting during the war and were competing in modesty. Mr Parker had a pronounced limp from a shrapnel wound, which didn't stop him playing golf, he said. Mr Seaton was missing the little finger on his right hand. Left it on the beach at Normandy, he said. Forgetful, as his wife was always telling him. Better than leaving something else behind, though, Harry, he added and they both laughed.

'Looks like our Jenifer's given the dog walker his marching orders,' Mr Parker said. 'She's got a mind of her own that one and doesn't mince her words. A real live wire.'

'That's one heck of castle they've put up in next to no time,' Mr Seaton said. 'Good to see our Timothy getting proper stuck in. He's not usually one for too much physical activity. More at home with a book. Needs to learn to stick up for himself a bit more, too, if you ask me. Can't have him getting bullied at school.'

'I bet you a pound to a penny that castle won't be left standing for long, if Jenifer's got anything to do with it,' Mr Parker said.

And so it proved: Timothy was busy inscribing the word 'Camelot' with his index finger when from behind him he heard a savage scream. Looking over his shoulder he saw Jenifer running at full pelt towards the castle. Leaping, she aimed a two-footed kick half way up its side and a great chunk of it fell away and slithered over her in to the moat. The sudden, unbidden act of violent destruction left him speechless. Her green eyes flashed, wild with excitement and pleasure.

'What are you doing?' he managed finally, stupified.

'Zaaaaas!' she shrieked, jumping up and laying waste the turrets with a series of karate chops. 'Zaaaas! Zaaaas! Zaaaaas!'

Within a minute Camelot was reduced to a shapeless mound of sand. Jenifer stood on the top of it, panting and breathless, daring him to say something with her wild green eyes. He could think of nothing but how beautiful, strong and invincible she looked staring down at him.

'Let's go rockpooling,' she said, jumping down. 'Last year I caught a crab the size of a plate. Daddy gave it to the cook at the hotel and we ate it for dinner.'

'How did he cook it?'

That night he had a dream that she was riding on a starfish as though it were a magic carpet, swooping around his head.

On the evening of the sixth day the Parkers invited the Seatons over for drinks. 'Aunty' Gigi had a French au pair who was happy to babysit Janet and so Mrs Seaton put on her smartest evening dress, made by herself out of taffeta, and she, Mr Seaton and Timothy set off on the short walk to the Radcliffe Hotel. He was told by his mother to be on his best behaviour because there would be 'important people' there.

As they entered the bar, Mrs Seaton felt as though she were taking part in a film. The Parkers were already there, lounging glamorously in their evening clothes. Jenifer was wearing a tennis skirt and blouse, still hot and impatient from her lesson. The hotel had its own grass court next to an eighteen-hole putting green. After being treated to glasses of lemonade, Jenifer was given two shillings and instructed to take Timothy for a round. Instead, she took him in to the grounds to play hide and seek, putting the coins in a small pocket stitched inside her pleated, wrap around skirt. In order to do so, she opened and closed the skirt in front of him in the same way his mother, trying on one of her new creations, used to do when he was smaller. ('What do you think, Timmy? Does it fit right?') Timothy caught a brief, shocking glimpse of her navy-blue knickers.

'That's thieving,' he said, his face burning. 'It's a sin.'

She smiled at him, wickedly, with her cat's-green eyes. 'You'll have to lie for me.'

'I can't. That's a sin too.'

'You'll have to. Promise me you will.'

Timothy felt a surging wave of devotion sweeping the prissy part of him away.

'I promise,' he said.

The hotel grounds were laid out in a series of thickly-planted terraces, sweeping lawns and small copses of exotic, foreign-looking trees. Jenifer, knowing every inch of them, was near on impossible to find. There were giant plants of a kind Timothy could put no name to. Some of them had enormous leaves shaped like elephant's ears and, as he blundered in hopeless pursuit, seemed to leap out at him like the ghouls in the ghost train his father had taken him on last year for the first time.

'Over here!' she trilled as he crashed through foliage to where the voice had come from, only to find nothing. 'Over here!' came the voice again and again until, on the point of giving up and bursting in to tears, she sprang at him like a tiger from out of a bush of rhododendrons, making him jump out of his skin.

'Did I scare you?' she said.

'It's not fair,' he said.

'Come on,' she said. 'Let's go to where Daddy says the hotel's going to fall into the sea one day.'

'It won't fall into the sea there,' he said. 'It'll fall in where the hotel is.'

'It'll fall in where the hotel is,' she parroted back. 'Who cares?'

And she led him down to where the grounds petered out just beyond the tall cedars, bent and crippled by the North Sea gales. There was a long wire and wooden post fence. A few yards on the other side a tarmacked path ended abruptly as though it were launching itself in to the setting sun. Before Timothy could remonstrate, Jenifer slipped through a gap where the fence had been uprooted and charged towards the edge of the cliff. Then, she sprang in the air and disappeared with a peculiar cut off shout.

'Jenifer!' he screamed. 'Jenifer!'

But there was no reply, only the shrieking of gulls overhead and the boom of the sea down below. Horror and confusion such as he'd never known made him bold. Slipping himself through the fence he walked gingerly towards the edge of the cliff. Then, as he got to his knees, preparing to crawl and peer over, her face popped up from behind a tuft of grass.

'Boo!' it said. 'Fooled you.'

She was standing on a broad ledge giving on to a perilous but not necessarily deadly descent.

'You scared me,' he said. 'I thought you might be dead.'

She scrambled back up.

'It was a test,' she said, squaring herself to face him, her brow scrunched up in a serious, examining frown. Then, 'Do you love me?'

'Yes,!' he said.

Jenifer bent over towards him and screwed up her eyes. Then, he felt her cold, wet lips on his. Dimly aware he was required to respond in some way, the best he could manage was not to withdraw.

This qualified as a kiss, his first ever, because she said in a brisk, business-like manner, 'That was nice.' And went skipping off.

The remainder of the holiday passed for Timothy in a prolonged, delicious swoon of devotion. He hugged his secret to himself and was careful not to exhibit any signs of the turmoil going on inside him. The thing was so precious and private that, were anyone to so much as suspect his feelings, he feared it would shrivel and die. He was sure Jenifer felt the same. She had given him a note which said, simply, 'I Love You.'

So, on the last day, they parted as if nothing more than ordinary friendship had passed between them; a friendship circumscribed by the adult world which ruled them, to be continued next year. The Seaton's and the Parkers, seeing as they'd enjoyed each other's company so much, had already booked the same chalets for the same two weeks in August. (They exchanged Christmas cards, no more. Holidays were holidays.)

'Bye. See you next year.'

And that was that. Crying inside, Timothy was led off, back to his other, non-holiday world.

He hid the note in a crack in the wall at the bottom of their garden. At school his secret made him feel superior and he became even less interested in boyish things, although he did try to join in football games to keep up appearances. By the following summer he had 'shot up' another three inches. So had Jenifer. Apart from that, she, (like everything else) was wonderfully, miraculously the same: impetuous, commanding, capricious, daring and, in Timothy's eyes, as bewitchingly beautiful as the gangly figure in his mother's photograph album (secretly visited) who stood beside him on the ruins of a sandcastle licking an ice cream cornet. For two whole weeks they carried on as they'd left off; she, still the inventor of challenges, adventures, he, still prostrating himself with facts. Although, on his visits to the outside lavatory behind the Clock Tower Café, Timothy now knew, dimly but irrevocably, what the crudely carved images on the door were depicting, he had no idea *why* people should do such things to one another. So, when she kissed him and he kissed her back, he had no sensation other than it being a sort of repeated seal on their feelings for one another. On the last day, she told him she'd decided they were to be married as soon as they were grown up.

'Bye. See you next year.'

Ten days later, Timothy was made to put on a blazer, a tie, and wear a cap on his head. He was given a brown leather satchel and some coins. Then his mother walked him to a bus stop where, dabbing at her eyes with a handkerchief, she waved him off on the journey across town to the boys grammar school he was to attend.

Arriving, Timothy found himself in hell. He was allotted to a 'form', which was then marched from one classroom to another where a succession of frightening men shouted orders and dictated facts about strange new things such as physics and geography. One of these facts was that something called "matter" could "neither be created nor destroyed; only transformed from one form to another". When Timothy, as had been his habit at junior school, asked a question, in this case what the word matter meant, he was told not to be 'impertinent' and the whole form laughed. Quickly, he learned not to ask questions or volunteer any opinion of his own. But the biggest shock of all was that girls had vanished from his life. Overnight they had become a remote and segregated species glimpsed through the bars of his miserable exile to a world peopled entirely by men and boys. To actively wish to have any contact with them was now regarded as perverse. That was for the boys at the secondary modern who had become distinct from him as well, as if, being a grammar school boy now he was expected to live on a kind of reservation for the mentally gifted. And anyway, he had no time for play. His evenings were filled with hours of homework. So, he simply became ever more devoted to his mother, and she in her turn used this to bribe him to 'stick it out', as is father put it. Mrs Seaton was painfully aware of his unhappiness but could do nothing.

'Please, Timmy. Be a brave boy for me,' she said every morning, straightening his tie and brushing down his blazer. 'Make me proud of my Timmy. My precious, clever Timmy.'

Dutifully, he adapted to unhappiness. He became meek and uncomplaining, and waited for the summer holidays when life could begin again.

At last they came. To his relief the clockwork toy sprang in to life and magic flooded back in to his own. Everything was the same. On the first night Mrs Seaton tucked him in bed (forbidden now he was eleven, but allowed this once because they were on holiday). For once he appeared happy. He fell asleep secure in the knowledge that Jenifer was there, in her own bed at the Radcliffe Hotel a few hundred yards away, thinking of him and their first morning back together. The year long wait was nearly over.

Arriving at the chalet, the Parkers were already there, although he couldn't see Jenifer. He assumed she'd gone off to buy an ice cream or something like that. The adults greeted each other warmly. Then Mrs Parker said, 'Jenifer will be joining us in four days. She's become quite smitten by ponies and absolutely insisted we let her go on a trekking holiday with her high school even though it clashed with ours. She'll be coming down by train with a friend. I'm sure Timothy will find her charming. They're practically inseparable.'

Timothy smiled, said nothing; showed no feeling. At that moment he lost all faith in the world. It became no longer possible to trust and all magic vanished from it. Early in the New Year the Parkers emigrated to Canada. Christmas cards were exchanged for a while and then contact was lost.

So, when he saw her daughter presenting on the television it came as a shock to find that feelings sharper than the familiar ones of pointlessness and self-loathing, the dull ache that lay just beneath everything he did, could still be aroused in him; feelings that could discompose, make his head spin. The last time he'd been unable to keep such things at a distance was when, in his late twenties, he heard his mother wailing hysterically down the phone that his father had just dropped dead of a heart attack. Since then, throughout his working life at the town library and the one he shared with his mother in the house he'd grown up in, he'd managed to preserve an inscrutable equilibrium. Frugal, abstemious, utterly self-contained he'd supported them both uncomplainingly in modest comfort for forty years.

'Timmy, come!' he heard Mrs Seaton's thin, palsied treble warble from the sitting room. 'Come quickly! It's the Radcliffe on the telly!' He was cooking their evening meal: grilled pork chops with mashed potato, her favourite.

'Not now, Mum,' he called, 'I'm in the middle of cooking. You wouldn't want me to spoil your chop now, would you?'

'It's the Radcliffe, Timmy! The Radcliffe!'

'Give me strength,' he said under his breath.

Recently, her mind had begun to wander in and out of the past with a will of its own. It had happened quickly. One day, it seemed, she'd been as sharp as a tack, the next she was telling him she was going to pick up a loaf of bread from the Co-Op which had been demolished in 1977. But he wasn't putting her in a home. Never.

'It's the Radcliffe! I swear.'

'Please, don't,' he called, half sarcastically. That was another thing: she'd started to use bad language. It just came out, like belching, for no apparent reason.

'He was a randy sod, your Dad,' she'd said the other day when they were watching Countdown. Terrible.

And Janet wasn't any help living on the Costa Brava with that second husband of hers. Timothy turned the gas down, wiped his hands on his apron and went in to the sitting room.

And there it was. The woman, tall, mid to late thirties, a bit on the horsey side, was talking to the camera standing on rocks beneath a cliff that was crumbling in to the sea. It was one of those programs – there seemed so many – featuring presenters trying too hard to conjure something extraordinary out of rotting heritage, as if anyone really cared anymore. Ciara's Coastal Odyssey, he remembered now from the Sunday Times supplement. He'd seen her before but never really taken to her, or what she was doing: tramping breathlessly around in a kagool, pointing out, in a voice pitched somewhere between dramatic suspense and holy reverence, underwhelming gems of the nation's past.

'…..I'm standing beneath a classic piece of mid-Victorian seaside architecture, which has a special significance for me,' the woman was saying in a voice that was educated and English but possessed also an underlying mid-Atlantic sort of burr, which wouldn't have been out of place in Norfolk.

'It was here, before they emigrated to Canada, that, as a young girl, my late grandparents brought my mother on many a summer holiday back in the nineteen fifties. Beside the fire, in our log-cabin retreat outside Vancouver, she would tell us stories of how she roamed the enchanted grounds, planted with rare species from all over the world by its eccentric former owner, the botanist Sir Henry Mildew, who went mad and hurled himself from the cliff one stormy night…a cliff that would have been a couple of hundred yards or so beyond where I'm standing. Mother, an adventurer herself and the author of several travel books under the name of Daniela Kildare, regaled us with descriptions of the hotel's grandeur, its faded but still palpable splendors; for grand and splendid it must have been…'

The camera panned upwards to where the Radcliffe now stood, teetering over the precipice, bearded with ivy, its windows boarded up, like a House of Horrors. Timothy looked on agog. Since the age of twelve, when his parents switched their summer migration to the milder attractions of Torquay, he had managed to keep the place frozen in memory; part of a mental vignette of the one point in time, as his life subsequently revealed, where he had been truly alive. Now this woman and her camera crew had shattered it. Bitterness jabbed inside him. So, she had become ordinary after all: married, had children. There was no doubt. The resemblance was clear: the large bony nose; the green eyes, slightly mad, seemed to be taunting, challenging him, as her mother's had done: the mother who had conceived her out of lust for a man. How could she have debased herself, surrendered to such a repulsive act when he had remained pure all his life? Women were there to be served, worshipped, obeyed; not plundered. She'd allowed herself to be plundered like the rest of them.

The woman was standing now in what looked like a tropical jungle.

'...and here is the real, the astonishing magic of the place,' she panted, gesturing around her at billows of colossal plant life. '...the fantastic samples Sir Henry Mildew nursed, kept lovingly alive, on his voyages back from Borneo, the Galapagos Islands a century and a half ago and planted here to be clipped and pruned by generations of gardeners...have, in a few short decades, been returned to their natural wilderness...amazing...'

'Bitch!' Timothy said. 'Silly bloody bitch!'

'Oooh, Timmy,' Mrs Seaton chuckled wickedly.

'Silly sodding bitch!'

'Oooh, Timmy! What language to use in front of your mother.' He smelt burning. Smoke was coming from the kitchen. 'Oh flippin' heck! Now look what you've made me go and do, Mother,' he said. 'That's not the Radcliffe. That's any old hotel, that is. You and your imagination.'

'It's burnt,' his mother said, when he returned with the chop and potatoes. He set them before her on the dinner table, tucking the napkin in the space between her blouse and the turkey wattle of her neck. Extreme age had, if anything increased her appetite, whilst at the same time turning her into a messy eater. But it still gave him pleasure to watch her eat, the act providing special confirmation that she was still there, alive and in good health. 'I can't eat burnt food.'

'It's only burnt a little bit, Mother,' he said, having recovered equilibrium. (For one stupid moment he'd actually thought of explaining his outburst. But no: she would never know someone had once competed with her in his affections.) 'Try it with a nice bit of chutney. I haven't got anything else in.'

The television was off. They never ate with it on because that was 'common'.

'Are you going walking tomorrow?' Mrs Seaton said between mouthfuls. 'Walking' was how she described his regular hikes in the surrounding hills and dales and which provided cover for his monthly visits to Derby. They were getting more expensive but his pension from the library was indexed linked and he had small pot of savings. There was a new lady arrived a few months ago from Lithuania: a tall, intelligent, powerfully built young lady with a look that could wither Cleopatra herself. The way she sat on her throne in the special clothes she wore just for him, eating the chocolates he brought her which she allowed him to pop in to her mouth - it took the breath away. He respectfully requested that she chastise him in her native tongue, which was a special thrill, and she knew instinctively just how far to go.

'I think I'll do Thorpe Cloud tomorrow,' he said, 'seeing as it gives fine. A wonderful view from up there. Right across the Trent Valley. You remember when we used to do it together?'

'It was bugger to climb,' she said.

'Oh, Mother,' he said, shaking his white head sadly. 'I wish you wouldn't. I wish you wouldn't...'

A couple of months later it went, as they said, 'viral'. They were watching the nine o'clock news, which these days always seemed to end with some assuaging piece of trivia. The newsreader, an Indian man in a turban, finished reciting his usual litany of failure, crisis, death, fear, and, in a voice less full of barely suppressed stupefaction, almost bordering on humourous, said, '...and we say goodbye to a grand old dame of our seaside heritage. The Radcliffe Hotel - once home to one of England's great eccentrics, the Botanist Sir Henry Mildew and for over a century the retreat of generations of well-heeled holiday makers – has finally succumbed to time and tide...'

And there it was, first breaking free from what was left of its foundations with a great rending crack, then bowling down the cliff in a couple of bounds before crashing on its roof into the sea. The tide was in and the rough sea began immediately to swarm around it like sharks in a feeding frenzy, ripping and swallowing, which made Mrs Seaton start laughing in that strange, whooping, idiotic way that had come upon her recently.

'Oh, Mother,' Timothy said, crying inside. 'I wish you wouldn't...'

After watching yet another of those programmes featuring amateurs competing to emulate the feats of Michelin starred chefs and being barked at and humiliated in the process, it was time for bed. Timothy dressed Mrs Seaton in her nightgown, tucked her in and planted a kiss on the forehead of the ancient, innocent little face that peeked over the pink fluffy eiderdown.

'Goodnight, Mother. Sweet dreams.'

Then, he went to his own room and, putting on his pajamas, climbed in to bed. On the table next to it was a copy of A Year With The Inuit, by Daniela Kildare. Every night now he reflected on the oddness of how, for much of his life at the library, she had been there on the shelves. He must have issued her, stamped her out, scores of times without realising. How could he have known? He had no interest in travel writing; no interest in books as such except as the medium of his employment. He opened the page where she was smiling wickedly down from the top of an igloo, wrapped in furs. How imperious she looked now he had forgiven her.

CARAVANNING

Happy families.

Dinner finished – shepherd's pie, baked beans, jam roly poly and custard – we sat down to a bit of telly.

'This is the seven o'clock news.'

The world was going up in flames, but they chose instead to lead with the by now tiresomely familiar spectacle of some hounded ex-celebrity fleeing a baying pack of paparazzi.

'My God,' my wife Janet said, 'Isn't that...? Didn't he used to...'

'Charlie Carrick,' I said, taking a sip of merlot and turning the sound up (my hearing was just starting to go), 'aka Champagne Charlie. Star and host of You're Going On Holiday! back in the early 'seventies. Remember, he used to show up on people's doorsteps waving airline tickets and a bottle of champagne. The payback was they'd agree to be filmed on the freebie to Benidorm or wherever and, on their return, competing studio panels had to guess what happened next when the film was paused. Did Ken a) choke on his (mistakenly ordered) starter of octopus? b) send it back to the kitchen to be cooked? c) palm it off on Marjorie? or d) hurl it in the waiter's face? That sort of thing. Quite novel for the times. Groundbreaking in its way.'

'I was just a kid,' Janet said. 'You'd be about twenty. Off on the hippy trail. How come you remember it so well?'

'It ran for a long time. Kicked off when I was still at school. Just. It was the bullies' catchphrase too. 'You're Going On Holiday!' they'd say to Gerrison or Powell before chucking him down the coal chute.'

'Mum and Dad used to let me stay up and watch it,' she said. 'It was the highlight of their week. They never got further than Bridlington.'

Like me, Janet came from a not so well-off family. We both 'came up in the world'. Came up together until we could afford a nice big house and the kind of holidays even Champagne Charlie himself couldn't have dreamt of.

The string of allegations was quite a long and shocking one.

'Looks like the only vacation CC's going on this time will be at Her Majesty's Pleasure. Bang to rights by the looks,' I said. 'Another one bites the dust.'

'How old!?' she said, suddenly outraged, her tone catching something of the newscasters barely suppressed disgust.

'Not looking good, is it.'

'Of course he's denying it!' she shouted at the screen, getting quite worked up.

'Well he does sort of have a right. Habeas Corpus and all that.'

'But there were so many, by the sounds of it. They can't *all* be making it up. You've only got to look at him. Look!'

I did. What I saw was a frightened old man with the dishevelled, bewildered air of someone who'd just been pulled out of a hole down which he'd been for a very long time. He made a belated effort to compose himself before being bundled into the car and for a brief moment I caught a glimpse of the dapper, wise-cracking peddler of the average housewife's dreams such as they were back then. And I felt sorry for the poor bastard. I couldn't help myself. Sorry for him, and in a way, sorry for myself that yet another of those household names of my boyhood would have to be airbrushed from memory. It felt like my youth, my time of innocence, was being gradually nibbled to nothing by an unspeakably horrid cancer.

'Castrated, that's what they should be! Castrated!' Janet squeaked in disgust, making repeated snipping motions in the air with her long, delicate fingers.

'I believe in some countries they are,' I said.

'Well jolly bloody good for them!'

I knew I should have been able to join in, but I couldn't. I'm one of those people who can't feel hatred towards individuals, no matter what they've done. I just can't. My hatred – if you can properly call it that - is reserved for systems, governments, corporations, movements. I'm a political animal. I respond to the collective not the singular.

A soap opera came and went. I had a little doze and was woken by Janet shouting up the stairs.

'Felicity love! You'd better come down now if you want to catch the beginning of your Dad's show.'

'Wot!?'

'I said your Dad's on! He's on in five minutes!'

She came back into the room, plonked herself down on the sofa and cuddled up. A good ten years younger than me, she kept herself in shape with lots of Pilates and Zumba-ing; the kind of stuff a saggy sixty-something bugger like me should have been doing but couldn't face. She was still beautiful, with good, clear, skin; hardly a wrinkle. I was a lucky man.

'Playing about with make-up,' she said, 'I bet you a pound to a penny.'

Sure enough, there was a rumble on the stairs and into the room sprang Felicity, our fifteen- year-old daughter looking like she'd done herself up for a shift in some knocking shop in Shanghai.

'Will someone turn the volume down on that girl's face.'

'You really are soooo predictable, Dad,' she groaned, flinging herself in to an armchair and tucking her legs under her, as young girls do.

And you're getting far too precocious, I was going to say, but didn't.

Felicity came along very late in the day. We'd been trying for years and years then, without trying at all, there she was growing inside Janet. It was that much of a surprise, we didn't find out until she was already two months gone. We did our best not to spoil her but I'm not sure we succeeded. She had enough kit up in that bedroom of hers to launch rockets. Mission Control is what I used to call it.

The jingle started and, in due course, there I was: Ted of Ted Time fame. Fame, I should add, very recently acquired and reluctantly borne. I suggested the name as a joke more than anything, it being a weak pun on 'bed time', the dread words the more conscientious (or lazy) parents of my own generation would pronounce at some ludicrously early hour of an evening that was just starting to hot up for their delicate offspring. A minimum of ten hours sleep was considered imperative if one wasn't to physically and mentally disintegrate before reaching puberty. Comedy series that had the whole nation rolling in the aisles; European cup matches featuring miraculously surviving British teams; even frenzied demonstrations of loyalty to the monarchy were all forbidden if they happened to be screened after the witching hour of eight o'clock. It's the reason why, when I got older, I used to refuse to go to bed before midnight. I was catching up on lost consciousness.

Anyway, the 'People Who Know Best', thought it inspired. Ted is my name: Ted Baxter and I was an educational and child psychologist. Still am, I suppose. The programme was all about dealing with kids and the problems they have with their parents and teachers, or, parents and teachers and the problems they have with kids. You'd be surprised how it often turns out to be the same thing. Like pretty well everything important in my life it came about almost by accident. Working backwards:

There was a big panic such as only the British media can whip up regarding children's mental disorders. They were on the rise. They were going through the roof, in fact. Their behaviour was becoming unsupportable. We had, if the various sources were to be believed, spawned a generation of depressive psychotics. The nation needed reassuring that this horde of budding psychopaths could be headed off at the pass before they reached adulthood with a dose of old-fashioned common sense and a bit of child psychology thrown in for good measure. Who better to administer it twice a week than good old Uncle Ted, the acceptable face of social-workerdom. I'd done a bit of radio, local then national, and it seemed to go down well. I connected because, instead of spouting gibberish from a trendy clinic I'd worked in and ended up running a number of institutions for what used to be known as 'bad lads'. As a spin off I also found myself on various televised panels of experts dedicated to handwringing over the burning 'ishoos' of the day, especially if they concerned disaffected youth, who didn't seem to hate me quite as much as they did my co-panelists. I had a talent for dealing with them probably because I'd been quite a bad lad myself, in a way. I came to the profession late in life having exhausted my reserves of fecklessness on building sites, caravan sites, travelling fairs and hippy trails; anything to postpone selling out or, some might argue, adulthood. It helped and it didn't. At teaching college, where I met Janet, and in my first posting, I was always given the nutters. And as any old hand will tell you, your reward for doing a decent job with them is – you've guessed it: to get given them again. So, I decided to make a proper go of it, retrained and pretty swiftly – there's not much competition – I was Head of this unit and Director of that. My own childhood was the usual East End cliché of the day: decent, hardworking parents, hard scrapping, truanting son ('oo luvd 'is mum), clever in a cunning sort of way, but wayward. Not very interesting.

So, on the whole, I think I was right to allow myself the mildest glow of pride at seeing the figure on the screen. The boy done well in the end. Are any of us entirely without vanity? We ought to be, if Felicity was anything to go by.

'You look about a hundred years old, Dad.'

'Cruel.'

'Like one of those ageing sixties rock stars.'

'Less cruel.'

And fairly accurate. I've never managed to completely shake off the influences of my youth. As soon as I left school the young teacher on our building apprenticeship piled a group of us from the tech college in to his camper van and off we went to a rock festival - the first ever Glastonbury as it turned out - and I got the hippy bug. The closest I've experienced to a religious epiphany, once it took hold, it never really left me. 'What's so funny about peace, love and understanding?'' as the song goes. Well, quite. Until fairly recently I wore my hair long, with enough of it to make a decent ponytail and I am, despite the many horrid things I've had to deal with, an optimist. I can't see the point in being anything else.

'Still a looker,' Janet said, planting a big wet I''m so proud of my man' kiss on my cheek.

It was - I have to acknowledge in all modesty - once said that I could turn heads. Being unusually tall helped.

'Yuk!' said Felicity. 'Gross.'

'Could we please focus on the content, not the eye candy,' I said. 'Or I'll have to report you both for sexism. We blokes are allowed to hold serious opinions, you know. We're not just a pretty face and taxi service.'

The content was me, basically, talking to camera for a snappy fifteen minutes twice a week in response to a set of pre-chosen questions from anonymous worried parents. With a total budget of a few pints and a cheese sandwich down the pub, you can see how it was popular with the bean counters. And the programmers got it right, for once: they gambled on viewers having had enough of gimmicks - Michelin starred chefs put to the galleys in some Hackney council flat; hang-gliding Nobel Laureates. They must have woken up one day and thought, here's a new one: why not have a bloke who knows what he's talking about talking about it to people who want to hear. We'll be back to The Third Programme soon.

What I was talking about on that occasion was what one distressed mother referred to as her son's 'sleeping sickness'. He was sleeping his life away. She couldn't get him up in the morning. When she tried, he'd lash out at her and use foul language. Of course, there was no husband, partner, or whatever to help out; not in situ, anyway. If there had been, and had it been twenty years ago, I'd have told him to drag the kid from the arms of Morpheus, chuck him under a cold shower and threaten confiscation of all his kit if he ever talked to his mum like that again. But there wasn't and things aren't quite that simple these days. So I was launched on a schpeel about teenage hormones and how, at that age, they're like hibernating animals storing as much energy as they can against the often violent spurts of growth the body has to cope with. I didn't get chance to hear the practical steps I was about to propose because there was a ring on the doorbell. Then another, longer one. Whoever it was wasn't going away in a hurry.

*

They were 'polite but firm', as we used to say. I told Janet it was to do with a kid who'd skipped his hostel curfew and gone on the rampage (I still worked part time, counselling for the unit I'd once headed). She was used to the law coming round and looked disappointed more than anything. Disappointed that one of our rare evenings in together had been spoilt. On the drive to the station I tried to get what it was all about out of them. (We, who are in charge of clearing up other people's messes, often get inadvertently hauled over the coals for not being perfect ourselves. Comes with the job.) But they weren't having any. It wasn't them who were in charge of the investigation, they said.

The DI who *was* in charge of the investigation was a small, tidy looking man; more like your average bank manager than a top Plod. Coppers aren't what they used to be. I blame it on getting rid of the minimum height requirement. He sat me down and showed me a photograph of a stout, not very happy looking lady somewhere in her late forties, early fifties who I'd never seen before in my life.

'And?' I said.

'That,' he said, 'is your accuser.'

Then, without giving me a chance to ask exactly what I was being accused of, he laid another photograph in front of me. This time it was a pretty young girl in her mid-teens. She was wearing a bikini which showed off a lot of curves.

'Now think very carefully, Mr Baxter,' he said, not unpleasantly, as though he were asking me to assess my ability to pay off that four hundred thousand quid mortgage, 'are you absolutely sure you have no recollection of this person?'

'I don't remember her,' I said. 'But I know who she is.'

It wasn't the girl that had put two and two together but the caravan she was standing in front of and the great wide expanse of sea sparkling behind.

My head had started to spin. He followed up with another photo. This time the girl was probably about nineteen and she had a little boy on her knee who, looked remarkably like me at a similar age.

'Is the kid my 'accuser' too?' I said.

'He's dead,' said the DI. 'But, if he were alive, we very much suspect that he would be your son.'

'I'm going to need a lawyer, aren't I?'

'You certainly have the right to one, but I think that will have to wait to the morning. And now Ted Baxter I'm arresting you on suspicion of...'

*

Truth be known, I'd done the odd night or three in the cells before. Back in the day when I was Jack the Lad. I'd had the necessary coping mechanisms then. Like being drunk, stoned, or still high on some demonstration or other I'd been hauled out from and given a kicking before being slung in the van. And I'd felt safe in the knowledge that it wasn't the end of my life as I knew it. The next day I'd be sober and as penitent as was necessary. There'd be a fine. Then I'd be back out there, on the road, on the tear. But on this occasion I knew before the door had closed behind me; I knew as soon as it dawned on me in the interview room of precisely what I was being accused; what, in fact, I had done - I knew that the life, the little family I'd built around the person I'd made of myself was gone forever.

We were burgled once: got home to find the house turned over and the telly, computers, Janet's jewellery all gone. It takes your breath away. Makes you feel sick. That was what it felt like: my life had been burgled, trashed and was never going to be returned.

Once I'd got over the initial shock, the nausea and then vomiting, I began to take in my new surroundings. What struck me about the cell was how state of the art custodial accommodation had become since last being compelled to avail myself of it. All done up in bright, cheery colours, everything was curved: the bed, the bog, the door frame, as if they were on the point of melting like those Gaudi buildings Janet had so much admired on our trip to Barcelona, or those clocks in that Dali painting. 'Surreal' is a lazy epithet but that's actually how the whole thing felt: having recognisable elements of the world I was familiar with but not in the right shape or configuration or even, sequence of time. After a not very long time, I was sure it was morning (there were no windows) only to be told it was midnight and that I should stop banging on the door and try to get some sleep. The notion of sleep seemed laughable. How could a man sleep when there was no recognisable time to sleep through? How could he wake when there was no recognisable world left to wake to?

Morning declared itself finally in the shape of scrambled eggs, mushrooms and beans on a thickly bevelled plastic plate, to be eaten with an unbreakable plastic spoon. Despite the eye that surveyed me fishily through the spy hole, I wolfed it all down. The body must go on a kind of autopilot at times of severe distress or mental disturbance, the most basic instincts necessary for survival coming to the fore, even though you don't particularly want to live anymore. I felt stronger by the time I heard the key in the lock again and one of the uniforms took me upstairs to where I was to be allowed private counsel with my brief.

The Channel had been busy. Word must somehow have got back to them. Perhaps Janet had done some reading between the lines. Anyway, I had at my disposal the spectacularly named Hermione Montefiore. For reasons of sheer proliferation, she had found herself specialising in my type of case, with limited but notable success. Not everyone had gone down. She'd managed to get that old pederast Roland Templar (Songs for Sunday) off, and in so doing added to the sum of human injustice, if you ask me.

'Someone's in a bit of a pickle,' she said, displaying at once her famous talent for understatement. HM, as she'd become known, had a certain bluff, manly heartiness that went down well with jurors. It was said to offset the sick, cringing, weasel-like image her defendants inevitably projected now they were mired by the accusation of The Worst Crime in The World.

'Yep,' I said. 'Should have seen it coming. Should have kept my head down. When all this hysteria first kicked off it came back to me like a bad dream. For decades I hadn't given it a moment's thought. I'd sort of just buried it away. It belonged in another place and time, another world, when I was another person which I thought I'd left behind. And now that person's come back to destroy me.'

'A bit early to be talking like that, Ted. It might not be much of a consolation but you should know that they've been trying to get you since the success of your first mini-pilot series. They've been digging away but haven't been able to nail a thing up until now. It would appear to be inconceivable to certain sections of the media that a man can work closely with children and not want to abuse them. You have to *prove* you're not a Nonce.'

'It doesn't come as any consolation at all.'

'But it could undoubtedly work in your favour: A man who chose to dedicate himself to one of the most delicate and, some might say, thankless of the professions for decades. A man who had unlimited access to vulnerable young people and yet, even in this climate of hysteria, not a single one has come forward with the slightest allegation of sexual malpractice.'

'That's because there wasn't a single incident to denounce.'

'You'd be surprised how irrelevant that's becoming.'

'Irrelevant or not it's true. I have absolutely no sexual interest in children. None. Zero. Never have had. I was, until my fifties I suppose, aroused by young girls. Especially when I was a younger man. That's to say, when they didn't seem, or feel, that much younger than me. Christ knows I had enough opportunities but I only succumbed once. To the girl in the photograph.'

'I believe you Ted, although I think you know we haven't got a leg to stand on in terms of disputing the woman's age at the time. We're not going to get a full acquittal. I have to tell you that now. It's borderline, but the arithmetic doesn't lie. The boy died in a motorcycle accident when he was still in his teens, but the mother will have kept at least some of his clothes for sure. There'd be no escaping DNA evidence.'

'I wouldn't want to,' I said.

'You're not going soft on me, are you?'

'It's not a case of going soft. I did what I did. I can neither deny nor excuse it.'

'But you have to provide some mitigating circumstance; some context that might make the affair less damning in the eyes of a jury. That's what we've got to work on.'

'What? 'She was gagging for it, Your Honour. I never stood a chance.' Please!'

'Well, wasn't she?'

'Yes. And so was I.'

'The woman's claiming you seduced and then used her on a number of occasions and that she was too young to know what was going on. Given her age at the time, the prosecution's going to go for turning that 'seduction' into statutory rape, and if they don't get it then they're still shooting from the high ground.'

'That's wrong!' I shouted, for the first time feeling anger at what was being done to me. 'I've never 'used' any woman sexually. It's not in my nature. Why is she doing this?'

'I expect that once she saw you on the screen doing quite nicely thank you very much, she convinced herself, or was convinced by interested parties, that it was you that ruined her life: lifelong psychological damage rendering her incapable of functioning as a normal social being. The usual.'

'Well I clearly didn't help to make it a bed of roses. How many runaway dads have I had to deal with in my time? Tried to get them to face up to what they ought to do. Make a go of things. And now I find out I was one myself. The lady didn't even have that going for her. Then just as she's done the hard yards the kid gets himself killed on a motorbike. I can understand her anger and her grief gnawing away at her all these years, but I can't see how taking me down for sexual abuse is going to help. That's a different thing. I didn't abuse her and I didn't use her. I can't do that to people. I wouldn't know how. I committed a crime, yes, but she's telling a lie.'

'I suspect the main reason she's bringing charges is simply because she can, or rather, because it's required of her. We're all victims of something now and we must have recompense whether we want it or not. It's the way of the world. So come on,' she said, mentally rolling up her sleeves, 'a bit of fighting spirit. You're not a bad person. You haven't turned in to a monster overnight. You...are...not...a...bad...person.'

If Hermione Montefiore, or anybody else for that matter, had said the same twenty-four hours before I'd have wondered what on earth she, they, were talking about. Sitting there in the sterile little interview room, beltless, and without shoelaces, it felt like very much like I *had* become a bad person, a very bad person.

'Let's start with some background,' she went on. 'You've got to do some serious digging around in your memory if I'm to be of any help at all. I know it might be a bit hazy through *the mists of time*, but you've got to have a go.'

*

RED FLAGS

The mists of time had to reach back to the summer of nineteen eighty. It was my last season on the North Devon caravan site I'd worked for four years. I was the odd-job man, doing everything from reception and welding repairs, to cleaning the bogs. In the evenings, I'd perform a few guitar vocal numbers in the club they had. I'd make a bit of extra giving private surfing lessons, when I wasn't surfing myself that was. It was a very sweet number: Bermuda shorts and flip flops, deep weathered tan and salt in my hair. They gave me my own mobile home for free (a misnomer because it was what we in the business called a 'static'. It hadn't shifted since the day it was delivered). I did it out with drapes and stuff until it was proper cozy. Happy days.

It went without saying that I wasn't short of female attention. There were many who came and went and, I think, were satisfied. I was a lover. I wasn't into notches on the headboard and all that macho crap. That just wasn't my scene. I didn't do any pursuing, seducing. On caravan sites, fairs, trails, you don't have to. They're all set up for free and easy loving if you're not a complete gargoyle, and I wasn't. There were a few girls who got a bit heavy, tried tracking me down after their week or so was over but I was off, away, of 'no fixed abode'. Return to sender, address unknown.

Quite a few of the punters used to come every year, especially families. Book the same unit, same week or two weeks of the summer. I became a fixture in their lives I suppose. They seemed happy to see me. I'd run the odd errand for them on my Norton when they'd first arrive. Help them to settle in. If my memory serves me rightly, my accuser belonged to one of those families, although she wasn't a woman then of course. She was a young girl, about twelve when I first started working there.

It's highly likely she had a bit of a crush. At the risk of sounding vain, that would have been understandable. (I had the same on one of the Red Coats at the Butlin's in Southend my folks used to take us off to every year. I was devastated when, one July, she wasn't there any longer.) The crush could have intensified as the years went by until, by the time she became sexually active, she'd decided to do something about it the last summer I was there. At least it might go some way towards explaining what happened that night.

It was raining heavily. There was a storm blowing outside, tearing down the Bristol Channel. The mobile was being buffeted, rocking on its blocks. That was a fact. A storm is a storm and can be meteorologically verified if necessary. The rest is a collage of mental pictures and dim echoes of verbal exchanges which may or may not correspond to the physical reality of that time and place but is all I have to go on.

There was a knock on the door and there she was, soaked through to the skin. Could she come in? Her folks had gone out to some club or other and forgotten to give her a spare key. She herself had been at some kind of party for the youth by the looks of it; probably had a couple of halves of cider. It sounds odd: I can't remember her face, the details of it that is. The photograph I'd been shown earlier didn't seem to correspond with my own memory snapshot. Mine was prettier with a lot of freckles. But the strange thing is that I seem to remember with certainty the very weird, intense light in her eyes and that they were black.

She had on a green party dress of a kind of stretchy material that clung to her body. It was verging on the see-through after the soaking she'd had. I knew exactly what she wanted from the moment I let her in. Had I been an older man, I'd probably have sent her packing. Had it happened today, I'd already have been sent on a month-long course in caravan site management and the pitfalls thereof before being issued with a whistle to blow specifically in the event of being importuned by young girls. But it happened then, in nineteen eighty, when I was twenty-five years old.

She stood there, too inexperienced to make the first move, mascara running down her cheeks. I gave her a towel and she started dabbing ineffectually at herself. It was then that I was overcome with the most powerful contradictory sensation of wanting to protect, to nurture and yet to ravish at the same time. I began to towel her down properly and then she was all over me and I was all over her. Again, I can't remember details, only that it was quite quick and that, afterwards she was pleased. Of that I am completely sure. There was no guilt on her part. As for me, it all gets hazy again. Despite her fully formed, quite large breasts and hips it seems improbable that I wouldn't have had serious doubts as to whether she was of age. But to have asked before or during the act would have more than likely elicited a lie anyway and to have asked afterwards would have, to the person I was then, seemed a very grubby thing to do. I had very little concept of what was 'right' and 'wrong' in sexual matters anyway. Loving sex was a wholly desirable thing and the more of it the better whatever form it came in. If I did have any qualms, misgivings, they must have been slight because we made love on a number of subsequent occasions – three, I think – before she left. She appeared to be given a very free rein by her parents. It can't be put down to a momentary rush of blood to the head. I was perfectly aware of what

I was doing. Clearly, I held a certain power over her, but so did she over me. It was very intense, very passionate; addictive. The whole thing probably meant a great deal more to her emotionally but that's not to say it meant nothing to me either. (I have never been to bed with a girl or woman and not felt some kind of affection. You can't do something as intimate as that just for recreation. I've never been able to understand orgies, wife swapping and the like.) It's highly possible she – or her parents - tried to track me down when she found she was pregnant but by that time I was off and away on the Norton for the grapes in Cognac and then on to Casablanca, spending my summer savings on Moroccan Brown before moving on in the spring to the fairground I worked in Perpignan. Like I said, 'Return to sender, address unknown'. I don't think I gave her, it, a second thought once I'd moved on. That's how things were for me then. Life was a succession of beautiful moments, enjoyed, and then let go. Until living entirely for myself got boring and I swung the other way. I've never been able to do things by halves.

'We could go for entrapment,' Hermione Montefiore said, after I'd finished. 'There is the slightest of windows there. Can you be absolutely sure she didn't threaten to cry rape if you didn't make love to her? It does happen, you know.'

'What? And cry it again? Three times?'

'Sexual blackmail on the part of the very young isn't unheard of. Why should her recollection of events be any less hazy than yours? It's quite possible in the eyes of a jury that your own memory may have blocked out something unpleasant that was done to you, or turned it in to something less disagreeable. We have to work on turning the thing on its head. The very isolated nature of the offence should work in your favour, too; that and your reputation, your subsequent, unimpeachable record.'

'I'm not having it,' I said. 'I was a fool but I knew what I was doing and I'm not going to be a filthy lying hypocrite just to save my skin. I couldn't live with myself.'

'It's not only your skin you've got to think of,' she said.

*

I knew my wife well, which is why I also knew from the beginning our marriage was effectively over. Janet was a wonderful, gentle creature, but on one issue could be utterly, almost savagely unforgiving. That was paedophilia. She had once had a school friend, a best friend, who committed suicide because of the sustained abuse she went through as a child. Janet blamed herself for not having done more to prevent the tragedy. To her there could be no degrees of depravity. We were all lumped into the same category; tarred with exactly the same filthy, undiscriminating brush. The coked-up rock star and his predatory nubile groupies; the serially abusing headmaster of the obscure boarding school, himself the object of abuse when young; the tortured priest, all were the same to her: 'filth'.

By the time she got to see me the press had already been busy spinning its poisonous floss of rumour and speculation. There were many reports of unsubstantiated allegations. An awful lot of things had been 'reported'. She had the right to know the truth. I owed her that much, at least.

I wasn't prepared for the extent to which she'd aged and didn't manage to muffle the low howl of horror and despair that got caught in my throat when she entered the room. Exactly how *I* was looking had completely passed me by.

'Darling,' she said, 'what have they *done* to you? Why are they doing this? Why?'

It was her implicit belief in my innocence that made me feel for the first time something of the self-hatred and loathing demanded of me. Just as I find it difficult, well-nigh impossible, to hate individuals, I found it - still find it - equally difficult to hate myself in the appropriate manner of the times. I had done wrong. I had been extremely foolish, betrayed the pact of physical restraint that our society rightly demands of the young and the no longer young. But I had not been predatory. What I had done was not 'evil' or the act of a 'pervert' (as I was to be conveniently labelled). If it had been, I would have known. I know what evil is. I'm not an evil person. Equally, it was impossible for me to hold myself responsible for having ruined someone's life. If, for example, I had refused to make love to my accuser, informed her parents of her designs and she had attempted suicide as a result, failed and crippled herself, would I be equally liable to the charge of having ruined her life? Teenagers live in their heads: live lives of Elizabethan intensity, swinging back and forth from terrible tragedy to hilarious bathos. If the rest of their lives were held ransom to those few short years, there would be no normal people left on this earth. No, the self-hatred came from having ruined Janet's life, Felicity's life, our life together. For having annulled everything we'd built; in short, for having lived at all. I would have given anything to have disqualified my existence in order to have given her another, alternative one; to have never been known to the world; to have passed out of it without a trace. But that isn't possible. We are what we must be.

I should have said what I had to say there and then but she just kept on talking.

'They've made me take leave from school. Felicity can't go to hers. She's being horribly taunted. Trolled. The most vile things ...'

'Stop,' I said, unable to stand it any longer. 'I'm guilty. It hasn't been made up. I made love to a fifteen-year old girl when I was a young man. Before I met you. She had a child which died. My child.'

I watched her beautiful face collapse. Crumple into the mask of a confused and haggard old woman.

Whatever sentence I was supposed to serve was handed to me in that moment and I will serve it for the rest of my life.

*

The actual, custodial sentence of three years was greeted with approval in some quarters, incensed disbelief in others. Disbelief, that is, as to its lightness. To quote but a small selection of the reporting:

'...the hairy freak showed no remorse....'

'...How Many More?...'

'...astonishing that a predatory paedophile should have been left in a position of unquestioned authority over vulnerable children for nearly three decades...Vacancy: Heart Surgeon - Only Knife Wielding Psychopaths Need Apply...'

'...Ted's Time...three years is a joke...'

'...Carry On Caravanning ...Thanks to our ridiculously lenient laws on sex crime, convicted paedophile Ted Baxter could be at a caravan site near you in THREE YEARS!...'

I suspect that the hairy freak showing no remorse trope was a reaction to my habit of smiling at the world. It's a Buddhist thing I trained myself in. We have an obligation to be, or at the very least appear, as cheerful as we can possibly be. It's got me in to trouble before (oo you smiling at!? Boff!) But the main reason (apart from not being able to feel what I was expected to feel) for not coming up with the agonies of contrition the occasion required was that I was freefalling. This wasn't fair on Hermione, who did her best to portray me in the most favourable light possible. Once or twice I caught her looking at me like a singer or lead guitarist looks at a member of the rhythm section who's too stoned or pissed to keep time. It wasn't much use because I'd given up, become out of time, well before I was in the dock. There seemed absolutely no point in trying to cling to whatever vestiges of my previous life might be left to me. There was nothing really left to salvage anyway. Even had I walked away a free man it was unthinkable that the world I'd previously inhabited would have welcomed me back as if nothing had happened. That world was gone.

It's a kind of 'out of body' experience, witnessing your own character being batted back and forth in public like a tennis ball. You may have thought that there was only one 'you' but, once in the dock, that very quickly becomes a ridiculously naïve assumption. I could be a shining example of devotion to public duty one moment and a black hearted villain the next, my past employments chosen solely to facilitate a more convenient ravishing of the nation's post pubescent females. I could be both a devoted husband and father and a predatory sex maniac. Then a group of people go and choose which of these you must be. Except in my case, the decision was irrelevant because I'd already chosen not to play ball.

Freefalling isn't about not caring. It's about removing all

obstacles to re-invention. All my responsibilities had been stripped from me. This was not my doing. I had been a responsible citizen, a contributing member of society and now I was no longer allowed to play that role. I could succumb to the pain inflicted by that deprivation by trying to remain the same person who had been deprived or, become someone else. I was absolutely free to choose who that person was to be. Since you are beginning a new life, so to speak, you are no longer burdened with the inhibitions of your old one. You are still required to suffer for whatever bad things you made happen – it's not about zoning out or self-absolution - but you can do it in your own way.

*

Freefalling isn't about dropping out either, but in my case, I didn't get the chance to do anything else. A bank robber, corporate fraudster, even a murderer, can start a new life. Not so for someone who's done time for 'peedo'.

You'd have thought that in a city the size of London it would have been possible to drift along unnoticed, even without the kind of involuntary makeover I'd had. My hair started falling out during the trial. By the second week of being banged up I was as bald as a coot. I became very thin due to not being able to properly digest my food, which made me not want to eat it. The screws thought I was going on some kind of hunger strike to begin with. But I kept smiling; smiling through. That's what they called me: 'Smiler Baxter' and when Smiler got out, he was looking very much a shadow of his former self. He had reason to be fairly confident that Joe Public wouldn't be able to connect the Ted Baxter - robust, hairy, hearty of health who'd briefly strutted upon the nation's stage and was heard no more - with the shrunken version before him. He was wrong.

At the reception of the hotel I'd chosen in Paddington as my first domicile back in the free world, all went swimmingly. The receptionist was a young Ethiopian lady. Ted Time had thankfully not become a syndicated hit in Addis Ababa whilst I was doing porridge. I signed my name and, along with my key, was given a lovely big white smile of welcome.

After a hot bath, my first in three years, I dressed and sat on the bed psyching myself up to face the world outside. I had no one to meet. One or two friends came to visit in the first few months of my stretch. They made nice noises about having a jar together once I was out, but I could tell they didn't really mean it. I wouldn't have wanted to importune them anyway. Janet, after having been obliged to take (very) early retirement from her job as a head teacher had sold our house and moved away to Cornwall. Once the formalities for getting the divorce through and sorting out the finances were over, contact was ceased. Felicity, as far as I could gather from her rather wacky letters (she was allowed to write), had dropped out after one term at university and was living in a caravan in Scotland with some bloke. But there was always the pub. I put on a big black overcoat, covered my shocking baldness with a beany hat and went out on to the early evening streets.

The first boozer I drummed up courage to enter was full of the kind foreign-looking people who stay in Paddington because it's cheap and convenient for the Heathrow trains. They didn't give me a second glance. The barman was a young Kiwi, judging by his accent. I ordered a pint of bitter and he served me pleasantly enough. Emboldened, I thought I'd take a stroll down to The Bishop's Miter, a proper local. I'd been in once or twice way back in the day although I'd never been a regular. As the landlord was yanking away at the pump, I caught him looking up from under his bushy eyebrows in my direction and when he handed me the pint he sort of looked away. I took my beer to a quiet corner and started reading the evening paper. This was something I'd looked forward to enormously: a pint and a read of the Standard with nobody bawling at you telling you to hurry up. From behind the sheets, before settling down to read, I took in the punters: builders, railway men, different specimens of White Van Man, standing at the bar throwing back the pints; students huddled around that peculiarly tatty, haphazard furniture of the typical London backstreet pub.

I've always been quick to pick up on sudden changes in the mood of an event, a gathering. During my brief period of mild celebrity, I'd walk into a room and there'd be this reverential hush, lasting a few seconds before people returned to their chatting. Out of practice now, it took a while before I noticed the very slight but perceptible dim in the volume of conversation. Smart phones were being consulted with those fierce scowls of concentration that suggest the object of the search is of some consequence. A certain amount of nudging was going on.

Eventually, one of the builders, the advanced guard of an early Friday knock-off shift by the smell and looks of him, came across and, in a voice loud enough for the whole pub to hear said, 'Scuze me, guv, but me and my mates couldn't help noticing you're a dead ringer for that Ted Baxter geezer what got done for peedo a few years back. Now don't take this the wrong way. If you are, no worries, we aint going to do you in. You done your time. A bit harsh if you ask me. It wasn't as if you wuz kiddy fiddling...but...'

'No,' I said, lowering my paper and looking at him over the top of it, 'I'm not Ted Baxter. Don't worry, though. I get it all the time.'

'Kosher,' he said, then, 'Any chance of flashing a bit of ID. Driving licence'll do. It's just we've got a bit of a bet on and...'

'Please,' I said. 'I'd like to read my paper in peace. If you could please leave me alone.'

I still had two thirds of my pint left. I could hardly get up and scurry out. The five minutes I took to finish it, hiding behind the Standard, were interminable. What had Jesus (no comparison intended) said to Peter before he was crucified? Before the cock crows thou shalt have denied me thrice? Well I'd already denied myself once, and I'd only been out a day. I was Jesus and Peter rolled in to one. This, had I been able to change my name, might have been truly liberating, but a convicted paedophile isn't allowed to change his name for obvious reasons.

I managed to rent a small flat in Tooting. The landlord was Iranian, from Isfahan originally. We talked about Persian poetry which had been an enthusiasm of mine way back, when I'd been interested in everything. He never let on whether he knew who I was or not and I wasn't going to ask. I was simply grateful for the chance to talk to someone normally. On the rare occasions this happened it was almost always with a non-native of my country. They were most likely ignorant of my 'peedo' status but this didn't stop me arriving at the conclusion that they were nicer than my own countrymen; gentler, certainly nicer than the woman at the checkout of my local Kwik Store when I went in for the first and only time. I put my basket down and took out my wallet ready to pay, but she didn't scan the items. She didn't say anything, just stood there refusing look at me, with her nose in the air like she'd detected a bad smell but couldn't blame it on anyone in particular. There was a queue behind which started getting restless. I had to leave without my stuff. A couple of days later I went to check my mail in the box downstairs and there was an envelope containing a dog turd.

*

I bought a second hand RomaHome. A peedo can be dispossessed of himself but not of whatever money he has left. This wasn't a great deal but with careful husbanding it could be eked out for a couple of years and then supplemented by my state pension when it kicked in. They can't take that away from you either. So, if you're thinking of becoming a peedo, don't worry too much about the financial side of things. Even had I not ended up as one, I'd still have bought the RomaHome. It was part of the retirement plan. Janet would still be working. I'd be free to nip off somewhere nice whenever the mood took me. Then we'd use it together in the school holidays. Same vehicle, different function: now it was to carry me into exile. They can't take your passport away from you either; not yet, anyway.

Once across the Channel no one French had the faintest idea who I was, but I kept to the most obscure minor roads just to be on the safe side, trickling down through France and then over the Pyrenees into Asturias. Here was freedom at last. Not a British number plate to be seen. I struck camp. It was still very early spring and I had the site to myself. There was a small town a few kilometer's cycle ride away where I could buy provisions and wile away the days drinking, reading and writing in the bars. My Spanish, a rusty remnant from all those hash-happy winters in Casablanca, started coming back. I got to know the old geezers in their caps and berets quite well. I was a fairly old geezer myself now, something I'd never envisaged happening to me for some reason.

Nights were spent cooking on the little stove, eating and then sleeping early. The first proper deep sleeps I'd had for years. Then one morning I was woken from one by the sound of English voices, very middle class. Peeping through the curtains I saw parked nearby a large caravan and two young girls swatting at a shuttlecock with badminton rackets. What I took to be the mother was frying something outside, bacon judging by the smell coming through my open window. Happy families.

Breakfast over, the mum was washing up, the dad poring over a route map and the girls returned to their swatting. I badly needed the shower block, and in my shorts and flip flops, flung open the door.

'Morning!'

(The RomaHome still had British plates.)

'Morning!' I said.

'Hope we didn't wake you, arriving like that in the middle of the night.'

'Not at all.'

'Been here long?'

'About a month.'

'Wow! You must like it then.'

'It's a beautiful spot.'

'Isn't it,' she said, dreamily, looking round her at the wooded slopes and towering rock face of the gorge we were in, the silver ribbon of shallow river running swiftly over the grey pebbles of its bed.

'With family?' she said.

'No, just me.'

I saw the features harden, ever so slightly.

'Angela,' she said, 'and that's my husband Philip.'

'Ted,' I said. 'Pleased to meet you both.'

And toddled off to the shower block.

On my way back I noticed that the girls were no longer gamboling about and the family had shut itself up in the caravan. I heard raised voices from within.

'But we can't stay here, Philip, you fool! With Felicity and Annabel!'

'You're overreacting, darling. Calm down.'

'I will not calm down!'

The following day I left before dawn.

Like a rolling stone.

RED FLAGS

BASHER BAITING

I can't blame Basher, really, as he sits there twinkling at me across a couple yards of polished black oak. He bided his time admirably and now it's his turn. The boot is on the other foot, a fact which the desk appears designed to emphasise. It is vast and empty, confirming that he, Dr Colin Briggs, Headmaster (and major stakeholder), does nothing other than make clean, and sweepingly final decisions; a space over which things are announced, not discussed.

'But, Chief,' I say, still reeling, 'I can't possibly teach Lower School. I was hired as a French literature specialist, not an ABC man. I haven't the skill set.'

Basher insists on us calling him 'Chief', sounding as it does less stuffy than Headmaster' but still managing to convey distinction of rank. Plain, egalitarian Colin, on the other hand, would be stretching things too far for Dashwood School in China, which is modelled on its English progenitor *circa* 1934. We are in the Age of Franchise which in our case comes with Billy Bunter blazers, a rousing school song and the wearing of gowns for the teachers on Speech Days. It is for a *frisson* of this caricature that the new rich fork out their enormous fees.

'Nonsense, Charles,' he soothes, 'these things can be easily acquired by any intelligent adult, not to mention an Oxford man such as yourself. Just 'get stuck in' as you used to say back in the day. You'll get the hang of it.'

'But Miss Paine's thirty-seven years my junior. Fresh out of uni, as they call it these days. She can barely speak the lingo, so how on earth is she going to get Ronsard over to the special Oxbridge entry set?'

'Be that as it may, but Miss Paine has a recognised degree certificate. For the time being, it would appear that you do not and until we can clear the unfortunate misunderstanding up with the Ministry you're going to have to drop.'

'But...'

'I'm sorry, Charles. I can't risk it. I'm sticking my neck out as it is. They're tightening things up concerning this kind of thing. I'm sure your validation will come through in due course but in the meantime...'

He picks up a silver fountain pen with his big hairy right hand, holds it delicately between thumb and forefinger then drops it on the leather-bound notepad, which is the only other object on the desk. He repeats the action a number of times. It is the signal that our meeting is at an end, yet I find I can't get out of my seat. Basher has hypnotised me again with his remarkable transformation. The bristling moustache, close cropped hair and piggy eyes twinkling with cunning have turned him into a supersized Joseph Stalin in a gown, capable of chilling the blood of any minion summoned to his lair for 'a little chat.' I still can't get my head around it and am caught off guard. I can tell he's enjoying himself immensely and knows exactly what I am thinking: how did our fortunes become so spectacularly reversed and how did I manage to deliver myself so meekly into his hands? But I do not blame him. In fact I am learning to love him, as I must. Fate has decreed that he shall be my redeemer.

All was very different back in the eighties.

*

It was Roddy who christened him Basher (one of life's ironies since Roddy refused to second him at first). The Wild Colonial Boys was, like Dubai itself in those halcyon days, a rather exclusive club. Cricket is the real religion of the subcontinent as everyone knows and had we operated an open door policy, we British, outnumbered by about fifty to one, would have been swamped by its celebrants. It was for that reason we founded WCB CC in the first place: so we could get a fighting chance of wielding willow and chucking leather ourselves. There were those of squeamish conscience who were troubled by what they viewed as a colour bar, but as President and a founding member, I was at pains to point out that they were confusing claims to racial superiority with a measure of purely practical necessity. And anyway, they could always leave, or not join. Surprisingly few did either.

Basher's was an exceptional case. I remember the day he arrived and introduced himself. Roddy and I had just put on a record fourth wicket partnership of a hundred and eighty-three and were both not out at the end of forty overs. We trooped off to applause from team mates, wives and girlfriends carousing in the shade of the splendid new balcony. Perhaps a brief digression describing the club and its environs might lend greater vividness to the scene:

The lease of the land was granted by the Sheikh in whose employ Roddy and I coached polo and served as advisors on a variety of equestrian matters. Ten miles or so outside the city, in open desert, it was a large disk of baked, compacted sand with a polished concrete strip at its centre serving as the wicket. The pavilion was an assembly of Nissan-style huts perched on a small sand dune. It had a bar and, just completed, a long, shaded balcony. At one end of this sat Basher, a can of Tiger reduced to a thimble in his meaty fist. Once we'd got the pads off and cracked a couple of Tigers ourselves, he rumbled over.

'Colin Briggs,' he said in a voice I found redolent of the Yorkshire dales (he was, in point of fact, originally from Hull). 'I've not long arrived. I was drinking in The Old Vic the other night and someone mentioned this cricket club in the middle of nowhere, so I thought I'd come along and offer my services.'

He'd clearly got the wrong end of the stick. You didn't just rock up and offer your services. There were formalities. You had to be proposed and seconded. You had to be of the right stuff. And from the outset there was something wrong about Basher. His origins, to be blunt, were on the mysterious side and likely to raise objections amongst those members who took the whole colour business a little too seriously. A certain Persian swarthiness, hints of the perfumed orient, didn't fit with a torso resembling a beer barrel (a barrel propelled by trunk-like, slightly bowed, stubby legs that, when he ran, appeared to have a life of their own so that he absolutely did scamper around the outfield in imitation of a headless chicken). It seemed as though one half of him was trying to disown the other, which rubbed Roddy up the wrong way. He *did* take the whole colour business far too seriously. In fact, it wouldn't be doing truth a disservice to say that Roddy was a racialist. I knew him better than anyone. We were at school together. The ties that bind. It was touch and go with Basher. How could I have known then that I was arguing for the man who would bring about my final redemption? We needed players. A number of big engineering projects had been completed which had led to a sudden exodus of members. We could no longer afford to be as choosy as before.

'It's the thin end of the wedge, Charlie. We can't have half-castes sneaking in through the back door under the guise of being Yorkshiremen.'

'My dear Roddy, (he wasn't the brightest button in the box and needed certain elemental distinctions of logic explaining, very slowly) you seem to be confusing the question of birth with that of nationality. The policy of the club with regard to the non-extension of membership to natives of the subcontinent is purely and simply to ensure that we, the few, get a chance to play cricket. They, the many, have their clubs against which we play and we have ours against which they play and all are welcome in the bar afterwards. The policy does not extend to excluding Englishmen on grounds of their race or colour. That sort of thing went out the window years ago. With Basil D'Olivera, in fact. And anyway, he may simply be a product of the Spanish Armada with a long Cornish ancestry. Remember Terret?'

The name stirred some fond memory buried in that dull brain.

'Terret! Christ did we have some fun with him! Remember that time I zipped him into my cricket bag and put him on the train to Exeter. He was very sporting about it.'

'Well, there you go. Perhaps we might have some fun with Mr Briggs, too.'

We did. It became known as 'Basher baiting'.

*

One of the essential requisites of being in a cricket team, if you're serious about it, is an ability to play cricket. Basher could not, but for some reason was convinced that he could play it better than anyone else. What made his ineptitude all the more hilarious was the fact that he was a teacher of physical education at some private school for sons of the newly oil-rich locals and a peppering of expatriate offspring. Yet it was from this absurd belief in himself as the natural heir to Gary Sobers that, in a spirit of facetiousness, our nickname for him sprang: 'Basher' implies the ability to bash; to put bat to ball and send it racing to the boundary or crashing in to the stands, whereas the only thing he was capable of bashing was thin air. This became apparent in his first game.

He turned up, fair dos, in immaculate whites, accompanied by his buxom and (to my loins) rather attractive little wife.

'What do you do?' said captain Roddy, who was clearly appeased by the get up.

'I'm an all-rounder.'

'We'll put you on second change.' (He had won the toss and put the oppo' into bat, which I remember protesting against on the grounds that I had a thundering hangover and needed a few cold ones on the balcony to straighten me out.)

'I normally open.'

'Well, let's get started first and then we'll see.'

We were going along quite nicely, bagged a couple of early wickets and were pinning them down. Then Basher was handed the pill and proceeded to bowl four consecutive wides. The first was met with the usual helpful noises from the field: 'Bowling Colin! Just finding your range, old son!'; the second with the obligatory 'Unlucky, Colin mate! Unlucky!' By the third an embarrassed fidgeting had set in. After the fourth I trotted up from deep mid-on and tried to impart some rudimentary principles of line and length, putting my arm round his shoulder in encouragement and explaining that it was most likely the unaccustomed heat (forty five degrees in the shade) that was causing him thus to stray from what I was sure, on normal occasions, was an arrow-like delivery. He threw my arm off. I still remember the furious look in his eyes. Then he squared himself and began his run up - more of a launch, really, than a run-up. Had the ball been released at the end of this extraordinary preamble with a corresponding speed and fury, the batsman would have been quaking in his boots. But instead, it plopped out of his hand in inverse proportion to the enormous effort involved and, being mercifully on line, was swatted to the boundary. The remaining deliveries – bar one – met with the same fate and we were on the back foot.

'It's that bloody concrete wicket,' he said, back in the pavilion at tea. 'I'm used to grass.'

'We all struggle at first, Colin,' I said. At that juncture he was still Colin. It took an even greater show of ineptitude with the bat for him to become Basher. Basher Briggs.

Fate saw to it that we needed a mere two runs off the last five balls to get us through and that he, in at sixth drop was to be the man to get them. After a lot of posturing on the balcony he trundled out to the middle, swinging his bat from the shoulder like a pro. The first delivery was played with a forward defensive stroke which, although classical in the elegance of its execution, as though he were opening on the opening day of a five-day test match, paid absolutely no attention to the trajectory of the ball, which was short and half a yard outside his off stump.

'What on earth is the man doing?' shrieked Roddy in horror, rising from his seat.

'A chap's allowed one to get his eye in,' I said.

He did the same again.

'For Christ's sake man! You're not opening at bloody Lords!'

'Patience, Roddy! Patience!'

The third stroke, a beautiful hook shot, again showed scant regard for the actual trajectory of the ball which flew through to the keeper. It was as if he were performing in some parallel game a set of physical manoeuvres, like Tai Chi.

'For Christ's sake man! Hit the bloody thing!'

By now we were all on our feet and getting very heated. He appeared to respond by dancing down the wicket to the next one in a show of lofting the ball pavilion wards. But it was precisely that: a show, a dance and the ball thudded into the keepers welcoming gloves. Then he was clean bowled. Stumps everywhere. We, or rather, he, had, as they say 'snatched defeat from the jaws of victory'.

To his credit, a lesser man would have been cringingly apologetic but Basher was of that stubborn breed who can find little or no fault in themselves. On that first occasion it was the sun and its unaccustomed glare which had been responsible for failure. On subsequent ones (and there were many) it was anything from movement behind the bowler's arm (we couldn't stretch to side screens) to – and I do not exaggerate – the sudden noise of a flock of migrating flamingos which had chosen to fly directly overhead just as he was facing his first ball. We had enormous fun. 'Good luck, Basher and watch out for those ants!' 'Plague of frogs forecast, Basher, so keep your head down.' None of it sank in. He was (or appeared to be, as I was to find out) oblivious to the guffaws from the balcony which followed him as he stomped purposefully towards the crease. Once, by the law of averages I suppose, he actually did make contact with one of his fantasy lofted drives and hit a huge six, which had pandemonium breaking out. We were absolutely helpless with laughter, made worse by the way he refused to acknowledge the unprecedented feat, swanning down the wicket instead to remove a bit of stone with his bat, as if hitting sixes were his common forte.

I had a job calming Roddy down. He was a sore loser. A fine bat but a sore loser. But he wasn't without his softer, more forgiving side once the Tigers had been flowing. And they flowed! The Wild Colonial Boys were a very fast, hard drinking set.

'You know,' he said, deep in to the night, putting his arm around the man who had lost us the game, 'you're a rum looking bloke but you can hold your drink like a true Yorkshireman (this was undoubtedly the case. He had an impressive capacity). I'm going to call you Basher.'

'Basher?'

'Because you couldn't knock the skin off a rice pudding, haw haw haw.'

'To our new recruit, Basher,' Roddy went on, turning to us all, can raised. 'To Basher Briggs!'

'To Basher Briggs,' we chorused back.

And that was that. He took it on the chin; seemed pleased even. Or so I thought.

*

To go with the bluntness, he also possessed to an almost pathological degree that other supposedly Yorkshire trait: he was inordinately tight. It was true he didn't command quite the same salary as most of our members who, like Roddy and I, were in the upper expat income bracket. But he must have been adequately remunerated for doing what, judging by his own performance in the field, could not have been an overly taxing job. Yet I never once saw him buy a round. Pay day always seemed to have been late or he had forgotten his wallet, or his wife had cleaned him out for the month, until we gave up trying. Then, by chance, I discovered the real reason.

He was sitting alone inside the club house one day hunched over and scribbling on a piece of paper. I had entered in stockinged feet (no boots allowed) and he hadn't noticed me. Curious to know the reason for his absorption I took a quick gander whilst he nipped to the bogs. He was in the process of drawing up some kind of balance sheet of his personal outgoings. The salary wasn't all *that* bad but the sheet contained calculations of such minute detail pertaining to domestic expenditure – rice (basmati) 6 Dirhams per week; one new carving knife 18 Dirhams – as to shame any man with claims to a normal attitude towards money. He was, in short, a 'Hoarder' of the most supreme order.

According to my own anthropological table of male expat society as it then was – rarely if ever disputed – people fell into three quite distinct categories: the three Hs - Hearties, Homos and Hoarders. Roddy and I were pretty typical examples of the first; the second had their happy hunting ground along the Beach Road and in certain enclaves of shopping malls. Basher, it was clear, was the absolute personification of the third and as such, could no longer be let off so lightly. I came up with a ruse.

I got Phil Brear, who was good at that sort of thing, to produce a counterfeit demand from the Dubai Municipality stating that all expatriates should now pay a flat resident's tax' equivalent to about a sixth of my salary but at least a half of Basher's. This was to be distributed amongst all members except Basher and brought along to the annual general meeting.

Proceedings over, we adjourned to the bar and on a signal from me Phil pulled out his demand and started to lament the passing of our tax-free status. Basher began to turn pale.

'I haven't received anything,' he stuttered. 'It must be one of their bloody cock ups again. Couldn't organise a piss up in a brewery.'

'What? You haven't received yours yet?'

One by one, others began to take out the document from blazer pockets and to bemoan their luck that, just as they'd managed to put a bit of clear water between themselves and the bank manager thanks to the fiscal paradise they had holed up in, the buggers had gone and put the kibosh on everything.

Basher snatched one, read it with a trembling hand and then let out the most extraordinary noise: 'Nooooooooooo!' he howled like a dog. I could have sworn there were tears in his eyes. I actually began to wonder whether I'd gone too far.

'I'm bloody ruined. I've just taken out a mortgage on an 'ouse. The missus is going to kill me. She'll say it was all my fault for not doing my homework. She'll kill me, she will. Kill me...'

The voice trailed off in a sort of whimper. I winked at Roddy.

'Only joking, Basher old son! Only joking!' and the bar erupted with laughter. We all slapped him on the back and I very pointedly bought him a double whisky. 'You've had a terrible shock,' I said, handing it to him.

'Yes, I suppose I have.'

Some men may have been ashamed to show their face after such an exhibition. But Basher was dogged. Determined, I see now, to prove to himself that he could cut it in a fast set; cut it with The Wild Colonial Boys. Dogged was the word.

*

Not anymore. 'Imperious' is more like it. Finally prising myself from my seat I steal quietly out of his office, leaving the faintest of smiles playing beneath the Uncle Joe 'tash. I am, as they say, 'toast'. I don't have a 'recognised degree certificate' and he knows it. I have a very good fake one, brilliantly done by Phil Brear and authentically dog-eared from passing muster with many Ministries during my years on the run. But that was in the days before international surveillance had become such a well-co-ordinated art. The world has caught up with me. Even an Oxford man has to prove his credentials now.

By the time Basher arrived at WCB CC it was well known that I had indeed been an 'Oxford man', but had not taken a degree. Back then, in the summer of my days, academic distinction appeared of little importance and I made no secret of having been sent down for good at the end of my second year. The white powders, The Furies, as I call them, had made their first decisive intervention in my career.

I was born a libertine. There was no choice in the matter. I believe we are created to fulfil a role which our future actions will unfold. In youth I was very beautiful and my mind, my hands, refused to labour. I have always done things with great ease. Languages, games, horsemanship, women; they just come naturally, settling on me like doves. The downside of this not having to try very hard is boredom, chronic in my case and it is upon this condition that The Furies naturally play. At Baliol I was the centre of a very fast set, but nothing was ever fast enough for *me*. They needed speeding up and before my disinheritance, my exile; before The Fall, I had the means to purchase the necessary in fairly stupendous quantities. But the necessary on its own proved to be an insufficient alleviate. I needed the extra thrill that came from dealing in it under the noses of those who purported to be supervising my education and moral welfare. I was reckless in the extreme and my luck finally ran out. After I had used her up it was not certain whether Arabella committed suicide, but the overdose was far too big for it to have been accidental. They managed to hush it up but our tight little set had been broken. They squealed like pigs. I was no longer an Oxford man.

All this is confided to Yi Li. His mind is the ledger on which I write the balance of my life. Yi Li was an artist, a poet and something of a dissident way back in the day. By the time he had his stroke, insufficient obeisance had been paid to the Party and once his wife deserted, he was left practically destitute apart from the attentions of a younger sister. He lives in what I can only describe as a cave in a one storey old house on one of the streets set just back from the canal that runs parallel to Shi Qiuan Jie. It is from this Spartan cell, stacked with unsold canvases that the sister wheels him every evening to sit outside our local Family Mart general store and watch the world go by. I do the return trip.

The Chinese capacity for enduring suffering is a humbling thing. He was deposited one summer evening just after I had arrived. I was sitting in my usual spot under the awning on one of the metal chairs they kindly provide for customers like me who like the fresh air (my upbringing was a sporting, country one and to this day I cannot abide being stuck indoors for too long). The Family Mart is on the corner of a busy junction which affords an interesting view of cyclists, scooter riders, and rickshaw men slowly churning the pedals of their battered contraptions. I had just begun on my daily cocktails of Tsingdao lager and sixty percent proof bai jiu (my replacement for The Dark Lady, more of whom later) when this old woman rocked up with a slightly older man in an ancient wheelchair, and left him there next to me. He neither moved nor spoke, like me it seemed, content to just watch the world go by but with a strange, intense light in his eyes. My Chinese is fluent, colloquial, a product of being largely cut off from my own kind for many years. Although he was a tiny husk of a man in a Mao era peasant suit, his face possessed great intelligence and distinction. I decided to enter into conversation.

'A beautiful evening.'

No words came back, but he bowed his head in what I took to be a polite agreement.

'Especially for this time of year, when I gather in Suzhou it is meant to be much hotter.'

The same again.

'Perhaps the rains will come early this year. More like down south in Guizhou where I have come from.'

Again, no verbal response but he bowed his head more vigorously this time and his eyes appeared to be smiling. (I was to learn from the sister that they were natives of that poor, lush and steamy province.)

Then the penny dropped. Having never before had discourse with someone who could not speak but could clearly understand every word I said, I felt it would be impolite to stop speaking simply because I had made the discovery. At the mention of Guizhou his eyes had lit up, so I began a long, fond monologue on the beauties of the place which appeared to please him greatly. By the time his sister came to pick him up again we were getting on like a house on fire. When, subsequently, she informed me of his previous life and profession I was in a position to tailor my monologues to his interests, which are mine too. They are supplemented by regular bulletins on the developing Basher situation along with 'the story of my life', which make his eyes shine with an extra, laughing brilliance.

*

I should have seen it coming. When the advertisement appeared, it seemed too good to be true. I had been scratching a living teaching English privately to frazzled businessmen, not particularly taxing in the pedagogic sense but a form of torture to any sensitive mind. There were also issues with the renewal of my visa, since the client who had been my sponsor abruptly ceased to be one when he discovered that his wife had conceived a passion for me. It remained a passion unrequited since, despite her obsessive attentions I did not give in to them. Although, thanks in large part to The Dark Lady, I am a rather shrunken version of my youthful self, I still exercise considerable power over women. However, I was, and have been for some years now, celibate. But my client was a jealous man and he withdrew his support. It left me in a bit of a hole.

I cannot return to my own country since I would be either instantly arrested or, if not, most likely killed. Provincial visa renewal can be a bit touch and go but if one has the right contacts a certain lack of rigour on the part of the authorities with regard to the inspection of documents can be arranged. Mine had deserted me. So, when, in a spirit of whimsy more than anything, I replied to the advertisement which was seeking a French specialist to teach university entrance students at a private school in Suzhou, it was with astonishment and relief in equal measure that I found myself straight away accepted. There was no preliminary interview. The school would see to the sponsorship upon my arrival. He had sprung the trap in which, dressed as a footman-valet complete with white gloves I now writhe. He has a memory every bit as elephantine as my own. Tit for tat. If you've dished it out you've got to take it.

*

The WCB CC Annual Ball was not an overly formal affair. It took place at the Ramada, which back then was one of only four spanking new hotels set in its own patch of desert. The surrounding neighbourhood was still in the early stages of construction so that it stuck out, like some freak survivor of a nuclear attack. We couldn't stretch to the hire of the main ballroom so the do took place in one of the less splendid function rooms where the wearing formal evening clothes would have appeared incongruous: which was precisely why we decided that Basher should turn up thus attired.

He was a terrible snob of the inverted kind. You might say that people like Roddy and myself were, in the Dubai that then was, simply taking our place in the natural pecking order of things that once existed *chez nous* in the old country. We moved unassumingly amongst the Sheikhs, Sheikhas and their offspring and were treated in turn with an easy graciousness. There was never any question of having to demand respect. Basher, on the other hand, was always banging on about his 'roots' and how he'd 'come up the hard way' etc...etc. Yet, at the mere sight of a dishdasha (the Sheikh and his sons would very occasionally come out to watch us play, finding the whole thing highly amusing) he'd go into a swoon of obsequiousness. It was toe curling to witness. Then, far from showing the kindred feeling you'd expect from one so avowedly belonging to a lower caste himself, he lorded it over our Indian bar steward Freddy and his two helpers as though he were back in the days of the Raj, addressing them peremptorily in a form of pidgin English, which I found both unnecessary and offensive: 'I ask for cold beer. This not cold beer. This hot beer. Now you go back bar and fetch cold beer. Geldi! Geldi!'

That sort of thing. He was fair game.

We had to exercise our powers of ingenuity to the maximum. A tailor was sought out who was to be in on the ruse. He was paid to run up an outfit of the kind of formality mentioned earlier, but absurdly over the top. In the weeks approaching the ball there had been much talk of the difficulty of finding a decent tailor who still knew how to rig one out in the necessary. Basher was in a bit of a state already, I could tell on account of the expense, but he was adamant he was not going to let the side down. I mentioned I knew a little place in Deira which would do the business for a not extortionate sum and told him to mention my name and the purpose of his visit.

We had given him a ticket with a kick-off time half an hour later than the actual thing so that when he arrived, we were all there, sans tux and dickie and getting nicely oiled. Roddy was at the door pretending to perform the services of a footman, announcing loudly to the room the names of newly arrived guests.

'Ladies and Gentlemen. Mr and Mrs Briggs.' (The latter, so to speak, was 'collateral damage'. I had been screwing her for some time so things could be patched up later. She took it fairly well anyway, being accustomed to belittling her husband in public at the slightest opportunity.)

A full twenty seconds went by before we were treated to his

eventual response. During this interval I was able to observe his soul writhing within him as torrents of laughter roared in his ears.

The get up was preposterous in the extreme and even included a crimson cummerbund tightly wound about his midriff. At first the expression on his face was one of stunned incomprehension. Then it changed to black rage. I thought for a moment he was going to be sick with it. He was trembling all over.

Then a strange calm descended on him and smiling, in a mock upper-class bray of a voice, he shouted, 'Ladies and Gentlemen, I give you Mr and Mrs *Basher* Briggs. And you are all bastards who I am going to drink under the table!'

He kept his head. He hung on. He showed himself the better man. Dogged.

We took it turns to slap him on the back. Mrs Briggs was looking more than usually toothsome in a satin gown which showed off to the full the humps and lumps I had already been privileged to explore.

'Did you reserve the room?' she said hotly in my ear.

'Yes.'

'We'll have to be quick.'

'I know. Hard and fast.'

She flushed. Like me, perhaps she was addicted to risk.

*

'Champagne, Mr Moncrief, if you please,' Basher says as I shimmy by. It is Dashwood School in China's Open Day for parents and we are all on show. I am on show to a much greater extent than my colleagues. He is talking to a very wealthy-looking couple who, being Chinese, do not find it in the remotest bit strange that they are being served by a middle-aged English man dressed as a butler. They do not 'do' jokes of this kind. So, to a certain extent, he is prevented from getting his full satisfaction, although I'm doing my best by entering into the role as enthusiastically as a limited thespian talent will allow. It being my first year, I discover that we, the staff, do indeed distribute drinks on this crucial occasion which - I think correctly - he deems the right personal touch for the exclusive establishment we are. (It also helps to cut down on expenses. Old habits die hard with Basher.) I, on the other hand, am the only one among us thus formally attired.

*

When I breezed in, a little late, to our pre-party staff pep talk the hilarity was not quite as uncontrolled as I presume he'd hoped it would be. My colleagues are considerably younger than I. To add to this age gap, I have acquired a reputation for eccentricity so some of them probably thought I really did consider the Jeeves get up appropriate. But it is fair to say that laughter was general. I could tell it had hit the mark. Basher, in his joshing way, likes to parade me at times as an old friend of mysterious origins. It all adds to his own mystique. I do not demur. That would never do. The joke needed no explaining, being taken for the latest in a series belonging to our riotous past together.

'Ah, there you are Charles,' he said as I tottered into his office fresh from a fatiguing last hour imparting the rudiments of my own language to very young and, I have to concede, very keen little minds.

'Glad you could find the time to help me out with a last minute *crise*.' (Gone is the Hull accent. He must have taken elocution lessons somewhere along the way. He sounds more like a slimy Conservative upstart minister from the early Thatcher administration.)

The catering company I was planning on using to dish out the grog tonight has cancelled at the last minute. I'm going to have to ask a few of our male staff to fill in. I know it might seem a bit OTT but would you mind decking yourself out in this?' He held up the costume. 'Ridiculous I know, but this sort of palaver goes down well with the parents. They lap it up.'

'Of course, Chief,' I said, more concerned that I should have time to down the contents of and replenish my hip flask before we go over the top. By rights I should have been with Yi Li at the appointed hour, making free with the Tsingdao and bai jiu cocktails. I rarely miss and forgot to tell him I would be late. He worries about me. I can see it in his eyes sometimes.

The fit was perfect. He must have done some serious measuring up in his mind. It is clear that, for better or worse, I loom large in that limited organ. The quality and cut weren't bad either. It must have cost him a pretty penny. Perhaps middle age is beginning to dispel his preternatural tightness. Live and let live.

*

I proffer the tray of bubbly with a discreet bow of the head, showing off to maximum effect my thatch silver-streaked hair with not a hint of bald patch.

Making to continue on my rounds, he says, 'Do stay a moment, Mr Moncrief. Mr and Mrs Fang this is Mr Moncrief, our oldest and most distinguished member of staff. He is an Oxford man and we are very lucky to have him.'

This is duly translated by his wife, the Yellow Peril as I call her in less guarded moments, although I know I shouldn't use such language, lumping me as it does nowadays in the same camp as Roddy (dear dead Roddy). She stands at his elbow, a sliver of greed and malice in Chanel, but mighty attractive nonetheless. He's batting way above his average, is Basher (which thinking back, is quite something since I recall it never got much above 3). Mrs Basher (Mark II) has one of those exquisite little dabs of a Chinese face, which, with a slash of red lipstick, scrub up very nicely indeed. Like many of the very pretty women I have known, she tends to hide her beauty behind a scowl as though trying to keep adoration at bay with a show of ill-temper.

'We played cricket together in Dubai in the 'good old days'. What was the name of the club?'

'The Wild Colonial Boys, Chief.'

'That's it! Dear old WCB CC.' I notice Mrs B skips this bit, it being beyond her powers (Basher, of course, speaks hardly a word of *zhongwen*, it being way beyond his). 'I don't play anymore, although I might have to get the bat off the shelf as we're thinking of introducing it into the curriculum. If your son should choose to finish his education at a university of your choice in England, it wouldn't do him any harm to be acquainted with our national summer game. Don't you agree, Mr Moncrief?'

'It wouldn't do him any harm at all,' I say.

'Mr Moncrief is a man of many parts, you know,' he goes on, sipping from the flute I have just proffered. 'He didn't take up an academic career upon graduating. Instead he chose to exploit his talents as a horseman. In our Wild Colonial days, he coached polo to the Sheikh and his sons.'

I can tell this is hitting the mark. Mr and Mrs Fang are impressed.

Their eyes widen with interest. Their pupils dilate. Long, long gone are the days of class struggle. Or, rather, the struggle now is to get class *back* and I am a useful ally in this war of regression, to be paraded, it is becoming clear, on this and similar occasions before being put back in my box.

'How long were you employed in that capacity, Mr Moncrief? Remind me now.'

He knows exactly how long. Not long enough. The Furies intervened.

*

Endurance racing, oddly popular in those desert climes, requires precisely the quality its name implies; a quality that can be greatly enhanced in both horse and rider by the administering of certain white powders. One of the young men in my charge, the third born son, was a great enthusiast but a sore loser, especially when it came to losing against other enthusiasts from rival Emirates. Losing was not taken in the jocund spirit encouraged at the kind of school I attended. I have seen swords drawn. Blood in those parts, like the climate, is very hot. Unfortunately, my charge was rather good at 'not winning', as I was careful to phrase it. Although the lion's share of the work is done by the horse it can only go as fast and as long as the rider urges and my charge, if not exactly sickly, was not the most robust of physical specimens either. Some artificial enhancement, he came to realise, was necessary, perhaps in the form of, as he put it, 'cockay'. Could I procure him some?

Now the main reason, apart from the money, I had washed up in those parts after several years of dealing to the *beau monde* in both the Old and New worlds was that 'cockay' was not on the menu, except on pain of death. I was offered more money in Saudi Arabia but that would have been pushing things too far. At least in the Emirates one could drink and I had contented myself with wrestling the Tiger, whilst waving goodbye to the Furies. But they are always there, mustering for another charge. He pleaded. He begged. He gave me a considerable amount of money. I gave in.

It was relatively straightforward. The horse used in endurance events – the Arabian Piebald – benefits greatly from a particular kind of feed deriving, if procurable, from pampas grass only to be found in a certain part of Argentina. Money being no object, it *was* procurable and Roddy and self had an agreeable jolly to the land of the Gaucho to firm up supplies. I booked myself a ticket for a follow up visit to check that we weren't being short changed. That was the official reason for the trip. The real one was to source and smuggle a consignment of top-grade Columbian to be concealed in the crates of feed. A few calls to old pals in the trade and all was fixed up nicely. Just like old times. That was the easy bit. What I hadn't banked on was my charge's prodigious appetite for the stuff. Despite my earnest pleas for moderation, tragedy inevitably struck. Whilst leading a race by a suspiciously large margin, the aptly named Pegasus collapsed and died under him. He followed suit shortly afterwards while waiting for the back-up train. There was, of course, an autopsy. The finger twitched. I didn't wait for it to be pointed. The Wild Colonial Boys were deprived of their middle order in one fell swoop, Roddy following me to Brunei Darussalam like the loyal friend he was.

*

'Oh, about five years, Chief,' I say.

'That's right,' he says. 'I remember you having to leave in

something of a hurry. There was a hint of a scandal somewhere. Mr Moncrief was never far from scandal back in those days. He's a reformed character now, though, isn't he dear, Ha! Ha! Ha!' Mrs B concurs with a rare tinkle of laughter. 'But our paths were to cross again. We both ended up working for, in our respective capacities, the man who was at that time The Richest Man in the World. In Brunei Darussalam, of all places.'

I can see this is going down very well indeed. Basher is playing his Man of the World card to maximum effect, with me as his subordinate partner.

'Didn't we, Mr Moncrief?'

'We did, Chief.'

He becomes silent, twinkling at me paternally. This is his usual manner of concluding our discourse.

Thus dismissed, I shimmy off to where a noisy group of rich people need their empty glasses replenishing.

*

The sport at which he chose not to excel next was golf. It is a pursuit that takes a lot of explaining to Yi Li. Cricket clearly taxed his powers of imagination to the maximum. Golf floored them completely. I can tell by the look in his eyes that my efforts are not meeting with success. Why would any sane human being spend large amounts of time and money - membership of the club I helped to build, even back then would have ensured his Iron Rice Bowl in perpetuity – for the privilege of chasing a little white ball around with a stick? I have to resort to physical demonstration, miming what was once a beautiful swing (I played off scratch as a Blue).

At the time, the ruling family was going through something of a schism. The Boss, as we called him, was a conservative in matters of religion and finance (comparatively speaking for a man who kept over a hundred vintage cars). Number Two, his slightly younger brother, was a libertine on a gargantuan scale and needed the right people to play with. It was towards his faction that I naturally gravitated. He preferred golf to polo which he played quite well when not incapacitated through excess (Roddy took care of the latter, coaching The Boss and his family). Before he could play it on his native soil a course had to be built and it was to this end that my services were offered and accepted. I had no prior experience but we were still (just) in the days of the gentleman amateur. To be on the safe side, I wired Phil Brear who came up with the necessary documentation.

Until recently, they were perhaps the least unhappy years of my life. When I was not busy bouncing about in my jeep supervising the rape of virgin jungle, I was piloting a speedboat to-and-fro across the South China Sea. On the outward trip my cargo was dollars, on the return, powders of various strength and provenance. There was little risk, the coastlines of Malaysia and Brunei being hardly policed at all. If they had been, Narcissus II would have burnt them off in a matter of minutes anyway. It was a very fast boat and I had great fun with her.

Narcissus I was the exclusive property of Number Two, an ultramodern yacht, stocked to the gunwales with fine vintages and women handpicked for their beauty, absence of conventional morals, and sense of fun. I was a frequent guest, occasionally taking the wheel when its owner was indisposed. He trusted me completely.

Then Basher arrived and, whether by coincidence or not, things soon went pear-shaped.

The broad vowels had by then already undergone modification but the voice which hailed me from the clubhouse balcony as I trooped off the eighteenth was unmistakeable.

'What's your handicap now,' it shouted, 'a permanent hangover or being just plain rubbish?'

As club Pro – a title bordering on the emeritus given the number of appearances I was required to put in – I had taken a foursome of Number Two's more distant cousins around with a view to ironing out glitches in swing and stance. Dusk was coming on and huge storm clouds were boiling up in the sky, shortly to release their pelting of warm rain. I had been looking forward to watching it alone, breaking over the course I had built, with a large G and T. All that was gone. I could hardly believe my eyes. Like the voice, the figure had undergone a noticeable paring down. I clattered up the stairs. He shook my hand like a very old and dear friend.

'Basher, what on earth...'

'I've not long arrived. I was drinking in the Orchid and somebody mentioned this golf club not long built by a bloke called Charlie Moncrief. I put two and two together and thought I'd pop along and see about joining.'

He'd got the wrong end of the stick again. The Royal Brunei Golf Club was, as its name suggests, not the kind of place you just wandered into and joined. It solicited you, if you were the right stuff.

'How did you get in?'

'The name Moncrief would appear to open doors round these parts.'

Basher had used my name.

It turned out he *was* the right stuff, of sorts. He'd managed to get himself a PhD in something called Sports Science and Psychology. Allied to a willingness to brave hostile climes, it had sufficed to land him a job in some vague advisory capacity to the Ministry of Education. The mind inevitably conjured images of the tiny nation's youth classically schooled in games of Empire, able to posture beautifully with bat, boot and racquet whilst holding the ball in high minded contempt.

He had also gone native, electing to wear the colourful *khamis* a button-less silk shirt with a round neck collar fastened with a single stud. It was by no means compulsory for non-natives to do so, but was rumoured to give our masters pleasure seeing us thus attired. In other words, he was 'brown nosing' as Roddy put it. Nothing much had changed on that score. We settled down to our drinks, which he ordered from Ali, our Indonesian bar steward, with the same brusque condescension I remembered from our WCB CC days.

'So how's it been since your abrupt departure from the sandpit?' he said. 'Prospering?'

'Getting by. Still in the gainful,' I said, gesturing to the course that stretched out before us under the sunset's last streaks of pink and rose.

'I hear there's some proper fun to be had here if you're in the right circles.'

As I recalled, fun and Basher'were not words often to be found loitering in close proximity, unless the latter was providing the former as the object of some kind of ruse at his expense. It was clear from the off that he was intent on reinventing himself as a man of the world and that I was to give the process a helping hand by introducing him to the 'right people'. The business of treating me like a long-lost friend began to grate but set against it I have a ridiculously overdeveloped sense of loyalty to people I have known in the past. I wasn't displeased to see him.

'Number Two knows how to throw a party, for sure,' I said, with some degree of understatement.

'Number Two?'

I took some time to explain the set up and the agreeably dissolute nature of the man to whom I owed my fief. He listened and I could almost hear the scribbling of mental notes.

'And Mrs Basher...' I said, finishing.

'Thriving,' he said, 'especially as she isn't working. Lady of leisure now.'

Whether this was a veiled hint at the extent to which he'd 'gone up in the world', or an oblique criticism born of his legendary tightness I could not be sure.

'Do give her my best.'

The prospect of taking up where we so abruptly left off was an encouraging one. I was beginning to tire of supermodel types and hankered after something more substantial.

'I certainly...'

Before he could finish his sentence there was a tremendous bang, like a shell packed with high explosive going off directly overhead: the storm had broken. He jumped out of his seat, which made me laugh out loud in the way I used to when watching him going out to bat. Perhaps there was still fun to be had. I phoned Roddy as soon as I got home.

'Basher!...Never!...How wonderful!'

'What say? I put him up. You second.'

'Absolutely.'

He sounded over the moon.

*

It was getting on towards the summer vacation when I got the summons I had been expecting. The staff room was abuzz with talk of how everyone was going to spend it. Tibet? Ankor Wat? Koh Samui? (I do love this enthusiasm the young have for travel; for just wandering around and seeing things.)

'And how about you, Charlie?'

'Oh, I think I shall just chill out here. Things to do.'

'Really?'

'Really.'

Of course, I can't tell them I'm on the run. When they ask, as curiosity dictates they should, about the last time I returned to 'Youkay', I have to lie. I have to lie about pretty well everything I've ever done. Only Yi Li knows the full story. Basher suspects but only Yi Li gets the God's Honest.

*

Everything was going swimmingly until the mid-nineties. There seemed to be this fount, this artesian well of money which Number Two was spending on great projects for turning the little place in to a fiscal and upmarket tourist paradise. The Royal Brunei Golf Club was but one of them, and indeed we had begun to attract the attentions of extremely wealthy golf-playing types, mainly from Japan. Narcissus II continued to cruise the South China Sea in wild piratical pursuit of fun, with myself increasingly at the helm. Number Two had begun to appear under some sort of strain and was compensating with all kinds of powders. The reasons became apparent when, overnight, the country collapsed. There was no more money left for The Boss to keep the people in the manner to which they had become accustomed. Number Two had spent most of it, off the books as it turned out. There was the most almighty row and Number Two was exiled. To London, where he was kept on a pretty tight leash by The Boss, said leash nevertheless extending to several private suites at the Dorchester and a regular supply of powders, supplied by myself. I decamped with him; became his private, his exclusive dealer. As previously stated, I have an overdeveloped sense of loyalty to friends and Number Two, along with quite a few of his entourage was in a hell of a mess. He, they, had fallen into the clutches of The Dark Lady; Lady Henrieta; Lady H. In the early stages of my intermittent career I had refused all entreaties to deal in her. But I could not bear to see him suffer. Then, perhaps inevitably, I too was seduced.

I have previously stated my belief that one is born to fulfil a role which one's future actions will unfold. There is no choice in the matter, and so it proved with The Dark Lady. She had been patiently waiting there for me. What started as a business proposition became, at the same time, a physical necessity and all went well for a number of years. It was a small scale, localised operation from which I derived a decent profit and all I needed to service my own habit. Then, overnight it seemed, the Russians arrived in force. I refused to deal for them. They threatened to kill me in various grizzly ways, and probably would had they not stitched me up instead with whatever bent Old Bill they had in their pockets at the time. While sourcing in the Golden Triangle I got it on very good authority that should I return to the old country there would be a reception waiting for me and I would go down for many years. That or turned into *borsh* (as they put it). I was marooned in a beautiful land, in a part of it no less where satisfying my habit was as easy as picking fruit off the trees. Until the money ran out.

*

'Won't you get bored?' they say.

'I never get bored these days.'

And that is true, although I cannot tell them why.

It is impossible to be bored when you are in the arms of The Dark Lady. Your whole being is devoted to servicing her. If ever you manage to divorce her, fully, unconditionally, then neither will you be prey to boredom again, because it is like getting a new life. Everything looks new. Every sight and sound become precious. So, it is a win-win situation, but I would never recommend you try it since the divorce is likely to send you out of your mind. I did everything I could to postpone it. For a while I stole. I even stole off the poor. Then the monks took me in and supervised my stay in hell with their no-nonsense approach until I came out the other side, a chastened but much hardened man.

For a while I thought of staying on, but the ascetic life would not have enabled me to atone for my previous one. I needed to be of the world and became a teacher of my own language which was much in demand. In my free hours I would give classes to the children of the poor.

*

'Enter!' I hear, in response to my knock.

'Ah, Charles. Good of you to find the time in between teaching the little ones.'

He sweeps his arm across the gleaming expanse of desk, indicating I am to sit opposite him.

'You do seem to have taken to them like a duck to water. Well done, well done. Which makes it all the more sad that I'm going to have to let you go.'

'Chief?'

'It's nothing to do with your performance, you understand. I have no complaints on that score. It's this business about your qualifications. HR have drawn a complete blank. We re-submitted for validation twice believing something must have got lost in translation and each time it came back negative. There is no record of your ever having graduated from Oxford.'

There is nothing I can say. I just sit there.

'It would appear you are a fraud. A complete fake. What do you say to that?'

'I was hoping no one would find out, Chief. A man's got to keep body and soul together somehow.'

'I appreciate that, Charles, but you've let me down terribly. Terribly. Had we been flash inspected we'd have been in very deep water. The new Minister is a terrier over this sort of thing. But, let's leave that aside for a while shall we. What fascinates me, what I want to know is, how does it feel to have gone through life as a complete and utter charlatan?'

'I've never really given the matter much thought, Chief.'

'Haven't you? Why ever not? Take a bloke like me,' he says, leaning back in his chair. 'Did I ever tell you that my mother was a common prostitute? A woman who consorted with sailors from all over the globe, one such being my father. The father I never knew. I was a Bernardo's Boy for most of my childhood. Did I ever tell you that?'

'I don't think you did, Chief.'

'Well there you have it. I'm glad it's out. Hardly the best start in life, eh? I might not be top drawer material intellectually, either, but I can derive a certain satisfaction from what I've achieved because I've earned it. Every single thing I've accomplished has been through struggle; through application of the will. It hasn't been easy and I've had to make sacrifices, not just financial ones but to my pride sometimes as well. You of all people will appreciate that. You...of...all...people!'

He rocks violently forward, pointing a hairy finger at me, before leaning back again and smiling, as though recalling some pleasant memory.

'But it all just made me stronger. The greater the sacrifice the bigger the man. Wouldn't you, at least partly, agree with me on that?'

'What you say isn't without wisdom, Chief.'

'I'm glad you concede that, because now take a bloke like *you*.' He rocks forward again. 'A man born with every advantage in life. Some might say with a silver spoon in his mouth. Heir, even, to a title. Such men are usually found in later life amongst the great and the good yet here you are at the age of fifty-nine, against my strongest wishes, about to be relieved of a post teaching your own language to small children. Not much of a CV, is it?'

'Is..it!?'

'I don't suppose it is, Chief?'

'Tell me, Charles, because I'm fascinated. How is it possible to live with yourself knowing that all your talents, all your many gifts, have born absolutely no fruit whatsoever? Knowing that you will never get a second chance. Knowing that you will die with nothing to your name but abject failure.'

'Some of us lose our way, Chief.'

He folds his big hairy hands over his chest and reflects on this for a moment.

'That, if I may say so, is fatalistic rubbish!' he almost shouts, rocking forward again. 'People don't just lose their way. It's insulting to those who don't give in. To those who have to push the world along. To the right sort of stuff. No, they fail because they're weak. They lack what used to be called 'strength of character'. They give in too easily. Give in to cheap thrills. Drugs. Cynical sex. The humiliation of those they consider inferior for their own facile amusement. But I'm departing from the main reason why I called you in today.'

'I thought you'd already stated it, Chief.'

He grows suddenly milder.

'Good grief, Charles. Did you really think I could cast aside an old friend over a matter of bureaucratic obstinacy? I have a proposition to make, but before I make it could you just answer me one thing?'

'Of course.'

'Why is your passport Thai? Why is it you can't renew your British one, or get a British visa in your Thai one, which would make matters much easier. Why is it you can't return to your country; to your country and your family?'

I feel a great relief come over me that I no longer have to lie.

'That's easy,' I say. 'I would be arrested on arrival as a known smuggler and dealer in heroin. I can't return to my family because I brought disgrace upon it many, many years ago.'

'Thank you, Charles for being so candid. It's confirmed what I thought. Now, are you still fond of animals?'

*

Watching Basher play golf was - as Roddy, in an uncharacteristic spasm of wit put it - like watching an ape conducting an orchestra. He was quite literally incorrigible. It is a game that cannot be learnt. You can take as many lessons; try as hard as you like, but if your circuit board is not wired for it you are wasting your time. Basher's wiring was all wrong.

When he wasn't abusing a beautiful game, he was doing the same to Ali and his two helpers. Working as a Minister, or for a Ministry (I could never work out which) had gone to his head. He appeared to think it was his right, his station in life, to take out his frustrations on them. It is well documented that golf can ruin a man's day. He takes to the first tee with a song on his lips and leaves the eighteenth green in a black rage. Such, inevitably, was the case with Basher. He would stomp into the clubhouse and pick fault with the slightest thing in that ridiculous pidgin he used. Once he even tipped his beer - which wasn't cold enough for his liking- over Ali's head, making out it was all in jest. It wasn't. He had to be taken down a peg or two.

We needed to proceed very subtly and Mrs B. (Mark I) had to be in on it also. This was not difficult. She would have walked over hot coals for me such was my hold over her.

One evening shortly after the beer tipping incident Basher arrived in the bar looking like he hadn't slept for days and in a state of some agitation.

'You'll never guess what happened last night,' he said, not offering a round and accepting his drink from Ali who served him with his usual faultless politeness. 'I got home to the villa and there on the porch was a dead and disembowelled rat in the middle of a circle of feathers all covered in blood.'

Roddy and I exchanged what they call 'significant' glances, conveying both surprise and serious worry.

'Are you sure?' I said. 'Are you absolutely sure that it wasn't a cat leaving an offering.'

'There's no way a bloody cat could have done that. This was arranged in a pattern.'

'Was the rat a black rat?'

'Why yes, it was come to think of it.'

There was a sharp intake of breath from Roddy. I gave him a look that said are you going to tell him or should I. It was Roddy who broke the news.

'Oh, dear, oh dear,' he said. 'Oh dear oh dear oh dear.'

Basher, not the most patient of men, shouted, 'Oh, dear, what!?'

'You would appear to have upset a tribe of Kayan. The black rat in a circle of feathers is their calling card so to speak. Their announcement that you will die through Keli Keli.'

'What's bloody Keli Keli?'

'The Kayan form of Voodoo. If they consider the honour of the tribe to have been insulted by cowardly acts in battle or the humiliation of any one of their number, they let loose the spirits on the perpetrator.'

'But I don't know any bloody Kayan. Why would I be mixing with a load of jungle bunnies?'

I gave a discreet cough, gesturing with my eyes in the direction of Ali. Basher went pale beneath his swarthy skin.

'You mean?...but I apologised. I was only having laugh. He knows that. Look at tonight. He served me with a smile.'

'You're still a bit green, Basher old son,' Roddy went on. 'Have you not noticed that whatever you do, whatever you say to these people they will always smile? It means nothing. It's a smile that can contain joy or murderous rage. I would say Ali's contains the latter.'

'But I apologised!'

'And the apology will have been accepted, superficially. Business as usual. But the point is, the tribe cannot forgive. To do so would be to poison their blood. Vengeance *must* be exacted.'

'Superstitious rubbish!'

'Quite,' I said. 'Don't give it any thought.'

'Just out of interest,' Roddy said. 'By any chance, you didn't keep getting woken up in the night by a peculiar kind of screeching?'

Basher went pale again.

'I didn't sleep a bloody wink as a matter of fact.'

Another sharp intake of breath and exchange of glances (we had paid the Indonesian gardener and night watchman of his compound to make the noise concealed in the bushes outside his window; Basher was not particularly liked there either).

'It wasn't like this by any chance?'

Roddy made the chilling sound of a screech owl. He was a man of many talents in his own small way.

'That was it exactly.'

We shook our heads.

'Not good,' I said.

'Fookin 'ell,' he said, the old rougher round the edges Basher making a return.

Most people would have thought it a good idea to get to the

bottom of the matter there and then and apologise; humbly request the offended party that the thing be called off, in which case we would have been stymied. But as previously stated Basher was of that breed that finds it near impossible to admit fault. He continued to insist that the beer tipping had been in jest and that he had apologised sufficiently already. That was what we were banking on. From thereon in it was plain sailing. At regular intervals we arrayed before him a variety of dead creatures and bloodied feathers: heads of monitor lizards, snakes, even a small ape (all roadkill since I am fond of animals). The *piece de resistance* was a shrunken human head that Roddy had purloined from a museum. Borrowing a spare set of keys from Mrs B, I managed to place it in the driver's seat of his car. We followed him out to the car park as he left that night. It was one of those very dark, still nights when you could almost feel the spirits brushing your face, so we couldn't actually see his reaction, but the short burst of screaming was enough to confirm the thing had hit home. He was on the point of breakdown. The time had come to put him out of his misery.

'I can't take it anymore,' he very nearly sobbed as we gathered round to see what was the matter. 'I can't stand it! I can't stand it anymore!'

Once we'd calmed him down, Roddy suggested how he might possibly remedy the situation.

'In exceptional circumstances a very special offering to the offended party might call it off.'

The following evening Basher arrived bearing a particularly rare species of parrot in a cage which he politely, almost humbly, offered to Ali who looked at him in utter stupefaction (he had not been in on the thing).

'Sah?'

'Please accept this gift, Ali, as thanks for your service.'

'Sah?'

'Please accept this gift, Ali, and call it off.'

'Sah?'

'The Keli Keli.'

'I do not know of Keli Keli, Sah.'

Roddy could contain himself no longer.

'You bastards!' the old pre-ministerial Basher shouted. 'You fooking bastards! You fooking fooking bastards!'

But he kept his head. He hung on. He was the better man.

*

'Whatever happened to that fool of a friend of yours? What was his name, now?' he says as I scatter chicken feed about the run. He is on one of his periodic inspections of the grounds. In these grounds there is a sort of miniature farm containing a variety of the smaller of Our Lord's domesticated creatures: chickens, goats, piglets and so on. Dashwood School in China prides itself on its 'rounded curriculum' and the farm is beloved of the lower school pupils who are brought out by their teachers occasionally to bond with nature (nature having been all but eradicated from their lives by the march of progress). My erstwhile colleagues have read between the lines regarding my disgrace and are a little embarrassed at having to call me Old Macdonald as the Chief demands the pupils should. The post requires no validation of qualifications since none are deemed necessary and I survive on a Chinese labourer's wages by living with Yi Li in his cave. I have enough for beer, bia jiu and a Spartan diet and so am quite content; more so than I have ever been in my life. Basher enjoys these 'little chats'.

'Roddy. He was killed in rather extraordinary circumstances,' I say.

He mimes shock.

'You remember he was very fond of the fancy dress parties that were always being thrown back then. Used to go to great lengths.'

'It's coming back to me,' he lies, since he was never invited to any.

'Well, on the night of his death he was attending one themed on film musicals and had chosen to go as the Tin Man from The Wizard of Oz. I got this eventually in London from the girl he'd been squiring at the time. She was accompanying him as Dorothy. Roddy had really gone to town. Positively clanking in metal from head to toe. Anyway, on the way there the most almighty electric storm kicked off. Roddy having many Tigers taken no doubt, felt in urgent need of relief, stopped the car on open, exposed highway, exited towards the bushes and, blue flash and bang...*exeunt* Roddy. There wasn't much left of him by all accounts. It was a hell of a belt. Far too young of course but it would have been how he'd have chosen to go.'

'Should have gone as The Scarecrow,' he says.

'Chief?'

'If I only had a brain,' he hums, rather pleased with himself.

Graceless. Utterly graceless. But I must love him. He is sick in his heart and I must love him.

I expect the twinkling, paternal dismissal but it doesn't arrive.

'I'm glad I've managed to catch you, Charles,' he says, changing subject. 'I'd like to raise a matter pertaining to my wife which you, with all your past experience might be able to help me out with.'

'I hope Mrs Briggs is well,' I say with genuine concern. She is perhaps the least generous in her nature of all the women I have ever come across, but it is only with love, with compassion can one counter such negativity.

'Oh yes,' he says. 'Perhaps too full of the joys of spring. Frisky, might be the word. At times I find it hard to, how should I put it, keep up with her. She is, after all, many years my junior.'

'You mean on the badminton court, Chief?' (They play badminton together in the school gym. Or rather she plays badminton and Basher lumbers around like a rhino, swatting air.)

'I mean in bed, Charles. I know I can be candid with you. We've known each other such a long time. I can rely on your total silence and discretion. That is what friends are for.'

'Naturally,' I say, a trifle bemused. This is the only matter on which I'd ever heard him admit shortcoming.

'Do you remember that craze in the seventies and eighties for wife swapping? I do. I've often thought perhaps that sort of thing might give her the satisfaction she craves. She's much younger than me and to tell you the truth it's getting me down. If treated in the right spirit of fun, of playfulness, wife swapping can hardly be considered adultery.'

'I'm not quite sure where I come into this, Chief.'

'Well, the odd thing is, she appears to have taken something of a shine to you.'

*

Of all the things I did to him, it was seducing his wife and keeping her under my spell which causes me now the most shame, even though I now see she was not entirely innocent. I did not need to do it. I could have had any number of attractive, unattached women at the time, but it was the risk; the thrill of sailing so close, so very close to the wind. He was, is, a big, strong man and could have ripped my head off if the affair had been discovered. But he chose not to because I see now that he knew all along. There *was* no risk. It was a put-up job. He was in on it from the beginning. The better man.

I was led to believe early on by Deidre (that was Mrs B Mark 1's name), once the Tigers and G and T's had been flowing, that his physical power was in no way matched by attributes deemed necessary to give a woman her full satisfaction. In fact, it was implied that they had lately become lacking entirely unless pornographic images of an esoteric nature were produced. Knowing what I know now of his early years, his ineradicable sense of having been stained at birth, rudimentary psychology leads me to conclude that he was and is a sexual cripple. A classic case. I, on the other hand, had a large and healthy appetite, more than matched by Mrs B's and we sated ourselves freely, recklessly. Once, not long before the collapse of Number Two's empire, he had us pretty well bang to rights.

He returned a day earlier than planned from a trip up jungle. I was about to get into my car when his came up the drive with the usual gnashing of gears (he drove as badly as he ran). Mrs B was on the porch, waving me off, wearing nothing but a diaphanous negligee. The driveway was too narrow for two cars to pass and I had to reverse into the car port, which was not. Mrs B had legged it back inside the villa but he must have seen her. I wound down my window expecting at the least a grilling, at worst a beating (a bashing), but got instead a cheery greeting and thanks for having responded to his wife's SoS that I come at once and flush out a small, harmless, but nonetheless disturbing snake that had taken a fancy to their downstairs lavatory.

'Bloody women, ay?'

*

So, it has all been engineered most discreetly, in the Chinese way.

Dinner approaching its end, Basher receives the call. (Some urgent school business he didn't wish to bore us with. No, Lili (Mrs B II) would not hear of throwing me out before I could sample dessert - she had been in an unusually good, almost playful mood and he wouldn't want to 'break up the party'. No, he couldn't say, exactly, what time he'd be back but it wouldn't be before midnight.)

And so I lie in silken sheets on this large circular bed. The room has a number of mirrors, guilt framed in appalling mock rococo. One of these - I know not which — will be a two-way mirror and will have eyes. Piggy little twinkling eyes. Outside, I hear the rapid click of high heels belonging to tiny feet approaching down the corridor, signalling my final redemption.

OLD BOY

'We killed him, Branston,' Tony Finch bellowed, fighting for their ears over the tremendous din of the Association's biggest turnout ever. All expectations had been exceeded, even those of Kevin 'Branston' Pickles himself. In the draughty barn of a Victorian Town Hall, two hundred and forty- three Old Boys were assembled. As President for the past decade, he'd chivied away on the website, the phone, through the post, e-mail, and therefore been confident of a decent crowd; but this…! Huddled round cast iron pillars, squeezed into alcoves, roaring on the open floor stood dense knots of elderly men with pints of beer in their hands, red-faced and merry. It was a triumph. There could be nothing like it again. A mathematical man, he'd done the sad arithmetic: In another ten years a third of them would be dead, exceeding in number those active members who hadn't managed to attend. No new generations could take their place. Evershed Boys Grammar School had ceased to exist in 1974; turned into a 'Comprehensive' by Labour. The line was extinct. So, he, Kevin Pickles, would go down as the most successful President ever.

'I think that's a *bit* of an exaggeration, Finchy,' he yelled back, gulping at his pint for support.

The ridiculous assertion had unseated him. They were supposed to be taking part in a celebration, not a critical seminar. It wasn't playing by the rules. The school couldn't defend itself against charges made now. It was what it had been and ought to be left alone to fond memory. That was how Kevin saw it, anyway. He'd naturally assumed that all active Old Boys took the same view (they certainly seemed to ten, twenty, thirty years ago). Otherwise, what was the point in being one? But Finchy, although the most vocal, wasn't the only dissenting voice he'd heard since the evening began. Some of them even appeared to be making fun of the old place. Was that why, in this, his hour of crowning glory, he'd begun to feel a little out of sorts? Or was he just tired? He was, after all, 'getting on a bit', and his phone had hardly stopped ringing for weeks.

Kevin tended to steer clear of people with revised opinions. His own had stopped forming decades ago. Retired now, he was able to live almost entirely in the past. In the back of his mind he knew he shouldn't but he found it increasingly hard to get his head round the here and now. It kept changing all the time. The past, on the other hand, stayed where it was, like a picture in a gallery, always the same, always there, and to him, deeply moving. On Armistice Day a few weeks back he'd even found himself close to tears. As the Last Post came on the Nine o'clock News, he remembered that same lone bugle call drifting in to Assembly Hall, over the ranks of schoolboy heads, bowed for once in complete silence. The Head Boy's solemn quaver: 'At the going down of the sun we shall remember them'...And now *they* were all going, the years picking them off one by one with the cold indifference of a sniper. He seemed to spend half his time writing letters of condolence or up at the Crematorium. But tonight, at least, for a few short hours, the best days of his life were still there in the shape of these shouting men; men who, despite the odd loose cannon, he was sure saw things his way. If not, why on earth would they have bothered to come? And he was still President until the handing over ceremony scheduled for ten.

'Yeah. Overstating your case, me old cobber. You always were one for cracking a nut with a sledgehammer,' Dave Ford hooted, siding, as he'd always done over half a century ago, with 'Branston' against the cleverest of the three of them.

By rights, Finchy should have gone to university but his family was poor and had needed him to be earning. Instead he'd done an HND in Engineering at the tech, part time, whilst working as a postman. As soon as he got it he was off, to Australia, Land of Opportunity; just like that, leaving his two best mates flabbergasted. They thought he'd been joking. He hadn't been back for forty years, not since he returned on a flying visit to bury his father, dead at an early age of asbestosis. When Kevin got the letter confirming his attendance, he was beside himself. The Three Musketeers, together again!

'Not really,' he persisted in that Sydney twang the other two couldn't quite believe was genuine. They spoke in the flat Midland's drone of the small brewing town they'd lived in all their lives. So, with varying degrees of strength, did most of those attending. No matter where you roamed it seemed to stick to you like a birthmark on the face. That it hadn't done so with Finchy they considered a kind of betrayal. Both were proud of their origins, of the positions of modest eminence they'd attained in their respective breweries, and of having had the good fortune to attend 'The Shed'. The best education a boy from a working class family could ever hope to get. All gone. And replaced by what?

'We drove him to it, mates. No doubt about that. He hung himself because of us. We might as well have fixed the noose round his neck.'

Kevin took a step back, glancing uneasily from side to side. It wouldn't do to see the President engaged in anything other than affectionate reminiscence. Where had all this argumentativeness, this seriousness come from? The few Australians he'd met at test matches weren't like it. He didn't remember the schoolboy Finchy being like it either. He was worse than the lot of them when it came to having a laugh, usually at someone else's expense. Something had changed in the intervening fifty four years. That was the way with some people, although he could never see why.

'Imagine what he must have been going through every day. The shame he must have felt in front of his colleagues in the staffroom. Every class must have been like going over the top in the trenches except instead of bullets he was met with a hail of 'faaaaat!!!'.... 'faaaaat!!!''

The impersonation of that unfortunate voice was as sharp as it had been back in the days of 4B when, as fourteen-year-olds they'd launched into the chant with the rest of the class at the moment he walked in to the room, three times a week, for nearly a whole term.

They were talking about 'Fat' Price. It was Finchy who'd resurrected him. On show, fussed over like royalty, were the very few surviving Masters still well (and willing) enough to attend. 'Fat' Price wasn't among them. He'd hung himself on New Year's Day 1964.

A teacher of geography, he arrived from somewhere down South. From the off he couldn't keep discipline. He didn't terrify. He was too nice. Of course, that meant nothing to Branston, Finchy, Drof and the rest of 4B. In war you do not, you cannot, regard the enemy as feeling creatures. This essential principle was lost on, or had not been sufficiently instilled in, 'Fat' Price. For a couple of fatal weeks at the start of that autumn term he betrayed a genuine interest in his pupils as individuals and a wish to be correspondingly liked.

To begin with, a few range finding shots were fired. It was Branston who first took the risk on behalf of the rest of them, farting extravagantly during a lesson on the formation of ox-bow lakes. Instead of – as his terrifying predecessor Ronny 'Skippy' Skipton would have done – dragging the offender by the hair to the front of the class and beating him with a cane, Fat Price merely sniffed the air and said in his tragically imitable voice, 'such noxious vapours do not please'. He didn't see that such a remark, delivered as it was with a complicit, humorous air as though sharing in the fun, was an absolute gift to the schoolboy's repertoire of catch phrases. From then on, any boy suspected of smelling - and even Fat Price himself, who was an overweight, sweaty, greasy-haired man – was greeted with 'such noxious vapours do not please'. And he couldn't back track since the remark, repeated in his presence, was slyly offered as a complement to his lofty wit. *Apres ca*, as Mr Wood, their psychotic French teacher might have put it, *le deluge*.

There were plenty of Masters of equally discouraging exterior. 'Peggy' Smith, Head of Latin, had a wooden leg (the original lost in the war). Arnie 'Maths' Jacobs sported a great mole in the centre of his forehead, as a Rajah might wear a jewel. Such things didn't matter. The point was, they could be terrifying when they wanted to be and had fearsome, slashing voices. Fat Price's belonged to the stage, or in one of the popular comic radio shows of the time - Round the Horn, The Goon Show. It was, as 'Peggy' might have put it, *sui generis*, pitched somewhere between the bleating of a sheep and a very feeble chainsaw. To make matters worse, for some reason, his 'ings' came out as 'angs',

'Stop chattang, please boys!'

'A little less chattang and a bit more listenang might be advisable, boys.'

As he stood there mouthing geography to empty air, some wag

would shout to another across the room 'Stop chattang!' to be rebuked with 'No, you stop chattang!' If, by chance, silence should happen to reign for a minute or so, it was soon broken by a bleat, and then another, and another, until the whole class was a flock of distressed sheep. Other Masters would have to come in from neighbouring rooms to quell the noise.

Finchy decided to ratchet it up a notch. As de-facto leader of the class (big, strong and sarcastic, something of a bully when he wanted to be) he ordered it to greet Price's entrance with what became a signature chant that pursued him from then on in, through corridors, in the playground: the sound of his own dreadful voice proclaiming his physical repugnance.

'One...two...three....faaaaat!!!.....faaaaat!!!...faaaaat!!!'

Dave could picture it even now: 'Fat' Price standing there, pinioned by the wall of noise, utterly at a loss what to do. He'd 'lost' the class completely. It was no longer his to control. It was in the hands of Tony Finch. He decided if and when it was to do any work. In any other setting the whole thing, even to a fourteen-year-old, would have been distressing. But Masters weren't ordinary, feeling human beings. They were Stormtroopers imposing their will, their authority, with iron and at times sadistic, discipline. As such, the routing of Fat'Price represented a stunning victory and had to be celebrated. Kevin pictured something else: a weakness justly punished. He'd brought it on himself. He hadn't conformed.

'He was too full of all that modern rubbish they'd started filling them with in the training colleges,' he said. 'Trying to get in with the pupils. He should have sought some advice from the more experienced hands.'

'What? About how to be a bastard? How to be a sadist? How to grind the little buggers down?'

'Now, come on, Finchy,' Dave said, 'that's really stretching things a bit far. They weren't bastards or sadists. They were just ordinary blokes doing their job according to the standards of the time. That was how things were.'

'And so were the Nazis.'

Kevin let out an incredulous groan and pulled the kind of face that footballers make when they can't believe the stupidity of the referee who's just flashed the red card.

'Now come oooonnnnn!'

'No, you come on, Branston! Didn't the Nazis beat people up for stepping out of line? Didn't Goebbels single out 'certain elements' for public ridicule? Just like The Beak at assembly picking on a 'long hair" or a 'shirker'.'

'Yes but...'

Accustomed only to reverence, Kevin was lost for words.

'...but times were different then, as Dave said. You can't judge the standards of the past by those of the present. It's unfair. I'm sure they'd have liked to have been nicer, friendlier people. Outside school they were. Remember Jacko, the music teacher; he collected stray dogs off the street and found them homes.'

'He took a chunk of my hair out, I know that.'

'That's because you deserved it,' Dave said. 'You kept dinging your triangle deliberately in the wrong places. And you made Martin Clarke stick two drumsticks up his nostrils and pretend to be a walrus.'

'I know I did. I was a nasty fucker.'

Kevin recoiled. He disapproved of strong language. The strongest word he used was the occasional 'bloody'. Were all Australians quite so foul-mouthed? Perhaps it was the beer that had gone to his head? They weren't used to English bitter.

'But the point is I don't make excuses for myself. I was a nasty fucker then. I'm a nicer person now. I've moved on. I've grown up. Ditto The Shed. What was it when you really think about it? A boot camp with a load of rote learning thrown in, that's what it was. 'Energy is the capacity for doing work! What is energy, Pickles!?' 'The capacity for doing work, Sir!'' He clicked his heels together and gave a parody of a brisk Nazi salute.

'Now it's a comprehensive where kids think things out for themselves, with teachers that don't beat and humiliate the pupils, and pupils who don't get pleasure out of stripping weak and vulnerable men of their dignity. Oh, and boys and girls together. Now there's a revolutionary concept. No, the world's a nicer, friendlier, saner, more understanding place. You should try living in it, Branston.'

He did, occasionally, but found himself increasingly rebuffed. He'd never married, lived with his widowed mother until she died, never had children. Perhaps that was the problem? Children were supposed to anchor you to the here and now. But he'd never had them and the manners and speech of that here and now were growing ever more foreign to him. The town had changed, too. It was full of foreigners. Not just Indians and Pakistanis and Jamaicans (they were alright, they'd come over in the fifties and sixties; there were even one or two there tonight). No, it was all these others from places he could hardly find on the map:

Romania, Slovenia, Lithuania. When he went to the library to chase up a bit of local history (he was putting together a slim book about the town's old tram system) he couldn't get on the computers. What were they doing there? If they'd come over to work, what were they doing in the library at eleven o'clock on a Tuesday morning? Did they all work nights? He'd actually asked one of them, politely, out of curiosity, what he did but didn't get an answer because he couldn't speak English. Even the Big Issue seller outside Sainsbury's he bought a copy off every week had been replaced by a Gypsy-looking woman who was Romanian. He knew she was Romanian because he'd taught himself to say 'Good Day' in her language and had received an ecstatic response. No, *he* wasn't one of those racist types marching through the town with their Britain First placards, giving it a bad name. It was just that he couldn't see what it was all for; all this mixing people up; mixing things up. What was it for?

'What about ISIS?' he said, trying to shunt the conversation towards more neutral ground. 'If the world's such a nice, friendly, sane place these days, what about ISIS?'

Finchy wasn't having any.

'What *about* ISIS? They don't count. They're just loonies. I'm talking about modern day society, not some idiotic recreation of the middle ages. Modern day education. What I can't stand is all this rose-tinted spectacles stuff. All this yesterdayism. You have to admit that The Shed was a savage place! What about all the bullying that went on? It was institutional. You remember Molloy? 'Stiff Head' Molloy. 'Stiff! Stiff! Stiff! Stiff!' We made his life hell, just like we did to Fat Price. And none of the teachers raised a finger to stop it. Some of them even found it amusing. Same as they did with Fat Price. Schadenfraude is what the Germans call it. Secretly relishing someone else's distress. Dog eat dog, that's what it was.'

Kevin thought he'd got him.

'And you know what Stiff Head became?' he said.

A pause. Dave smiled. He knew what was coming.

'The Head of the Bank of Hong Kong, that's what he became. He was on the telly the other day talking about Asian markets.'

'Your point being?'

'My point being that it couldn't have done him any harm. May even have spurred him on. Being called after a pickled relish never stopped me from getting to be a Head Brewer, either.'

'Aha! The old character-building canard! Doesn't wash, I'm afraid. The fact that you succeeded *despite* your educational experience isn't a justification *for* that experience.'

Kevin stood with his mouth half-open, bamboozled. He was a diligent but not a clever man and felt the weight of his own sluggishness on his tongue.

'Bloody hell, Finchy,' Dave said, 'it's enough to make you wonder why you made the effort to come if the place was so bloody awful.' He felt duty-bound to protect his friend from disappointment. They met only rarely, once or twice a year, if that. Dave had a wife and a busy family life being 'Super Grandad' as he fondly lamented, but he knew how much the Presidency, the whole thing, meant to Branston.

'I came,' Finchy said, softening a little, 'mainly out of curiosity. Like most of us here, I should think. Let's be honest. It's kind of irresistible. See how we've all turned out. That's the real reason, if we're honest with ourselves. I'm having a bloody good time, don't get me wrong. No worries on that front, mates. It's great to meet up after all these years. And the missus is loving the old town,' he lied for the sake of convenience. 'Can't get enough of it despite the fucking awful weather.'

It was late November and a very cold one. There had been snow. The ancient heating system wasn't up to the job. Whatever simpering of warmth it generated rose straight to the cavernous ceiling and out into the night. It was a chilly, draughty barn of a place and a good many of them had dressed accordingly, wearing chunky woollen sweaters under coats and jackets, some sporting reindeer or Santa motifs in what Finchy – a snappy dresser himself - presumed was in early anticipation of Christmas (although he had the feeling, he didn't quite know why, that they probably wore them all year round). Some of the blokes looked positively down at heel, as if this was their first public outing in a long time. The odd one or two he thought may have been let out of, or even escaped from, institutions of a caring nature. It had been a good call skipping off to Oz when he did, no doubt about that. A very good call. If not, he might have ended up like them: out of shape, shabby, untouched by the sun, shambling about like a forgotten tribe. What he'd seen of the town so far hadn't impressed, either. He remembered it as a spruce and thriving place despite the industrial grime. It, too, appeared to have let itself go. The High Street was full of vacant lots, betting shops, charity shops, even a couple of pawn shops.

'It's not been at its best for you,' Dave, a great connoisseur of weather, said, like an octopus squirting ink. 'We haven't had an early winter quite like this since 1981. You remember that one, Branston? Bitter it was. Ground frozen solid for weeks. The Albion had to cancel three home games on the trot.'

Kevin said he did remember, then quietly, almost to himself, but with an air of finality, 'Anyway, we didn't kill him. And that's that.'

He felt an urgent need to get away from Finchy; to not have to think anymore. He wasn't used to thinking. Not like this, anyway. The fact was they were no longer the Three Musketeers. Why on earth had he imagined they still would be? People changed. He didn't. Was that, he'd begun to ask himself in less guarded moments, on long winter evenings with no association work to do and nothing worth watching on the telly, why he had so few real friends?

'Call of nature, I'm afraid,' he said, and broke away.

'Branston! Come and join us!'

They were on him immediately, like wasps that wouldn't go away.

'Bring on The Branston!'

'Would you kindly grace us with your presidential presence, Branston, for we shall not have the honour much longer?'

'Branston, you old bugger! Get over here!'

Pleading a more pressing engagement somewhere else in the hall, he gave them the slip. They didn't seem to mind. Some of them were already quite drunk. He needed a few moments peace and quiet but there wasn't anywhere to hide. He felt worn out. Was it Finchy upsetting his equilibrium like that or the effort of his labours finally catching up with him? Only the other day he'd felt his heart give a little jump in his chest and then patter about a bit before settling down. It had never done that before. Whatever it was, he found his thoughts retreating to the quiet of his study, the cosy pool of light cast by the angle lamp; his slowly growing opus on local trams. For a moment, the thing he'd looked forward to for years, he half-wished to be over; to be safely confined to the past. A man with absurdly thick spectacles swam up to him for inspection, peering with hugely magnified eyes like a fish in an aquarium, demanding, with a stupid smile on his face, to be identified.

Briefly, Kevin thought about escaping, running outside, then pulled himself together, rummaged around in his tremendous memory for faces, placed the one in front of him and was off again, 'Bull 1961-68. You won the Fourth Year chess prize for Wellington House...went on to play for the County...'

A little into this exchange there was a sudden dimming of the roar, as though someone had tweaked a volume switch ever so slightly. History itself had finally arrived in the shape of the guest of honour.

It had been touch and go whether he'd arrive at all (a bout of bronchitis, enough to carry off any man in his mid-nineties). But he'd got over it just in time, and here he was: still ramrod-backed (although walking with a stick), a full head of crisply-parted white hair, spotted handkerchief in the breast pocket of an immaculate blazer, silk cravat loosely knotted at the neck - Squadron Leader Andrew 'Wings' Hervey, the oldest surviving Master who, by rights, none of them should ever have known. As a Spitfire pilot, he'd been shot down over the Channel in the Battle of Britain and twice again in the course of the War, before, it seemed at the time, parachuting himself dramatically from nowhere into the town as the school's Head of English, in 1950. A Cambridge scholar and Double Blue he could have taken his pick of jobs anywhere in the country and, of all places, chose The Shed! It was like having royalty actually electing to live amongst you.

There was never any question of his needing to exercise

discipline. Order, respect, came automatically, with his reputation. Perhaps because he'd cheated death on multiple occasions, he was a man of supreme good humour. No one ever saw him lose his temper. Not once. He took great delight in the kind of clowning beloved of boys: slowing down the trumpet alarums on LP recordings of Shakespeare; occasionally whipping off his jacket and using it as a matador's cape on boys who misquoted The Bard. On Speech Day it was a custom, permitted by The Beak, to allow the school to express its – good-natured – approbation or otherwise of the Masters by booing or cheering as they trouped on to the stage in their ermined gowns. Those with a reputation for harshness would be booed like pantomime villains, others of more gentle dispositions cheered. 'Wings' was cheered to the rafters. It was no exaggeration to say that he was loved. And here he was, miraculously still alive; the nation's finest hour, incarnate.

Abandoning Bull-61-68 without a word of apology, Kevin shot across the room.

'Mr Hervey, Sir. So glad and honoured you could attend. It's made the whole reunion. The icing on the cake.'

A perfectly timed pause. A keen, appraising, sceptical eye. Then, 'You always were prone to hyperbole, Pickles. Especially when it came to your atrocious performances on the cricket field.' Extreme age had reduced the once suave baritone to a piping treble. 'To appropriate Churchill,' it said, 'dodgy icing, *some* cake. You are to be congratulated, Pickles. I don't think I've ever seen so many reprobates gathered in one space. You wicked, wicked little boys!'

The men Kevin had brushed aside laughed in a knowing, proprietorial way. With extreme unction, he ushered his prize away from them towards the seated area reserved for the Masters.

'What's it to be, Sir? What's your poison these days?'

Fifty years ago, it had been whisky. In rather large quantities. Especially on Fridays. The forms who got 'Wings' on a Friday afternoon were in for a treat.

'A large, a very large Scotch and water, if you don't mind, Pickles.'

'Coming up,' Kevin lied.

Why on earth hadn't he planned for that?! Along with the beer, there was a limited quantity of wine for those few who preferred it, but no spirits. What an appalling oversight! Remembering there used to be an off-licence in one of the adjacent streets, he grabbed his overcoat and dashed towards the exit.

'Leaving us, Branston!?'

'Spot of fresh air?'

'Are we to be left without our Great Helmsman?'

Kevin flapped a hand at the voices following him out of the double doors.

'Back in a jiffy. Cock up on the booze,' he bellowed over his shoulder.

Outside in the square it was bitterly cold. An irascible wind was blowing grit and litter about. He bent into it and began marching away from the hall, down a street of handsome Edwardian villas now chopped up into flats. At his back, the noise of what sounded from outside like a riot pursued him for a hundred yards or so, fading to something more like a demonstration marching out of earshot. Soon, there was just the sound of his footsteps on the frosted pavement and wind whipping through bare branches of great century-old town oaks. He was glad of the break, the solitude; would have liked to have kept walking for a while longer if he were to be honest with himself.

The off-licence was still there, and open. One of those old-style off-licences he liked that didn't belong to a chain. Beating down his more frugal self he bought a whole bottle of Haig, stuffed it in his coat pocket and hurried back the way he'd come, the wind this time seeming to propel him towards the hall.

He could only have been gone about ten minutes but something behind the noise seemed to have changed. The demonstration had swung round and appeared to be coming *for* him; shouting *at* him. It was a most strange sensation, as though he no longer belonged to the thing he'd spent years organising. He had no idea of where the feeling had come from. Finchy, upsetting him like that? The sight of Pete Bennet, once Captain of the 1st XV, who had some terrible wasting disease and sat in his wheelchair like a bag of bones? No, it was more general than that; out of time, out of place, like a great chunk of meaning had broken away from him, a sort of mental landslide. He'd felt a bit the same – a queer, disorienting, floating sensation - when, at the age of fifteen, he quite suddenly realised there was no god and that the hymn he was singing in assembly was a hymn to nothing; just words.

He paused for a while under the names of The Fallen inscribed on a tablet above the great double doors. Perhaps they might set him right? Put some sense back in to him?

'Pickles! Where on earth have you been? A man could die of thirst here.'

'Someone polished off the scotch I'd got reserved for you, Sir. I had to nip outside for a refill.'

'God and all his angels cast their blessings upon you,' Wings said, taking a good gulp at the glass of straw-coloured liquid. A small court had already formed around him. Its chief courtier appeared to be Finchy, who was looking pleased with himself.

'You were saying, Andrew?' he said.

Andrew! Andrew! You didn't go around calling people like Squadron Leader Andrew Hervey, Andrew. Not in England, at any rate. Kevin wanted to intervene; put things back on their correct footing but the old man appeared perfectly at ease.

Extraordinary things were being said: 'No, you are quite right to question what went on at The Shed, Finch. Quite right. Don't get me wrong. I enjoyed my time there. But speaking as a socialist there were all sorts of things to pot with the system that made it hard to take the whole thing seriously. I know you chaps feel you owe it a lot, and I'm honoured to have been a part of something that means such a great deal to you. But, leaving aside the fun I had, for my part it was plugging a hole which shouldn't have been plugged. We were just tinkering. We missed our chance between '46 and '54. We should have gone for broke. Gone properly comprehensive then, wholeheartedly. You were the 'lucky thirty' as they used to say. What about the other seventy percent who didn't pass that ridiculous, that iniquitous intelligence test at the age of eleven? Didn't they realise that young boys' intelligence develops at different speeds, in different ways? You can't decide the kind of life a person's going to have on the basis of whether they can articulate what melted chocolate will reconstitute itself as when it solidifies again. Or what's the fewest number of triangles a square can be broken up in to. That sort of trickery. At the age of *eleven*! Pure wickedness! And they're trying to bring it *back*!'

He appeared to be quite angry. What shocked Kevin most, though, were the number of heads, mostly bald, nodding in agreement.

'How many 'O' Levels did you get, for example…er…Payne?' Wings went on, pointing shrewdly at a wizened-looking man in his seventies. 'I remember you were a C streamer. How many?'

'Two, Sir,' said the man called Payne (reputed to be a millionaire) rather sheepishly, to hearty guffaws.

'Precisely! And that was going it some. In a bad year, half the C stream left with none at all. Now why do you think that was?'

'Don't know, Sir. Perhaps because we were a bit thick.'

'Wrong. It was because of sheer, rank bad teaching. In a lot of cases, it could hardly be called 'teaching' at all. If you didn't get the point of something first time round you got it explained again in exactly the same terms, if you were lucky, and if you weren't you had pieces of chalk thrown at you. You couldn't teach in the proper sense of the word, you see, because that would imply understanding of individual needs, which in turn would imply empathy, which would immediately be taken as weakness. And then you'd be dead in the water.'

Kevin felt, vaguely, that he ought to protest but just as he was about to open his mouth, he realised he didn't have anything much to say. Things didn't seem to matter in quite the same way they had even as little as three hours ago.

That clever, twanging voice got in first anyway, 'You might say we succeeded *despite* your best efforts, Andrew.'

'*You* might say that, Finch, but you'd be being hard on us.'

Sitting at the same table were three other old Masters, all

sprightly and equally lacking in an appropriate spirit of respectful nostalgia. In fact. Kevin couldn't even be sure they weren't actually laughing at their former selves; at The Shed, as though it were something you couldn't quite credit with ever having been allowed to exist, like driving when drunk or smoking on buses. It wasn't supposed to be like that. It wasn't supposed to be *funny*.

'The point is we all did our best given what it was. But what it was, was all wrong. Real learning can never take place in an atmosphere of mutual fear, and, despite occasional appearances to the contrary, that was what the whole system was based on: fear. It put terrific strain on the heart, having to maintain discipline all the time. Having to keep you buggers from making our lives hell, by scaring the living daylights out of you. A whole lifetime nearly of having to be someone you're not. We're the lucky ones. How many of us retired and then a year or so later simply dropped dead?'

He gave a roll call of those of Masters who'd died before they were seventy. There were quite a few.

'And it was always heart. *Always* heart.'

'Do you remember Mr Price, Sir,' Kevin heard himself saying.

The hall was brightly lit, but Dave Ford swore later to his wife that he actually saw a shadow cross the faces of the four old men. It was eerie, he said. Like Fat Price's ghost had swooped down from the rafters.

'Peter Price was a tragic example of everything wrong with the system. A young teacher full of drive and ideas who was just too bloody nice. And it crucified him. I was on the panel which interviewed him. For years I felt partly responsible for his death. I should have told him there and then to pack it in and be an inspector of buildings, or a public surveyor or something like that; something loosely connected to Geography. I could see straight away he didn't have what it took to be sufficiently mean when he needed to be. But he was so damnably keen. And well qualified too.'

'So, you don't blame us, Sir? Only Finchy here says we practically hung him ourselves.'

'Good grief, no. You were just doing what you'd been conditioned to do. Some of us offered to help but he wouldn't hear of it. Neither would The Beak do anything. That would have been tampering with the natural order, you see. Terrible man. I'm not keen on doling out advice but if I had one particular piece of it to give before I croak, I'd say never stop questioning what you're told is the natural order of things. You make your own life.'

So, Finchy had lost the battle, but won the war. The odd thing was that he, Kevin, didn't really care anymore. It was that feeling again. Like he no longer belonged to the person he'd been only three hours ago.

'Thank you, Sir,' Finchy said. 'I suppose we all have, in our different ways.'

The man called Payne, sensing a need to lighten the mood again, said, 'You remember that time you caught us in the saloon bar of The Saracen's Head, Sir? When we were supposed to be out on cross country...'

'A question of who was the guiltier party, I seem to remember...'

Wings' memory was astonishing.

And they were off...

But Kevin, although smiling, wasn't really listening. His mind was somewhere else, going round and round in a maze of its own making. If he, Kevin Pickles, thought differently to Squadron Leader Andrew Hervey on matters that had defined the tenor of his whole life, didn't that make him, Kevin Pickles, all wrong? Was it conceivable that he'd backed the wrong horse and the rest of the punters had simply been too polite to point the fact out? Discretely, he detached himself from the court of 'Wings' and drifted quietly away to the gents.

They were, like the main hall they served, an example of magnificent redundancy. A dozen enormous urinals, beautifully tiled, stood to attention like soldiers on parade. (Kevin himself had got up a petition to keep them there. It was the job of the council to preserve such things, not to bloody tear them down!). Alone, he chose the fourth from left, relieved to be excused the kind of public urinal banter he hated. He didn't feel up to that. He didn't feel up to anything much. Washing his hands, he raised his head and in the great, rust speckled mirror, caught the reflection of someone who was, and at the same time was not, Kevin Pickles. A memory surfaced of a boyhood trip to the seaside; The Hall of Mirrors at the end of a pier, his mother, father and elder sister laughing at his grotesquely distorted image. No matter where he moved. he couldn't get back to himself. He didn't understand and had burst into tears. The same sensation of being un-selfed was happening now. His face was the same but it transmitted no value.

Its mouth opened and he heard a voice say, 'You arsehole. You wanker. You prick.'

'Talking to yourself, Branston!' another voice said. It belonged to a man non-too steady on his pins who was weaving his way towards the urinal basins. 'First sign of madness, so they say. Or seven pints of Carstons. Bloody good stuff. But better out than in, though. Syphon the python. You're on by the way. It's ten o'clock.'

In the hall, shouts of 'Bring on The Branston!' were going up. Then he was standing on the stage where a band of musicians had assembled. A banner proclaimed them to be The Shed Hot Stompers. Next to him was the man who he was to hand his president's chain over to.

'I should have known something was up,' Dave Ford said to his wife a few days later. 'He'd prepared a speech, see. He'd showed it to me. A bloody great long thing it was, full of jokes and stories. But all he did was say 'Over to you, Richard,' and hung the chain over Richard Prevert's shoulders. We all put it down to the occasion being too much for him. But then he started dancing to the band. Dancing! Branston! A sort of Charleston. All on his own. His arms and legs going everywhere. It was horrible. 'Just a bit pissed,' we all said. 'Letting his hair down after all the responsibility.' I should have known something was up. I should have taken him home. But he wouldn't stop dancing. Couldn't get him off the floor. Kept on shouting he was making up for lost time and talking about emigrating to Thailand. Thailand! Branston! Anyway, he isn't going anywhere now. My old mate. We'd known each other since we were nippers. I should have known something was up. But you know what I can't get out of my mind. It's all those empty oblong spaces on the walls when I'd crowbarred the back door in. I knew instantly. He'd taken all the school photographs down, see. He used them to remember all the names. Empty oblong spaces all over the house...'

'You can't blame yourself, love,' his wife said, pouring him another cup of tea. 'You phoned twice. You went round twice. You didn't see any empty bottles or packets or anything like that. There wasn't any note. They always leave notes. You see, the autopsy will say it was a heart attack. You said yourself he'd been complaining of feeling a bit giddy. It was just a heart attack, brought on by all the excitement probably.'

'Empty oblong spaces' Dave said, shaking his head. 'Scores of them, all over the house.'

THE B.I.L.F.

Extracts from a Journal of a Literary Festival

By

Elisabeth Victoria Anne Brown

April 10th 2017

The brochures arrive today from Beijing - *'With Luv n Hugs from Paddy'*, both of which I wish he'd stop sending. I only slept with him a little bit and that was over three years ago. He got laid, I got the job. A perfectly businesslike transaction involving, in the light of our difference in age, a great deal more give on my part than his. Paddy doesn't see it that way, however. Few older men do. They start mewing about meaningful relationships of the kind their wives can no longer provide. All very flattering but I'm not that sort of girl. When it comes to men, I try to keep the meaningful at bay.

It's the usual routine with The Man from China Post; a different one every year. He gives a little jump backwards as I fling open the door and tower over him in all my tousled early morning glory. Then he starts quacking in his local dialect, holding the mailbag out to me in a manner that suggests there may be some confusion in my mind that it is in fact a mail bag and not, say, the head of John The Baptist. I jabber back in my atrocious Mandarin, affirming that I have indeed understood the true nature of the object and his mission of delivering it into my hands. He hands me his chit. I sign it. Then he scurries off at the double, perhaps afraid I've put a spell on him and his wife's babies will come out the same colour as me, or he might start turning black himself, or upset his ancestors; maybe all three. There's no end to it. Sisters of mine: if you're narked about turning heads for the wrong reasons in, say, Inverness, I suggest you try being a black lady of Amazonian proportions here. Out in the country, infants burst in to tears at the sight of you, children pull your hair to see if you're real. Paddy's no fool though. He took a gamble hiring me to run the place and it's paid off because, what works out in the sticks works for different reasons with the students and rich arty types here in the city. Here, I am the ultimate in chic. They flock to the court of Queen Bess. Heavy Dub now booms in the lobbies and elevators of all those brand-new boutique hotels their daddies own. My curried goat is the talk of the town. Brixton (pre-gentrification) is the new Black. It's all there in The Explorer:

> Beth Brown hails from Brixton, South London. Since taking over the Biblio-Bar three years ago, she has transformed it from a sleepy enclave for book lovers who like a drink into a centre for gastronomic, musical and intellectual exploration. The old cosy atmosphere is still there in the book-lined walls, rough wooden floors and 1920s lampshades but now pulses to the sounds of her native Jamaican roots. The menu is an authentic taste of the Caribbean. Be sure to try the famous curried goat. Don't miss the International Literary Festival which runs over the last two weeks of April, with world renowned authors passing through, all under the formidable rule of 'Queen Bess' herself!

And all very gratifying. From jobbing EFL teacher to international literary hostess.

Re-arranging my Kimono (from which I fear a generous booby may have peeped during aforementioned encounter with Postman Pat) I

lug the mailbag over to the bar, and get some coffee on the go. It's a lovely sunny morning, unusual for April which normally throws it down all month. Light is flooding through the Chin filigree windows I got Paddy to restore to their original glory. Peace perfect peace. But not for much longer. The Festival is upon us. No escape. It's Paddy's baby. His way of re-affirming annually what we're supposed to be about. And what is that? Well, according to P it's to do with 'cross-cultural dissemination...
breaking down barriers...sharing heritages...providing a forum for the free interchange of ideas between the international and local communities.' He's a bit of a dreamer. He's also a businessman. One that must have got tired of making money because, despite the glowing praise, if my branch is anything to go by he must, in a very good year, be just about breaking even. True, Beijing and Chengdu are bigger operations, but my guess is size just serves to widen the circumference of the black hole he's pouring his *Kwai* into. But the odd thing is he doesn't seem to mind. I think it might all be a tax dodge for his other enterprises. On his rare visits he measures success by the number of bums on seats discussing Song Dynasty poetry whilst eking out a pot of green tea for hours on end. All very picturesque but I don't get a salary. I'm supposed to live off the bar and food takings. I know we shouldn't indulge in such disgraceful stereotyping, but it has to be said that Johny Chinaman and his money don't like being parted unless, that is, in parting he's going to see a lot more of it further down the line. This, unfortunately, doesn't apply to my range of fine wines and craft beers.

    Braced by the first of the day's strong black coffees and cigarettes I take the scissors to the mailbag. The brochures slither onto the bar (With Luv n Hugs from Paddy on a big red cardboard heart I suspect he may have made himself). What ship of April fools will we be sailing this year? I have no say in the matter. The format has always run like this:

Our three branches are assigned the same three 'writers in residence', spending two weeks in each. The Festival warms up with us in Suzhou, zigs West over to Chengdu, finally zagging up to Beijing, the whole thing lasting six weeks. One WiR deals with poetry, another with kids' stuff, the other oversees the fiction side of things. They tend to be lightweights who nobody, including myself, has ever heard of. They get a free air ticket, meals but no cash, and need bigging up. The bigger names, such as they are, announce themselves and flit in and out as their busy writerly lives permit. Along with holding workshops and generally being on hand to chat with the punters, the WiRs are responsible for introducing the talks of their better-known peers and chairing the subsequent Q and A sessions. Even if you may not be familiar with the extreme touchiness of the breed, you will still spot the potential in this set up for a certain amount of tension. So, it is to our WiRs that I first turn, since it is they whose egos I shall be alternately tiptoeing around and massaging for the coming fortnight.

Donald Dunn is a young Scottish poet who describes himself as a 'post-modern patriot'. Originally from the Highlands, his family moved to Glasgow when he was in his teens. His debut collection: *A Load of Gorbals* deals with his deep sense of longing for the wild background in which his boyhood was spent whilst at the same time lovingly exploring the seedier side of his adopted city. It is a heady brew of both the beautifully naturalistic and edgily urban. He is also an acclaimed poetry performance artist.

Christ! And a ginger to boot. Not my type *at all*. Drinks a lot by the looks of it. Definitely not having the guest room.

Linda Werweeweea is an Australian Aboriginal children's author who illustrates all her own work. She is bilingual in English and her native Warlpiri. Her many works appear in both languages. Her most recent book *The Amazing Adventures of Ricky Roo*, a lovable, mischievous baby kangaroo which lives in the suburbs of Wollongong won The Wollongong Children's Writers Gold Star Award. Linda divides her time between writing, drawing and visiting schools.

Looks like a younger, paler, madder version of my Aunty Essie with a bit of a drinker's face too. Sorry, Linda but no guest room for you.

Our fiction expert, on the other hand, is a well-groomed and attractive blonde, albeit with that rather chiseled countenance belonging to driven American women who spend half their lives in a gym. At least, by comparison with the other two, she looks sane and, when not facilitating, will probably be off running half marathons. So, she gets the futon. I read on:

Felicity Blaise won instant critical acclaim in 2007 with the debut novel *Too Good To Be True* which deals with violent delinquency and suicide in small town Wisconsin. Described by the Washington Herald as a 'lacerating voyage through the black hole at the empty heart of a vacant generation' *Too Good To Be True* is Holden Caulfield on crystal meth with a loaded AK-47 in his school bag. He is currently at work on a collection of short stories.

Well, there goes our first typo. Not as bad as last year though, when a venerable poet, one of our bigger names, was billed as 'the farter of Malaysian Modernism'. In comparison to which, a little slip of gender is excusable. La Blaise would seem to be a step-up in caliber from last year's incumbent, it has to be said. She was Welsh, published by her husband, and spent most of the time going on in print and in person about what it was to be a Welsh woman in Wales in the 1980s. Not a page turning crowd puller whereas, although I've never heard of her, Felicity comes with genuine credentials. The Washington Herald is not the Aberavon Gazette. A slight doubt over the ten year gap in the follow up, though. 'Currently at work' could mean anything. I am also impressed at how daring Paddy and the team at HQ Beijing have become in their choice of authors. Crystal meth! Ak-47s! Whatever next? There was a time when Winnie the Pooh would have raised the censor's eyebrows. Perhaps the place really is opening up?

April 15th

5 a.m. I'm at Arrivals, Shanghai Pudong International, jostling for space at the barrier with about fifty other greeters all brandishing their often rather touchingly inexact placards: Welcome John'... Beard For Holiday Inn ... Honorable Professor...

Mine says:

FELICITY BLAISE-BIBLIO-BAR ILF

A number of flights must have arrived at the same time. It's a sluggish river of happy to be home Chinese on which bobs a thin flotsam of first time foreign, anxious *weiguoren* faces. One by one my fellow greeters are picked off by these *weijy* who appear pathetically relieved to be met. Time goes by. The river dwindles to a trickle, then to a dry bed and I'm left standing alone. I'm about to give up when out of this emptiness steps the solitary figure of a (taller than me!) beautiful, serene man in his early thirties carrying nothing but a slim briefcase. He strolls calmly up to me.

'I'm sorry to keep you waiting,' he says in a slow, soft American voice. 'My suitcase didn't arrive.'

'I'm sorry,' I say back, batting my eyelashes and smiling. 'But I'm afraid I don't know who you are.'

'Obe Ostler.'

'But you're supposed to be a woman.'

'Felicity Blaise is my pen name. Didn't they tell you that?'

'No, they didn't. And in the brochure picture, you're a woman.'

He claps a hand to his forehead.

'Hell, they must have gone and *used* that photo? I told them I don't do photos. Ever. They wouldn't take no for an answer. Kept pestering. I sent it as a last resort. Out of exasperation. It's the photo I always send.'

This is said with the appropriate note of apology lacking, as though he's describing the action of somebody other than himself.

'Well, that's not going to help much but at least it kind of makes sense,' I say steering him across the hall. 'Ten to a pound Paddy...Pa Di Li...he's the owner of the bars...the main man...doesn't have a clue Felicity Blaise is a pen name. Neither will any of the Chinese staff at HQ in Beijing. They're very literal-minded people. It's the kind of cock up that can only happen in China. Paddy's a businessman. He likes to patronise the arts, but doesn't actively engage with them. He doesn't read, *period*.' I pause, rather proud of the Americanism (where did *that* come from?). 'He wouldn't know James Joyce from Desmond Bagley. But the punters at the festival take their literature very seriously. The brochures have already gone out. This is going to take some explaining.'

'The punters?'

'The people who'll be paying to attend your activities. They're going to get the same kind of shock I've just had. It's all going to take a lot of explaining. They might not show it but they're quick to take offence if they think they've been made fools of.'

'I'm sorry.'

'I suppose it's my fault, too, for not having read your book or anything about you either. It's just that I've been terribly busy and I don't get...'

'That's OK. No problem. You don't have to explain. It's my stupid fault. I have a horror of the publicity machine. I believe in primacy of text.'

'Quite. Although a bit early in the morning for me. Well, at least you're not a transgendered person. Not that I have anything against transgendered persons, of course. But if you were one it would be pushing the envelope a bit *too* far. You aren't, are you? I mean, part time, so to speak. I mean the photo's pretty convincing.'

'No, I'm not.'

'That helps. I know it's all the rage in the States, but unfortunately China's still got a lot of catching up to do. We have to tread carefully if we're to keep our license.'

'Suits me fine. I don't much care for faggots dressed up as women either.'

Such is my level of conditioning and the odd nature of our discourse to this point that for a moment I can't believe my ears.

'Are you by any chance winding me up? Because if you are, I should warn you I'm not at my most even tempered at five thirty in the morning.'

'No,' he says, quietly, evenly. 'I don't like faggots who dress up as women. I find it disturbing. I'm just articulating what I happen to think. I believe that's important.'

'Well, you'll have to restrict yourself to just thinking it for the two weeks you're with me. I should warn you there'll be quite a few *faggots* attending your workshops. I tend to attract quite a – discreet – gay crowd. It all seems to go hand in hand with good taste. I don't quite know why. They're nice people.'

'Fine with me. If you say they're good people I'm sure they're good people.'

We've got off on the wrong foot. I need to get things on the right one.

'Good,' I say. 'So long as that's understood, we'll be fine. Incidentally, what did you say your name was. I can't go around for the next fortnight calling you Felicity.'

'Oberon Ignatius Ostler is my full name. My father, Robert Ostler, the dead poet, was a strange man. People call me Obe, as in 'robe'. Say, do we have a car? Is it far to where we're at? I could sure use some coffee and a shave.'

Our driver, a warty man with terrible breath (the best I can afford) is chain smoking by his equally unimpressive vehicle. There's already a small mound of buts built up at his feet. Before setting off on the two hour drive he clears his throat extravagantly of phlegm, loudly depositing it as a sort of garnish for the fag ends. Now, most Americans I know out here usually squirm at all the hawking and spitting, but not Felicity/ Obe. He remains icily unbothered. Nor has he vented over the trauma of being separated from his luggage, which would have had *me* ranting. He is unnervingly serene.

Pretty soon we're bowling along nicely, although at 6 a.m. the traffic's already starting to build. A wet, grey dawn is spreading over the wilderness of concrete and steel. Obe regards it in silence, his face giving nothing away. I don't think he's big on small talk. Silence in company makes me feel uneasy. I'm a bit of a gabbler. I could never live in Finland.

'I have to apologise again for not having read your book,' I say, unable to stand it any longer. 'I don't read as much as I should these days. Running the bar seems to take up all my time.'

'That's OK.'

'I gather it's pretty violent in parts.'

'I was a violent young man.'

'So, it's autobiographical, then?'

'Not in any factual sense.'

'Is there any other sense?'

He smiles. He hasn't smiled before. It's actually quite a nice smile.

'Ever wished you were someone else?'

'Er...once or twice, I suppose.'

'I wish I was someone else all the time. Say, you talk kinda funny.'

We're getting somewhere.

'It's posh South London,' I say.

'Sorry.'

'Black aristocrat. Where I come from. we're practically royalty.'

'Gee. How come?'

He appears a strange mixture of remoteness and naivety, this beautiful young man.

'Grandpa Arthur came over with the first Jamaicans to avail themselves of the British Nationality Act. On the Empire Windrush in 1948. In Brixton he was regarded as a kind of elder. I was christened Elisabeth Victoria Anne Brown. They stopped short at cramming in Boadicea. There was a tremendous reverence for all things British. My father, for example, is Winston Stanley Neville Brown. That's like calling your son Theodore Woodrow Franklin Delano Ostler. Both my parents were brought up with a rod of iron. Speaking the Queen's English was a part of it. It rubbed off on me. They're incredibly god-fearing people, too. Baptists. That didn't rub off on me, thankfully.'

'My great grandparents were emigrants, too,' he says. 'German. Stallknecht. The family changed its name to Ostler, the English homonym, during the first war. Which was a good thing. I wouldn't have liked to have been called Oberon Stallknecht.'

This is almost approaching light banter. We're starting to connect. Then he goes and ruins it.

'My mother was a very intense, religious woman, too. But she lost her faith and drank. My father was an alcoholic and believed in nothing, eventually. Not even poetry. That's maybe why they killed themselves in their different ways. I never did get to find out. Say, I'm kinda tired. Will you excuse me whilst I take a nap?'

'No problem.'

I look out the window, feigning indifference. But there *is* a problem. I'm stuck in a car, and for the next two weeks, with what would appear to be either a sociopath from a family of manic depressives, or, a compulsive liar. When I turn back, he's fast asleep.

He is, though, very beautiful and it's a long time since I slept with a really beautiful man. They're thin on the ground in these parts. And I'm not getting any younger. I feast my eyes.

He dresses well: a grey suit of light material, and tailored black shirt. The body it clothes, lean and hard, could almost be chiseled from marble. His sleeping head is twisted to one side so the sinews of his long neck stand out like Michael Angelo's David. A dense twenty-four hour stubble bristles on the square jaw and hollowed cheeks. The lips are full and the lashes long. He sleeps silently, hardly breathing. 'Let the winds of dawn that blow, softly round your dreaming head, such a day of welcome show…'

We shall see?

April 17th

A long day. The last of the late-night punters has been shepherded out the door. I'm putting my feet up in the boudoir with a glass of Pinot and leaving the WiRs to it downstairs in the bar. They're in celebratory mood. Linda's reading went down quite well with the six O'clock kiddies crowd. Ricky Roo was a big hit. A masterstroke of mine to get in that nerd from Dulwich College with the perfect *putonghua* to do a running translation. I might let him run a few errands for me as a reward. It's remarkable how slavish some of my admirers can be. I shouldn't take advantage but I do.

Donald's reading was a bit touch and go in the sense that nobody could understand much of what he said. He speaks a language which is just about recognisable as English to someone like me, whose final year thesis was The Great Vowel Shift in Early Middle English Poetry with Specific Reference to Langland (Distinction), but to your average Chinese might just as well be Hungarian. He pulls it off by being a burly, flamboyant performer, which is doubly important because, like previous BILF poets, the actual poetry, that is to say, the words on the page, don't seem to make much sense either. Sample:

NIGHT IN

pizza in the matchbox

fitbah on the telly

tin of bevvy in the hand

chaser hits the belly

party elsewhere getting louder

howling at your door

you've led your lamb to slaughter

now can you make it roar?

Make of that what you will. I won't go on. The main thing is he looks the part. The tartan shell-suit (a 'post-modern' piece of irony?) along with the bushy ginger-red beard has them all nicely on board. Bring on the kilt and sporran!

Obe hasn't read any of his stuff yet on account of it being in a suitcase, possibly in Tokyo although no one at Pudong International is really quite sure. The punters get the story behind the brochure photo mess up straight. I simply tell them what he told me at Arrivals, which they accept quite readily. They're an earnest bunch, as serious about their literature as Obe. The sweater I leant him, a couple of sizes too small, clings to the beautiful torso and has clearly given the *faggots* the wrong impression. This also helps things along and should guarantee more bums on seats in the days to come. He is remarkably patient with everyone and reads quite beautifully from a selection plucked from my shelves, giving simple and clear explanations of why he thinks it is good writing.

So, on the whole, a relief.

Then, I sense a dramatic change in the mood downstairs. Donald's voice becomes raised in anger and instead of being a sort of muffled gargle I begin to pick out the words. I won't transliterate because it's too much effort but in the Queens:

'...Your whole nation was founded on a deliberate act of genocide! You're worse than they murdering English bastards... You hunted them down like animals...'

'Calm down, Donald!' (From Linda).

A chair is tipped over.

'Donald, sit down!'

'A nation founded on murder and slavery! Land of the Free!'

A glass shatters. I rise from my divan and trip lightly down the three flights of stairs. Donald, drunk, is standing over the calmly seated Obe, snorting with fury, fists bunched at his sides. Obe smiles up at him serenely, smoking a cigarette.

'What on earth's going on?'

'Donald is telling me the truth about my country.'

'Why are you doing it so loudly, Donald? And smashing up my bar?'

'Because the patronising fascist shit insulted mine.'

'I didn't insult your country, Donald,' Obe says, lazily, smilingly. 'I just happened to say what, on balance, I believe. Namely, that Scotland was a very backward place before the Act of Union; that the Scottish Enlightenment could never have happened without it and that, in yet again seeking independence from the United Kingdom, you will not become a nation again but rather, a tiny little vassal state of the European Union.'

This smooth reiteration does nothing to calm Donald down.

'Vietnam!' he yells and points a dreadful finger. 'Chile! Nicaragua! Iraq! You're just a bunch of murdering fascist bandits! And you dare to lecture *me* about freedom!'

'I'm not lecturing you, Donald. Just saying what I think.'

What happens next, changes my whole perception of Obe. Donald lunges his considerable bulk at him. Without appearing to exert himself, Obe somehow manages to tie it in a knot and lower it to the ground with its arms pinned behind its back. This seems to calm Donald down. It's as though he's met an irresistible force against which it is useless to struggle.

April 19th

Donald is no longer speaking to Obe. This is understandable but makes the breakfast meeting a bit awkward.

Linda and Donald leave the Spartan confines of the budget hotel I booked them into and breakfast chez moi, during which, in theory, we're supposed to discuss strategy. Tomorrow is the first of Donald's two performance poetry sessions billed as a 'full frontal assault on conformity'. We've sold a lot of tickets. However, he needs to be made aware that this assault can involve most things but must stop short at any criticism of the Party. And there can be no mention of the two Ts- Tibet and Tianmen. From the depths of his hangover, I extract a grunted assurance that no such *faut pas* will be allowed to pass his lips and he stomps off with Linda in tow (I think there might be something developing there), probably in search of cheap drink from the local Family Mart. I am alone at ten in the morning, sharing coffee and croissants with this beautiful man who is wearing one of my dressing gowns. He smokes lazily whilst reading a collection of short stories by members of the Suzhou English Writers Club who will be meeting him for lunch. This is nice of him. I've never managed to get past the first page. He's quite sweet, really, whilst at the same time managing to be frightening in some hard to define way, as though the slow speaking voice and languid exterior is only just holding at bay a violent force. I do wish he'd open up about himself a bit, though. Expand a little on the occasional nuggets of personal information he allows to escape. I'm well in to my autobiographical repertoire already whereas he might just have emerged fully formed, as from an egg.

I have another go, 'Where did you learn those neat sort of *wrestling* moves?'

'I'm sorry?'

'You know: last night. The Pacification of the Scot,' I say, hinting that I may just be finding the whole Donald the Brave persona a tiny bit ridiculous. I know I'm not supposed to show bias towards my WiRs but Donald really is a bit of a dick. I mean, aren't we supposed to be People of the World these days? Haven't we moved on? If *we* have, Donald certainly hasn't.

'Oh,' says Obe, flatly. 'The military.'

'The military!?'

'I served my country. You know, some of this writing is really very good. Honest. Utterly uncontrived. I like these Chinese people. Good people. They aren't afflicted by irony. Ironists.' he says with something approaching emotion, 'I'd cut their throats if it didn't land me in jail.'

He would, too. Obe takes his writing very, very seriously. Nothing else would appear to matter. Certainly not sex. I have been wearing my most alluring outfits. Take this morning: I was up with the lark and into my made to measure, figure hugging, red silk Chinese one piece with the slits up the sides. Short of actually doing a pole dance in his face ('my hump my hump my hump…my lovely lady lumps'), it's as close as it gets to non-verbally announcing my intentions. But nothing doing so far.

'You wouldn't stay out of it for long in my country,' I say, resigned to the fact that perhaps the only way to his dick is through his head.

Time to dust off my First.

'We're the Olympic champions of irony,' I continue in Senior Common Room mode. 'It seeps into everything we say and do. It's one of the reasons I left the magazine in London and started a new life here in China. All those nasty little in jokes from middle class hacks writing for the 'proles'. I blame it on Swift.'

'He has a lot to answer for,' Obe says into the magazine, lighting another cigarette.

'A Modest Proposal kicked it all off.'

'I agree,' he says.

'That's good,' I say. 'Now we've established I'm serious about literature too, we can we go upstairs and bang each other's brains out.'

Except I don't. I must tread softly; be patient.

'Where did you get your education?' I say instead, as casually as I can into the buzzing silence that keeps settling between us like flies on a cowpat every time I stop talking. If he wasn't so beautiful and mysterious; if he was, say, Donald, I'd have emptied the coffee pot over him by now.

'I was homeschooled. I read nearly every book in my father's library. Where did you get yours?'

I tell him the prestigious name of my alma mater. Not a flicker of surprise. Most whiteys give themselves away with a momentary dilation of the pupils that says: 'you…a…went to!?' But with Obe, not a flicker.

April 20th

I witness something I've never come near to experiencing, even during my extreme youth hanging out with the uber-pretentious of St Martin's College in the mid-nineties. It comes in two parts and the upstairs auditorium is full. He might be a prat but Donald is pulling in the punters. They don't seem to pick up on these things. To accommodate the overspill, I get out the little plastic stools we normally use for the kids.

Part One consists of Donald intoning his strange words but this time to the accompaniment of some sort of lute. It meets with wholesome applause.

I turn to Obe who has been standing next to me at the back, smoking in his usual languid way.

'Quite a success.'

'Good people. Honest people,' he says. 'I like it here.'

'Thank you.'

'I like you, too.'

His hand brushes mine and I give it a squeeze. He doesn't retract. Then I trip lightly down the stairs to try and stop Donald consuming my limited selection of spirits during the short interval. He's been at it all day, and is one of those unfortunate drinkers who tip, very suddenly, over from the amiable to the aggressive. This may account for what nearly happens in Part Two.

From behind a screen which is now displaying random, faintly disturbing images, Donald emerges wearing a kind of one piece, figure hugging kiddies' romper suit with a tight-fitting hood. Certain sections of the audience may have misunderstood the intended mood. The 'piece' is billed as 'Counting Down', which has no obvious comedic undertone, in fact, if anything, comes with a slightly apocalyptic one. But such is the outlandishness of his appearance that he is greeted with more than a few titters. In front of him is a large piece of plastic sheeting taped to the floor and ringed by pots of paint of various colours. Onto this he steps and begins to make the motions of a primitive man stalking prey, whilst all the time gazing wildly around him and sniffing the air. Then, picking up a pot of red paint and examining it with convincing Neanderthal curiosity he suddenly tips it over himself. The same sections of the audience greet this with unabashed laughter of the kind you don't think Chinese people are capable of until you hear it. He carries on. Perhaps he can't hear over the noise of the piece of early Pink Floyd which functions as the soundtrack, or is too absorbed in his performance to notice. Pots of yellow and black paint are dashed over the sheeting and he begins to wallow around in the mess, making noises which I assume are meant to imitate primitive speech.

'What do you think it's all about?' I say to Obe.

'It's a verbal, visual, musical fusion of the ascent, or if you like, *descent*, of man. Donald's responding spontaneously to the images and music, creating at the same time an abstract vision in paint by using his whole body as his painting tool. The performance is designed to symbolise the oneness of primitive man with his world. The 'noble savage', if you like. The resulting finished work will be all that's left: an abstraction; a testament to man's ultimate alienation from that world, to make of what you will.'

This is said without the slightest hint of irony. He takes all creative enterprise very seriously. His workshops are conducted in an atmosphere of near priestly reverence for the written word. All offerings, so long as they contain no hint of irony or cleverness, are treated with equal respect and enthusiasm. He and Donald have a lot in common in that regard. Despite Donald's strenuous attempts to fall out with him, he refuses to be fallen out with, and has even engineered a *rapprochement* between them. They're back on speaking terms. This is a refreshing change from the bitchiness of festivals past. It's a respect that is about to be tested and cemented further.

Having done a fair bit of wallowing and intoning, using a lot of paint along the way, a 'work' of sorts is beginning to take shape. Donald stands up in the middle of it and the music stops. Then he begins to scamper about observing what he's produced so far in a dumb-show of incomprehension. Unfortunately, due to being barefoot on a now very skiddy surface he slips over, flat on his backside. This really is too much for that unsophisticated section of the audience who like a bit of slapstick with their performance art. There is volley of laughter which this time he can't ignore. He springs to his feet, the oval of face ringed by the hood twisted in rage. One of his wobblers is coming on. The fists are bunched at his sides. He's snorting. He's going to charge. This is an emergency. I'm a big, strong girl but still not up to stopping a charging Donald. As though reading my mind, Obe weaves gracefully through the now quaking audience interposing himself between it and the artist.

'It's taking shape, Donald,' he says. 'A work of art's being born. You mustn't abort it now.'

There's an awful silence during which I still think he's going to explode and Obe will have to do his wrestling moves again. Then the music kicks in; music of different kind, and he climbs back into character.

I'm beginning to think that Obe has special powers. If aliens ever do get to walk amongst us they will be like Obe.

April 21st

How to describe the events, or to be more precise, non-event, of late last night without wanting to curl up into a ball and die?

The remembrance of the hand squeeze, that feeling of his warm skin and bones held in mine with all it might promise, has me tingling as we sit nursing our nightcaps at the bar. Outside, heavy rain is drumming on the porch roof. Inside is dry and cosy, bathed in the soft red glow of the lamps I've left on. I'm wearing my red, slit pencil dress, showing a generous expanse of thigh. I'm positively drenched in Chanel Number 5. Chet Baker is oozing from the speakers. I am wittily flirtatious. Yet, nothing happens. Perhaps he is 'spoken for'? Perhaps he harbors old-fashioned notions of fidelity capable of withstanding even the blow torch of my sexual force field turned up to full blast? Perhaps he is a repressed homosexual? I really don't know. He talks so little about himself.

I take the plunge. 'Anyone special in your life back home, Obe?' I say, casually twirling at the ice in my Long Island Iced Tea. 'Are you *carrying a torch*?'

He gives one of his misty smiles.

'No.'

'Anyone carrying a torch for *you*?'

'No. No torches.'

'But you must have…someone…I mean we all have…you know… *needs*?'

'I'm a celibate.'

'Er…OK…but…isn't that a bit unfair on those who might want to make love to you…I mean…after all, you're a beautiful man?'

'I don't think so. I'm unable to have sex with women for whom I have feelings of affection. I find the two incompatible. I used to screw around. Stupid one-night stands with drunk girls. But I recognise that such behaviour is bad, so now I don't screw at all.'

I can safely say I've never been in this position before, and lose my head. 'Well, *I'm* feeling a little drunk tonight. Couldn't you relax your regime? Just for old time's sake. Ha! Ha! Ha!'

'Please, Beth,' he says. 'I like you too much. You've been kind to me. This has been the most wonderful week. I feel at home here. At peace. Please.'

April 22nd

The suitcase arrives a full week after its owner, along with the news from HQ that Zhengyu Fang has had to cancel. His visa didn't come through. This is a disaster. Zhengyu Fang is...was, our biggest name. The biggest we've had so far. His Inspector Song crime novels, set in the Beijing of the eighties and nineties have been translated into practically every language under the sun and televised in a number of countries. He's a US citizen, settled in New York, having managed to emigrate just after the Tianmen crackdown. In short, The Real Deal. He's been allowed a number of visits since the thaw but must have said something injudicious in the interim. This leaves a whopping great hole in our programme which is going to have to be filled by Obe. I'm curious as to whether his stuff might be anywhere near up to the job. So, taking advantage of one of his walkabouts (he likes to join in with the Dancing Grannies in the park down the road. He really has been bitten by the China bug. It happens that way with some Americans) I sneak a peek. Two dog eared copies of Too Good To Be True are on the floor next to the futon. I haven't got much time so I open one at random. I'm dreading finding yet another example of what I call the Creative Writing School of Writing, a style which, these days seems to plague the young. It all reads the same, like they've attended the same course that has coached them to avoid ordinary language at all costs in favour of twisting and bending it in to weird shapes. A simple sentence like 'Bill quietly crossed the room and poured himself yet another mug of hot tea' comes out as 'Tea needy Bill ghosted linoleum and brimmed a mug of steaming brew.' That sort of thing. Exhausting after a few pages. Obe's writing, thank God, isn't like that at all. It's simple, precise and reserved, without making a fetish of it. A bit like him, really.

There's also a large, loosely-assembled manuscript of what I assume is the work in progress. In the middle of a story titled Night Raid

I come across the description of a murder:

'The knife went in under the ribs and found the heart. After a slight sensation of resistance, he found himself stirring at nothing; a void. In seconds the body was still and the shocked eyes turned milky. He pulled out the knife and moved calmly on to the next room.'

April 23rd

In the evening Nelson James arrives.

Some name, some guy. His grey hair's down to his shoulders this year and he's wearing what he must think is his trendiest gear. (Skinny jeans on a what...fifty-seven year old? I think not). He's the academic from the university. As part of its 'outreach programme' and, as he puts it, 'a bit of a scribbler' himself, he collaborates yearly with the BILF by guaranteeing a full lecture hall of hungry young literary minds for our main turn. I have to break the news that Zhengyu Fang won't be that main turn.

'What do you mean, he's not coming?'

'Er...he's not coming.'

'But he can't be not coming.'

'He's not coming. His visa didn't come through. They kept him hanging on till the very last minute.'

The whole kerfuffle is almost worth it for the look on his face. Normally a grinning mask of suspect bonhomie, it collapses into the features of a man who's just been told his wife's run off with the postman. (Actually, his wife did leave him for someone else two years ago, because he's a selfish old boozer).

'Oh bollocks!' he says. 'Bollocks. Bollocks Bollocks.'

'Chill, Nelson. All is not lost.'

'Bollocks. Bollocks. Bollocks.'

'Never mind the bollocks,' I say in a moment of inspiration, showing my astonishing breadth of popular cultural knowledge, 'here's Oberon Ostler. Ha! Ha! Ha!' Obe comes through the door just on cue, refreshed from his session with the Dancing Grannies. 'Obe, I'd like you to meet Nelson James from the university's English department.'

'Hi.'

'Pleased to meet you Obe,' Nelson says, in his superior way. 'Are you here for The Festival?'

'Yes.'

'In what capacity, may I ask?'

'Writer in Residence.'

'I see. I see.'

'I don't think you *do* see, Nelson,' I say. 'But you are excused. Obe is Felicity Blaise. And he's going to be Zhengyu Fang on the 25th.'

'But Felicity Blaise is a woman.'

From behind the bar, I run through what is by now my well-rehearsed schpeel.

'I see. I see.'

'Stop saying I see, Nelson, and get yourself outside of that,' I say, handing him a bucket of Long Island Iced Tea, his preferred 'tipple' as he calls it. I notice his hand is shaking.

After a few gulps he begins to regain some composure.

'I have to confess I'm not familiar with your work,' he says to Obe, in his fruity academic's voice. 'Being a teacher of literature, I have so little time for reading.'

I hear this sub-Wildean quip every year and it doesn't get any funnier.

'That's OK. Do *you* write?' Obe says, getting jiggy with it as he likes to do.

'Oh,' says Nelson, wafting his cigarette about. 'I scribble occasionally.'

Previous WiRs have happily let the old fool off the hook at that, which is clearly what he's expecting. Not Obe.

'Have you published?'

'Published? Good heavens, no.'

'What do you write?'

'What do I write?'

'Yes, what do you write?'

(I ought to intervene but am transfixed by the long, solitary hair protruding from Nelson's left nostril. How can he not notice that?).

'Well...I suppose...er...literary fiction...so I'm told.'

'Told by whom?'

'By whom? By whom? Is this an interrogation?'

'No. I'd just like to know what it is you write and for whom. Perhaps I can help you.'

'Help me?'

'Yes, help you.'

'Why on earth would you want to do that?'

Time for the bell.

'Enough, gentlemen! To business. Do you, Oberon Ostler agree to fill in for Zhengyu Fang at Nelson James' university on the 25th April?'

'It would be an honour, as I said this morning, Beth.'

'And do you, Nelson James agree to Oberon Ostler filling in for Zhengyu Fang.'

'Well...I suppose...not much...er...choice...really...oh bollocks!'

'Fantabulosa!'

April 24th

Linda spits the dummy over having to play second fiddle to another Linda, Linda Chen, who is a much bigger fish in the world of kiddy's pic-lit than the creator of Ricky Roo. Puddy is a young panda known outside of Wollongong; of international fame, in fact. Ricky doesn't belong in the same ring. It doesn't help matters that his creator, in addition to being a Chinese-Malay, ex-beauty queen and mother of two perfectly adorable children, was also, until quite recently, married to a famous Asian actor. Puddy is, so to speak, the fruit of that highly publicised and bitterly dissolved union, Linda C cashing in by showing the world, through her adorable creation, that she isn't just another Barbie doll thrown on the scrap heap. We are incredibly lucky to have her. It has been whispered, however, that the many adventures of Puddy may not all have issued from the pen and stencil of Linda herself. In fact, Linda Werweewea goes even further, maintaining that her namesake doesn't 'know a pen from a f***ing fishing rod'. This towards the end of the packed Q and A session to all the other yummy mummies she has been unsteadily chairing. Donald, in a remarkable reversal of roles has to spirit her away before sustained damage can be done. She's fallen off the wagon as I knew she would as soon I met her. I always thought there was something a bit suspect in the rather flayed look her face has. Junkies, alcoholics, always carry the scars. Full marks to Donald, though. I think I may have been a bit harsh on him.

April 25th

Nelson, as in years gone by, is there to greet us at the front of the Uni. He sits on the plinth supporting the giant bronze statues of Confucius, Plato, Wagner and some modern Chinese poet whose name I don't know. With the skinny jeans and pointy boots, he's wearing what I call his magician's jacket, a black velvet thing with, for reasons unexplained, a broach in the shape of a beetle pinned to one of the fancy lapels.

'Looking dapper as usual, Nelson,' I say, as we make our way towards the lecture theatre.

'Most kind of you to say so, Beth. Most kind.'

'Just one eeny weeny little thing I feel I ought to point out, though. I wouldn't mention it but the press is going to be in attendance.'

'Point away. Point away.'

'You have a long grey hair protruding from your left nostril.'

'Good god! How horrid.'

'It is a bit. So...' Fishing in my bag I hand him a pair of tweezers and he dives into the foul- smelling gents (the fees are astronomical. You'd have thought they could stretch to a bit of bleach).

The theatre is beginning to fill up with eager young bookworms. Having been kept in the dark, they're still looking forward to their first glimpse of a properly famous living writer. Nelson is to conduct the interview and quickly briefs Obe on the questions he'll be asking. Obe is completely nerveless and nods with his eyes half closed in that semi-stoned way of his. At 8.p.m. sharp the lights go down and the two of them take their seats on the stage to a rustle of whispered confusion.

'Ladies and Gentleman. You may by now have gathered that the person sitting next to me is not Zhengyu Fang. For reasons beyond his control Zhengyu Fang is unable to fulfill his engagements in China at this current period in time.'

Delicately put Nelson. In place of the howls of disappointment this announcement would have elicited elsewhere, there is a knowing silence (they know they know they know).

'No. The person sitting next to me is Oberon Ostler, better known by his pen name of Felicity Blaise. Those of you who attended my lecture on George Eliot will be familiar with the device and the reasons for its employment. Oberon, or Obe, as he prefers, is the author of Too Good To Be True, a profound treatment of violence and alienation amongst the young of America's heartland which has been likened to a latter day Catcher in the Rye with which many of you will be familiar through my module on the Modern American Novel. Before we begin our discussion of your work and views on literature and writing, Obe, perhaps you'd care to give us a brief autobiographical prelude...'

I'm expecting this to be met with at best the scantiest of revelations, at worst, downright refusal, Obe being a great believer in the 'primacy of text over context' and all that. Instead, something quite astonishing happens:

'Thank you, Nelson. I was born, an only child, in Ripon, Wisconsin to alcoholic parents who, in my thirteenth year, both killed themselves. My father, Robert Ostler, was a poet, belonging to the Wisconsin Group which achieved some degree of celebrity in the early 70s. He blew his brains out with a hunting rifle shortly after my mother had gassed herself, leaving me in the charge of an aunt. She was a fine lady but I turned bad and took to dealing drugs with all the violence that came with them. Fortunately, I was never apprehended by the law and was therefore able to join the military in time to serve my country in both Afghanistan and Iraq where, as a Navy Seal, I was often engaged in combat duties and killed many people. Upon returning to civilian life I transformed my experiences into the fiction which, together with a small legacy from my father, provides me with enough money to live off and I hope to continue writing until I die.'

You can hear a pin drop. Nelson, for once, is lost for words and his face has turned that greenish colour people have when they've just stepped off a particularly sense-scrambling fairground ride they hadn't quite bargained for. I feel a little bit queasy, too.

April 27th

It's time to say goodbye. Linda and Donald are leaving on the night train to Chengdu. They are now officially an item. Donald has declared that after the festival he is taking the fight for Scottish Independence to Wollongong where he intends to live with Linda. Obe is taking tomorrow's late-morning train. He wants to have one last session with the Dancing Grannies and say goodbye. They've taken to him as he has to them, practically adopted him. In the process his Chinese has really come on.

The taxi arrives. Linda and Donald bundle themselves into the back of it. Ungenerous I know, but I can't help comparing them to a couple of bag people who've fallen in love. They've become inseparable in a way I shall never know. I'm too selfish. They and Obe are nourished by what they do and lead completely authentic lives of the kind I shall never know, either. Although I think I shall keep up the journal every year. It may provide some amusement in years to come.

We wave them off until the taxi turns the corner at the end of the street.

'Byeeeeeee!'

Then, suddenly, I'm overcome with an immense weariness and desire to be alone.

April 28th

Obe doesn't make it down to breakfast. His train's at eleven forty five and it's already nine thirty. I climb the stairs and give a polite, inquiring knock on his door. There's no reply.

"Obe,' I trill, in a cheerful, chivying way, 'it's nine thirty. Your train's at eleven forty five. Better get your skates on.'

'Obe? Speak to me Obe!'

Still no reply.

I open the door very slowly, just wide enough to poke my head round. It is my gaff, after all.

He's lying propped up on the pillows, naked except for his shorts, gazing ahead with a blissed-out smile on his face. Tears are streaming down his cheeks.

'Are you OK, Obe?'

'I have seen my life,' he says to a point on the wall about a meter above my head.

'What do you mean 'you've seen your life'?'

'I have seen my life before me and it takes place here.'

'No, it doesn't, Obe. It takes place in America. This is just an interlude.'

'No,' he says, with a hint of firmness, 'it takes place here in this country, in this city, in this bar, with good people, honest people and with you by my side.'

'This is fanciful nonsense,' I say in my sternest voice (which can be quite stern when I want it to be). 'Now get your passport and shoulder your pack, soldier.'

He springs to his feet in one fluid movement, like a flame leaping. The tears have stopped and the face is the old serene, half-dreamy one I first swooned at.

'I don't have a passport. I threw it in the canal half an hour ago.'

'You threw it in the canal! But you can't board your train without a passport, you div!'

'I know. What's a div?'

'It doesn't matter what a div is! You can't go anywhere without your passport!'

'I know.'

'Stop saying 'I know'!'

'OK,' he says, and lights a cigarette.

'Oh, Jesus wept!'

'We can work this out, Beth,' he says, snaking lazily towards me. 'It can all be worked out. You must believe in what I say.'

And the tips of his long, delicate fingers softly touch my cheek.

To Be Continued....perhaps...

THE DOGHOUSE

Penelope Wagstaff was in the habit of opening her husband's private correspondence. It was a way of getting him to notice she was there. He didn't seem to mind. Whether this was out of trust or indifference she couldn't be sure. Brian Wagstaff was not a demonstrative man. He had a long fuse. Try as she might, in over three decades of marriage she'd never succeeded in making him properly lose his temper. If only he would, then she'd have something to shake back in his face, that placid mask with its very occasional martyred look of 'haven't I given you everything you ever wanted?' But no: instead, he continued to tiptoe around her moods, her drinking, neither, she suspected, loving nor hating.

Penelope's nerves, always on the delicate side, were made worse by not having anything much to do. The boys had long since flown the nest, following their father into the City. Not that she'd been a particularly doting mother. Money had seen to that: nannies and boarding schools setting her free to peck away at charity work, gardening and a litter of abandoned correspondence courses aimed at various forms of self-improvement but never quite hitting the spot. It was as though the act of marrying Brian had both fulfilled and exhausted her capacity for serious enterprise in one fell swoop. The decision to accept his proposal was the last thing of any real consequence to have happened to her. It had been made in haste. Now, alone in the country with too much time on her hands, she was repenting at leisure and leisure, along with drink, was not in short supply.

With the drink came bitterness and the urge to blame. Old

enough now to assign herself a role in history she decided hers was to be a victim of its necessity. It was all the fault of the eighties. Had they not come along she would never have married out of her class. Too late: the world of her girlhood, of blue-blooded families on their uppers cadging favours off one another was gatecrashed by new money. Barbarians were suddenly at the gates and they had been flung open because they sought not to plunder, but to spend. In the vanguard of this Golden Horde were young men like Brian Wagstaff; men who often came from out of the North and wore vulgar off-the-peg suits. Men who not only talked about strange new things like derivatives, hedge funds and 'exponential risk but actually seemed to make money out of them as well; a great deal of money.

They met at Ascot. The young Penelope – pretty in the mannish way of upper-class girls, not overly bright but expensively finished - was fiddling at a job an uncle had procured her in Corporate Hospitality, then quite a new thing. The slightly older Brian, out on a jolly (but not very jolly), was in her charge. She made it a rule not to flirt with clients but there was something about him which touched off a kind of mothering instinct, tinged with sex. Yes, he was good looking (in a rough sort of way) with a strong, square shouldered frame. But what really set the whole thing off were the top hat and tails. Clearly rented for the occasion, they appeared to be wearing *him*, and with a certain amount of ridicule at that. He looked out of place, like a man who'd arrived at the wrong fancy dress party. She was reminded of one of the very few lines of poetry she could recall: something about silk hats on Bradford millionaires.

'What is it you do, exactly?' she said when they found themselves alone together, away from the herd and able to exchange more than semi-yelled pleasantries.

'I make money,' he said in his flat, droning Northern voice.

'Do you make a great deal?'

'Half a million, last year.'

'Baldock and Crewe must have been terribly pleased,'

'Not really,' he said. 'That's the bonus they paid *me*.'

'Golly,' mouthed Penelope over a rumble of hooves as the field flashed by in a sudden blaze of colour. She had no proper concept of money. A sufficiency had somehow always just been there without ever being referred to. Hearing it spoken of now in such blunt terms came as a shock; relieved it of its mystical quality, at the same time making it seem more necessary.

'What do *you* do? Apart from this, I mean,' he said.

'This is all I do.'

'And what do you *want* to do?'

Penelope found herself looking shyly down at the turf. She wasn't used to such directness. He seemed incapable of small talk, the kind of tittle tattle she'd been schooled in.

'I mean,' he said, gesturing towards his fellow tail-coated, top-hatted corporate fools, imposters to a man. 'You can't tell me stuffing this lot with champagne and canapes is what you *want* to do.'

'I say, isn't that a bit jolly rude.'

'It might be, but it's true.'

She was unseated. He was breaking the rules. One was not supposed to say what one meant. One was meant to say the opposite, or preferably say nothing at all in as nice and amusing a way as was possible. And how could someone so lacking in command of his appearance, be so completely assured of the truth of what came out of his mouth? She would have to take him in hand. A new and powerful urge to groom, to improve a man to whom at the same time she felt herself surrendering, swept her away. She became unguarded for the first time in her life.

'It *is* true,' she said after a long pause, kicking at the grass, still unable to look him in the eye. 'I *don't* want to do this. I'm thoroughly *sick* of it. What I *want* to do is get married like everybody else I know, be a wife and have children.'

'Thought so,' he said.

Things happened quickly after that. There was little objection. She was the youngest by far of five sisters. A happy accident, her mother said, although as she grew older Penelope wasn't so sure. The older daughters were all successfully married off in quick succession during the sixties and seventies. Her childhood seemed to have been spent entirely in bridesmaid's service to these fortunate siblings; a dizzying time of bells, bows and confetti; of engagement and wedding balls. But when *her* time came there were no longer enough eligible and solvent Mounts, Grenvilles, Fettiface Smythes to go round. They'd all been 'soaked' by Labour. The Urquhart's themselves were practically down to the family silver. They were open for business.

The meeting with Daddy had been a bit sticky, but he'd come through in the end.

'And what does your father do?'

'He drives a bus,' answered Brian, excruciatingly, 'bus' being one of those words which lent themselves so perfectly to his unreconstructed northern vowels. (She could muck about with his clothes, his hair, his table manners but she wasn't having his voice. He drew the line at talking 'posh'.)

'A bus!' said Daddy with great enthusiasm. Then, with wonderment: 'a bus, indeed. Yes, yes, of course, a bus, a bus,' followed by a frown of intense concentration.

'So, he is a bus driver.'

'That's right.'

Brian's future father-in-law nodded to himself vigorously, and carried on doing so for some time until Penelope said, 'Brian got a double First in Greats, Daddy.'

This feat of brilliance appeared as nothing beside having been born to a man capable of piloting large four-wheeled vehicles for the purpose of transporting the general public.

'Clever chap. Clever chap,' he managed, finally.

'And he's with Baldock and Crewe. They give him oodles of money just for managing theirs.'

'Actually, that's not true, Penelope,' Brian said. 'I'd been meaning to tell you.'

She looked at him in panic as if he'd been lying all along and was about to reveal that *he* drove a bus as well.

'I've been headhunted.'

The old man came to his senses. He'd spent time in Northern Borneo as some sort of Governor during the Emergency in the 'fifties.

'By Cutt's.'

The two words used in conjunction: headhunted and Cutt's, the latter denoting the nation's oldest and most snobbish merchant bank, acted like smelling salts.

'Headhunted by Cutt's, by Jove!'

'Yes. They've offered to double my bonus and thrown in options as well.'

'Baldock and Crewe paid out half a million last year, Daddy,' Penelope said, dangling the figures in front of his nose, and let basic arithmetic do the rest.

No, what major objections there had been had come from within; from the suspicion that what she was doing wasn't quite right. She was marrying out of the clan. It felt like a betrayal, one which was being enthusiastically sanctioned but a betrayal nonetheless. Then, of course, there was the name. It wasn't becoming. No one she knew was called Wagstaff. What on earth did it mean? Where had it come from? A Smith shod horses, a Cartwright mended carts. What did a Wagstaff do? Wag his staff? At what? Why? It was a ridiculous name. The night before the wedding she cried and cried.

She was on the point of bursting in to tears now. Was this another of his tarts stringing him along; another attempt at blackmail? The two envelopes, both addressed in large old-fashioned handwriting had arrived at the same time. One contained a letter - more of a statement than a letter - in the same handwriting. It read:

Dear Brian

I shall be coming to stay shortly.

Hamish

The other contained a typed document done on an old-fashioned typewriter. It appeared to be some sort of covenant:

I, Brian Wagstaff, do solemnly pledge eternal allegiance to thee, Hamish Pelham, poet, painter and genius. In so pledging I swear that such moneys, provisions and shelter I possess shall be freely laid at your disposal as long as we both shall live.

Signed on the 10th of November 1977

Brian Wagstaff

In the presence of

Hamish Pelham

The signatories had sealed the unequal pact with their thumbprints, not in ink but in blood. Penelope shuddered, wrapping her dressing gown round her as though she'd been brushed by a ghost. The paper also contained a large, riotous wine stain.

Penelope had the whole day to brood. Her husband wouldn't be back from town much before eight in the evening. Then she would confront him. But for now - banned for drink driving - she was marooned in the enormous house with only her bad nerves and this revolting document for company. For a moment she considered tearing the thing to bits but then thought better of it. It was ammunition; a way at least of claiming his attention.

Too early for drinks, she swallowed instead one of her special pills the doctor had prescribed for panic attacks. From across the fields there came the faint but inescapable noise of barking dogs. They were at it again, barking, barking all day long. She was sure those dreadful people who'd moved into The Gables were keeping kennels on the sly. She'd raised the matter at the latest Parish Council meeting but nobody seemed to take her seriously since the driving ban. People, especially young mothers with children, gave her a wide berth. The Land Rover had narrowly missed a crowded bus stop. She was in the doghouse. Brian was supposed to have had a word on her behalf, but hadn't. She'd confront him about that, too.

She woke with a start to the crunch of tyres on gravel. The room was suddenly swept with light. Somehow, twelve hours had gone by and she couldn't remember how. Hurrying to the drinks cabinet she poured herself a neat gin, drank it off in one go, mixed another large one with tonic and, before the key could be heard in the door, was curled up on the sofa apparently engrossed in a book.

'Hello, darling,' she said languidly, without rising. It was his job to stoop and plant the frigid kiss on the offered cheek. He looked tired.

'Hello, darling.'

'Hard week?'

'Disastrous.'

'How so?'

'Lost a packet on Kazakhstan and it looks as if China's going into meltdown. The market's been dumping derivatives like confetti.' He threw himself into his favourite chair. 'Any beer?'

'I'll fetch you one.'

She returned with a can of his 'bitter' and placed the two papers beside it on the coffee table.

'These arrived this morning,' she said. 'Now I know you're going to tell me it's my own fault for spying on you, darling but don't you think you owe me some kind of...'

Penelope didn't get to finish her sentence. She was shocked into silence by his face which had turned very pale and wore a curious twisted expression she'd never seen before.

*

Explanation? She wasn't having one yet. He needed to explain it all to himself again. He wanted to hug the memories, now he'd been given the excuse; to hear the echoes of his other voice, the one he'd begun to cultivate forty years ago and then killed off. He picked up the two papers and his beer and took himself off to his study, pleading 'a few odds and ends from work to tidy up before the weekend.'

Locking the door, he opened a small wall safe and took out the key to the bottom drawer of his bureau. He hadn't read the diary for years. It was too painful, being not a diary in the strict sense of the word but more a record in fond vignettes of a love so brutally terminated he'd never properly recovered. They were the sole remains of the new person love had once managed to coax out of the old one. The entries were nearly all made the day after the events described due to alcoholic incapacity. He went straight to those recording the more riotous exploits of their brief year and a half together.

10th of November 1977

Early yesterday morning we sealed our friendship for life after a second successful raid in two weeks. This was the form:

Hamish hung about the quad where the senior's common occupies two ground floor rooms tucked away in a corner and partly hidden by a great rhododendron bush. When he was sure the way was clear he began to make the loud, bellowing noises of a drunk undergraduate. Under cover of this racket I smashed the small square pane nearest to the window latch, freed it, shoved open the sash window and, climbing inside with my swag bag cleaned out the cupboards of whatever alcohol was there. This turned out to be a lot. More than even we could get through. By the time a weak winter sun was creeping over the lawn outside these dear rooms we had drunk ourselves sober. I was frying sausages on a primus stove whilst Hamish opened a bottle of the surprisingly good Burgundy the Post Grads kept.

'Brian,' he said, spearing a banger. 'You know I haven't any money.'

'You never have any money, Ham.'

'I don't mean now. I mean at all. In my account. I've spent it all and Papa, who is a brute, refuses to let me have anymore. So, I'm going to have to ask you to give me some. Either that or we rob a bank.'

'I'll give you some. I don't feel like robbing a bank today.'

'My situation is so terribly precarious. The more I have the more I simply have to spend or give away. To do otherwise would be a gross betrayal of my nature. I shall have to send myself down before the term is out and take holy orders as Mama preferred.'

I could not countenance such a thing and so proposed a pact that I share everything I have with him. Once I had typed it, we each made a small cut on the palms of our hands and clasped them together. Then, dipping our thumbs in the blood we each made our seal. It was a most affecting scene.

2nd of February 1978

Yesterday we held our first meeting of The William Etty Society in the back room of The Black Boy. It is not an agreeable pub being full of the kind of proles from whose clutches I was recently delivered by my brilliance. But the boy on the sign outside bears such a striking resemblance to Etty's The Missionary Boy that Hamish said it would be 'heretical' to convene anywhere else, despite the manifest dangers.

'We are here to drink the health of the greatest draughtsman who ever lived,' he said in his beautiful, cutting voice, momentarily stopping conversation at the bar. We were carrying, for identification purposes, a large framed print of Male Nude With A Staff. This, in proximity to Hamish himself who was wearing for the occasion a blue frock coat with matching felt hat, attracted a fair amount of attention. We ordered beer, bitter, which I am teaching him to drink. Nobody came, which was the plan. We remain a society of two and so the meagre funds granted by the college should, in theory, last much longer. That was the intention, sadly betrayed. We dined at the Waverly off oysters - which Hamish is teaching me how to eat - and roast beef with wines to match. The bill exceeded slightly the society's funds and we were unable to afford a cab back to college, taking instead a bus. Explaining that the man driving it belonged to the same profession as my father and that all last summer I had been a conductor, a 'clippy', for Bradford Corporation Transport, Hamish was enchanted and asked for a demonstration. This I duly gave, to the confusion of the passengers. Then Hamish held a collection for The Society, taking his hat round the top and bottom decks declaring that to give towards the restoration of Etty's reputation was an act of 'supreme good taste and its own reward'. We made 10p. Alighting, we found ourselves in urgent need of relief and hurried into the underground convenience opposite the stop, our favourite, where the late Victorian brick and porcelain work contains some exquisite detail. Such was our haste that we did not notice we had been followed. Our assailants were evidently of the opinion that Hamish and I were homosexuals, perhaps intent on using the convenience for purposes other than its proper design. Hamish remonstrated most politely to the contrary but to no avail and was landed a blow in the stomach. I sprang immediately to his defence and employing the brute street fighting skills I had reluctantly to acquire in the course of my unfortunate upbringing, knocked both of them down perhaps exceeding the bounds of self-defence by kicking them repeatedly in the testicles and once or twice in the teeth. And so to bed.

14th of April 1978

A big win! Funds have not been forthcoming of late and we have taken to spending the dismal afternoon hours between closing and opening time at the bookies in – until yesterday – unavailing attempts to restore a measure of dignity. Wine had vanished from our table, a privation mildly irksome to myself but to Hamish a personal disaster. The bookies is one of the few independents left and abounds in wonderful old characters whom Hamish has charmed with his tales of the turf (the Pelhams being breeders and highly respected in the racing community). Alas, this familiarity with the secrets of the turf rarely - on reflection, never - gains due financial reward, despite much scholarly consulting of the green and yellow papers. I proposed, therefore, a less strenuously considered approach, suggesting that for each of the five races we place one pound on the horse with the very highest odds. My proposal was accepted rather scornfully, Hamish conceding with 'the grace of omniscience'. The first four races saw our nags wheezing across the line some considerable time after the rest of the field. The fifth and last was another matter. About half-way through, a strident note of excitation from the commentator began to attach itself to the name of our last hope, Gala Lad. It was coming up on the rail with what appeared to be a rocket up its anus. As the final furlong approached this changed to the high-pitched ululation of a man in the throes of a violent apoplexy as Gala Lad began to pull clear of the field. Hamish fell to his knees in extravagant attitudes of prayer. There was no need for divine intervention since it was clear the beast was uncatchable and indeed streaked past the post some distance ahead to the utter disbelief of all assembled. It had won at the preposterous odds of 75-1 (perhaps not so outlandish after all since we discovered later it had only one eye). We were rich and, before the pubs opened, gave thanks to the statue of St Cuthbert in the little chapel just off Snag Lane, an appropriate object of thanksgiving, St Cuthbert having been trampled to a pulp by a troupe of horses at the command of the Emperor Valerian. Details of subsequent events are vague although the presence in my bed of a stuffed badger of remarkably similar appearance to the one occupying a glass case in The Cross Keys suggests that a minor act of felony may have taken place at some point during the course of our revels.

November 14th 1978

Yesterday was the anniversary of Etty's death and we began our commemorations early at The Black Boy, moving on to The Pheasant, The Blue Post, The Rising Sun and finally The Green Man. In each of these Hamish's panegyric to the greatest draughtsman who ever lived was received enthusiastically although contributions towards our restoration fund were meagre. By eschewing luncheon, we succeeded in achieving the state of worshipful intoxication appropriate to the occasion. Forcibly ejected from The Green Man into the chill of a gloomy November's afternoon Hamish proposed we test our devotion with a swim in the fountain pool at the centre of which, in a state of shocking disrepair stands Etty's statue. We set off, expropriating along the way a bottle of cognac from the shelves of a ghastly new supermarket. Disrobed and suitably fortified we breeched the icy waters, arms outstretched and chanting 'William William William Etty'. Then we began our swim oblivious to the cold but not, in time, to the sizeable crowd of onlookers gathered around the pool. This in turn was joined by two large policemen who began to beckon to us in an urgent and rather preoccupied fashion. Hamish rose from the waters and, like magnificent Poseidon melding with his new element into warlike Ares, confronted these petty officers of the law.

'Constables! How good of you to bear witness to our devotions. As you have observed we are engaged in a sponsored swim, the purpose of which is to raise funds for, amongst other things, the restoration of the monument you see before you in all its scandalous neglect. Perhaps you yourselves would care to make some modest contribution before we resume.'

'You're not resuming anything, Sir,' said the more punctilious of the two, 'until you can produce your licence for carrying out this activity. Failure to so do will put you in breach of the peace and you and your friend will be asked to accompany us to the station.'

'But Constable, we have no need of the services of British Rail.'

'Most amusing, Sir, but lacking in originality if I may say so.'

'We seek only to serve beauty, Constable. Have pity please.'

'If you don't want to be serving it in an overnight cell, I suggest you re-unite yourselves with whatever clothes you have and hop it.'

Returning to the bench where we had deposited our clothes, we found they were no longer there, stolen no doubt by some souvenir hunter. Fortunately, the bottle of cognac hidden in a recess of a nearby wall had not suffered the same fate. Its remaining contents saw us regain the college precincts in good spirits despite several hostile encounters along the way with the more prudish members of the general public.

*

'No,' he said across the dinner table, with as much animation as she could remember him showing for a very long time, 'it wasn't a *gay* affair. Why *is* it women always assume sex has to be at the root of everything? There was no sex. Hamish wasn't interested in sex of any kind, hetero, homo, whatever. Come to think of it, neither was I much.'

'As I found out, rather to too late, darling,' Penelope said, biting into a sausage.

'I gave you children,' he said.

'If it wasn't gay, then what on earth was it? Why do you insist on being so bloody cryptic all the time?'

She was already well down the nightly bottle of Chateau de Puilly.

'Alright,' he said, loosening the tie of his habitual reserve, 'I suppose it was a *kind* of love. For my part at least. As for Hamish, I couldn't say. He came from that class, the same lot as your lot, that don't - or didn't - show what they feel. Far too common, feelings. Keep them below stairs where they belong. All I know is we hit it off straight away in our first week there and became inseparable. It may have had something to do with opposites attracting and all that stuff. Along with us both being outsiders in our different ways. The last thing I wanted was to hang around with other scholarship boys from Rotherham, Barnsley, places like where I came from. I'd worked my balls off to get *away* from them. The thought of anything remotely connected to that old life filled me with horror. I was the opposite of homesick. Anything that reminded me of 'home' gave me the creeps. I hated the place and I hated my class. Couldn't get out of it quick enough. And Hamish despised his lot, too. Horse-faced fools, he called them. So you could say we were made for each other. We were certainly chalk and cheese. I was a clever little bastard, naturally gifted, a loner and a grafter to boot. Didn't go down too well with the bully boys on the estate. I was a grammar *toff*. Had to run a gauntlet after school. It did me a favour. I learned to give as good as I got. In a sense I literally had to fight my way out of Bradford. Once I'd succeeded, I wanted a new identity, so I could really leave it all behind. It *is* possible to do that, you know. But I couldn't do it on my own. Then Hamish came along. He was everything I was not: self-assured, a dandy, an aesthete. There was something saintly, other worldly about him, too. He used to give his money away, when he had any, to a bunch of tramps who sat on a bench opposite one of our locals. He was completely his own man and if you think about it that makes you free, or freer. The freest spirit I ever knew. So I basked in his shadow, hoping a bit of it would rub off on me. And it did.'

'What was in it for him?' Penelope said, aware that this was perhaps the longest and most earnest piece of speech she could recall him uttering since their brief courtship. She wanted him to go on. He was talking about his past. He'd always refused to do that. It was as if he didn't have one; as though he'd never been young or loved. For all practical purposes, he might have been raised by wolves.

'Hard to say. It wasn't the pleasures of slumming, if that's what you're thinking. That wouldn't have been like him at all. Slumming implies snobbery and Hamish was no snob. If anything, I was the snob. There was a bit of Jeeves and Bertie about it, that I do know. I was always getting him out of scrapes. He was like a red rag to a bull to some people. It helped me being handy with my fists. The Bradford Brawler he used to call me. And, of course, we both had a huge appetite for drink and a capacity for holding it. We found that out on the night we met.'

Penelope took another sip of hers. She had the adulterous sensation of beginning to rather fancy this other, roistering Brian his boringly sober counterpart was introducing to her. The Brian she knew had never been much of a drinker. How she would have liked someone to go head to head with over all these years. Get a bit tight together.

'Tell me about some of the things you got up to.'

'Oh, the usual undergraduate, sub-Brideshead stuff. Not interesting.'

'Try me.'

'Can't remember.'

'Surely?'

'It was nearly forty years ago.'

He was drying up on her.

'Why didn't you remain friends?'

For the second time that evening she thought she saw his face twist in pain.

'He left the university without telling me. He just vanished. I wrote to his London address but got no reply. I thought about going there, turning up on his doorstep, but bottled out. More than likely I'd have been told to piss off by some butler or footman or whatever kind of bouncer your lot used to employ to keep the oiks at bay. So, I settled down to being a brainbox again. A grafter. A first-class scholar. He did me a favour. I wouldn't have got the double first otherwise. Baldock and Crewe only went for double firsts in Greats. Without it I'd have ended up as some poxy schoolteacher or something.'

Penelope helped herself to another sausage and a dollop of mash. She had the hearty, untroubled appetite of her class. At least that hadn't deserted her, and the local supermarket did wonderful ready meals; much tastier than she could ever produce. Why bother fiddling about with pots and pans when you could just get Dali Cars to take you to Bellrose once a week for a big raid on the freezer.

'So he thinks he can just invite himself to stay and you, we, will welcome him with open arms?'

'Evidently. I told you. He's a solipsist. They need a lot of looking after.'

'But why? After all these years *why* should he suddenly want to make your acquaintance again?'

Brian knew exactly why. He had run out of money. Run through whatever inheritance he'd come into and was calling in the pact. It wouldn't strike Hamish as at all odd. Of course, he couldn't mention that to his wife. That would frighten her. It smacked too much of blackmail. There had been a problem some years back concerning one of the tarts he employed occasionally to minister to his peculiar, unhappy needs. She'd been using a hidden camera. He'd managed to bring things to a satisfactorily muted conclusion, but it had been an upsetting time for her; terrible if the boys, then at Harrow, had been dragged into it.

Instead he said, 'I should imagine he's got a bit sentimental in middle age. Happens to us all.'

'But why send that revolting document?'

'His idea of a bit of a wheeze, more than likely. He loved pranks.'

'For how long does he intend to stay? I can't share my house with a complete stranger. A drunk probably? A madman? You can't just bugger off to town for the week and leave me with him.'

'Don't worry, darling. I'm sure it won't be for long. He really is perfectly harmless. And you can always put him in The Doghouse if he turns out to have the same habits as those I remember.'

The Doghouse was the large wooden shed - more of a bungalow than a shed - they'd had built for the boys to entertain their friends from school and university when they came to stay. It had beds, a cooking stove, running water even. It hadn't been used for years.

The meal finished, Penelope lit one of her long, thin cigarettes, exhaled and exclaimed in self-congratulation, 'The Pelhams! I *do* remember them now. I was about fifteen. It would have been 1979. I remember Daddy telling me a story about how he and a friend called Teddy Pelham used to hunt wild pigs in Borneo when they were tight and that he'd been killed in a shooting accident. That would have been roughly the same time as your friend went down!'

For once, Brian felt he underestimated his wife. When it came to genealogy, she was a terrier. It was in the blood, he supposed. Their precious bloody blood. In his heart he'd known all along that Hamish had come into his inheritance and no longer needing him, Brian Wagstaff, had simply done a bunk. He had the duty of spending it which needed to be immediately discharged. Besides, he had no interest whatsoever in academic study and, once he'd inherited, no need of furtherance through the pursuit of it. He knew the upper classes lived by a separate code of feeling and that he, Brian, had no place in it. He wasn't stupid. It had been part of the attraction anyway. But they'd been so very close; inseparable. Could he not have stayed on for the sake of that friendship? Or at least kept in touch?

'You could be right,' he said. 'What does it matter now?'

Brian watched her mood brighten, as often happened at the apex of her drinking before tipping over. The sudden change was like a riptide. One minute she'd be a gaily coloured beach ball bowling along on a shore-bound wave, the next punctured and swept out to deeper, darker waters.

'I say, darling, isn't this all rather thrilling. To begin with I was frightfully upset. I thought we were dealing with a queer version of one of your tarts. Now I'm curious to meet him.'

'Don't count your chickens,' he lied. 'He might not turn up. He may simply have been in a whimsical mood. Like I said, pranks, whimsy, persiflage were what he lived by.'

'Don't you *want* to meet him again? Aren't you just that *little* bit curious?'

'Not really. Like I said, it was all silly sub-Brideshead stuff and a long time ago. Besides, he made me look a fool. I hated him after that.'

He was lying, of course. He'd tried to hate him but only succeeded in hating his class, his kind. To have hated Hamish himself would have been a betrayal of the one period in his life when he'd felt capable of love. Instead, he'd realised too late, marriage to Penelope had been a sort of oblique revenge. He'd done his little bit to fuck up their blood. They fell silent.

Then, 'Oh shut up! Shut up! Shut up!' she began to moan, scrunching up her eyes and stubbing out her cigarette, grinding and grinding until it disintegrated completely. The tide had turned.

'Shut what up?'

'Can't you hear it!?'

'Hear what?'

'The bloody barking! The bloody dogs!'

He cocked an ear pretending not to hear, carrying ever so faintly across the fields on the night air, what sounded like a pack of hounds on the scent of quarry.

'You're imagining it, darling.'

'I am not bloody imagining it!' she said in a strangulated scream. 'You said you were going to do something about it.'

'Did I?'

'Yes, you bloody well did. So, bloody well do it!'

*

He arrived on a Sunday. They were just sitting down to lunch in the big, redundant kitchen: two Bellrose ready roast dinners with all the trimmings. There was a ring on the front doorbell, insistent, slightly mad.

'I'll go,' Brian said, his heart thumping. He'd thought about little else but this moment in the two weeks since the letter arrived. It was typical of him not to have specified any date or time. He'd always held time and its keeping in haughty contempt.

On rubbery legs Brian made his way down the hallway towards the door. Through the frosted- pane he saw a tall shape, fuzzy yet instantly, shockingly, recognisable: the ghost of the only bit of his past he cared to remember was beckoning. For a moment he lost his nerve and stood fidgeting before it. Another angry summons on the buzzer pulled him together and he flung open the door.

'Ham! How are you? Long time, no...'

Except for the hair, which was silver, he appeared, in essence, not to have changed at all. He swept into the hallway with exactly the same flourish on imaginary trumpets that used to announce his entry into Brian's college rooms. Then he'd stand, as he was doing now, blinking his remarkable pale blue eyes, the bearer of momentous tidings completely forgotten. It really was as though forty years had never gone by.

'Good God. That's Etty's Incomplete Pandora,' he said finally, peering at the large framed canvas hanging in the hall which contained a number of beefy nudes, mainly female. 'Terrible daub.'

Greetings, formal salutation of any kind, had always been dispensed with.

'I'm still fond of the old bird,' Brian said, slipping as if by sorcery into his old voice. 'It came on the market so I couldn't resist.'

'Funds are forthcoming?'

'You might say so. Took a hammering in two thousand and eight but clawing my way back. I take it the reverse holds for you.'

It certainly looked to be the case. Despite the summer afternoon dozing outside in the fields, an overcoat that had seen better days was hanging off his tall, spare frame. On his feet was a pair of cheap running shoes. The long, delicate fingers of his right hand gripped a battered leather valise belonging in a TV adaptation of some tale by Somerset Maugham.

'I have been prodigal.'

'How prodigal?'

'All gone.'

Brian needed no further clarification. Hamish had never dealt in degrees.

'Come and meet my wife.'

'You have a wife?'

'Is that so extraordinary?'

'Unthinkable until now.'

'Excuse me, gents!' another voice said from the doorway. 'Sorry to butt in but I've got another fare waiting and...'

'Ah yes,' said Hamish. 'Brian, would you do the necessary. A hundred and forty-three pounds fifty I believe.'

Penelope had done her homework.

'Lord Pelham. Such a pleasure to make your acquaintance,' she said, offering her hand.

Brian noticed she'd replenished her lipstick along with her wine glass and, having already downed a number of sherries before lunch, was approaching her apex. A good job, he thought. She could be 'amusing' in such a mood to people who dealt in her kind of badinage.

Hamish wafted away his title with a dismissive flutter of his long fingers.

'Hamish, please.'

'Penny Wagstaff.'

She pronounced her married name with irony, not exactly disowning it but implying she hadn't the faintest idea how it had become attached to her.

'Lunch,' Hamish said, eying the table hungrily.

Brian remembered his ravenous appetite; the room-bound winter afternoons spent watching him shovel down platefuls of crumpets toasted on an electric bar heater. He'd been one of those tall, thin men who no matter how much they eat and drink, could never put on weight; still was by the looks of it, although Brian suspected that, these days, this had more to do with hunger than an insatiable metabolism. Although in no way suggesting despair, his cheeks had something of that famished hollowness he saw in the droves of homeless camping around London's tube stations. It occurred to him that he, Brian, on his way to and from the bank, may all this time have even been walking past the huddled shape of his lost friend. The clothes, certainly, recalled those of an earlier generation of down and outs. A shiver ran through him of that instinct to protect which had bloomed in his heart when they first met and which he'd never managed to feel again quite so tenderly; not even with his own sons.

'I'm sure Penny can have a rummage around the freezer and come up with something,' he said. 'In the meantime, can I get you a drink? Gin and vermouth if I remember rightly? When funds were forthcoming, no?'

'Water. I seldom take drink these days.'

'Doctor's orders?'

Brian received the glare of barely suppressed rage reserved for people who fouled the air with boring remarks. How often had it been directed at his nineteen-year old self until he learned not to make them? Could he, should he, be bothered to learn the rules again? They were men now, surely? Or was becoming a man simply the process of becoming dull, to be avoided at all costs; something Hamish appeared to have achieved? Apart from the hair and rather down at heel appearance, he seemed to have been untouched by life. The cheeks, although hollow, retained that excited pinkness he remembered. His movements were still crisp and eager, the voice fluting and musical. Brian felt that if he were to run his hands over that face, that body, he would be touching his past.

After a short performance of pinging and whirring on the microwave, Penelope returned with their own reheated dinners and one more for Hamish. He immediately set to. His contempt for all kinds of social convention still, Brian noted, encompassed a complete disregard of table manners. So polished in every other department, that bit of his upbringing appeared to have been ignored; perhaps considered too trivial or 'bourgeois', to merit attention. Oysters, knocked back like Russian toasts in vodka were the only comestibles he was comfortable with. Other foods were ingested with the random success of a toddler let loose with a spoon for the first time. Once finished, and if not satisfied, he'd begin on whatever remains others had left on their plates, occasionally misinterpreting a pause or a trip to the gents so Brian would return to his to find it empty and Hamish looking sweetly, innocently, guilty.

'Will you not take a little wine, Hamish? I do so hate to drink alone,' Penelope said, unfazed. The frenzied shark attack over, he was sitting wordlessly, exactly as Brian remembered, gazing into space as if focusing exclusively and with intense concentration on the process of digestion.

'For you, Penny, I shall abandon my regime,' he said, snapping out of the trance.

Brian was still in the dark as to what had imposed it. Had he kept up the same ferocious boozing for even a few years after their time together, radical cures would have become necessary. But the Hamish he remembered, had drunk for fun, not out of despair or predilection. So perhaps the fun had stopped, or the drinking itself had become a bore. He had a greater horror of boredom than of sobriety. Brian wondered how on earth they were to fill time now they no longer boozed. He remembered how quickly and hilariously the hours had flown by when they had; how completely natural it felt to spend whole days in each other's company doing nothing but booze and prank. Somewhere along the way he'd completely lost his taste for people. They bored him. He avoided, if at all possible, any kind of social event which precluded an early departure; any gathering which ran the risk of his being marooned in company. He had no real friends to speak of. How had that happened?

He needn't have worried for Penelope's sake. He was relieved to find that, as hoped, she'd fallen under his spell and was captivated by what he was saying in reply to her request that he recount 'the adventures that have resulted in this temporary problem with liquidity'. Brian even felt a pang of proprietorial angst. Hamish was *his* friend, not hers.

Of course, it was all about money. It always had been.

'... after the Madagascar fiasco, I found myself in possession of a hotel on a small Polynesian island. The terms of the lease were generous, the natives pacific to the point of docility and the climate sympathetic in the extreme. A paradise in fact, which I ran accordingly on strictly utopian principles the staff applying themselves to running the place in a manner befitting their individual talents with all profits distributed communally.

Remarkably, it turned out that no profits were forthcoming. Furthermore, in stubborn contradiction of Marx himself, the simple joy of performing their duties without being in the least compelled to do so proved to be insufficient recompense in itself. In short, I was required to resort to monetary inducement, to wit wages, in order to retain their services. Pretty soon telegrams of a rather peevish tone began to arrive from my bank. But what drove a stake through the heart of the thing was the tremendous typhoon of '97. I emerged from the cellars – still mercifully well stocked - to find myself *sans auberge* but with a twenty-year lease round my neck. So, my Man Wednesday – I found him face down in a gutter in Kota Kinabalu on that day of the week – my Man Wednesday and I took to the high seas once more...'

And so on. At intervals, Brian kept on hearing a most curious noise, as though someone else was in the room with them who couldn't be seen. It was the dry, incredulous bark of his own laughter surprising his throat. There'd been no need to worry after all.

Having drunk much more than he was used to, he retired to bed early and left them to it, pleading a crack of dawn start and a tough week ahead.

*

Before the crash they'd owned a large townhouse which, along with the villa in Antibes, had to be sold in order to straighten things out. Like pretty well all of them, he'd been caught napping: too many eggs, not enough baskets. He was left still a rich man but not *as* rich. For over two decades it really had been like picking the stuff off trees. Then, enter the age of austerity; the very public non-acceptance of fat bonuses. The top brass had to sit on the 'naughty stool' for a while. They were in the doghouse. A show of solidarity was required. He bought a studio flat in Richmond and crashed there Monday to Thursday. It was poky but handy for Heathrow and at least it meant Penelope didn't come up in person anymore. Instead, they did a weekly Skype, during the course of which, without exactly threatening suicide, she did her best to make it clear that life held no great attraction for her. Today was different.

'I've been taking down Hamish's memoirs,' she was saying in a confident, slightly matronly voice. 'We started yesterday. It was an idea that came to me over breakfast whilst he was daubing his face with marmalade. Of course, he's never written anything down in his life and can't type a word. So, he dictates to me. It comes out in this remarkable stream. We're making terrific progress.'

'Where is he now?'

'In The Doghouse.'

'You told him he had to stay there?'

'Quite the reverse. He loves it; says Uncle Tom's Cabin is the only work of fiction he ever read with pleasure and if a wooden cabin was good enough for old Uncle Tom then it was good enough for Hamish Pelham. Or something of the sort. I can't keep up some of the time but I'm learning fast.'

'Has he mentioned when he might be leaving?'

'I'm not sure he *is* leaving. He's got nowhere to go. He seems to have no family left as far as I've been able to make out. He doesn't appear to have any money either. No money *at all*. Of course, *I* can't ask him. That would be terribly rude. Didn't he say anything to you about it?'

'Not in any detail. The usual stuff about 'temporary problems with liquidity', but that could mean anything.' Brian needed to dissemble.

Too much of the truth might set her against the arrangement. He didn't want to lose him yet.

'Oh well,' she said, breezily. 'It's not so bad. Nice in a way to have someone around the place for a change. I say: the rate we're going we may have moved on to that bit of his life where you feature. Now that *will* be interesting. Very interesting. Talking of which, I can see him coming up the orchard now. It's time for our third sitting of the day. Golly, I feel quite worn out, but in a nice sort of way and I haven't had a drink all day. Got to go. Bye, darling.'

There was a noise, like a genie being sucked back into a lamp, and she was gone. Brian was left alone to ponder his own image in its little box on the screen. His worn out, puffy face which sneered at him every time he found himself alone with it: 'Money bags', it said. 'Empty money bags. Forgotten how to live you have. What's the point of you? What *is* the point of you?'

On Friday he left the office early and glided the Bentley westward through a baking summer afternoon. The Cotswolds shimmered in the heat and fluffy white clouds hung motionless in a sky of china blue. On one such afternoon he remembered Hamish trying to cure his aversion to classical music. Strapped to a chair, in the shade of a great spreading chestnut tree, he was fed white wine and strawberries whilst being made to listen to Beethoven on a portable gramophone. It hadn't worked but he got pleasantly drunk. Such images were still pin-sharp. All week, he'd found them running through his head on a loop. Perhaps the past was retrievable after all. Now Hamish was installed in The Doghouse - contentedly if Penelope was to be believed - they wouldn't have to live too much in one another's pockets. It would be like having college rooms again.

'Back early, darling,' Penelope said. She looked different, like someone who'd returned from a long summer vacation.

'Not much going on,' he said. 'Bank Holiday on Monday. Thought I'd beat the traffic. Lovely day.'

'Isn't it. Drink?'

He noticed she didn't have a glass in her hand. This again was different.

'You know, I fancy a gin and vermouth. With lots of ice.'

She returned with his drink and still nothing for herself.

'Hamish about? He hasn't been pestering you with all this *Memoirs* stuff I hope?'

'The reverse, actually. I find it all quite stimulating. Not to mention funny. We're on to preparatory school. Did you know he managed to get himself expelled from three?'

'I didn't. Like I said, we only traded in the present. The past bored him. This penchant for memorialising is new to me.'

'Why don't you pop down now? Take him a G and V. He's been painting all day. He drove us in to Bickerly and bought canvas and paint. Or rather I did.'

The Doghouse was nestled in a glade of silver birches at the end of the cherry orchard, above a deep, fast running stream that ran through the grounds. The door was open and Hamish, barefoot, stripped to the waist, what looked like an old school tie keeping up his trousers, was applying himself vigorously to a long oblong canvas that he'd nailed to the end wall. With a shock, Brian - who prided himself on his 'eye' - immediately recognised that rare thing: complete lack of affectation. The bit that was already worked up somehow managed to recall the cave paintings at Lascaux, depicting not animals but human beings engaged in whirls of activity. Yet the style was not the least bit 'primitive' and the setting distinctly modern: an underground railway station, perhaps? There was also a beautiful Chinese simplicity to the strokes. Minutes passed. Standing there in silence, watching the tall, spare figure, framed in sunlight, absorbed so completely in its task, Brian knew he was in love again. The feeling consisted simply in wanting more of the presence of the loved one; an inexplicable, nourishing hunger. At last he gave a little cough, and Hamish wheeled round, brush in hand.

'Interesting brushwork. Tang. Dunhuang school. Especially the little floating figure on the left. Am I right?'

'How very *sharp* of you, Brian. One borrows as dishonestly as one can and is rarely found out.'

Brian handed him the gin and vermouth.

'Thieving was once my besetting vice,' he went on, after smacking his lips in approval at the strength of the drink. 'Objects of beauty one simply had to possess if only for a while, returned in due course. It led to a short stretch in the Scrubs. An unfortunate misunderstanding. The owner of a rather valuable vase convinced herself that I took it for its monetary value. I have since confined myself to filching discretely from the Masters. The farther back in time the better. But you have rumbled me. I hope we can keep it our secret.'

'Have you exhibited? I've never seen you on the circuit. Unless I include your contribution to that exhibition we put together for the Etty Society.'

'Good God! 'I Thought Canaletto Was An Ice Cream Until I

Discovered The William Etty Restoration Fund Exhibition'.'

Brain gave his rare, single bark of laughter.

'You remember it!'

'My dear, Brian, I remember *everything*. I am cursed with the memory of a whole herd of elephants. That is why I prefer to live in the present. If I didn't, I'd be trampled to death in a stampede of nostalgia; or shame. Recently, though, I have become confessional. Why, I don't know. Intimations of mortality? I have certainly not merited so much life. I have been selfish and unkind to people whom I loved. I am grateful to your wife for assuming the role of confessor so uncomplainingly. Did she tell you she is taking down my memoirs?'

'She mentioned something of the sort.'

'It must be a terrible bore for her.'

'On the contrary.'

'That *is* a relief. In answer to your earlier question: no, I have never exhibited. I have not been prolific and my few completed pictures I have given away. To creditors mostly.'

'Perhaps it's time to restore *your* reputation, *a la* Etty.'

'One cannot restore something that has never been.'

'I liked your early stuff.'

'You are too kind.'

'And I like this stuff. I like it very much. I have a proposition. I'd like to commission you for a series...'

'...No, I insist. If this *menage* is going to work at all for however long it's to endure, it needs to be put on a proper footing. We can agree terms over dinner. I'd be grateful if you'd join us. Nothing fancy, you understand. Bellrose's finest. We don't stretch to oysters, I'm afraid. Oh, and on Saturday Penny and I are down for the Quiz Night at The Plough. Her thing, mainly. Gets her out of the house. We nearly always come last. Perhaps you'd like to beef us up a bit.'

*

They won. Hamish's appetite for trivia, Brian was pleased to discover, had remained undimmed. Unless absolutely unavoidable he would read nothing but newspapers and poetry. The Sun and The Times were devoured with equal voracity. Winter Sundays in College were spent in bed together, under a spreading quilt of supplements, reviews, magazines, sporting focuses. The two of them would have cleaned up, had there been quizzes back then. Funds would have been very much 'forthcoming', as they were tonight (and as quickly spent). Hamish was busy at the bar buying the whole pub drinks with the pot they'd scooped, ferrying them to tables of defeated rivals, commiserating. Volleys of laughter went off at each one he visited.

'Trailing clouds of glory do I come,' he said, returning.

'More than can be said for Brian,' Penelope snorted derisively. 'I mean, really, darling 'who is Lady Gaga?' You need to live more in the world.'

She was well watered as always but with a happiness that wasn't there before. The apex had been reached but there was no sign of the riptide. She was merrily bowling along.

It was a warm night with a full moon and the sky crammed with stars. The better to prolong it, Hamish suggested they buy a couple of bottles of wine as takeaways and walk the two miles back, tippling along the way. Brian, unusually merry, agreed and to his surprise Penelope, never much of a walker, did too.

RED FLAGS

Leaving the pub, they came across the new people at The Gables who were decanting themselves raucously into a taxi. Earlier in the evening, in a break between the Picture and the Sports round Brian had found himself queuing for drinks with the man of the house and taken the opportunity to broach the subject of his dogs' incessant barking, politely explaining that the noise was beginning to wear his wife down. The man - early-forties, flash, faux cockney, pissed (a trader perhaps, Brian knew the type well) - very impolitely pointed out that they were in the 'cantry' and that if dogs couldn't bark in the 'fackin cantry' where could they bark and that that was one of the reasons they'd bought their gaff in the 'poxy fackin cantry' in the first place. There 'was no fackin law against it, was there?' Brian politely retired, for once feeling very much on his wife's side.

The man and his wife were accompanied by a muscular youth with a bald head, wearing several rings stapled to the lobes of his ears; the son, presumably. As the taxi pulled away, he wound down the window and sticking his head out barked 'woof! woof! woof! woof!'. His mother and father found this greatly amusing.

They set off at a jaunty pace. The road cut through fields folding one in to the other in a gentle swell. Brian was puzzled to find it lurching under his feet. Completely out of practice, in trying to keep up, he'd somehow managed to get drunk; properly drunk. And it was enjoyable. He was enjoying himself. He even gave voice to a snatch of punk rock that had swum up out of nowhere.

Penelope stopped suddenly, cocking her head to one side.

'Listen,' she said, 'they're bloody well at it again. At this hour!'

Sure enough, from across the fields came the barking.

'I've got an idea,' Brian said. 'Since we're up and about and with supplies let's go and give them a taste of their own medicine. Let's go and outbark the bastards!'

'Yes! Yes! Yes! That's more like it! The Bradford Brawler returns to the ring!' Hamish cried, scenting sport. 'Let slip the dogs of war! Silence the brutes! *Avante!*'

The Gables stood alone on a parallel road a few fields away which they cut across, following a path trampled out by ramblers. The house was ringed by spiked iron railings and accessible only through a large electrically operated gate. As they approached, the barking became frenzied. The dogs, three in total, of some warlike German breed, began to hurl themselves impotently at the railings, teeth unsheathed, eyes blazing. On the count of four, Brian, Hamish and Penelope began barking and howling too. The noise was appalling. They kept it going for a full two minutes, paused for a slug of wine then started up again, louder than before. Hamish was jumping up and down in a kind of war dance, enjoying himself enormously. It was then that Brian felt something fly out of him. The sensation of relief was almost physical, as when he'd passed, quite painlessly, a recent kidney stone. He felt suddenly lighter, and enormously happy.

Lights were still on in the house. The family had only just got back. Perhaps they were on the point of going to bed. So much the better. They kept up the cacophony until two burly male figures emerged from the front door and began making their way across the lawn with a menacing tread.

'This your idea of a joke?' the father spat through the railings.

'No,' said Brian. 'It's our idea of a protest.'

'Well you better piss off or else.'

'Or else what?'

He didn't have an answer.

'It's all right, Dad, I'll sort it out,' the son said.

'I wish you would,' said Brian, ambiguously. He felt that pounding in his chest, the sudden adrenaline rush that used to precede violence. The son lumbered over to the gate, pressed some buttons and it swung open. Brian closed in on him.

'Be careful Brian,' Penelope twittered, 'he may be armed!'

'I'm warning you, Grandad,' the son said. 'Fack off or I'm gonna 'ave to give yuh a slappin'. I don't want to but...'

He didn't get to finish the sentence. Brian's right fist connected flush on his chin. There was that wonderful sound he remembered, like the splash of overripe fruit thrown to a stone floor and the son went down. Picking him up, Brian rammed his head through the railings.

'Goodnight, sweet Prince,' he said. Then, to the father, 'I'd keep them muzzled if I were you, me old cockney sparrer, or there'll be a bit more of the rough stuff coming *your* way.' For good measure, he gave the son a kick up the backside, signing off with a couple of expletives he hadn't used in conjunction for as long as he could remember.

*

The next morning Penelope appeared in Brian's bedroom carrying a breakfast tray, something she hadn't done for years. Flinging the windows wide she almost sang, 'Can you hear it!'

'Hear what, darling?'

'Silence. Beautiful silence.'

'Refreshing. I'm happy you're happy.'

She planted a kiss on his forehead, another thing she hadn't done for a very long time.

'How's your poor head?'

'My head?'

'You two put an awful lot away last night.'

'Oh, I've never suffered from hangovers.'

'Impressive.'

'I'm a dark horse, me.'

Hamish, who'd never suffered from hangovers either, was already at work when Brian surprised him with a mug of coffee. The heatwave was holding and he wore only a pair of old undershorts. There was something oriental in the way he moved with vigorous grace in front of his creation; a monk practicing Thai Chi.

'It's beautiful,' said Brian from the doorway. 'And it's alive.'

'I feel so too,' Hamish said, taking a few steps back. 'It is very rare but there are times when the canvas seems to be painting itself. A good sign.'

'You're going to be properly recognised. I shall use my contacts.'

'You are too kind.'

'It's not a question of kindness. You are an investment. It's a matter of necessity. If we're to keep doing ourselves well that is. There's another crash coming.'

Hamish quivered. Mammon was speaking through his prophet.

'A crash!' he said, hungrily. 'Like the last one?'

'Much much worse.'

'Cataclysmic!?'

'Apocalyptic. China's shot its bolt. Pretty soon it'll be calling all its assets in. Time ladies and gentlemen please, ain't you got no homes to go to? Remember that? There'll be no more assets worth speaking of, just bad debt with no one prepared to pick it up this time. It's like pass the parcel. Whatever money there is left to go round will be in the hands of those who saw it coming. This time I have. Don't breathe a word to Penny yet, but I resigned last week. I liquidated whatever stocks I had months ago. They're in gold in a vault in Switzerland. Should be enough to see us through. The world is to become very simple again. Early Medieval. There will be the rich, the poor and nothing in between. Just kings and paupers. We shall be kings.'

'Munificent kings, I hope.'

'Of course.'

'Shall we bathe, Brian?'

Forty years ago, on such a morning, they'd strolled at sunrise through fields lush with buttercups and cow parsley to the stream that drained the land behind their college, and bathed in its cool waters. The one that ran behind The Doghouse was equally deep and narrow, gliding swiftly to the Avon a mile or so downstream. From the bedroom window where she stood brushing her hair, Penelope watched the bodies of two men in middle age, drifting on their backs with the current. An eddy brought them together and, for a moment, they joined hands before spinning apart again. Then a bend in the stream took them out of sight.

STRANGE AS FOLK

Apartment 7 Floor 5

Building 32

Primorsky Boulevard

Odessa

Ukraine

20/03/2040

Dear Mr Floyd

Thank you for your kind wishes. In answer to your question: no, I am not in the least bit put out by your request that I explain why my writing career started so late and what made me start it. As someone who loiters obstinately on the fringes of the literary scene, I am always flattered that anyone should consider it worth their while to read my stuff. That someone should undertake to write a PhD thesis on it bowls me over.

To be brief, apart from the obvious reason of having led a busy life, until I reached fifty I didn't feel I had anything of particular interest to say. Then I got in with a crowd of Russians when I moved to Odessa to develop my business as it then was. They seemed to have stories coming out of their ears and I felt that I was somehow letting England down by not keeping my own end up. My first attempt to do so resulted in a sort of epiphany that sparked the whole thing off.

We live in an age of Pygmies. Of that, at least, my Odessan friends and I were in agreement. It was a theme to which we returned again and again over beer and vodka in the bar of the Londonskaya Hotel (well worth a visit if you're ever in this neck of the woods). The Six O'clock Club was the name this after-work gathering of well to do middle aged men went by. Amongst other things, it provided a mildly drunken forum for them to indulge the Russian passion for storytelling. Each had his yarn to spin of preceding generations witness to titanic struggles, appalling suffering and enduring love, until I, an Englishman, began to feel pygmy-like myself. English life, as its literature on the whole attests, does not lend itself readily to the grand narrative. Its dramatic tension lies in its parochialism, its furtiveness. Of this, it occurred to me, my own family, perhaps even myself, were near perfect *dramatis personae* with which to illustrate the point. The intricacy of a personal reminiscence, with its secrets and lies, might, I thought, act as a counterpoise to their more sweeping canvas. I had no notion of what form it might take and simply began with the earliest significant memory I possessed and let it led me from there.

It should be pointed out in my defence that I was - am not - as a rule, given to such autobiographical ramblings. However, there is a depth of seriousness to Slavic people - entirely lacking in my own countrymen – which encourages the same unguarded quality in oneself, making a weakness for the first person excusable. In their company, one could almost have been back in the Mead Hall, ancient sagas rising to the smoke-filled rafters as the cup is passed round (although the smoke was that of expensive, lightly scented Russian cigarettes and the cup, a bottle of premium quality vodka). Spoken aloud my story began to draw *me* in with its oddness, gathering in momentum, as though I were being spoken through. Once finished, as is sometimes the case when waking from an agreeable dream, I was seized by the need not to let it go. Back in my apartment, for the first time since boyhood, I began to write. Transcribed and fleshed out here in English, with only the occasional imaginative liberty taken to join up the gaps in memory, it appears stranger still; the more so with the passing of thirty-four years. Yet it is true.

It has never seen the light of day and might possess a certain scholarly, if not literary, interest. Please feel free to use it as suits your purpose. I would, furthermore, consider it an honour should you wish to continue our correspondence.

I notice that you write from Glasgow, the place in which I assume you reside. I spent many a shore-leave there in my Navy days. Not a city to be trifled with.

    Kindest regards,

    Gerry Denison

*

After lunch Uncle Ned usually spent the rest of the afternoon in his study. 'Fooling around on the airwaves' was what Aunty Mag called it when, one Sunday, at the age of six, I asked what he was doing up there. I was none the wiser. He was, my father scoffed, 'a radio ham', which left me even further in the dark since ham — his twin sister's horrible fatty version of it - was what I'd been forced to eat earlier; 'every last bit' so my mother said, before I was allowed down from the table. Why should the stuff have anything to do with radios, or my uncle for that matter? I decided to investigate.

I liked Uncle Ned and his 'funny little ways'. My parents warned he could be 'moody' on account of what happened to him in 'The War' but with me he was always a big, jolly man who never made me eat things I didn't want to eat, or scolded me for eating things I did, too fast, or with the wrong side of my fork or with my elbows sticking out. I knew he wouldn't mind and, pushing the door open slowly, poked my head into the darkened room.

'Hello Tiger!'

'What are you doing, Uncle Ned?'

'I'm having an affair,' he said, taking off his headphones.

'What's an affair?'

'It's something that makes you feel all wobbly at the knees.'

'How do you have one?'

'Come over here and I'll show you.'

His body – which always made me think of the pictures of elephants in my colouring books - filled the little box room with its rumpled bulk and the smell of the tweed suit which had clothed its six and a half feet for as long as I could remember. In front of him was a large radio with lots of knobs and dials on it, giving off a spooky green light. Beside it was a device, the like of which I'd never seen before.

'What's that thing? Is it for the ham?'

'It's a Vibroplex transmitter. Semi-automatic key. A thing of great beauty.'

'What does it do?'

'Hop aboard,' he said.

I climbed on to his lap and he put the headphones over my ears. Twisting my head upwards I got a close look at that side of his face and neck where the skin was shiny and smoother than the other. It also had an ear missing. There was just a hole with knots of skin around it. I was told never to ask why.

'Regardez et ecoutez,' he said, and pressed a little paddle type thing to the left with the knuckle of his index finger then to the right with his thumb, which sent a weight sliding along a bar. Through the headphones I heard the sound for the first time:

'dit...dah...dit...dit...dah...dit...' It went on for about half a minute whilst outside I could just hear Uncle Ned singing in the same deep-throated slowed down wonky way he'd play his gramophone jazz records at the wrong speed to make me laugh:

'After...you've ...gone...and...left...me...crying...'

'More! More! More!' I said.

'Hang on a minute, Tiger,' he said. 'Takes two to tango.'

There was a silence, then, from out of a huge nothingness, the reply: '...dit...dah...dit...dit...dah...dit...' and I pictured a little bird, lost in something vast and infinitely empty, straining to be heard.

'What's it saying?'

'After...you've...gone...there's...no...denying...' he sang in his wonky voice.

'Why can't it just say it?'

'Aha!' he cried, 'there's the rub. Tiger's hit the nail on the head.'

'Where's it coming from?'

'From The Forest of The Big Bad Bear.'

'Where's that?'

'Over there,' he said, swivelling us in his swivel chair and pointing at an imaginary horizon, 'but you can't see it because it's hidden behind a huge great iron curtain.'

'Why?'

'To tell you that would take a hundred thousand days and nights.'

'Wow, that many!'

'And then another hundred thousand.'

'Coorrr!'

'By which time we'd both be as old as the hills.'

'How old are the hills?'

'Very old. Now run along. Nuncle Ned's got to finish the song.'

I slid down the twisty banister of the staircase (one of my favourite things) and fizzed in to the lounge where the grown-ups were drinking coffee from special little cups and my sister had her face full of the bottle I would sometimes give her to stop her crying.

'How's Uncle Ned?' my mother said.

'He's having an affair,' I said.

They burst out laughing and carried on laughing for quite some time, which made me feel like I'd done something good for once.

A visit to Uncle Ned's and Aunty Mag's was to enter a world utterly at odds with our own. Theirs stood for order and hygiene ours for chaos and dirt. My father, though he had given up farming for scrap metal well before I was born, was ineradicably a man of the land. A great deal of this land somehow always managed to get into the house by way of his boots, causing my mother to wail in despair at the Sisyphean struggle with 'muck' which marriage to such a 'mucky man' had condemned her. Even at the age of six, despite her fierce efforts, I sensed our domestic standards were not quite up there with those set by the chintzy interiors my school friends inhabited when I visited for tea. And while they had nice, stroke-able animals for pets we had two slavering dogs on chains that kept noisy sentinel over the yard.

Our large, damp bungalow, which adjoined the yard, was, if my mother's protestations were to be believed, under constant threat of being overrun by the forces of anarchy that surrounded it. We lived in the shadow of a mountain of twisted metal at the top of which sat, as zany as the hats worn by the ladies to our famous local racecourse, a shifting display of disembowelled, sawn in two cars. Under this mini alp of rusting filth my mother crouched, dressed for battle in her apron and rubber gloves, repelling the invader with an assortment of brooms, mops and buckets of bleach. It was war. So was her marriage: a series of yelled engagements punctuated by tender truces. During one of the latter my little sister must have been conceived. More noise. And an ever-present string of nappies flapping on the clothesline in what passed for a garden.

Uncle Ned's and Aunty Mag's marriage, although I didn't know it at the time, was war too, but a secret, silent one. Entering the house they'd had built to order in 1952, five years before I was born, was to step in to the hush of a country church smelling of Brasso and wood polish. Rather than being used, lived in, it had the air of waiting to be used. The furniture, floors, curtains, potted plants and silverware all gleamed immaculately in anticipation of a ceremony that was indefinitely postponed. This was not entirely metaphorical since the house, quite a large one, had been built with children in mind but the children never 'arrived'. Over whose fault this was, I caught my parents arguing one evening at an age when such things were dimly beginning to make sense to me.

'She's a cold fish, is Marion,' my mother had said, in that insinuating tone she used to wind my father up. (She was right of course. There was little femininity, softness, warmth there. It was impossible to picture her and Uncle Ned embracing and laughing as my parents did after they returned from a visit to the pub.)

'Never, ever speak of my sister in such a way again,' I'd heard my father thunder back. He was extremely protective of her. They were very, almost unnaturally, close. Aunty Mag seemed to come alive in his presence, and he in hers. My mother must have felt an intruder. I'm not sure that she even liked Aunty Mag. Certainly, she never seemed properly at ease in her company. Again, as I got older, I began to realise it all had something to do with their different backgrounds. This was hinted at in an earlier response of my father's, to a typical piece of wearisome quizzing from my early boyhood period.

'Mummy, why do you call Nana Slack, 'Mam'?' I remember

asking. 'And Daddy, why do you call Nana Denison, 'Mummy'?'

'It's a question of upbringing,' came the reply.

'What's upbringing?'

'The way you're taught to behave and speak.'

'Which is better?'

'Which, do you think? You're a Denison, not a Slack, aren't you?'

My mother remained silent. Daughter of a miner and a seamstress who lived in a council house (one of the first to have been built in our town before the war), she deferred to him in all matters of an abstract nature, especially those pertaining to her own social class.

Entering Nana and Grandpa Slack's house was to trespass on a realm so devoted to order and cleanliness as to relegate even Aunty Mag's efforts to Silver on the medals podium of Olympic strivings with mop and duster, except for the fact that they could never have been entered for the same event due to Aunty Mag having someone called The Char to help her. Nana Slack's devotions, on the other hand, were unaided and took up her entire waking life. One of her favourite sayings was 'I've never stopped', prior to setting to again on the tiny interior with its Spartan collection of furniture and black leaded fireplace. Meanwhile, Grandpa Slack sat in his chair coughing up sputum from his wrecked lungs.

'Where's the joy, Beryl!?' my father would wail as he sped us away from these painful visits in the Austin. 'Where's the *life*!?'

'Don't go exaggerating in front of Gerald, Geoffrey,' my mother would peck back. But even as a very young boy I could see that he wasn't exaggerating. Nana and Grandpa Slack did not appear to take pleasure in anything. There seemed no point to them at all.

A visit to Nana Denison's, on the other hand, was pure joy. The four days we spent there every Christmas I was given the run of the rambling old, falling to pieces house and its grounds. For once, dirt and its eradication from the premises or possible incursion on to them through the agency of either me or my father ceased to be of dominating concern. The place was full of it: dust cloaked the gigantic furniture, cobwebs hung in curtains from the ceilings of arctic bedrooms; mice nibbled at the wainscoting and left their droppings everywhere. I loved it.

'Yappey Mastrisch!' Uncle Ned said, one of these Christmases when I was nine, going on ten.

'Knaythou!' I said, and began tearing at the wrapping paper which concealed a large oblong box.

The garbling and jumbling of letters and words was our private joke, our 'funny little way' of getting back at those who had overlooked, or wilfully ignored my dyslexia. Teachers were too busy or insufficiently trained to attend to it. Although unusually bright at arithmetic, and a precocious young master of the sketching pad, I was put in a group for slow learners all the same. The Slow Learners Set it was called. I was SLS. My father, who thought that any ailment could be cured by an application of willpower along with some shouting, bought me extra spelling books and then shouted at me when I filled them with semi-gibberish. It was left to Uncle Ned to diagnose and do something about my condition.

Ever since that first introduction to the mysteries of Morse, I'd taken every opportunity to badger him to let me try it for myself. This didn't take much doing. I think he actually preferred my company; had the knack of tuning in to what excites the imagination of children.

'You say it reminds you of a little bird. A lone bird, chirping out of a black forest that goes on forever and ever.'

'That's right. Maybe a thrush.'

'But I say it's a dolphin that's got separated from its family calling out across a vast ocean.' He made the clicking noise dolphins make which he then translated in a tender, quavering voice, 'is there anybody out there?...Can anybody hear me?...Mum?...Dad?...I'm still alive you know!' And his big, craggy, scarred face with its bushy eyebrows became suddenly pained and sad. I saw a tear gather at the corner of one of his extraordinarily blue eyes and race down his smoother cheek.

'Silly old Nuncle Ned. Now let's have another go shall we.'

He was infinitely patient. Operating the Vibroplex, or 'bug' as it was called, required powers of dexterity normally beyond those of a young child but he and I persevered until I could, with a painful slowness, 'dit' and 'dah' simple phrases which he would dictate, usually absolute nonsense that would have me in stitches.

'The bottomless hippopotamus boogied to a band of jumping beans...'

But the miracle was that, by transcribing the dots and dashes back into letters of the alphabet - as he encouraged me to do - I found I was forming, without the slightest effort, perfectly spelt words and, eventually, sentences. Then, when I tried to read them, by some quirk of chemistry in the brain sparked by the transliteration process, I found the letters no longer jumped about. He had discovered - whether by chance or design - a partial cure for my dyslexia.

I suspect it was by design. He was an intelligent, perhaps a brilliant, man, spoke several languages (often greeting me in Russian), and worked in a Ministry so important he was not allowed to talk about it. But to my boyhood self he was just funny Uncle Ned.

Then came the day when he announced I was ready to have a go for real. He was going to introduce me to a lady whom I was to call 'Jill' and who lived in the Forest of The Big Bad Bear. I was to introduce myself as the nephew of Jack. After some preliminary coding of his own (about twenty times the speed of mine), he placed the headphones on my head and I duly coded what I'd been told.

A pause, and then the greatest thrill of my life, 'It is a great pleasure to speak to you, Gerry...'

I was hooked.

Unwrapped, the box turned out to contain a brand-new short-wave radio and Vibroplex identical to the one Uncle Ned used. This was all my Christmases and birthdays rolled in to one. For a moment I was speechless, highly unusual for me at the time.

'Wow!' I managed, finally, then, 'wow!'

'Enough of your wowing,' my mother said. 'Say thank you properly.'

'Thank you, Uncle Ned,' I said, and he raised a forbidding palm, dismissing all notion of formal gratitude. Instead, he said, palm still raised, and instructing me to do the same,

'Repeat after me: "I, Gerald Samuel Denison... (I repeated) do solemnly swear....to conduct myself...in a manner befitting...the responsibilities conferred upon me...by the ownership of this radio...so help me Dog".'

'Edward!' Aunty Mag, snapped, cutting me off before blasphemy could pass my lips.

'Sorry, dear,' he said. She was a religious woman.

'So help me, *God*,' I said, rescuing the situation.

'That's alright then,' he said, 'because to use Morse you're supposed to have a licence, which, being the young whippersnapper you are, is out of the question, but a nod's as good as a wink to a blind man, eh, Geoff.'

My father had been watching all this with his usual humouring air, eyebrows raised over a face creased in a condescending, quizzical smile. Not being in the least clever himself, this was the mask he usually hid behind when confronted with someone who was.

'Ha ha!' it said, 'you can't get one over on me. You may think you can, but you can't.' This time, though, it betrayed something else: the tiniest trace of envy, of bitterness even, and I realised that inadvertently, Uncle Ned had eclipsed his gift to me of a bicycle, discovered earlier in Nana Denison's cellar.

'Oh, Gerald,' he'd said very matter-of-factly, 'Pop down the cellar would you and fetch up the turkey.'

A new bicycle, one with gears, was what I'd been lobbying for since the summer. It was the custom to pile our presents on the large table of what was called The Scullery, the room which Nana Denison inhabited and in which we ate and performed the usual Christmas family rituals. A bicycle was obviously too big to fit on the table but the absence in this room of something swathed in wrapping paper corresponding in size and shape to this pinnacle of my desires had got me nervous. Was I, for the first time, to be denied my Christmas wish? Was this to be another painful lesson in 'growing up', the stoical acceptance of thwarted desire being, I was given to believe ('Stop your blubbering boy and grow up!')

an essential part of this process. Not so. I harrumphed my way down into the icy cave where perishables were kept in metal containers left over from the war and there it was, although not exactly new, as I was to discover once my feverish tearing at the paper was done.

Was my father's scrap business the root cause of his refusal to employ any new object when a serviceable old one would do? Or was it this incapacity that had led to him to choose the scrap business once farming, for some mysterious reason, had ceased to be possible? Which came first, the chicken or the egg? Such reflections were immaterial to my then self, compelled as I was to defend against the mockery of my friends whatever second hand imposter of their new things I'd been given: a bandaged cricket bat so old it could have belonged to W G Grace? It had special powers! A hand-crafted catapult made out of an old paint brush? It had extra accuracy! It would be harder to explain the innate advantages of the hybrid racing bike, with its Raleigh frame, Carlton gears and suspiciously pre-war-looking brown leather seat. But it was a racing bike all the same and, for several minutes, before Uncle Ned had trumped it, my father and mother had been the most generous parents a boy could possibly wish for.

'Have to rig up a mast, though,' Uncle Ned went on. 'Shouldn't be a problem finding the wherewithal in that old rag and bone yard of yours, Geoff.'

It wasn't. Whatever my father's shortcomings may have been, pettiness and spite never figured among them and he rose magnificently to the challenge. For decades our bungalow sailed beneath the rigging of a thirty-foot high mast which gave me an almost perfect reception with which to conduct my passionate affair.

That particular Christmas was when I began to realise there was something not quite right with Uncle Ned; that his funny little ways might be a way of coping with some inner disturbance. On Boxing Day, it was our custom to take a long walk across fields our family had once farmed. Except that year, 1967, we couldn't because there was something called 'foot and mouth'. Instead we had to stick to a narrow winding road skirting the farmland. A mile or so along it an unpleasant smell came wafting towards us, slightly sweetish yet putrid, which I'd never come across before. Then, rounding a sharp bend, a great stinking pile of dead cows revealed its origin; a small mountain of them tapering at the top to which a digger was adding more from its bucket. They were not like the living cows I knew, but terrible sacks of bones with huge staring eyes and tongues protruding stiffly. It was a horrible sight and I heard my father utter a grown-up word which children should never ever utter on pain of a 'thrashing'.

'Don't look, Gerald!' my mother cried feebly and far too late. It was indeed a scene not made for children's eyes and it has stuck in my mind ever since but, horrible though it was, Uncle Ned's reaction seemed out of all proportion. They were, after all, only cows, but in the face of them he stood still, quivering slightly as if a mild electric current was being passed through him. The quivering turned to shaking and he let out a prolonged, low moan. Then he turned and set off back down the road at a jog trot, still moaning.

'Ned!' my father cried, as if to a runaway horse. 'Come back, Ned! Think of Marion, for God's sake!'

'Let him go!' Aunty Mag trilled in a dramatic quaver, herself starting to shake. 'God, I can't take it anymore. I really don't know if I can take anymore.' And she began to sob. My father put his meaty scrap man's arm around her shoulder.

'It's alright, Marion. It's alright.'

Then Aunty Mag shrieked a string of words so out of bounds to children as to turn her, in my eyes, into a witch.

'It'll be _____ Belsen! All I get is _____ Belsen! All I've ever had is _____ Belsen. And that _____ Ministry that owns him. Belsen and cloaks and daggers and secrets and lies! Why the hell couldn't I have married John!? We were so right for each other John and I. _____ religion! Instead I married a man not right in the head. But how was I to know, Geoffrey? How was I to knoooowwwww!?' And she buried her head in my father's chest, howling like my sister did when I'd done something unpleasant to her.

The true import of the words of course meant nothing to me. But I remember how foreign and exotic the word Belsen sounded to my ears. That, and the revelation that my Uncle John – she couldn't have meant anyone else - might possibly have once been associated in some romantic capacity with Aunty Mag. I noticed my mother was smiling to herself, as though hugging a secret. When we got back, she explained that Uncle Ned would be having one of his 'migraines' and I should not disturb him on any account.

Uncle John was my Godfather. He still farmed. In fact, his farm was the largest around, the Cecil's having taken over the Denison's tenancy when Grandpa Denison died suddenly in 1947 and, for reasons never explained, my own father was not allowed to take it on. All I was permitted to know was that Uncle John had behaved 'very decently,' and allowed Nana Denison to stay on in Brackley House, which came with the tenancy. To make ends meet, she was obliged to take in lodgers. Brackley, as my father always referred to it, was so big that these lodgers - a total of three and always single men - were seldom seen, appearing unexpectedly, ghostlike, in passageways and, like ghosts, wordlessly vanishing into their rooms. I recall one of them had the same name – Heath - as the British prime minister who, to the general approval of all but Uncle Ned, had come to office not long before my fourteenth birthday. By this time, the whiff of mystery (possibly even scandal!) that clung to our family history had begun to arouse the teenage sleuth in me.

I had blundered once as a child and been frightened off, 'Daddy, why did Grandpa Denison die? Was he killed?'

'Shut up, Gerald!' my mother had snapped in her panicky voice from the front of the Austin. (Most of my quizzing seemed to go on in the car.)

But, as I began to acquire a fledgling intellect to go with the fluffy down on my cheeks, this wall of silence became something I was determined to breech. Not being a real uncle, merely my father's oldest friend, Uncle John was the obvious weak spot. He drank a lot. Perhaps, if I was sufficiently cunning, I might winkle something out of him one Sunday when he came round after a few post-Mass whiskeys at the Barley Mow.

Sundays at Brackley were proper, church-going Sundays. This was alright by me because, recently confirmed, I was going through a spasm of piety. To get my full money's worth I would even attend eight o'clock communion before we set off in the Austin, arriving just in time to pick up Nana Denison and ferry her to the one that took place in Brackley village Church at the more humane hour of ten-thirty. There she would be, rain or shine, at the end of the drive, wearing one of her floppy homemade hats. Tall, big boned, with a long, strong, bony face, she was a formidable lady, belting out the hymns in her music hall falsetto. She was also an accomplished organist, sometimes filling in when the occasion demanded.

An organ, late Victorian with an array of stoppers and two candelabras fixed at either end, sat in the corner of The Scullery.

'Give us a tune, Fay!' Uncle John would yell (she was profoundly deaf by then as well as partially blind). 'One of the good old ones.'

'Nay, John. I've not got the bellows for it anymore.'

'Rubbish, Fay!'

'Nay, John.'

But soon the room would be loud with Berlington Bertie; Who Were You With Last Night; There Was I Waiting At The Church.

Uncle Ned rarely joined in. His famous migraines seemed to have got worse and more frequent. Sometimes he didn't come to Brackley at all. Aunty Mag would arrive shockingly alone at the wheel of the Hillman Minx and my spirits would sink. There would be no Morse talk. No swapping of frequencies. There was a large globe in The Scullery and it thrilled me, on the occasions he was free of migraine, to point out to him the cities I'd visited on the airwaves. Vilnius. Tirana. Gdansk.

'Very interesting,' he'd say, stroking his chin. '*Very* interesting.'

'They're 'iron curtain,' right, Uncle Ned?'

'Indeed, they are.'

'Russian sphere of influence, right?'

'Very much so.'

'In The Forest of The Big Bad Bear.'

'Your memory does you credit.'

Cured of my dyslexia, spy novels were now my thing. When I wasn't actually devouring them, I was picturing myself brilliantly wrong-footing the dastardly agents of communist evil. I even began one myself. It had my Scout Master as head of a Soviet ring. I showed it to Uncle Ned.

'Tops,' he said, handing it back. 'Dib Dib to the power of ten.'

He was lying. I had taken the precaution of very lightly gluing a couple of pages of the notebook together and they were still stuck. I had even managed to outwit Uncle Ned, who I had begun to imagine as a master spy himself. On which side, I was still undecided. A rather lonely boy, I began to live increasingly in the web of fantasy I wove round a world which seemed intent on persecuting me wherever I turned.

The problem was that I was misplaced. It was all to do with my father's insistence on upbringing. He wasn't able to send me to the kind of minor public school he himself had attended in palmier days when Grandpa Denison must have been a prosperous gentleman farmer like my Uncle John. It didn't take much to work out that we weren't, and were never going to be, rolling in money. The fact was loudly proclaimed during my parent's almost nightly rows which my sister and I were not supposed to hear. The Yard, as the business was referred to, always seemed to be struggling. There was even mention of having to get rid of Tom and Will, The Hands, leaving my father to do 'the heavy stuff' himself.

None of this would have been a problem had I been left to assume the broad regional accent of my school fellows at the local grammar. But my upbringing, rigorous and unstinting, had branded me with a voice and manner of speaking that could have passed muster at Eton. Consequently, I was a 'snob'. Throw in an aversion to games, coupled with a rather detached, dreamy nature, and I was even a 'poofter'. The name Gerald didn't help matters either with the Kevs and Keiths, the Steves and Daves who bossed the corridors. It all had the effect of turning me further in on myself; of cultivating a stance of Gerald *contra mundum*.

And it was all Grandpa Denison's fault! His death and its shattering aftermath also clearly had something to do with the unlikely coming together of my parents. How else to explain it? By now, living up to the accusations levelled against me, I was busy *becoming* a snob, imbuing myself with the archaisms of English social class. Why on earth had my father chosen to marry so blatantly out of his own, causing me, his son, to be marooned on this island of his still-lingering pretensions? I began to work it out for myself, since clearly no one else was going to fill me in.

He was a proud, fiercely independent man and could never have worked in an office. Was it that he simply needed a good solid woman who saw nothing lowering in scrap? It was hard to imagine the rather grand ladies of Uncle John and Aunty Megan's County Set embracing, as my mother had, the life of a not overly prosperous scrap merchant. But surely, there must have been one or two eligible debs left on the shelf whose family money might have eased his mysterious falll; kept him in a manner befitting his own upbringing? Or had he simply been as 'pig headed' as my mother claimed he was, turning his back on them to marry her, out of reckless spite (the thought they may actually have loved each other was too preposterous and embarrassing to consider)? Or was it that he had been left with no choice: some terrible scandal surrounding Grandpa Denison's death placing the son beyond the marital pale? I had to know.

On one such musing Sunday, Uncle John was particularly 'merry' and I decided to seize my chance. His ruddy, good humoured face was verging on crimson and the veins stood out more than ever on his slightly bulbous nose. As usual, he stood with his back to the coal fire that heated The Scullery (and the groaning water boiler from which a scalding trickle would emerge in the tub of the arctic bathroom on my rare bath nights). He was wearing his Sunday best and his special tie. This was patterned with exactly fifty identical, tiny depictions of a Lancaster bomber.

It had been my father's job to explain that Uncle John was a 'War Hero'. The fifty bombers represented the fifty missions he had flown. Such was the extreme danger that the chances of surviving twenty-five sorties were three to one. By the time he got to fifty he was supposed to have been dead several times over and was the only surviving member of his original squadron.

'Wow!'

'I'm not entirely sure whether 'wow' is appropriate or respectful of his deceased comrades, but yes, it was an exceptional feat of courage aided by enormous dollops of luck.'

What he didn't tell me, which I later deduced, was that it was also aided by a lot of whiskey and that he had become an alcoholic in the process.

Nevertheless, my father was in awe of Uncle John and his war record. Born in 1921 he'd gone through the 'whole shebang' whereas my father, born three years later just caught the 'tail end of it.' I brought all my formidable powers of deduction to bear.

'But you were nineteen by 1943, Daddy. That was before D-Day.

Why weren't you on the beaches?' I said. (I was a prig as well as a snob.)

'I have Grandpa to thank for that. He went through the whole of the first show. He knew there was nothing 'dulce et decorum' in getting blown to bits. Of course, I wanted to join up as a private as soon as possible and have a crack at Jerry but he calculated that going for a commission would buy me precious time. He was right. I just missed the landings. We were eventually posted to what became Yugoslavia to mop up Jerry deserters and keep the Jug commies and partisans from shooting each other up. Not without its hazards but not the sharp end either. Thank Grandpa you're here.'

I didn't thank him at all. It smacked to my Boys Own mind of shirking. And anyway, I was never sure how genuinely felt these sentiments of his were. I detected a sense of inferiority emanating from him when the subject of the war came up amongst his contemporaries. On such occasions he was quiet, deferential, something which diminished him in my eyes. No boy likes to see or feel his father diminished. And it was all Grandpa Denison's fault, again! How could that matinee idol in officer's uniform staring blithely down at us from his regimental photo on the bookshelf have cocked things up so spectacularly?

Whereas Uncle John had had a 'good war' in his way, Uncle Ned, some seven years older than him still, had had a bad one. Again, it was left to my father to explain what had been 'bad' about it. By now I was too old to be told to shut up.

'Ned had a shocker. Lot of cloak and dagger stuff in France in the very early days. Spoke excellent French, Ned, and got parachuted in to help the Resistance. In exactly what capacity, I don't honestly know. He doesn't like to go on about it. It's all a bit vague - like the section of the ministry he works for - but from what we can gather there was some mix up and he had to cut and run leaving several Frenchies to the tender mercies of the Gestapo. I think it rather preyed on his mind. He may have lost his nerve. Who's to tell with a highly-strung chap like Ned? Anyway, he changed tack and got a commission in the 11th Armoured Division. Tanks. Challengers. Tommy Cookers is what Jerry called them. They certainly made a pretty good job of cooking Ned. But at least he managed to get out before his went up. Not so the rest of his crew, apparently. That was in Normandy. Anyway, he got himself patched up – after a fashion as you see – rejoined his outfit and helped spearhead the drive into Northern Germany. Liberated Belsen. Not a pleasant thing to have had to have done. I think it's stayed with him ever since. Understandable. Those images. Appallling. Bastards. Absolute bastards!'

I was now allowed to hear (but not use) certain swear words as part of what he must have considered an appropriately staggered induction into manhood. A glass of wine, on its rare appearance at table, was also allowed me. That Sunday was one such occasion. Uncle John was often in the habit of turning up just as we'd sit down to one of Grandma Denison's erratically cooked lunches, his own domestic arrangements being 'somewhat bohemian' in Aunty Mag's words. 'Banquo's Ghost,' as she called him on this and every other lunch sabotaging visit, held forth merrily from his place in front of the fire, feet splayed, whisky glass in hand, as we gnawed at near raw joints of beef. As a Catholic, he liked to poke gentle fun at my grandmother's past dabbling in spiritualism, a short-lived consequence of her sudden bereavement.

'Been in touch with any spooks lately, Fay!?' He'd yell.

'I'll spook you, John Cecil! I'll spook you so help me I will, you

Papist renegade!'

'Haw! Haw! Haw!'

Could their religious differences have been the cause of Uncle John's and Aunty Mag's thwarted romance? Or was it again something to do with my dead grandfather? I was determined more than ever to get to the bottom of the matter once and for all.

I waited until lunch was over. Uncle John, as was the custom on his particularly 'merry days', was taking a nap on a divan in the lounge. This was urged upon him since there was considerable worry about his being able to drive his 'jallopy' in an acceptable fashion now that something called The Breathalyser had been introduced. After what was considered a sufficiently sobering period had elapsed Aunty Mag dispatched me with a mug of strong black coffee to wake him up. The lounge was a grand room with a grand piano in it that Grandma Denison would play on the rare occasions she would receive guests. Being hardly ever used, it always seemed exceptionally cold even by Brackley's polar standards. Uncle John was oblivious to this arctic blast as he lay on his back on the divan snoring like a Titan.

Waking this bear of a man always filled me with dread. After prolonged prodding the bloodshot eyes would suddenly fly open and cast around the room in confused horror, before he got his bearings back. Once he had even shouted 'Bail! Bail! Bail!'. This particular awakening was comparatively gentle.

'Coffee, Uncle John.'

'Thanks, old man. Must have dropped off. How long have I been out?'

'About an hour and a half.'

'Good god!'

He was still 'merry', I could tell.

'Pass me my pipe, there's a good chap.'

Pretty soon a convivial fug was building up between us, Godfather and Godson enjoying a close moment (although I always suspected I was something of a disappointment to him, his own sons being rugger playing types).

'Uncle John, you know earlier you were ribbing Grandma about the spooks.'

'And rightly so, the silly dear woman.'

'That's spiritualism, right?'

'Nothing spiritual about it, old son. A bunch of loonies shoving a glass around a board isn't going to bring anyone back. Understandable though, under the circumstances, God bless her. I think she went a bit off her head for a while, Sam popping off so suddenly.'

'How *did* he go, Uncle John? Was it an accident or was it…did he…'

Before I could get it out his eyes went dead. He stopped being Uncle John and became a man, full of the sort of cold contempt men can reserve for other men who've let them down. The look told me he knew full well that I had tried to catch him out in his cups; that in doing so I had betrayed the deference the boy owes to the man and, in effect, could no longer to be trusted. That look was the first real stamp on my passport to adulthood. The second was Uncle Ned's vanishing.

The news, or, rather, the fact, was postponed and then eventually fed to me with the usual obfuscations. His increasingly frequent absences from the Brackley Sunday, I was used to. I myself, now considered old enough to be left alone in the bungalow without burning it down, was allowed not to attend from time to time. Increasing piles of homework to get through as the school leaving exams approached excused' me. But I did miss Uncle Ned's company. He had been the first to talk to me as something other than a boy. My passion for Morsing had proved to be a lasting one. It had not gone the way of my other enthusiasms: God; good deeds, spy novels. The thrill of trawling in the lives of total strangers from exotic, forbidden places; the sense of exclusivity the skill conferred, remained as strong as ever. Before he vanished, we had also begun to talk about politics, a fresh interest of mine inspired by the spectre of economic and social collapse that was stalking the land. My own were, predictably, dictated by an indignant awareness that there was something not quite right with the way the world was ordered, a sentiment robustly ignored by my father but shared by Uncle Ned. With his usual patience, and lack of condescension he'd begun to explain why things were as they were and how they might be different. I had come to rely on his intelligence as a bolster to mine and then suddenly he wasn't there anymore.

'Uncle Ned not coming *again*,' I said one compulsory Sunday, slouching against the organ and stroking one of its candelabras.

'I'm afraid Aunty Mag's got something to tell you, Gerald.'

'You're *afraid*, Daddy?'

'Oh for heaven's sake, will you stop poncing around like that and grow up a bit!'

Growing up was now roughly synonymous with behaving like my father, something I found myself unable to do. I had become cleverer than him. We were growing apart, and, no longer able to shout me back into line, he was at a loss how to deal with me.

Aunty Mag lit another of her long thin cigarettes, took a sip of the drink that never seemed to be out of her hand and said in her taught, theatrical voice, 'Edward's had to go away.'

'Go away?' I said, the lounging aesthete deserting me.

'That's right, go away.'

'You mean he's...you've...'

'Gerald!' my mother trilled in horror from across the room.

'It's quite alright, Beryl,' Aunty Mag continued through her brave, bright, stiff smile, 'Gerald's old enough and perfectly within his rights to ask such things. Let's face it, pretty well everyone else has. But, in answer to your question, no, he hasn't left me. Neither have I left him. Not in the conventional sense, anyway.'

I stood gawping. This was a considerable speeding up of my induction. Especially coming from Aunty Mag, whose halo my father had been polishing all these years.

'You do know Edward's not been well for quite some years now. His funny little ways – you remember - got worse and there comes a time when a person like that needs looking after with more care than a wife can give. So he's gone to a place where he can rest, so that I can rest, too.'

'You mean an asy...'

'Gerald!'

'Of course, in time, you'll be able to visit but for the moment we think it best he's left alone. I'm so sorry, Gerald. I know how fond of Edward you are. I'll keep on keeping you posted,' she said with a near hysterical brightness, 'don't you worry.'

But I never did get to visit. There was never any intention that I should. And she never did keep me posted.

Grandma Denison died a year and bit after the announcement. Brackley was sold. My father made unavailing attempts at persuading Uncle John to keep it on. Some scheme to turn it in to a guest house was proposed but by this time even Uncle John was short of money. His drinking was worse and his heart was no longer in farming. His own sons showed no inclination to follow him into the fields. I think that he never properly recovered from having to put his herd down in '67. So, the house was sold along with practically all its contents. The only thing my father kept was the organ that stood in the hall of our bungalow, un-played, its ornate grandeur a painful rebuke of his own shrunken circumstances.

In reality, we had always been an ordinary family, just getting by like most families but as long as Grandma Denison had reigned over Brackley it was possible to believe otherwise; to believe in a mythical past of entitlement; the nobility of land, of old blood. With her death, the myth vanished and we became authentically ordinary. My father never got over it. I took leave from Naval College to help him with clearing out the house. On the day we finished, just before we left it for good, I surprised him, standing alone in the bare scullery. He was crying, his shoulders heaving and tears streaming down his face. I had never seen him cry before and I crept away.

The choice of a Naval career may seem odd in one who had spent his adolescence in open rebellion against order and cleanliness. I had been on the side of Brackley and its tipsy championing of genteel decay; of dust and cobwebs over spit and polish. True, it was a shock to me at first that there existed gradations of order and polishing which would have held even Grandma Slack in awe. But pretty quickly, like the rest of my cohort, my bed linen resembled an exercise in advanced origami. The buttons of my crisp white tunic were a blaze of polished brass and my black boots dazzled the sun.

Looking back, I didn't have much choice. The Navy chose me. Although widely read, I was neither 'arty' nor particularly technically inclined and had no real taste for academic study. University would have been pointless, a waste of three years, but the prospect of going to work in a bank or an office was equally distasteful. And there was absolutely no question of following my father in to the 'Yard'. I had made that abundantly clear. A romantic streak coupled with my roving of the airwaves, had, however, bred a healthy restlessness and general longing to 'get away'; to explore the vastness of the world as quickly and intensively as I could. The Navy seemed the obvious, indeed the only, way to do this.

The decision came as a shock to my father, accustomed as he was to having a human sloth as the fruit of his loins. Then something like joy came over him. I had reawakened his own romantic muse. To have a son roaming the high seas in Her Majesty's service was not ordinary. It was not ordinary at all. The Denisons were becoming extraordinary again. Of course, my mother was horrified, but was roared down.

I breezed through the various entrance exams. My proficiency in Morse all but humbled my instructors. I held, in no time, the rank of Sub-lieutenant on a vessel called, oddly enough (it was the nickname the few friends my father had called him by), HMS Ironsides. The world was duly seen and I became a man.

Christmases were more often than not spent riding at anchor in tantalising sight of land or drinking in such ports – Colombo; Djibouti;

Valparaiso – as proximity permitted. On board, ships company Church Parade on Christmas Day was a compulsory affair, as had been my attendance at communion in the latter Brackley days although by now, whatever vestiges of religious belief may have clung to me then, had completely vanished. This made attendance at Aunty Mag's preferred Church on the Christmas morning of 1983 something of a chore. That year we were dry docked and given a whole week's leave. I was informed in my mother's neat, schoolgirl writing, that much of it was to be spent at The Morgue - our little joke (... 'I know this will not be to your liking, you being all grown up now, but Daddy is so looking forward to us all being together again just like in the old days at Brackley'...).

Letters from my father, bluff and hearty, had done nothing to prepare me for Aunty Mag's decline. I had not seen her for over three years and the change was shocking. By now myself a young veteran of the grape and grain I took in immediately the extent of her devotion to them. Her voice, crisp and theatrical as always slalomed tunelessly through the carols, badly out of tempo. On Boxing Day, the time-honoured turkey soup came seasoned with sugar. Through a fierce, Maori Warrior-like bulging of his eyes my father managed silently to communicate that nothing must be said, although my sister couldn't suppress a fit of the giggles and had to leave the table. The brisk afternoon walk was eschewed in preference for liqueurs' but my father declared eventually that he had to 'get some air'. The house, as always, was terribly overheated, and for once he had no difficulty in persuading my mother and sister to accompany him on this tedious route march. I was to stay behind and keep Aunty Mag company. So, tipsily pouring us two enormous brandies she sat down to field the inquiry that she must have known was coming. After ten minutes or so of trivial banter I decided I'd had enough.

'Look, Aunty Mag, how *is* Uncle Ned? I mean, how *is* Uncle Ned *really*?'

'Oh, much the same, Gerald. Much the same.'

'Now look,' I said again in a no-nonsense, I want to get to the bottom of this once and for all voice, 'I don't think it's fair that I should be kept in the dark like this. I was very fond of him as you know. I often think of him. I can understand your reluctance to give me the details when it all just happened. It must have been very raw and I was very young. Daddy's obviously taken some kind of vow of silence, too. But I'm a big boy now. You can tell me.'

The bright, tense, brave little smile that used once to hold her whole being erect and together was no longer there. Without it, she slumped in her armchair like a puppet on slackened strings. But her diction was as cut glass as ever.

'You want me to tell you exactly how loony he is?'

'I suppose, if you put it like that, yes.'

'Do you think it matters? He's a bit loony? He's very loony? Loony's loony.'

'But can he come back? Is there any possibility of him coming back?'

'I shouldn't imagine so.'

'Where, exactly, is he...he being kept? I should, if at all possible, like to visit. Perhaps before I take ship again. I've got a hire car.'

'I would strongly advise against that,' she said, lighting up again and closing one eye against the rising stream of smoke. This made her look sly and mannish. 'Besides, the ministry doesn't take kindly to visitors. Can't have any old Tom, Dick or Harry just popping by to have a chat, not in Edward's state. You never know what might slip out. What *do* you do when one of your top decoders goes doolally? Better not ask. Mum's the word. Don't forget, they're keeping my ship afloat as well, if only just above the water line,' she said, gesturing at the room with its faded velvet curtains and chair covers. 'If you'll pardon the nautical expression, Captain.'

'Was he always...unstable? I mean to say, you did *marry* him, Aunty Mag. There must have been some...feeling...attraction.'

'What an awful lot of questions.'

I ploughed on. 'Which deserve answers. Honest answers. This family's been lying to itself for too long.'

'I didn't love him, no,' she said, suddenly, and with the kind of resolution, finality, normally reserved for conveying precisely the opposite sentiment. 'I loved John. It's very possible John loved me. We grew up together, John and I. Played in the fields as children. Attended the same balls. During the war it was me he would write to with his real, his private feelings. It was me who shared his grief at the loss of all those pals of his, all those lovely young men cut off in their prime. But he was Catholic, see. The Cecils were Catholics, an old Catholic family, unbroken, going back centuries. They would never have allowed it; would have cut him off. And then along came Megan. Of impeccable Catholic stock, our Megan.' She laughed, drily, wheezily. 'And not short of a shekel either.'

Now she'd got going, it all came out with astonishing directness and speed.

'John was never the same after the war, anyway. None of them were who'd been properly on the sharp end. Today there'd be battalions of psychiatrists and wot not to help them over it but back then it was left to good old English stiff upper lip. Edward, to begin with, seemed to have that in spades. And he was a *man*. It wasn't quite as bad as after the first war, but there *was* a distinct shortage of eligible bachelors around and I wasn't getting any younger. When the ministry moved his bit of it out to our part of the sticks, he must have wondered what he'd done to deserve it. He'd had a shocking time and then he finds himself in a small market town in the shires with a bunch of yokels. Brackley must have appeared positively *beau monde*. So, I suppose we were both grateful for each other's company. But it wasn't love and never became so.'

It was my turn to flinch from honesty. There must be pockets of ignorance, of untruth, left in our lives for life itself to be bearable. I was grateful for the brandy.

'Courting was agreeable enough and he was perfectly honest about the extent of his burns. That was never an issue between us. There was no incapacity, you understand, but after we were married, I can't pretend the whole business filled me with relish. And then, of course, there were the nightmares and the sudden and vicious bouts of depression that would come completely out of the blue. It's only when you begin to live together that these things announce themselves and then it's too late. I used to believe that it would get better: the healing balm of time and all that guff. But there are some things, which, to people of heightened sensibility – and Edward was not a man of ordinary mental powers, which often comes at a price - ...which are...must be... so devastatingly horrible to have witnessed that the horror just enters their soul forever. His Division was the first to enter Belsen, as you know. He would talk about it once he was sure I was prepared to listen but he could never find sufficient words for it to properly come out. Talking didn't really help at all. And bear in mind that Belsen came on top of his earlier failure to save his Resistance comrades. I doubt if he could actually have done anything to save them. It certainly wasn't his fault that his cover had been blown. But he regarded saving his own skin as a kind of betrayal. And, of course, one shouldn't forget the small matter of watching, hearing, your best pals being burned to a crisp before being blown to bits. Poor Edward. Poor John. Poor the lot of them.'

She seemed now to be tiring with the effort of it all and I saw my chance slipping away.

'All the same, Aunty Mag, he must have been a bit of a catch, no? You were married in '48. It was '47 when Grandpa Denison died and everything changed. Uncle Ned was an outsider. Someone not particularly put off by his suicide...the scandal surrounding it.'

Again, as had occurred many years before with Uncle John, I had miscalculated; misjudged the power of the heavy drinker's code of honour towards the most sacred parts of his or her sober self. Aunty Mag gave another of her dry, wheezy laughs.

'That was very naughty of you, Gerald. Very naughty of you indeed to think you could catch your Aunty Mag napping like that. No, it was *not* suicide, if you *must* know, although suicide might have been preferable. But I owe it to your father not to tell. If it is to come from anyone it must come from him. And now, if you don't mind, I should like to have a little doze.'

There was nothing on the television except the usual overblown Christmas specials and tired old comics trying too hard to make people laugh. I went upstairs to have a look around the empty rooms I used to squirrel myself away in as a boy. More than ever the house felt entirely pointless, with un-sat on chairs, un-viewed pictures, all in the same place they had been for decades, frozen in time. The door to Uncle Ned's study was not locked. There was his short-wave radio, his Vibroplex Semiautomatic and headphones. The sight of them, exhibited like pieces in some dusty corner of a provincial museum, filled me with an awful sadness at the loss of such a fine mind; at the loss of all the things I never got to say to him, to share with him as I grew in to a man.

It took Aunty Mag six more years to accomplish what she had set out to do years before. She died of liver failure in the winter of 1989/90. The winter all the walls came down. Being at sea, I was unable to attend the funeral. The new exalted rank and role I had taken on made it even more difficult to get shore leave. I had shifted to naval intelligence, coordinating the attempted decoding of a blizzard of traffic coming from Russian vessels. Everything had gone very wonky very quickly and everyone, on both sides, was extremely jumpy. Maximum alert. Missiles bristling in their silos. Subs circling deep, deep down waiting on the word. It was no exaggeration to say that my opposite numbers and I, bobbing up and down in the Baltic, the Barents, were arbiters of the great game of mutual assured destruction played at its highest pitch. One very bad misunderstanding and kerboom! Stimulating but ultimately exhausting.

Old Morse, for intelligence purposes, had been largely superseded by something called 'Squirt'. Messages could now be compressed into dense, garbled bundles of code. The equivalent in physical terms would be to compress a dry sponge in to as tiny, as solid a ball as possible. In order for it to be useable, it needs to be released with water to find its own natural state. Such a releasing is what we were in the business of doing, but with sounds, rather than solids. It was an exercise in monumental tedium. Then there was the stuff we called 'chaff', very occasional messages in deliberate old-style Morse designed to sound off-message from some amateur but just credible enough to have you thinking 'hang on, what have we here?'. Designed, in other words, to distract. It was while taking a break from assessing this 'chaff' late one night in that crucial winter that contact was made. For years I'd been convinced that something more complicated than mental instability had been behind Uncle Ned's vanishing but not had the time or the inclination to follow my hunch. Aunty Mag's death had set me off again. I turned to a Moscow land-based frequency and 'fished', as we used to call it.

'Hold that tiger...hold that tiger...hold that tiger...hold that tiger...'

Decades ago, he had used it to 'tag' me, his then protégé. The refrain was from Tiger Rag, his favourite jazz number from which his nickname for me as a child had derived. After a minute or so his 'calling card' came back. There could be no doubt it was him. Nobody else could possibly be using it.

'Hatt regit dolh...hatt regit dohl...hatt regit dohl...' Part of our running joke at the expense of those dunderheads who had written me off as educationally subnormal. After seventeen years we were talking again in that terse and exclusive language. I nearly fell off my stool.

'Location?'...'TFOTBBB.'...'Can't believe.'...'You betcha.'...'Not in loony bin?'...'A question of interpretation.'... 'Still can't believe.'...'You betcha.'...'You went over?'...'I was having an affair.'

All of it made sense; became suddenly obvious. It had belonged in one of those dark pockets of willful ignorance and now, released, shone with solving clarity. He excused himself unsentimentally. I absolved him. We bantered as tersely as possible, eager to maximise what might be a unique and possibly final encounter, both aware he could be intercepted at any moment.

'You…prosper…in…HMS?'..'Yes.'…'Rank?'…'Captain.'…'Proud.'..'Thanks.'…'Married?'… 'No.'… 'Wise….Aunt Marion?'…'Dead.'

There was a pause.

'When?'…'Eleven days.'…'Cause?'…'Drink.'

Another pause.

'Mea culpa mea culpa.'

'RIP.'…'Yes. Peace.'

'Retired?'

He was, by then seventy-five years old, although whether, in intelligence, you can ever be said to retire, is debatable. What you know can't simply be packed away in a box like the contents of an office desk.

'Extinct.'

That was pure Uncle Ned. He seemed not to have changed at all.

'Bear treating you well?'

Then the noise I'd been expecting any second separated us: a softly howling blizzard of aural snow; the sound of infinite space. I never heard from him in person again.

So, that was it: what had first occurred to me as a boyhood fantasy had been true all along. The lie had been so consummately well told and maintained. I had not questioned it but neither, I now realised, had I fully believed it. I felt no bitterness. In going over he had sacrificed his life to an ideal that had, in its turn, betrayed him. He had probably suffered agonies of loneliness and remorse ('...I say it's a dolphin that's got separated from its family, calling out across a vast ocean...'.) I remembered the tear, running down the smooth side of his face. The pressure he'd been under must have been immense, yet he had patiently given me the greatest gift of my life.

'For Christ's sake, Daddy,' I said, at the first opportunity that occurred a month or so later on shore leave, 'you might have told me. Of all people, you might have told *me*. What a stinker of a lie to have kept up all those years.'

He had aged considerably. All the vim, the punch, had gone out of him. Aunty Mag had been the last remaining vestige of his life before The Fall (Uncle John had died of a heart attack some years back.) Now he was left alone with my mother. She could finally claim him; all of him. He was defenceless. Her reward for putting up with a married lifetime of playing second fiddle had come at last.

'Your Aunty Mag, married to a *traitor*,' she said, pityingly. 'How *could* we tell you?'

This was skilfully barbed. My father roused himself in the old fashion, 'Be silent, woman!' he roared.

But it was the roar of a toothless lion. She had him now.

I took us both to the pub. Away from the house he cheered up a little but it was clear his grief was final.

'Ned was never right for Marion,' he said with some bitterness, once we'd got ourselves seated. 'He was too clever by half. For all her sophistication, Marion was a gentleman farmer's daughter. We stood for the land, he stood for the mind. He was all brain and no heart and he took the fun out of her. You never knew the real Marion; the one that used to laugh and loved to dance.'

In my uncle's defence I wanted to point out that it had, perhaps, been six of one and half a dozen of the other; that Aunty Mag had not been entirely honest when making her vows, but that would have been another betrayal. What would have been the point, anyway? He had a right to his black and white world. I could, however, come to Uncle Ned's defence when it came to accusations of not having a sense of fun. I had always had a hoot in his company.

'That was typical of Ned,' my father retorted. 'He found the child's fantasy world more interesting than the grown up one. Double lives can't bear too much reality, I shouldn't think. Look at all those clever Cambridge chaps from before the war playing Russian hide and seek. They couldn't have believed in it all, truly believed, surely?'

With a shiver of regret, I realised I'd underestimated his levels of insight. There had always been a distance between us. We had never been able to say what we really thought and meant.

'What *exactly* was it Uncle Ned did?' I said. 'I mean, we all knew it was secret stuff, but you must have known the gist of it.'

'I honestly don't know. It was never talked about. He never talked about his work, even to Marion. Imagine that: a married lifetime of being cut off; shut out. My own guess is it had something to do with codes and all that sort of jiggery-pokery. He was a mathematician at Cambridge before the war, as you know. Quite a brilliant one by all accounts. Like I said: all brains and no heart. If he had one it was in the wrong place. Given over to that Marxist-Leninist rubbish, it turned out. Poor Marion.'

He lit another of his powerful cigarettes. Always a heavy smoker, he'd given up on giving up even though the doctors had started to sound grave warnings.

'How *did* he go over?'

'How? How? How does anyone go bloody over? Don't ask me. I'm a scrap merchant.'

This was no longer strictly true. He'd sold the business along with the bungalow a couple of years back; for a reasonable sum, as far as I could gather. They lived in a smaller, neater one now, still on the fringes of the town. He kept the dogs. On my infrequent visits, in these shrunken, tidier surroundings they appeared to me like wolves in captivity.

'Marion said he went on one of his trips to London and simply didn't come back. It was left to the Ministry to break it to her. And then to shut her up. To buy her off. To be perfectly honest, I think it came as something of a relief. Poor Marion. What a waste of a life.'

I left the following morning and never saw my mother again. It seemed cruel somehow that, just as she was settling down to enjoying exclusive nagging rights to my father's life, she should have dropped dead like that. It was my turn to grieve, although mildly, it turned out. She had become bitter over the years, and it's hard to love a bitter person. No sooner had I taken ship again than the news came through.

On the train up from Portsmouth, a full three months after the funeral had taken place, I had plenty of time to reflect on how, for the bachelor, death picks away at the once rich tapestry of a life crowded with family, leaving it starkly simplified. My sister had emigrated to Canada. We were practically estranged. I had no wife and family of my own. There was only my father left.

Without my mother in it, the bungalow was in rampant revolt against the regime of order and hygiene she'd finally been able to impose. The sink was stacked with unwashed crockery, and saucers brimmed with cigarette ends. There were empty wine bottles under the dining table. Outside, the tiny square of lawn was dotted with piles of uncollected dog mess.

'You're getting a Char in,' I said, in my new voice of command. (How suddenly age and helplessness reverses roles.)

Lear-like, he railed against this diminution of his authority.

'I will have no such bloody thing!'

'You bloody well will! You can't live like this!'

'Like what?'

'Like this,' I said, gesturing at the spectacular mess. 'It's an insult to Mummy's memory and I'm not having it.'

He backed down. I had won the opening skirmish in our war of attrition, I for once on the side of order and cleanliness, he, enlisted in a barbarous rampage towards his own extinction which took, remarkably, another fourteen years. He wasn't going quietly. By the time he did go I had left the Navy and the geopolitical map of world had changed utterly.

De-commissioned, I was able to visit much more regularly, shuttling backwards and forwards from Odessa where I'd used my Russian to set up an export-import business, something unthinkable in the good old bad old days. We became closer, almost friends, boozing till late into the night. On my last visit I knew he was hiding something from me. There was a yellowish tint to his skin and I came across new boxes of pills that were obviously not being taken. He sat in his chair smoking more furiously than ever. Yet, there was at the same time, a curious calm about him.

'I think I should tell you something, Gerald,' he said. 'It's been wrong of me to keep you in the dark all these years.'

I knew what was coming. I'd given up on ever finding out the truth. With time the whole thing had become of academic interest anyway. Yet I felt my pulse immediately quicken.

'My father, your Grandpa Sam, died in the most terrible way.'

'You don't *have* to tell me, Daddy.'

'I must,' he said with something of his old fierceness. 'I must! It must be told!'

'OK.'

'He was on the Board of Agriculture, you know.'

'I didn't.'

'During the war and then after it. Attlee's lot. Not a bad chap, Attlee, on the whole. He was open to new ideas and one of these was investment to be made in new, more efficient ways of fertilising. Gave the Board its head. Father was put in charge of developing the use of the slurry tank. Involved a lot of toing and froing down to London for consultations and so forth. Sometimes he'd be away for a week or so. I'd just got myself de-mobbed and was pretty well running the farm on my own. With the hands of course. We had four back then! Imagine that now. Our first tank was delivered whilst he was away. I had already got one load out of it and was about to fill it again.'

He stopped, staring straight ahead, gulped back something catching in his throat, and carried on with fierce determination.

'Father had managed to get away a day earlier than expected and didn't phone to tell mother. Wanted to surprise her I suppose. Christ knows how, but he must have arrived by cab from the station, found the house empty, gone out to inspect the new tank and climbed down the ladder inside. At the same time I came back to the yard, closed the lid and started pumping a new lot of slurry. I didn't hear a thing. The tractor's engine was running and the pump's engine was deafening.

His suitcase was there in the hall of the house, so obviously there was a big panic; Mummy beside herself. Police on the look-out everywhere. I didn't find him until three days later, once the fertiliser mix had had a chance to work properly and I'd drained the tank for the fields. It had half consumed him by then. Christ. Christ! What a thing to have done.'

'It's alright, Daddy,' I said, pouring him another scotch.

'But that wasn't all. Father was a gambler. We all have our Achilles heel and his was the gee gees and the cards. Up here in the sticks he was able to manage it. Down there in The Smoke he must have got in with a fast set. Out of his depth. Long story short, he started embezzling Board money. Rather a lot. So, what was a simple farmyard accident became the subject of an inquiry. Naturally, suicide was suspected, disguised as an accident to lessen the suffering of those left behind. In order to deny the rumour, my own part in his death had to come out. The local press got hold of it and then the Nationals. An appalling time for the family. We were ruined. Your Uncle John, the Cecils, even had to put up the money for the bungalow and the Yard. There, you have it. You have it all.'

I couldn't find anything to say that would have come even vaguely close to matching the occasion. There was a long silence.

'You did well to recover, Daddy,' I managed, finally. 'You gave us all a good life. Started again from scratch. Built up the business. We never wanted for anything. Mummy was a lucky woman to have married you.

She didn't like to show it, but I know that's how she felt.'

He sat gazing ahead, cigarette held out in front of him, drooping ash.

'It's a terrible thing to say, Gerald, but I never really loved your mother,' he said, eyes still fixed on some patch on the wall. 'She deserved a better man. Someone to love her with all his heart. We had a sort of life together. Made a decent fist of it. But the only woman I truly loved was Marion. Does that sound odd?'

'A little.'

'When the school holidays came round, I could hardly wait to see her again. Play in the fields. Hide and seek in the house. And I never stopped loving her in that way even once she grew into a woman. You know, she never once blamed me for father's death. I blamed her for marrying Ned, though and that was wrong. Very wrong.'

'It's alright, Daddy,' I said. 'It's alright. It's all in the past now.'

He hung on another month. The Char found him one morning still in his chair, having refused all entreaties to get to hospital. It was kidneys. According to the autopsy the lungs were, miraculously, perfectly functioning organs.

I would appear to have inherited something of their robustness. They are impervious to the damp Odessa winters as indeed am I. They don't get me down. I love the city, with its Potemkin Stairs and proud, down at heel public buildings; the ever-present whisper of the sea.

For every Navy man there is a particular thrill once his ship is safely out of port, has gathered speed and is racing towards open sea. All the kerfuffle involved in leaving shore, of correct procedure, of casting off, is behind him and clear water beckons with its promise of simplicity.

RED FLAGS

I was hoping that my new unencumbered life might be a mirror of this: that once I'd sold the bungalow, tidied up my father's affairs and bundled his, the family's life, into neat, safely compartmentalised boxes of memory, I'd be free, really free to get on with my own. Instead I felt orphaned. My bachelor's resolve began to weaken (to be a bachelor by choice, takes true resolve and a certain amount of nerve in the face of the gamble one is taking).

It was in such a mood that I began thinking of Uncle Ned again. It was a long shot, but I began to cling to the hope that he might still be alive. When I first made the move to Odessa and decided to make it my home, it had occurred to me that I might be in a position to find out if he was still around. If so, why not make contact again, although this time, face to face? Immediately, the odds against this being possible started stacking up. He would have been given, or have adopted, a new name, presumably Russian. It wouldn't be a simple question of looking up Edward Kentish in the phone book. We were in a new era of entente but it wasn't quite that *cordiale*, yet. If I were to petition the relevant authorities for information on the bearer of that name, alarm bells would start ringing straight away. The whole thing would take considerable reserves of patience, not to mention the time involved. I gave it up before I'd even begun.

Then, one unusually cold evening in December with the snow piled up in the streets, I was working late in the office on some bills of lading. There was a knock on the door, very faint. Apart from the janitor I was alone in the building and that was not his knock. Who on earth could it be?

'Come in,' I said.

The door opened slowly and a tall, distinguished looking old woman entered the room. She was swaddled against the cold in an ancient fur coat and hat. This was nothing out of the ordinary. In winter, half the pensioners of Odessa wandered about the place looking like extras on some movie set for a Cold War thriller circa 1950. What *was* exceptional, sent me reeling in fact, was that pinned to the lapel of the coat was a brooch which, in the Russian style of women of her generation, contained a daguerreotype image of a man, perhaps her deceased husband. The image was, unmistakably, that of a young Uncle Ned.

'We have met before,' she said in clear Russian with a slight Moscow accent, settling into the seat I'd offered her. 'You will perhaps not remember me. You were very young. I was your very first 'tag'. My Morse name was Jill. Your Uncle Edward was known to me as Jack.'

'Good God!'

A smile lit her face. It was the face of someone who had been very beautiful once, and still, even at her age, possessed the serenity of extreme beauty.

'You will no doubt have many questions you wish to ask. Edward was very fond of you as a boy and you of him, I know.'

'He is dead?'

'He died two months ago at the age of ninety-four. He was lucid although housebound for the last three years of his life. He wished me to make contact with you and explain some matters concerning his past.'

As I handed her a glass of tea I noticed my hands were shaking. I poured myself a glass of vodka to go with mine and offered the same. She refused.

'How on earth did you meet?' I said, knocking back my shot and pouring myself another. 'Were *you* running him?'

She broke into outright laughter at that.

'In a very different sense, yes. We met during the war. I was a young journalist on Pravda. As you know, Belsen had a large contingent of Soviet Prisoners of War of whom about twenty thousand perished. Not gassed, you understand. There were no chambers at Belsen. Just left to perish. We did the same to their bastards after we'd encircled Paulus's army. I spoke, or claimed to speak, some English, so when news came through of its liberation, I was sent along with an advanced military detachment to liaise with the British and Canadians and report back. When I got there, I found I could barely understand a word and was perfectly useless. Edward's Russian, on the other hand, was excellent and he managed to get himself temporarily seconded to the unit I was a part of. His Division had been the first in. The first to discover the full horror. The bodies. Piles and piles of them. The experience had affected him greatly. He had nightmares till the last. I was less affected. We were used to such horror by then. For several weeks Edward and I were inseparable. He was the first foreigner I had met. Utterly different from the Russian men I had known. I fell deeply in love with him and he with me. Does that sound strange? Perhaps the least romantic backdrop to an affair imaginable.'

'I'm trying,' I said. 'I'm trying very hard. Please go on.'

'Of course, we knew we would never see each other again once our duties had been discharged but that didn't stop us. We were young. The war was not yet over. Death was everywhere. We took what good things we could when we could. Everybody did. Our people even made love during Stalingrad if the opportunity presented itself, despite the best efforts of the commissars. Edward loved jazz, as you know. He taught me to love it too. He'd carried around with him a number of his favourite sides. There was a gramophone in the farmhouse we'd commandeered. We danced until our feet were raw. Before parting, he gave me the records. We also exchanged 'calling cards' and favoured frequencies. I don't think we really thought we could meet again. But it was something to lessen the pain, the sadness. Of keeping some faint hope alive. Yet we did meet.'

'When?'

'It was '53. He'd been married some time by then.'

'To my Aunty Mag.'

'So I gathered. An unhappy woman. I never married. My work was enough. But not one day went by without thinking of Edward. Our affair was the most beautiful thing that had happened to me in a very hard life. Some people can only fall in love once. And then we made contact.'

'It must have been hazardous,' I said. 'For you especially. You must have risked losing everything.'

'Of course, we could not speak candidly. We would, for the most part communicate in the words of the jazz songs he had left me and others I had managed to get my hands on. A code within a code.' She broke into a surprisingly authentic jazz voice. 'You'll miss the cutest gal that you ever had.'

'Absurd to think of now,' she went on. 'What an utterly absurd time that was. The Cold War. What a perversion of the human soul.'

'Did you know at the time he was in intelligence?' I said.

'Not at that time. I found out when we finally met: in London.'

'You *met* in *London*?'

'In '65. It is not as surprising as it may seem. I was very senior on the paper by then. Absolutely by the book. Trusted by the Party. I had no problem getting foreign release. We were able to meet on a number of occasions.'

A picture of Aunty Mag alone at the wheel of the Hillman swam into my head.

'Was Uncle Ned really a spy? Was he passing information through you?'

'Not of any significance,' she said, bluntly.

'I find that hard to believe.'

'What information he gave me to take back was largely obsolete. Edward was not in the very top echelons. It is even possible that he was under suspicion and that whatever *he* was fed was false, designed to have us barking up the wrong tree. The important thing was that he was giving *something*. If I was to get him over; if we were ever to have a normal life together it was necessary for him to be seen as being one of us. I had to offer them something. You have to understand that in those days, for the most part, it was not so much the quality of the information that was important but the willingness to give it. He was a very small catch, but a catch all the same.'

'Was he real a believer?' I said. 'I remember him explaining the essentials of Marx to me when I was about sixteen. At about the time he...'

What *had* he done? I was lost for the appropriate word. Defected? Absconded?

'Joined you. You know my family gave me to understand he had been put in an asylum.'

'So I gathered. Perfectly understandable. Common procedure with our dissenters at the time; some of our finest minds. The joke was we may have been falling behind in the quality of our consumer goods but not in the quality of our lunatics. In answer to your question: yes and no. Like the rest of us. Once Khrushchev let the cat out of the bag it became impossible to really believe in the concrete side of things. One lived in a dream of abstractions.'

It was getting very late and I began to worry about her accommodation arrangements.

'I have a perfectly comfortable hotel,' she said, in answer to my entreaty that she should stay the night in my apartment. 'One last thing Edward wanted you to know was that you made his reputation in Russia. He became well-known for his treatment of dyslexia. The Morse Method. It was entirely his idea. He said he piloted it on you.'

'He did,' I said. 'His patience was quite phenomenal. In many ways I owe my literacy, my love of books, my life as it turned out, to him.'

She got up to go, buttoning her coat with bony hands. I took one last good look at his miniature image taken before his burns, the face young, full of life and handsome; his regimental beret set at a slightly rakish angle.

'I'm assuming you found me, the business, on the internet,' I said.

'That is so,' she said.

'Perhaps we might keep in touch. Perhaps I might be able to…'

She cut me short.

'My doctor would counsel against that. It may be a waste of a train ticket. Besides, Edward despised the internet. He said it had taken the wonder out of life. I tend to agree.'

I offered to accompany her to her hotel. She refused.

'Goodbye, Gerry,' she said, smiling. 'It has been a great pleasure to meet you again after all these years.'

RED FLAGS

The tale-telling season begins in September when the new young faculty have just arrived and the weather is fine. This part of China has a fickle climate but for a few short weeks after the sopping heat of milky August, the air becomes dry, clear and pleasantly warm. Coinciding as this does with the start of our academic year it lends sprightliness, a brief touch of colour to the place, before the real drudgery sets in and the city assumes its dominant hue, which is grey; very grey. I imagine it reminds them of that other, longer hiatus, the 'gap year', obligatory amongst the younger generation these days. The nights are starry and Victor's stays open till the early hours. We might almost be in some side street in Hanoi drinking beer lao and squatting on our backpacks.

Victor's is a shop selling luxury western goods. It has a large selection of beers with a few tables outside around which to consume them at shop prices. Huge competing rounds are bought to help with the thirsty work of recounting how they were stoned for months on end in Goa or robbed at gunpoint in Guatemala. It's hard work for an oldster. I wish the talk would take a more general turn once in a while. Age might well tend to flatter memory on occasions as I zimmer into my early sixties, but I nevertheless *do* distinctly remember youthful discourse transcending the bounds of personal anecdote. Views on literature and politics, for example, were batted about, often quite heatedly. It may sound trivial but an attempt on my part to steer the conversation in that sort of direction ended up depressing me rather.

At the end of a monologue by a man from Minnesota relating how he was adopted by a tribe of head hunters in Borneo, I remarked that his story seemed to have leapt straight out of something by Evelyn Waugh. The comparison was meant to be flattering but, with a certain measure of impatience, he confessed he'd no idea who that author was.

'Evelyn Waugh?' I said, appealing to the group around the table. 'Decline and Fall? Scoop? The Loved One? He's very famous.'

It turned out that not a single one of them knew who he was either but they would, they said to save my blushes, 'google him later'. And suddenly I really did feel old. It had never occurred to me before that to them I might be a relic of a bygone age. Yet there it was, plain: I did not and never could, belong. My time had gone and it was over to them now, with their googling and We-Chat and tales of tramping round the poorer parts of the world.

So, when Terry arrived, I thought at first that here might be a drinking companion a bit more on my wavelength.

Due to complications with his visa he got here late, at the onset of winter. The plaza giving on to Victor's was swept with icy rain. I was the only person sitting under the concrete overhang by the door where the light cast from inside is sufficient to read by. The younger folk had vanished at the first touch of cold. Where to exactly, remains a mystery to me since there's nowhere else to go for a beer after work for miles around. I was alone with my books again which is fine by me but it *is* nice to have someone to talk to occasionally in the evenings. Whoever does stop by for a quick drink has my ears. Despite appearances to the contrary, I'm not a bookish man. I like a bit of company but it's thin on the ground when the winter comes down and I'll be damned if I'm spending whole evenings in my flat. I've always done my reading in bars, pubs and cafés anyway. Until recently this was considered perfectly ordinary behaviour. Not so nowadays, judging by the way requests to join me are prefaced with awed expressions of reverence for the act itself as though I were deep in translation of the Book of Kells. Quite why this should be the case, given that we're all working at universities and live in something called the Higher Education Town, puzzles me. 'You're reading a *buk*!' they say before reciting the title as though having just learned to read themselves. 'The... Collected...Poems of Alfred...Lord...*Tennyson*. Wow!' Not so, Terry.

He came winging in across the Plaza like a bird of prey, with an extraordinary quick step, bouncing on the balls of his feet.

'G'day mate,' he said, noisily pulling up one of the painful metal chairs Mr Victor sees fit to provide us with, 'you must be The Chairman, right?'

'I'm sorry,' I said. 'Not quite following.'

'They said at the Language Centre you're always here. Just ask for The Chairman, they said.'

'Did they?' I said. 'Well it's nice to be known as something I suppose.'

'Can I get you one? What's your poison?'

'Well, if you insist. A Leffe Brown, please.'

'A little helper to go with, maybe?'

'Well...er...'

'A little Ballantines. They said The Chairman's partial to a splash of firewater with his beer.'

'That's very kind of you, but please,' I said, reaching for my wallet, 'let me help you...'

'...out,' But he'd already dived through the door.

So, I was The Chairman. This was news to me. Did the nickname imply a certain ironic respect, recognition of leadership in the art of getting pissed; a doffing of the hat to The Great Helmsman himself, or did it simply describe an odd bloke who sat outside a shop in all weathers drinking beer? Had I become that most pitiful of things: a 'character'?

He came back out, scattered four miniature bottles of whisky on the table along with the beers and flung himself into his chair. It was difficult to tell whether this clumsy vigour was a deliberate affectation or drink fuelled. He looked sober enough, but then again had black rings around his eyes, the whites of which were of a yellowish, jaundiced colour. Red flag, I thought.

Picking up the book I'd been reading, he scrutinised the cover. 'The Diary of a Country Parson...by...James Woodforde,' he said in his Australian voice, which had all the charm of a chainsaw going at a particularly recalcitrant log. 'Heavy shit.' Then, dropping it back on the table, 'Terry Docherty,' he said, and offered a brutal looking hand. He was a big, heavily built, bouncing man, somewhere in his late forties.

'Peter Latimer,' I said. 'And what brings you to these parts, Terry?'

At this innocent opening gambit, a dam seemed to burst inside him. My hopes that here might be a person with whom dialogue of a non-personal nature may be possible were immediately shattered. In place of the platitudes it was intended to elicit came the most extraordinary outpouring. Without the slightest preamble and with only the briefest of pauses to go at the whisky and beer, I was treated to the story of his life.

He was born and bred in Brisbane and started out as an electrician working mainly on overhead high voltage power cables. Due to the unusual level of danger involved he was much in demand and made good money which he was soon relieved of by a predilection for drink, hard drugs and fast women a succession of whom came in and out of his life with unpleasant consequences. Then an accident and resulting compensation led to his studying for a degree in modern languages at which he excelled, becoming the master of five, including two obscure tribal dialects, one African, the other Indonesian, in addition to the more run of the mill Spanish, Russian and Hindi. Armed with this formidable gift of tongues he then set about assuaging a wanderlust the scale of which reduced Marco Polo to the status of a day tripper. Along the way he hobnobbed with all sorts, from drug barons and warlords to minor royalty, all the while swatting off exotic foreign beauties. Here, in a nutshell, was a man of the world *par excellence*.

But there was a twist in the tale. Approaching fifty he'd tired of the prodigious life. It had taken its toll. He realised that if he was to survive into something approximating to old age he had to settle down; become a family man; beget children.

'So,' he said, leaning over the table and sticking what I'd come to regard as a rather unpleasant face into mine. 'You know what I did?'

I had no idea. By this time my mind had begun to swim. Over the course of what must have been a good thirty minutes, it had only been permitted a few seconds to gather itself at intervals as he paused to drink. It didn't matter because the question, like everything about him, turned out to be rhetorical.

'I went to Thailand, picked a wife and I impregnated her,' he said.

I was lost for words.

'I picked a wife,' he said again, 'and I impregnated her. Twice.'

'Well, well done,' I said. 'That must be marvellous for you both.'

This seemed to satisfy him.

'And now I've got two little monkeys to bring up,' he went on. 'That's my life now.'

'Are they with you?'

'No,' he said. 'The bastards are being difficult with their visas. But they will be. I can't leave them to Nid to bring up. I was training her, see. But now I'm not there to keep an eye on her, fack knows what might happen.'

'Nid being your wife?'

'Yeah. She's pretty clueless. Sometimes I wonder whether she's got a maternal instinct at all.'

'I presume she had some say in the matter of conception?' I said.

He let out that awful noise that in the five months I knew him came to be the one thing above all which made me want to put his eyes out with a red-hot poker. It was the utterance he made indicating he hadn't fully understood something:

'Aaay?'

'I mean, I'm assuming she was keen on having children, too?'

'She wasn't complaining.'

'Well, there you go.'

'They're my life, now, see,' he sawed on. 'I'm here to give them the best start in life possible. I reckon, when I get promoted to Tutor D, I'll be able to pay the house off in Bangkok in two years. Then, I can set about sending those two little monkeys to a good private school. You won't be seeing me out sucking piss once they arrive. But I wouldn't want anyone to think that Terry Docherty had led an ordinary life.'

'Well let's hope they get here sooner than later,' I said. 'Now, if you'll excuse me, I'm off to point Percy.'

I headed for the bushes that we're obliged to use once they close the shopping precinct after nine in the evening. Relieving myself as the rain lashed down, I had chance to weigh up the situation. Undoubtedly the most graceless person I'd ever met in my life had got it into his head that we were to be pals. Apart from ceasing my nightly frequenting of Victor's, the one thing that keeps me going here, it was impossible to see how I could avoid him. I was a sitting duck. For the time being the only thing to be done was to give him the benefit of the doubt and hope he might improve upon further acquaintance. Returning to the table, he held out a brief glimmer of hope that this might prove to be the case, just as quickly extinguished.

'You got kids?' he said.

Apart from establishing who I was, this was the only thing he'd come out with so far which suggested I might be of interest to talk to rather than at.

'No,' I said. 'We never had kids.'

'Married?'

'Not anymore.'

'She binned you or you binned her?'

'My wife died a long time ago.'

'Cancer?'

'No. From a tropical disease when we were working together in Africa.'

'Sorry to hear that,' he said. 'Heavy shit.'

'That's alright,' I said, relieved. Had he gone on to ask me what kind of tropical disease I would have had to have thrown what was left of my beer in his face.

He picked up his can.

'Suck more piss,' he said, draining it, clearly expecting me to return his round.

I began to feel a little sick.

'Look, Terry,' I said, 'Let me get you one, but then I'll have to love you and leave you. I'd been here a fair old while before you arrived and my feet are beginning to feel like blocks of ice.'

'Pilsner,' he said.

I got what he'd asked for along with a miniature of Ballantines and made my excuses again.

'Hasta manana,' he said. 'They say The Chairman's always here.'

The rain had eased off but I still needed my plastic cape for the five-minute electric scooter ride home. It felt especially wet and cold. Arriving back at the flat I found myself in a foul mood. Not an overly cheerful living space even when I was in the best of tempers, the place seemed to be *trying* to plumb impossible depths of dreariness. The chicken stew on which I largely subsist tasted like something Ivan Denisovich might have turned his nose up at. My nightly half bottle of Shiraz failed to warm me. I was unable to concentrate on the YouTube documentary I'd been looking forward to watching. I kept seeing his face leering at me, coarse, fleshy yet oddly androgynous, like that of an overgrown baby: features calibrated precisely to repel rather than attract the sort of women to whom he was apparently irresistible. I calculated that he must have been three parts lying, in my experience the usual ratio of truth to reality given to people who live entirely within their own self-myth. But that didn't explain why he'd felt the need to tell me, a total stranger, the story of his life, largely invented or not. Had I become a void into which people felt comfortable pouring themselves? I *had* begun to notice over the past two years or so how some colleagues appeared to single me out as someone 'safe' to vent their frustrations on, both professional and personal. Was that me: a sort of confessional box of absolving emptiness? I had a bad night's sleep.

By the following evening the rain had cleared and we were now in the grip of a freezing mist. Out of it emerged his bouncing blob closing down on me across the empty Plaza. Once he was noisily seated, fearful of a terrible sequel, I threw out some chaff intended to deflect any immediate repetition of last night's monologue.

'I see you're dressed for it, Terry,' I said. (He was wearing a charmless ensemble of luminous outdoor rainwear, Gortex hiking boots, and carrying a backpack). 'I hope you haven't forgotten your emergency flare.'

'Aaay?'

'The clobber, old son. You look like you're off to conquer an alp.'

He remained silent, with a suspicious, defensive half-smile dribbling down his chin. I'd hit on his Achilles heel: facetiousness. If I could keep up a constant stream of it, that dreadful chainsaw of a voice might be silenced indefinitely. He might even go away.

'Not many hills round here as you've probably noticed. We're sitting on a reclaimed marsh. Fifteen years ago, none of this existed,' I gabbled on, gesturing at the wilderness of concrete, glass and tarmac. 'It has a certain nostalgic Soviet era charm, don't you think. On a night like this, with the mist down, I like to think I'm playing a part in some adaption of John Le Carre. I probably am for all I know. I've been here an awfully long time. It gets to you sometimes. Of course, there is topography of the kind you appear to be seeking but it's not easy to get to…'

I found myself quickly running out of steam. Then, a man passing by us cleared his throat, depositing a large gobbet of phlegm a couple of yards from where we were sitting. It gave me more ammunition. 'Aah, the Olympic Chinese gob,' I said. 'Round here, it being fairly middle class, we're a bit more restrained when it comes to sluicing the pavements with our sputum. But if you venture into the older parts of town you'll find yourself wading through rivers of it…'

It was no use. I couldn't keep it up. He wasn't really listening anyway. As I came to learn, when he wasn't actually talking himself he was plotting what he was going to say next. In company he'd sit there like a Buddha with a thin, self-contained smile on his face as if in meditation. Then his right leg would start going ten to the dozen. Then out it would come, often interrupting the other person in full flow: some infinitely boring competing anecdote: 'When I was in Nicaragua…' or, 'That reminds me of the time I was…'

'I skyped this afternoon,' he said, finally.

'Oh, well done. Was it a good connection?'

'And you know who I got on the other end?'

'Your wife?'

'Sophie.'

Sophie was the eldest of his two daughters. She was three and a half years old.

'A precocious child,' I said.

'Now there's a red flag, I thought, straightaway.' He went into an impersonation of himself talking to his daughter and wife on skype and them talking back. "Sophie, where's Mummy?' I said. 'Mummy's upstairs sleeping.' 'Well go and fetch Mummy now.' So down she comes. 'Jeezus facking Christ almighty,' I say. 'It's four o'clock in the afternoon and you're *asleep. Upstairs.* With those little monkeys running about.' 'I was tired,' she said. 'I'm not paying for everything for you to be sleeping all day,' I said. 'I took you out of the gutter. I gave you a house and children and this is what I get. Wee Willy Winkie."

'No maternal instinct, see,' he almost yelled at me, this time, in his own voice. 'I'd been training her. We'd been making progress. She was starting to get it. And now she's gone back. I fear for those little monkeys.'

There was more in this vein. Then I saw Quaker coming towards us. Normally, I'd have pretended to be deep in my book, or examining an ant on the table, or dead; anything to avoid the prospect of Quaker joining me.

Quaker is called Quaker because of his gargantuan appetite for cereal of all kinds. He's an American of a size and girth that puts the average American fatty to shame. A great galleon of a man, he sails along in his specially made clothes which billow about him as he goes. His actual name is William Oates. The sheer felicity of the conjunction of diet and surname I found irresistible. Hence, Quaker Oates, which still makes me laugh. I can't help it. Frivolity, facetiousness are my besetting vices. Quaker didn't find it funny. As far as I can make out, Quaker doesn't find anything funny. I've never once heard him laugh or, come to think of it, seen him smile. Furthermore, he appears to be utterly devoid of mind, unless he's reserving it all for some magnum opus he's beavering away at on the quiet. I doubt it. I suspect, as someone once said of a famous actress, he has 'hidden-shallows'. He's been here as long as me, arriving single and getting immediately snaffled by one of the Chinese secretaries employed at the centre. Married now and with two kids, he's let out very occasionally to strip Victor's shelves of Shreddies, Coco-Pops and whatnot.

'Quaker!' I said, as though to a long-lost friend. 'Come and meet Terry. He's just arrived.'

'Gotta go shop first,' he said. 'Then maybe I'll have a beer.'

'Quaker,' I said, once, with great difficulty, he'd become seated, 'meet Terry. He's a father of two, same as yourself, although due to visa problems his family are unable to join him at present. I'm sure you'll have some advice as to how to keep them entertained round these parts.'

He didn't, but it turned out not to matter because Terry was soon off, expounding the Docherty method of child rearing, and berating his wife for not 'getting it'.

For the second night running I made my excuses and left early, hoping that this might send out the desired signal that perhaps he and I were not destined to be, as they say nowadays, 'besties'.

It didn't. And shortly after, things took a terrible turn for the worse.

A year ago, perhaps out of pity, I was relieved of my teaching duties and put in charge of the newly formed Writing Centre, which serves the Language Centre and university at large as a (supposed) panacea for the weaker student's inability to string two sentences together in English, the medium of their instruction. Its real function is to give burnt out teachers from the LC a break from waving the board marker before being thrown back into the fray, rather along the lines of pulling shell-shocked troops out of the trenches in order to preserve them for future slaughter. The atmosphere is, unavoidably, somewhat tense at times. We are an open plan office area and those of my team that had made it in for nine on a Monday morning heard a loud shriek of horror coming from my own cubicle. Denise, a terrible alcoholic from Cork on her last warning, came rushing over, perhaps recognising the post weekend heebie jeebies of a fellow sufferer.

'What is it, Peter? What is it?'

'It's OK, Denise,' I said, closing the offending e-mail. 'I'll be alright in a minute.'

It wasn't alright. The e-mail, from my boss at the Language Centre, read:

'...please welcome Terry Docherty on your team. He'll be with you for the immediate future until he takes up teaching duties in the new semester...'

Half an hour later he came bouncing in. He smelt of booze.

'G'day, mate,' he said. 'Reporting for duty to The Chairman himself. You didn't tell me you were running this outfit.'

I was tempted to say 'that's because you didn't even effing ask what I did here' but restricted myself to, 'Welcome on the team, Terry. Let me show you to an empty workstation. We've got quite a few. You can take your pick. We're still expanding. Oh, and by the way, it might be an idea to knock all this Chairman stuff on the head whilst we're working together. It's fine for Victor's but some of our colleagues might not get what you're on about and we're an open house with students free to wander in and out, and I'm known as Peter to them, too. First names are the norm so feel free to ask them to call you Terry. Not Mr Terry, or Mr

Docherty, or Honourable Teacher. Plain Terry will do.'

'When I was in Japan, they had trouble with the Rs. I got facking sick of being Telly, so I just got them to call me Mr T. If it was good enough for the Japs, it should be good enough for...'

'...I'm sure that was fine, and you can call yourself the Sultan of Brunei for all care. I'm merely pointing out how we go about things here. It's all about relaxing the students. Bringing down the 'affective filter' as they say. And a little extra practice with the pre-palatial dental fricative won't do them any harm. But up to you...'

Up until then, I'd only encountered him in the Great Outdoors, so to speak, where his clumsiness was restricted to orchestral scraping of Victor's metal chairs and the occasional knocked over can of Pilsner. In the confines of an office he proved himself a whirlwind of destruction. Within a week the AC and printer were out of action. He was a man against whom inanimate objects conspired in the most unexpected of ways. The very opposite of what might be expected of an electrician. He even managed to blow up the office kettle.

But this was minor stuff compared to the havoc wreaked by his voice. Contrary to office etiquette he refused, or was unable, to keep it down. All through the working day it buzzed and sawed around us: '...that reminds me of when I was...'

'Mate,' he said, appearing at my shoulder one morning about a couple of weeks into being with us, 'you've got to look at this.' Thrusting his smart phone in my face he repeated the words on its screen. They belonged to one of those unfortunately spelt or phrased signs you find in hotels and the like which have come to be known as Chinglish, 'Please hang your wet *shit* in bathroom not bedroom'.

'We all make mistakes, Terry,' I said.

'Please hang your wet *shit* in bathroom not bedroom,' he repeated, wheezing with laughter.

I nearly lost it.

'For Christ's sake, Terry! It's only a missing letter! A missing R! It isn't fricking funny!'

Heads peeped from over cubicles.

'Yes, but...hang your...'

'Alright! Alright!'

Neither, it turned out, was he any less graceless with those students assigned to him. Tutorials took place in a set of closed cubicles running along a corridor near our workstations, the glass walls of which were sufficient to keep in the sound of the normal spoken voice. Not so with Terry.

I took to spying on him. I was, after all, his immediate boss and had a duty to see that standards of conduct were being upheld. They weren't.

'Nooo! You're not getting it! Your word forms are all over the place. I told you to go away and study a bit of basic grammar. It's all about mental discipline. If you want to do it, you will. You carry on giving me this crap and you're going to fail. F.A.I.L. Fail! I am a *failing* student. *Failure* has consequences. Why do you *fail* to see this? Adjective, noun, verb. Basic stuff...'

Once, when I was coming out of the toilets at the end of the corridor, a girl exited his cubicle in a terrible hurry and came running towards the ladies. Sudden urgent call of nature I assumed; very common. But no, it turned out she was crying.

I could have reported him. Or I could have had a quiet word with Robert at the LC to the effect that here was a man who it might be better to 'let go' at the end of his probationary three months. Looking back, that was the point at which I could have saved his life. In the end, I did neither.

One Friday evening shortly before the Christmas break, when the office had emptied, he stuck his face over my cubicle. It had a salacious grin on it.

'What do you do for a root, Chairman?' he said.

As a roundabout way of establishing whether I really was the old poof a lot of people take me for, the enquiry came as no surprise. The surprise was it hadn't come much earlier in our unfortunate acquaintance. I decided to play him at his own game.

'You mean a fuck, Terry?' I said.

'Yeah,' he said. I was curious at how bashful he sounded. Wasn't he supposed to be a man of the world *par excellence*?

'I tend to lean towards abstinence these days,' I said. 'But if you're truly desperate there's a whole load of girly bars down on Shi Quian Jie. It's a good forty-five minute cab ride though.'

It turned out I'd misjudged his intentions. 'What say we take a little trip down there, you and me, after a few cold ones at Vic's. Get the old todger in the mood before taking a taxi.'

This really was too much. The thought that he might regard me as a potential accomplice in what for him was adultery made me feel sick. I was seized by the impulse to run away, like the student who'd fled his tutorial; to lock myself in the karzi until, in the manner of the proverbial spider in the bath, he might somehow condescend to vanish from my life. But such things a man cannot do if he is to remain a man. I was trapped;

wriggling on the pin of his deeply unwanted, limpet-like attentions. Despite my glacial *froidure*, he hung on, oblivious. I had nowhere else to go and I could hardly tell him to fuck off now I was his boss. Besides, one grown man can't tell another to fuck off unless he's been either grievously insulted or wronged.

'I'll take a rain check, Terry,' I said. 'Things to do tomorrow.'

The Christmas break came. It's always a nice time for me. I stay at the university and save the ten days for an extended Chinese New Year when I have a whole three weeks to work on our house in Cap D' Agde. Mary and I bought it shortly before she died. It's a work in progress. Always will be. Working on it helps to keep her alive. Meanwhile it's nice and quiet round here at Christmas. They say it's a lonely time for people without family but I never get lonely. I carry Mary around with me inside, so how can I be lonely. I was looking forward to it. Most importantly, Terry would be straight back to Thailand to renew the training of his wife in the proper rearing of his 'little monkeys', who by now I felt I knew almost personally (he was forever whipping out his phone and showing me the latest snaps). This, as they say, was all my Christmases rolled into one.

'What day are you flying out,' I asked him, in a spirit of seasonal good will. He appeared to be in a foul mood. I discovered why.

'I'm not,' he said. 'They've facking facked up with my facking resident's visa. It's not going to arrive on time.'

There followed a diatribe on the hopeless inefficiency of Chinese bureaucracy, by now a familiar trope but this time, perhaps understandably, of a particularly foul-mouthed nature.

'Looks like I'll be joining you,' he said, finally, once he'd blown himself out. In an unguarded moment, once I'd established he wouldn't be here, I'd told him of the quiet Christmas lunch I ate on my own at Jack's Home, the only restaurant in a conurbation of six million souls that could knock up a reasonable approximation to such a thing.

On the Eve, they hold a midnight carol service at the church down by the lake. It's a big, mock red-brick building in the evangelical American style. In the courtyard stands a huge statue of a smiling Jesus with his arms held out like a football player rushing towards the fans in celebration of a goal just scored. It's a much-favoured spot for young Chinese newly-weds to have their snaps taken. This says an awful lot about how far the place has come since the days of the real Chairman.

It's a very broad church. So broad, in fact, that finding God in it must be near on impossible. Instead, Jesus is the star turn and there's lots of playing guitars, banging percussion instruments, singing and hugging, which makes it all quite jolly. I stopped off last year on my annual Christmas Eve walk and stood at the back for a while by the door. In my black overcoat and trilby hat I must have appeared as the Grim Reaper. 'Please, join us' they said. 'Come and be with Jesus'. I didn't. I couldn't. I would have been an imposter. My faith deserted me when Mary died. It was tested and found wanting; vanishing at the first real persecution life had thrown my way. No John Knox, me. I resigned my Orders, returned to England and did a P.G.C.E. in English as a Foreign Language.

This time I gave the happy clappers the swerve in favour of just walking and drinking from my hip flask. The whisky, star-freckled sky, moonlight on the water, all contrived to put me in a good mood and, as my own token gesture of goodwill to all men I resolved to try and be nice to Terry the next day. After all, he had had a big disappointment. He was human and presumably suffered like the rest of us although it was hard to see how. The only emotions I'd seen him display, apart from dribbling imbecilic mirth at his Chinglish discoveries were anger, frustration, impatience, self-absorption and congratulation.

On Christmas morning, as a form of anaesthetic, I got through a quarter of a bottle of single malt before swinging by his building in the cab I'd pre-ordered. Hopes that he may have drunk himself into oblivion the night before were dashed. He was waiting outside in his habitual hiking gear but wearing one of those Santa hats in place of the usual woollen beany.

'G'day...hic...Chairman,' he said, clearly as half cut as me.

'Compliments of the season to you, Terry.'

'Aaay?'

'Merry Christmas.'

'Oh, yeah. This reminds me of the time I was in Serbia during the Balkan war and I'd got the day wrong. They don't celebrate it on the same day, see, and I...'

We were shown ceremoniously to my usual table. Mr Jackie had done his usual good job: plastic holly, balloons, paper streamers everywhere. The place was quite full, mostly families of fat American dads, Chinese mothers and nice well-behaved kids. Carols were playing in the background but not loud enough to drown out his awful voice. His language was entirely inappropriate to the setting, as though we were sat outside Victor's in the open air. Faces began to turn in our direction with beseeching looks on them.

'Keep it down a bit, Terry,' I said.

'Aaay?'

Food began to arrive, which provided some respite along with considerable spectacle. I'd never seen him eat before.

His soup was gone almost before I'd put out my cigarette and picked up my spoon, a third of it down his throat, the other in patches about his person and the tablecloth. Such was the frenzy of consumption that tiny specks of it managed to reach the lapel of my jacket. Then he hurled himself back in his chair with a look on his face that suggested that if I didn't get a move on with mine, he'd claim it for himself. I'm a slow eater which seemed to perplex him sufficiently to delay his next monologue for at least a minute. Once launched, however, it buzzed along, pretty well uninterrupted, until the arrival of the turkey and trimmings which he went at with an ogre-like fury. Only after the Christmas pudding had been despatched did I feel myself safe from inundation. Then I had one of my attacks which afflict me from time to time right out of the blue. The absurdity of it all boiled up in my head in a thunder cloud of despair and hopelessness. I began to laugh in a mildly hysterical way.

'Terry,' I said, 'you're a terrible person...a really, really terrible person...but for the sake of humanity I must learn to love you.'

'Aaay?'

Then, rising unsteadily (I was already on my second bottle of claret) I planted a kiss on his forehead before staggering to the refuge of the bogs for a few minutes respite.

The Chinese New Year break came and went. I returned refreshed and relieved to find his workstation vacated. The long wait was nearly over. His wife and children were due to arrive shortly after the spring semester began. It was late March and the temperature had gone up a notch, enough to tempt a few colleagues out of hibernation. I was no longer quite the sitting duck I'd been over the winter months. The great load that was Terry could now be shared with others patient enough to bear a part of it and then, I assumed, we would have to bear it no more. Since his return from Thailand we'd heard nothing but Terry the *pater familias* elaborating his system of child rearing and how, now she'd had him in situ again to demonstrate, his wife Nid was finally 'getting it'.

So, it was with some surprise that at ten-thirty on a Saturday night, just as things were getting rowdy, he arrived with the whole Docherty tribe in tow. It was immediately clear to me that here was a profoundly dysfunctional outfit. Whatever iron regime he may have expounded in theory was not finding practical expression. Most of the facts of his life I'd managed to expose as pure fantasy in the course of gentle interrogation; so gentle that he perhaps didn't notice or, more likely, was unable to take on board. (He had, for example, no idea who Danny Ortega was, nor could he say a word in Russian to the PhD student from St. Petersburg I once introduced him to). But here at least was incontrovertible evidence that Terry Docherty was indeed the father of two children. He was determined, as it were, to lay it before the jury despite the hour being way past what any conscientious father would regard as bedtime.

There was something in the spectacle which conjured in the mind a troop of medieval acrobats arriving in a small village bored of its own company. One almost expected minstrels, plucking on lutes, announcing his glorious paternity. The youngest daughter, Emily, was bouncing on his shoulders, the slightly older Sophie gambolling about his feet and yelling to herself. His wife followed a few paces behind, wheeling a pushchair.

She looked exhausted and deeply unhappy; almost terrified.

Setting Emily down, he pointed in my direction and said. 'Look, Emily, it's The Chairman. Go and say hello to The Chairman.'

This she did, attempting at the same time to mount my knee and leaving a trail of snot on one trouser leg. Neither child looked particularly clean, as though they'd been sleeping in their clothes for days. Only a year separated them and they appeared almost as twins. The mother stood helplessly by as they began to do unwanted things to the three other colleagues seated at our table. Terry looked on approvingly.

'My little monkeys,' he said.

Chairs were found for them to join us. His wife refused to sit at first. She was on permanent tenterhooks watching her daughters as they darted under the tables, but unable to exercise any form of command. It all seemed too much for her. Terry was too absorbed in his own triumph to notice that they were pissing people off. Neither had he bothered to introduce his wife, which I found grossly impolite. It was almost as though, to him, she wasn't there. As if she'd been a mere receptacle for the propagating of himself and now, her job done, was an encumbrance. It was all deeply disturbing.

I did the necessary myself, 'Hi, I'm Peter,' I said, insisting she sit beside me. 'You must be Nid. I've heard a lot about you. Lovely to meet you at last.'

She seemed suspicious of kindness; suspicious of everything around her in fact. This was understandable given that it was most likely her first time out of Thailand. But there was something deeper to it than mere 'culture shock'. Very young, slight and pretty she sat perched like a little bird taken from its nest and put in a cage.

I tried again. 'You have two beautiful daughters,' I said. 'They look much more like you than Terry.'

Suddenly she spoke:

'He very bad man,' she said. 'He drink all time. He no give me money.'

It was country-bar girl English, simple and to the point. 'He bring me here. He lie. He say we have apartment two bedrooms. It only have one. In Thailand I have house. Big house. Why he bring me here? My children happy in Thailand.'

This was spoken with some vehemence. 'China food disgusting,' she went on. 'I get sick first day. I cold. No one speak English. People spit on floor. Toilet disgusting.'

This was a fair summing up of my own feelings and experience upon arriving in winter eight years ago. I wanted to say that the place might grow on her like it had on me once my guts and aesthetic radar had had time to adjust. Then I realised this would be pointless. Her mind had already slammed shut. I'd seen it many times before in 'trailing spouses' as they're known; most of them better travelled than her. It was hard to think of anything to say which might placate her. By any objective standard the place isn't easy to live in. Half the time I don't know why I stick it out myself. Habit, I suppose. And the money's good. That's been my life: sticking things out. I noticed there was a large bruise where her neck joined her collar bone.

At that moment, Terry broke off whatever monologue he'd been delivering. I'd underestimated both his powers of taking things in and the true extent of his awfulness:

'Will you stop facking moaning and go and see what those little monkeys are up to. I'm trying to have a beer here.'

That was it for me. My faith in God had vanished years ago, but I've always tried, even in the most trying of circumstances, to keep my faith in man. Even the worst sort of person is deserving of some attempt at understanding. If that goes then, it seems to me, the devil really is getting the upper hand. In the case of Terry, despite all my best efforts, old Nick had finally won hands down. I began to to wish him ill.

And then things got, briefly, worse. Much worse.

I live in a large, soulless complex of hotel apartments. The flat above mine had been silent for some weeks. Like my own, it has two bedrooms and is normally occupied by the one child Chinese family unit. As a single man I'm prepared to pay for the extra bedroom which I use for my occasional painting, portraits mainly. Recently, I'd begun one of Terry, taken from his official university photo, infusing it, as a hopeful form of catharsis, with all the dislike that had built up inside me towards him. Then one Saturday morning I heard the voice of its 'sitter' coming through the ceiling. At first I thought I may have been hallucinating aurally, my obsession having tipped the balance of my mind, but it proved to be wishful thinking. They had moved in.

Throughout the day, the noise grew steadily, the children scampering, yelling and hurling objects on to the tiled floor. From time to time a shrill remonstrance from Nid could be heard, countermanded by the equally ineffectual Terry chainsaw at full blast. His language towards her was of the grossest kind and she gave as good as she got, shrieking back in Thai. This went on day after day until I became virtually exiled from my own flat during daylight hours. But I had to sleep somewhere and what happened at night was even more horrible.

RED FLAGS

Around about midnight, just as I usually drop off, it would begin. First Terry's muffled buzz-saw would come through directly overhead, demanding something which became subsequently clear. Then Nid's near hysterical twitter of refusal would start up. This went on for some minutes, getting louder and more impassioned. There would then be a brief pause followed by the rhythmic drilling of a headboard banging against a wall, going faster and faster. Then, a muffled sobbing, and, finally, silence.

They didn't know I was under them. You can go months without bumping into your neighbours. People keep themselves very much to themselves. I toyed with the idea of making an anonymous complaint to the reception desk but that would have been cowardly and I don't like cowardice.

In the end, I did nothing, until by the law of averages I eventually ran into Nid in the lift. It stopped, the door opened and by her expression - shock, morphing into deep embarrassment and shame - it was clear she had grasped the situation straight away.

Since her arrival, I'd become a kind of friend. Nocturnal family visits to Victor's had been fairly frequent, and since our first encounter she'd almost warmed to me, berating her husband's and China's shortcomings in an urgent whisper, whilst at the same time hymning the beauties of Thailand. That's me: I'm a 'good listener'. She may even have looked forward to the excursions as her only break from the horrors of family life with Terry. This hadn't gone unnoticed. 'I think you might be in there, Pete,' a slimy colleague from Birmingham said in his slimy voice after one of these occasions, and everyone round the table laughed.

'Why you no say?' she said. I noticed she had a blackening around her left eye.

'I thought I'd let you settle in first,' I said, feeling cowardly and ridiculous.

'I make you Thai food.'

'That's very kind, Nid. But save it for the children.'

'Terry eat pizza all time. Like pig. I hate he. I hate he.'

There was more in the same vein until we reached the ground floor. An unhappier person, I couldn't imagine. Still in her pyjamas, she was off to the corner shop.

'Bye, Nid,' I found myself saying, 'and cheer up. It gets better here once you get used to it.'

Pathetic.

On the electric scooter ride to work I did my best to imagine the helplessness of her situation. It was obvious to me she was the poorest kind of country girl for whom marriage to a *farang* was probably the only way out of poverty. The arrangement may have been encouraged by her family in the hope that some of the husband's money might also come their way. It was highly likely that at some stage she'd been enlisted in the legions of working girls staffing the go-go bars of Bangkok. Perhaps the prospect of a lifetime submitting to the demands of Terry in the singular, had seemed at the time preferable to one of submitting to him, as it were, in the plural. Such are the choices of the very poor. Either way, she was trapped.

It turned out, not for much longer.

The Sunday morning shortly after our meeting in the lift, after a particularly ferocious shouting match during which furniture sounded as though it were being hurled about, their apartment went quiet. I made myself some breakfast and, enjoying the unusual tranquillity, sat down at the computer to read the report on the latest slaughter of my football team. There was a faint knock at the door. It was Nid. She was wearing a short nightie. Blood was coming from a cut on her upper lip and pouring from her nose. There were ugly bruises all over her body. She was shivering, but not with cold. It was a hot morning.

'Come,' she said. 'You must come.'

The moment had arrived when I was going to have to hit him. Still in my dressing gown I followed her up the flight of stairs and into their apartment.

The first thing that struck me was my calmness. I'd seen a lot of death on my ministrations in Africa. It walks among you there with a casual swagger. But I'd not witnessed *violent* death, murder, first-hand since during the Falkland's campaign, when as a young Captain not long out of Sandhurst my *sang froid* had resulted in a decoration. Thirty-nine years is a long time, yet I took in the situation straight away and was already calculating what I had to do to save her. Terry was lying in his underpants, half on and half off the sofa with a large kitchen knife stuck in his chest. By the look on his face, death had been instant. It wore that idiotic look of surprise mingled with profound disappointment that I still saw occasionally in my nightmares.

The second thing that surprised me, less to my credit, was how little I cared he was dead. In fact, I was glad. He was an awful fellow; a wife beater, and once I'd done what I knew I was going to do, I knew life would then return to normal.

'Sit down, Nid,' I said. 'I'm sorry but I can't clean you up. We need to show the police exactly what he did. Now I want you to tear your nightdress. Tear it as violently as you can.'

She didn't understand, so I had to do it myself. Once I started, she sat meekly, looking up at me in a pathetically complicit manner. She understood, now. She was a country girl, with all the primitive cunning that poverty nurtures. It was the first time I'd seen a woman's naked breasts close up for a long time. After Mary died, I tried to rekindle an interest but it all felt wrong somehow and I gave it up. Nid's were quite beautifully formed. For reasons I couldn't fathom I seemed to be coming alive in parts of me I'd thought dead; the 'man of action' parts, which a life of quiescence and routine I'd thought had killed off.

'It's alright,' I said. 'I'll take care of everything. Don't worry.'

I used the apartment phone to call reception.

'Send the special police...you understand...the *special police*... to B2 1113, immediately,' I said in my quite good Chinese. 'There's been a fight. A very bad fight. Someone might be dead. I need also a policewoman. A policewoman. You understand.'

'Zidao! Zidao! Zidao!'

They knew me well. I was respected and no questions were asked.

There was a large police station a few blocks away and they arrived in minutes: the real guys in crisp khaki uniforms, not the Keystone Cops that dole out parking tickets and harass the street vendors. All this time the children had been silent and now they began to howl. The policewoman bundled them away.

The Detective Inspector spoke in the most broken of English, worse than Nid's. During the interrogation which took place on the spot, I acted as interpreter. I explained I was their neighbour from downstairs and related what I'd heard, adding that it was a regular occurrence and that on frequent occasions I'd seen bruises on Nid's face and body. There were no prints of mine in the apartment except for the on the phone I had used, which would be corroborated by reception. It was an open and shut case.

In the days that followed, things proceeded with the swift decisiveness that can happen here when there's a will. My evidence in court was conclusive. Nid was released and allowed to return to Thailand with the children. Terry's body was cremated in China. It turned out his embassy could find no one in Australia to accept its repatriation. Except for the functionaries I was the only person at the ceremony. The embassy had done a thorough check on him and records showed that apart from the occasional vacation and the few years in Thailand preceding his arrival here, he'd spent most of his life in Brisbane. I hadn't been wrong.

Thankfully, my life didn't return to normal. I adopted the family. I send money and visit the apartment I bought them as often I can. The 'little monkeys' have ceased their hyperactivity and communicate with me sensibly in the charming English of their private Thai tutor whom I pay via We-Chat, which I've now mastered. Meanwhile I'm learning Thai. They laugh when I use it. Nid and I don't sleep together but we hug a lot. Slowly, I'm coming alive again. I know in my heart Mary would approve. I'm no longer The Chairman.

ABOUT THE AUTHOR

James Nelson Roebuck was born and grew up in Burton-upon-Trent, Staffordshire, where he still has his home. For most of his working life he has lived abroad in places as diverse as Brunei, Saudi Arabia and China.

For details of our other books, or to submit your own manuscript please visit

www.green-cat.co

Printed in Great Britain
by Amazon